The Propagandists

A Political Thriller

Steve Jaffe

A Weaver of Tales Press Publication

www.aweaveroftalespress.com

A Weaver of Tales Press

38368 Crocus Lane

Palm Desert, Ca. 92211

A Weaver of Tales Press

ISBN 978-0-9819410-8-0

Dedication

I want to thank the investigative reporters, Senators, and House Members who helped put some realism into this story. I also want to thank the law enforcement agencies that help me add believable procedures and terminology for this tale.

And last, I want to thank Nancy, my best friend, and partner. Without her support and encouragement, I would not have completed this story, especially without your "Red Pen."

A Note from the Author

Attempting to bring characters from *The Architect's Manifesto* and *The Plantation* into this final chapter in the Corrupted Intelligence series was the hardest storytelling I've ever tried.

I had to coin new words such as *Corrupted Intelligence*: The abuse of entrusted power. As well as *Dog Whistles*: Figuratively, a 'Dog Whistle' is a coded message communicated through words or phrases commonly understood by a particular group of people but not by others. The last descriptive words I used were *Verbal Terrorist*, which speaks for itself.

The racial hate within the United States has been escalating for over a decade now, and it doesn't appear to be slowing down. Our verbal terrorists are giving the ultra-far-right permission to kill people of color or elected officials they disagree with. Political violence and un-American activities, if not stopped will be the eventual downfall of our great democracy.

The final chapter in my three-book fictional series on hate in America is The Propagandists.

Prologue

It was the third anniversary of Albert Dunham's, known as *The Architect*, tragic death. Professor Cochran felt it was time to resurrect his plan for the new Confederate States of America. His Domestic Revolutionary Group had had too many setbacks that began with Charles Stone eleven years ago, and his believing Haven House Plantation could become the White House in the south.

Cochran decided to turn on the evening news before he went back to his meeting notes for his upcoming White Supremacy Convention. He started clapping joyfully as the reporter played a video of one of his Domestic Revolutionary Movement supporters shooting over a hundred bullets from his AR-15 rifle in a shopping mall. The Professor did not know this young man with Swastikas on his forehead and chest but seeing him carrying the DRM flag got his heart racing.

As the video showed him opening fire on a group of twenty-five Black shoppers, primarily mothers and children, in a minority suburb shopping mall in South Los Angeles, Cochran felt pride radiate over his entire body, especially when he saw the twisted bodies lying in large pools of blood. The Professor felt a sadness blanket his body when he saw the young White Supremacist lying face down in the street, killed by LAPD SWAT.

Then, the reporter switched to another mass shooting at a Black church in Brooklyn, New York. The reporter focused her camera on two men with shaved heads and Nazi symbols tattooed on their arms and face, motionless outside the church. Then the camera shifted to the fifty-five churchgoers riddled with bullets from the automatic weapons these two men used on them while they prayed. Cochran once again applauded.

7

He turned off the television and returned to his meeting notes for his upcoming Convention of the Domestic Revolutionary Movement rally. This would be the first convention of the new White Supremacist Political Party in the United States. Over the last thirty years, fifty militia groups around the country had become the DRM's paramilitary wing. They had carried out over twenty-five mass shooting events around the United States.

Professor Cochran knew the time had come to merge every White Supremacist militia into one organized and formidable army.

During the last ten years, Professor Cochran skillfully orchestrated lies and conspiracy theories telling his followers that the Jews were trying to replace all White men with people of color. As membership in the Domestic Revolutionary Movement grew, the new, younger members who wanted to prove their loyalty choreographed mass shooting events against people of color. He was pleased that his *We Won't Be Replaced* campaign became the motivating chant his supporters marched to as it elevated the DRM inside America's far-right political party. Republicans who leaned right were forced to support their movement and show loyalty or their families would suffer.

President Thaddeus Thompson, the first Evangelical Christian President ran on the platform that God loves all his children, even all the White Supremacy groups responsible for over twenty-five racially motivated mass shootings. Dog Whistle phrases on social media had become normalized as political expression helping to grow the membership inside the DRM allowing it to grow into a powerful political party.

Cochran knew that after twenty years of failed attempts to start his civil war, the time was ripe for it to happen while the United States was in a polarized state. The Professor was delighted that his allies inside the West Wing and Halls of Congress believed the DRM members were loyal patriots exercising their right to political discourse.

The Domestic Revolutionary Movement's leader had the ear of the new President and had him chasing his tail, trying to stop the isolated attacks on innocent Americans. While this was going on, it kept both Federal and State law enforcement busy, allowing Cochran to prepare for a series of significant attacks that made 9/11 seem like child's play.

The United States, for the first time in its history, was at its most vulnerable, and the country's enemies, both foreign and domestic, had begun to exploit these weaknesses. Sporadic attacks throughout Europe, Africa, and the Middle East had started escalating from Neo-Nazi groups. These groups were well-financed by some European billionaires.

Cochran's upcoming meeting with twenty White Supremacist leaders would be the key for him to finally have the new Confederate States of America, a place for all like-minded White Supremacists to live and prosper.

The Professor dialed the great-grandson of Adolf Hitler, the new leader of the Global Neo-Nazi Movement and who had his home base in Argentina.

"Wilhelm, our civil war is about to start. We will be laying the groundwork for your invasion in sixty days. If phase one goes without a hitch, millions of innocent men, women, and children of color will be dead in the streets as you roll across the southern and northern borders."

"Professor, my great-grandfather would be proud of what you've accomplished these last thirty years. Our sleeper cells are in place, eagerly watching and waiting for the signal to open the doors of hell on the country that had turned its back on the White race. I hope you have a solid plan to kill Sam Collins and Tiffany Glass and that reporter bitch Paige Turner. I do not want them alive when the invasion takes place," Wilhelm ordered. Before The Professor could respond, the phone went dead.

"It's already in the works," Cochran said to himself.

1

Six months into his first term, newly elected President Thaddeus Thompson had called a special meeting with his Attorney General, FBI Director, Homeland Security Secretary, and Defense Secretary to discuss a recent news article and a disturbing podcast by Paige Turner. What had the President furious was that he was being criticized for passing the new *Freedom to Privacy Act* that had become a firewall for all groups that wanted to protest, especially White Supremacist militia groups.

Turner had placed President Thompson on her Corrupted Intelligence list. She accused him of using Dog Whistles aimed at his Evangelical supporters and members of the Domestic Revolutionary Movement. She also came down hard on the President for abusing his power with conspiracy theories to help pass his legislative achievement.

The Freedom to Privacy Act prohibited any federal law enforcement agency from having spies inside organized political action groups and militia groups. This new legislation made it next to impossible to get a search warrant before a crime was committed, even if law enforcement knew that a crime was being planned and set in motion. The new legislation had gone through all the courts and finally had been deemed constitutional by the conservative majority on the Supreme Court. These court battles and wins emboldened the Domestic Revolutionary Movement to move forward with their new Confederate States of America scheme.

With increasingly more DRM followers and supporters being elected to the House and Senate and appointed by President Thompson inside his Cabinet, the United States was slowly eroding the constitution and chipping away at democracy.

President Thaddeus Thompson, an Evangelical minister during his first six months in office, was under pressure from Professor Cochran and his DRM donors to pass numerous bills with specific wording that would legitimize the White Supremacist movement as well as destroy almost every protection a woman has under the constitution. The third legislative triumph had been to create a national federal education curriculum for grades K-12 that would teach the Evangelical history of God and how the importation of slaves to build America was a God-given right for White people.

Before President Thompson could start his meeting, Chief of Staff Cliff Williams burst into the Oval Office. He did not look happy as he slammed the *Washington Post*, *New York Times*, and *Wall Street Journal* on the President's desk.

"Thaddeus, we have a problem. Your job approval ratings are tanking below 15 percent," Williams said, trying to catch his breath.

The President remained silent as he glanced at the headlines:

PRESIDENT THOMPSON IS IN BED WITH EVERY WHITE SUPREMACY GROUP – *WASHINGTON POST*

AMERICA'S EVANGELICAL PRESIDENT WANTS TO MAKE THE UNITED STATES A WHITE CHRISTIAN COUNTRY BASED ON EVANGELICAL VALUES – *NEW YORK TIMES*

PRESIDENT THOMPSON LIED ON THE CAMPAIGN TRAIL. HE HAS TAKEN DONATIONS FROM WHITE SUPREMACY GROUPS – *WALL STREET JOURNAL*

President Thaddeus Thompson projected his frustration as he opened the meeting by first screaming at the FBI Director and ignoring the three newspapers on his desk. "Please explain why you can't keep your agents from giving interviews and criticizing me?"

FBI Director Leeland Johnson, his hands shaking, replied. "Sir, these complaints are bigger than what my agents say in the media. With her loyal followers of ten million plus, Paige Turner has been pushing her Corrupted Intelligence theory about the Abuse of Entrust Power inside your administration and putting you front and center on her weekly podcasts," Director Johnson said.

"How can I stop her?" the President asked.

Attorney General Thomas Hall jumped in. "Sir, I think you know the answer. I can, if you'd like, begin to open an investigation into her work and tie her up with subpoenas that will keep her small media company busy, so they won't have time to talk about her Corrupted Intelligence theory."

Sitting away from everyone was Vice President Shannon Graham, a left-leaning Republican who liked to listen before talking. "Mister President, I've read about Paige Turner, and she's a real American hero who can chew gum and investigate a story at the same time. We need to have her on our side. She exposed Albert Dunham, *The Architect*, while her life was threatened numerous times. Burying her with subpoenas will only make her mad and look deeper into your administration and its ties to your White Supremacy donors," Vice President Graham said.

"Damnit, Shannon, you need to pick a side. I hope it's mine?" the President shouted.

"Sir, I'm on your side and America's. I want this administration to work and move away from the radical right and White Supremacy movement that's taking over our country," Graham said.

President Thompson did not have a comeback to his Vice President's remarks. Doing his best, he tried to control his temper as he dismissed everyone except for his FBI Director, Attorney General, and Chief of Staff.

Once the Oval Office had cleared, he began to speak. "I think I have a real problem with my Vice President. She's always arguing about my agenda and what I want to accomplish. She's not a team player," President Thompson said. "We need to figure out how to replace her. I need someone in her position who's loyal and supportive."

Attorney General Thomas Hall replied, "Sir, we need to forget about the Vice President. You've only been in office for six months and replacing her will make you appear as a weak leader. There are rumblings around the DOJ that the Domestic Revolutionary Movement is planning something massive. We can't afford right now to have another civil war started. Our economy is too fragile after what Albert Dunham, *The Architect*, almost accomplished four years ago. I know we can't investigate this group before they do something, but we need to act," the Attorney General said.

President Thompson looked pissed with his Attorney General. His anger was boiling. "Are you loyal to me?" he asked, his eyes growing wide as his face turned red. "We must respect my Freedom to Privacy legislation and follow it to the letter." With that last remark, the meeting was over.

Chief of Staff Cliff Williams stayed behind. He had more to tell the President.

"This is bullshit," President Thompson blurted out as he kept skimming each article. "God has a plan for me, and I won't deviate from that plan."

Cliff Williams plopped himself down on the bright yellow floral couch bordering the Presidential Seal carpet and leaned his head back on the sofa cushions. "You need to speak again to The Professor and order him to call off his militia groups and let things cool down for a while. Cochran's inflammatory rhetoric can be linked to the current uptick in White Supremacy attacks on people of color," the Chief of Staff said.

Thompson stood up, moved around his desk, and sat across from Williams on a matching couch. "I just spoke with The Professor a few hours earlier, and he assured me that nothing is going to happen in the near future," the President said. "He's a good Christian and wouldn't lie to me."

Williams was shaking his head. "You can't believe anything that sociopath says. He's lied to you before you got elected, and he's lying to you now. The FBI and Homeland Security know something is brewing but can't do more with your crazy legislation you approved for The Professor," Williams said.

Thompson stood and asked his Chief of Staff to leave. He needed time to pray and ask God to guide him.

* * * * *

President Thompson, an hour later, was on the phone with the leader of the DRM. "Cochran, I know what you told me a few days ago, but I've been informed you are planning something big with your group?"

"Mister President, so nice to hear from you. I don't know who is feeding you this load of crap, but we are just having our first Confederate States of America convention. Is your FBI spying on my group again?" the Professor asked, his tone hostile.

"I'm not sure how we got this information, but is it true? I can't afford any problem right now," President Thompson said.

The Professor paused before answering. "There is nothing for you to worry about," Cochran said. "I just hope you don't have a spy in our group. It could mean trouble for you."

President Thompson cleared his throat. "You know I can't do that after I got your legislation passed two months ago, so don't threaten me. I am the most powerful man in the United States and the world."

The Professor sighed loudly, holding back a laugh. "Sir, was that all you called about? I have to prepare my speech."

President Thompson did not like the control The Professor had over him. He sucked in a deep breath and replied. "You have nothing to worry about from this office," he said and hung up.

2

The cigar smoke hung in the air above the chatter from twenty businessmen in black suits and crisp white shirts that hid their racist tattoos from public view. It was the first day of the Domestic Revolutionary Movement's new convention. Over seventy-five Senators and House Members openly attended this White Supremacy caucus for the first time.

In a large meeting room away from the auditorium, Professor Albert Cochran met with his council and a few key Senate members and House Members who had been helping his White Supremacy movement for almost three decades.

"Our movement has been dealing with setbacks for many years until today. We are ready to strike the first blow, so everyone will understand that our race will not be replaced by all the non-Americans of color, including the bastard Jews. Today our followers will see the light at the end of the tunnel, and our Confederate States of America will be restored to its once national glory," The Professor said.

"There will be three separate mass casualty events beginning in two days. My hope is that the Blacks, Hispanics, and Muslims will be fed up with the lack of law enforcement helping them. As the riots get out of control and local SWAT units begin killing protesters, it will start a race war that will keep the illegitimate government busy putting out all the fires we'll be creating. I hope all of your paramilitary militia groups are ready to take back our South?" Cochran asked. He glanced at his watch and realized it was time to address the convention.

As Cochran walked onto the stage, stopping behind his podium, his loyal followers become quiet. Today was the first time the leader of the DRM had come out of the shadows to take charge of their movement. It was a choice he never wanted to make, but he was forced to come out of seclusion after the failure of Charles Stone ten years earlier and then Albert Dunham, *The Architect*, four years ago. During the last twenty-four months, he was confident he had resurrected the DRM, expanding their membership around the country and inside the Federal and State governments and law enforcement. This was something he had set in motion with the help of Hitler and the ex-patriot Brown Shirts exiled to Argentina over fifty years ago.

Professor Albert Cochran, a leading historian of the South, was once the invisible leader of the new White Power movement in the United States. Now, he was about to unleash his army of White militia to restart his vision of a new Confederate States of America, as his elected government officials molded legislation to allow for an easy overthrow of the United States of America when the race war started.

Today's conference at Blacks Landing, a historic Southern plantation in the backwoods of Mississippi, was the motivational catalyst for the audience's one hundred and fifty patriots. It was a strategic location where thousands of slaves were unloaded and put on the auction block in the seventeenth century. After the failure of Charles Stone at the plantation at Haven House, The Professor needed a new motivation symbol and a new command post for his group of patriots. This location was the perfect spot for the new Confederate White House.

Each member in attendance controlled approximately twenty-five thousand well-trained soldiers eagerly waiting in twenty-eight states for their signal, a Dog Whistle, to take back their country that they'd never stopped believing was illegally taken from them.

After Charles Stone failed to initiate their civil war, Cochran rallied his support around Albert Dunham, *The Architect*, one of the richest men in the world, confident he would rectify Stone's mistakes. Unfortunately for The Professor, Dunham could not get out of the way of his ego and grand idea to become the sole ruler of the United States, which ultimately led to his death and pushed the movement back a few years.

Everyone in attendance was there to hear about the final solution that would create a new nation for White Supremacists. Professor Cochran was able to see all the men in the audience and smiled at the enthusiasm he witnessed on their faces. The lights began to dim as he leaned in, his mouth almost kissing his microphone.

In a calming voice, Cochran asked his audience to quiet down. "Gentlemen, today marks a time that our country and those of our patriotic allies will finally take back what is rightfully ours." Professor Cochran paused, taking in a deep breath. "A nation of pure White Christians. This is what our founding fathers envisioned for our new country. For over seventy-five years, we've been working toward a much-needed new civil war. With my leadership now, our first phase will begin in a few days with multiple strategic mass casualty shooting events. It will turn the United States on its ear. Then a few days later, before law enforcement can figure things out, we will set off bombs at places of worship." He paused and sipped from his glass of water.

"If we all do our jobs with precision and cast the blame on every sub-human of color, law enforcement will begin busting heads and it will trigger rioting, looting, and structure fires in all the cities in the north. Further, with our hand-picked elected men and women in high office supporting us, they will call us patriots and further incite the minorities to continue to destroy public property." The Professor paused and drank more of his water. "If everything goes according to plan, all we will need to do is sit back and watch." He sucked in a deep breath, waiting for the applause to die down. Everyone in the audience was on the edge of their seats, waiting for Professor Cochran to continue.

"Our job is straightforward now. Scream from the top of your lungs absurdities, lies, and false facts, so we can get the silent minority of Whites to commit atrocities for our cause." The entire room exploded with hoots and racially obscene words that went on for over ten minutes.

When The Professor quieted the group down, he continued speaking. "Our loyal Senators and House Representatives that are with us today as well as our new President who helped neutralized the FBI with the anti-spying legislation passed six months ago open the door for us to begin our civil war. While we initiate our attacks, the FBI and DOJ will think twice about infiltrating the DRM and other paramilitary militia, giving us a head start to rewrite the constitution." Cochran paused to observe how his remarks were playing with his audience. What he saw caused him to smile.

Professor Cochran continued speaking for the next two hours, giving his group important details they'd need to do their jobs in approximately twenty-seven states.

After walking off the stage, he glanced at his watch and realized it was time for Paige Turner's weekly podcast. He loathed that woman more than anything and wanted her dead after she exposed Albert Dunham's manifesto. "I hate you, bitch," he shouted at the television in the conference room as she appeared on her show.

3

A marine layer blanketed the beach in front of Sam and Tiffany Collins Del Mar beach house. While it had been almost eleven years since they were in public life, the two of them watched from a distance how America had changed and had become so polarized. It was getting too difficult for them to watch the news, with all the conspiracy theories and blatant lies from the far-right political fringe.

Every morning, they took their two children on a sunrise walk by the shoreline and its pounding waves. Tiffany had their ten-year-old daughter Irene by the hand, and Sam had their five-month-old son Michael in his snuggly pack facing forward, strapped to his daddy's chest as they walked slowly south.

"Tiffany, what do you think about the Domestic Revolutionary Movement now becoming a political party? This group has become a popular White Supremacist offshoot of a new Neo-Nazi division. It's as if Charles Stone was resurrected. On top of everything else, they seem to be supporting a handful of militia groups that are functioning as their paramilitary wing."

Tiffany did not like talking about this subject in front of Irene. "Sam, let's table your question to when we're alone," she said, picking up her pace.

Sam tried to keep up, but Michael started squirming and pointing toward the waves that were coming closer to them. This was his morning ritual to want to get close enough to feel the saltwater spray on his face. "You want to jump in?" his daddy teased. Without waiting for an answer, they were jogging over toward the pounding surf. When a large wave crashed on the sand and Michael felt his face get wet, he started his incessant giggling that made everyone laugh.

Sam did not see a small motorboat paralleling them as they played. The thick marine layer had gotten worse, masking the small boat that held four heavily armed men.

Tiffany stopped walking with Irene and waited for Sam to catch up. Her face was registering a sadness that only her husband understood. Since having Michael, she drifted almost daily into a depression, remembering the child she had given up for adoption when she was sixteen.

She had been careless with her high school boyfriend and being a mother at sixteen years was not in the cards for her. Never a day went by during law school she did not think about the daughter she gave up for adoption. When Irene was born, her feelings exploded about her lost daughter and then when Michael was born, it knocked the wind out of her sails. Tiffany wondered if her daughter still had the Saint Christopher medal she had left her before she was taken from her at the home for unwed mothers.

When Sam reached her, he noticed immediately what she was remembering and kissed her cheek. "Sweetheart, the memory is back?" He noticed her nodding. "Maybe it's time to search for her. We have the resources, and locating your daughter could be easier than you think."

Irene, for a ten-year-old, always paid close attention when her parents talked. "Find your daughter?" Irene questioned. "I'm right here."

Tiffany lifted her daughter up and kissed her on her forehead. "Yes, you are, sweetie."

Irene always knew when her mother and father tried to distract her. She wasn't buying it today as she wrinkled her nose, unhappy that she was not told the truth.

Sam and Tiffany switched directions and headed back to their house.

* * * * *

Wiley Jordan slammed his fist on the bulkhead of the boat he was sitting in. He put down his sniper rifle and dialed The Professor. "Sir, I couldn't kill the fucking Collins family. The marine layer was too thick."

"Get back here now. We have more important things to accomplish. The two of them can wait for a better time," Professor Cochran said.

* * * * *

Later that evening, after both children were asleep, Sam and Tiffany relaxed on their large wooden deck and sipped from their glasses of wine. This was their favorite time. A calm house, a beautiful clear sky, and watching the sunset on the horizon.

"Tiffany, we need to talk about how our country has become so divided and allows White Supremacy to become mainstream," Sam said.

"What do you expect when the electorate accepts all the lies they are being fed and votes for White Supremacist candidates or supporters of these animals? You do know that our current President is one of the biggest supporters of the Domestic Revolutionary Movement?"

"I'm very frightened about what has happened to our country," Sam said.

"I am too, but what can we do now?" Tiffany asked, trying to act brave.

"There is a new political group in its infant stages called the *We the People* party created by Dean Miller. Maybe we should contact him to see if we can get involved?"

"I do remember him and Paige Turner. They were truly great American heroes. I just don't see us getting back into politics, especially in this current environment. I'd rather be in the background fighting these assholes."

Before Sam could respond, Michael started screaming. "Let's table this conversation for another day," Sam said as he rushed off to see what was going on with his son.

4

Paige Turner had five minutes before her podcast would air. It had been four years since she had left her investigative reporter position at the California Media Network, CMN, after the death of Albert Dunham, *The Architect*.

She still experienced PTSD from the attempts on her life by Dunham. Over the last four years, Paige woke up frequently from nightmares that played over and over the near-death experiences she suffered. The country she loved was heading toward a slippery slope it might never return from, and she needed to be able to report the news as she saw it. She needed to have the freedom to investigate all politically sensitive stories without any interference from her network executives. Her goal was to expose all the lies, conspiracies, and the rampant abuse of entrusted power that was polarizing America.

Since leaving CMN, she had amassed over ten million followers from around the world. Her influence and popularity among Americans from both political parties scared a lot of high-powered people. She needed to continue her work with her *Corrupted Intelligence* theory so she could expose the truth and educate every American on how to see through all the lies they were being fed.

Exposing the lies men in power flooded the airways with frustrated her the most. What they said was being accepted by a large portion of a very unhappy electorate. She had been studying the case files Sam Collins and Tiffany Glass had written about another corrupt individual, Charles Stone. She made a mental note to call the high-profile couple for an interview at their Del Mar beach house as soon as possible.

Seeing her administrative assistant rush into her office carrying a thick manila envelope started her heart racing wildly as she grasped at the package that was addressed to her with no return address. The thick yellow envelope brought back horrible memories of when a thumb drive of *The Architect's Manifesto* was mailed to her. Because of her bulldog drive to investigate Albert Dunham back then, many of her friends and colleagues lost their lives. She never anticipated how much her life would change after she received the thumb drive and started her investigation into Albert Dunham. Staring at the thick envelope felt like she had been punched in the stomach.

Four years ago, as Paige got further and further down her rabbit hole, she could not stop herself from wanting to destroy this sociopath. Tearing open the package with her shaking hands, a folded note fell out. The note was short.

Please Save America Again!
An Admirer

She read about a new evil that was rearing its ugly head. Now she had to decide whether to jump into the pit with new and more ruthless men or bury the information staring her in the face and give it over to the FBI and let them deal with it.

After reading the first ten pages, she knew what she had to do. Paige recalled what Albert Dunham almost accomplished, which made Charles Stone's failed civil war at his Haven House Plantation seem like child's play. Now, this new information about a more heinous plot to destroy American Democracy left her no choice but to investigate.

Paige's investigative instincts had always pushed her to expose the corruption within corporate America and Congress. Sadly, every common thread between Charles Stone and Albert Dunham led her back to her Corrupted Intelligence theory. It was like a plague spreading across all levels of life in the United States. Reading more pages inside the package convinced her that there was enough information for her to start an investigation and attempt to uncover the real leader of the Domestic Revolutionary Movement.

For the last two years, Paige had been reporting that the White Power militia groups were successfully recruiting new young, uneducated followers, even with all their past setbacks. These groups were spread across the United States and had several hundred thousand followers. That number did not include their white-collar members who had been elected to state and federal positions and controlled some of the largest corporations based in the United States.

After delving deeper into the file, she stared, stunned that another brewing revolution was about to happen with a more organized, ruthless leader. Unable to ignore what she had gotten, Paige started jotting down notes, as she did with *The Architect's Manifesto*, to uncover the new leader of the Domestic Revolutionary Movement. She knew she would need help from Dean Miller.

Paige was startled by a loud banging on her office door. "Ms. Turner, you're live in two minutes," her producer shouted. She started mumbling to herself: "Today's topic *Corrupted Intelligence and how men in power can control the masses with their lies is a perfect starting point for today.*" She knew the leaders of the top three White Supremacist militia groups watched her broadcast. The threats toward her escalated after each podcast. The risks to her life only motivated her to expose the animals inside these groups. Today's podcast topic she hoped would send these traitors scurrying out from under the rocks they hid under once they realized she would expose their plan.

Like she did with every broadcast, Paige spoke in simple-to-understand language. Today's focus would be on Charles Stone and Albert Dunham, as well as the mystery man who mentored them and to interject this new information about an upcoming attack on American soil.

5

Commander John McAllister was shocked to hear what his retired FBI friend, Jacob Stein, whose undercover name was Jack Petry, recorded at the DRM meeting. He wished he knew all the locations and where these bastards were going to attack. However, what he taped would be a great first step to figuring the attack out.

He glanced at Bubba Jackson, noticing he was jotting something down in his notebook. "Sergeant, anything you care to share with me?"

"I did hear about some rumblings that something big was going down in a couple of days. It confirms what your CI told you. I want to talk to a few of my own CIs to confirm your friend's suspicions. If an attack is being planned, they would know where and when."

"Fine. Let's first listen to Paige Turner's show today. Earlier, I received a text from Turner's production manager that the podcast has some breaking news she's going to release when she airs."

McAllister signaled Bubba that the podcast was starting.

* * * * *

For the first time while opening her podcast, Paige Turner was not smiling. She appeared stressed; her face drained of color.

"Good afternoon and welcome to my series on Corrupted Intelligence, The Abuse of Entrusted Power," Paige said, her voice cracking. *"Today, I want to share with my ten million listeners something that was sent to me by an anonymous source. While I haven't fully vetted what I'm about to tell you, I felt*

it was urgent enough to expose this possible attack by domestic terrorists that could harm our country in the next few days."

McAllister and Bubba noticed her hands trembling as she spoke, something uncommon for her. "I've never seen this woman so nervous before."

"Not sure of the exact date, but the Domestic Revolutionary Movement is going to initiate three, maybe four mass shooting events in Manhattan, Los Angeles, and Washington DC. I've attempted to tell the FBI and the Oval Office, but I was laughed at and accused of being an alarmist," Paige said. *"For everyone who knows me, you can be sure that I love my country and will do everything in my power to keep every American citizen safe and secure with my reporting."* Paige sucked in a deep breath and sipped water from a perspiring glass at her desk. *"I'm hoping to have an exact date of these upcoming attacks by the end of the day today."*

Paige kept talking emotionally for the next hour, talking about specific men Americans trusted and who were currently abusing their entrusted power. Paige got excessively specific, targeting current political leaders on both sides of the aisle, spelling out examples of all the lies they continued to broadcast in the media. No one was spared. While she talked, her phone started ringing. Her administrative assistant passed a post-it note that read: President Thompson wants you at the Oval Office ASAP.

Paige ended her show as she did every week. *"Thank you for supporting my Corrupted Intelligence podcast. It's time to hold everyone to the truth and rethink our tribal mentality. Our democracy is coming apart as more and more Americans accept lies as fact. I welcome all my followers to verify everything I've said, as well as verify everything the men and women you've given the power to so you can make informed decisions. See everyone next week."*

Before Paige could get up from her desk, Rebecca Burns, her Chief of Staff and ex-FBI systems analyst, sat on the corner of her desk. "Boss, the President is pissed at you and all the shit you stirred up today. He's getting calls from the FBI, CIA, and Homeland Security demanding you turn over everything you have on these unsubstantiated attacks you told the entire United States will happen any day now. What you just did is currently affecting the New York Stock Exchange."

Paige leaned back in her chair, her arms locked behind her head, as a grin formed on her face. "Great. I was hoping to stir up some action from our docile President. I wonder if he's getting calls from his White Supremacist supporters, too. Tell President Thompson I can be in DC in three days. I have an interview I must do first in Del Mar, California."

Rebecca was shaking her head. "He's going to come unglued. He's not used to anyone telling him to wait," she said.

"He's one of the Corrupted Intelligence men who is currently abusing the entrusted power his supporters have given him. Maybe I should focus on him on my next podcast?"

Rebecca jumped off Paige's desk, her hands cupping her ears. "I'm not listening to you."

6

Commander McAllister and his team put down their beers and had stunned looks on their faces after listening to what Paige Turner said on her podcast. Everyone was talking when the Commander's cell phone rang. He waved his hand to have everyone pipe down. In a whisper, he said. "It's President Thompson. Let's be quiet."

"Yes, Mister President. My team and I can be at Camp David tomorrow. What's this regarding?" he asked, already suspecting it was about Turner's podcast.

"Yes, sir. I did listen to her. What she's saying has some merit, especially her Corrupted Intelligence theory," McAllister said.

"What the fuck do you mean her reporting has merit?" the President screamed. "She had National Security information that she did not feel obligated to tell my FBI, CIA, or Homeland Security directors. I know she's not a team player, but what she said has put our country in a downwind spiral."

"President Thompson, what would your directors, even you, have done with her information if she brought it to you?" asked McAllister.

"I know we would not have blabbed it to millions of citizens before we had time to verify her information," President Thompson said, his voice getting louder as he spoke.

"Sir, if I may be blunt. We all know that you and Congress have tied the hands of the FBI, forbidding them to spy on any White Supremacist group or end up being tried for treason. That was the most insane piece of legislation you signed into law," McAllister said sarcastically. "My sources tell me that what Turner said has a lot of truth in it. I was about to verify what I know and then talk with Turner to see what she has in her possession. I think I should come to Camp David later in the week and hopefully bring you accurate intelligence."

"Fine," President Thompson said, slamming his phone into its cradle.

McAllister looked at Bubba Jackson. "We need to verify what Turner said and then set up a meeting ASAP to see what actual intel she has."

"John, I think we need to visit Collins and Glass first and get their take on all of this. This smells like a Charles Stone, Albert Dunham plot," Bubba said. "I'll call Sam and see when they're available."

* * * * *

"Sam, Bubba Jackson here. How are you and Tiffany doing in Paradise? Using enough sunblock?"

"We're both fine. Being slaves to our two rug rats is keeping us in shape. But this is not a social call, right?"

"I'm sure you listened to Paige Turner earlier today?"

"Yes, we did. She's something else, isn't she?" Sam said.

"Never met her, but she's a brave woman after what she did to save our country from *The Architect*. What I'm calling about is that John and I want to meet with you and Tiffany and get your perspective on what she uncovered."

Sam laughed. "That's a coincidence. Turner just called us and wants to meet tomorrow at our home to discuss what she was given by an anonymous source. I'm not sure I want to jump back into another White Supremacist debacle as we did with the White Angels and Stone."

Bubba ignored Sam's last remark. "That could work out okay for all of us. The Commander wants to meet and have a friendly chat and maybe see what Turner has to say. President Thompson is demanding answers and asked John to help," Bubba said.

"Fine. See you tomorrow at around noon," Sam said and ended the call.

Bubba seemed puzzled as he looked at McAllister. "Weren't you going to clue Sam and Tiffany into the recording we got from the Blacks Landing Plantation meeting the DRM held?"

The Commander shook his head. "Not at this time. Our assignment with the ATF made us agree to keep what we uncover confidential at this time. Let's wait and see what Sam and Tiffany think and what Paige Turner has in her possession," Commander McAllister said.

"Then I'll check with the NSA and Homeland Security to see if they've heard any rumblings on social media that might confirm what we know," Jackson said.

"Good luck. They are so scared of their own shadows, not wanting to be accused of spying on domestic terrorists." McAllister's response was filled with sarcasm.

7

After thirty minutes of watching Turner's podcast, Cochran was in shock. *"How, in God's name, could she know about our upcoming attacks? She's a pain in my ass and needs to be dealt with,"* he mumbled to himself. He was on the phone with Wiley Jordan, Charles Stone's brutal enforcer and leader of the White Angels.

"Your speech was very motivating today," Wiley said. "Now, what do you want?"

Cochran did not like Wiley, but needed him when someone needed to be eliminated. "Paige Turner, if I didn't know better, knows of our entire plan. I'm not sure how she found out. She can't be allowed to stop us again. I need you to find out what she knows and who gave her our blueprint. Then get rid of her and the traitor."

"A professional security team protects her now. It won't be easy getting to her," Wiley complained.

"Are you saying you can't do this job for me?"

"No. It will just take some planning. I need to put together a strong team."

"Okay. Let me know when the job is done."

Professor Albert Cochran could not control his temper. While he was pissed that the reporter knew what he was planning, the good news was that she did not know when all of it was going to happen.

Paige Turner's podcast ignited flashbacks of the last eleven years of setbacks for the DRM. He remembered how the reporter exposed *The Architect's Manifesto,* which led to his untimely death. He closed his eyes tight, wishing for those memories to disappear, but his brain was on overdrive. His heart started

31

racing as Sam Collins and Tiffany Glass occupied his thoughts and how they stopped Charles Stone's civil war.

The Professor slowly opened his rage-filled eyes, his jaw tense, wanting to kill somebody. He had started tapping his cane, a nervous habit he had when he was upset. He imagined the bitch tied to a chair, just like Charles Stone was before he lost his head, and with one swift pass of his sword. She too would meet with the sweet justice that was part of the DRM's rules for traitors.

With a few rapid blinks of his eyes, Cochran needed to get back to the task at hand. He made a few strokes on his keyboard and was on a Zoom conference call with his Domestic Revolutionary Movement board of directors, some of the richest and most influential men in the United States. He hoped Wiley had formulated a plan to rid his world of Paige Turner.

Cochran positioned himself in front of the camera built on top of his sixty-inch computer screen. Once all twelve members signed in, he started the meeting.

"Gentlemen, I'm sure all of you listened to the news on Paige Turner's podcast. I think we need to move up our targeted attacks. What that bitch Turner just did might force President Thompson to grow some balls and put a stop to us before we even get started. Any thoughts?" Cochran asked the group.

Senator Jenkins, one of the original founding members of the Domestic Revolutionary Movement, was the first to respond. "We can't act on our emotions at this time. It didn't work for Charles Stone, and you know what happened," Senator Jenkins, with his Southern drawl, said. "My contacts inside the West Wing overheard President Thompson talking to Commander McAllister. If this asshole is helping the President, we might just be up shit creek."

The Professor did not like what the Senator told the group. "I'm afraid that if Turner has more complete intelligence about our plan, President Thompson and Commander McAllister might already know the time, place, and day of the first attacks."

"If what you say is true, then postponing this first phase might turn the tide on Turner and make her look like an alarmist," Senator Jenkins shot back. "It would be great to see her fall from grace."

Professor Cochran was deep in thought. "We still have the cable news stations who support us currently calling Turner a liar. If we hold off, then we need our patriots to hit the social media airways and begin getting them to blame the CIA and FBI for fabricating what's about to happen," The Professor said.

Wesley Jones, pastor of The White Supremacy Church, with a nationwide congregation of over fifty thousand, got into the debate. "The most recent national poll numbers show our White Supremacist movement has over a 43 percent approval rating with White male and female Christians. These White Christian men and women are portraying us as American patriots trying to restore our country to what our founding fathers envisioned for our kind." He paused to clear his dry throat. "I vote to postpone our attacks and let the opinion polls work for us."

"I can live with that. Maybe we use our fleet of police cars and have our militia groups wear police uniforms and begin stopping Blacks and Mexicans. They can either beat them silly or shoot them when they try to run away or fight back," The Professor said. His voice had no emotion. "This could work right now. We have enough Congressmen and Senators, as well as federal judges who believe in our *'We will not be replaced'* movement. Hundreds of thousands of Americans are fed up with the direction our country is going and will support anything we attempt to do, even the attacks we are planning. They believe a needed civil war will bring the country back to its greatness. At this time, our warriors will be hailed as heroes, not terrorists. Each of you needs to coordinate with your followers and let me know the time and place each of these events will happen in encrypted emails," Cochran said. "Historians will record this as the time American Democracy blossomed and the second revolutionary war started."

The meeting lasted almost an hour. Several of the other DRM directors wanted to pause what Cochran was proposing, feeling the heat from Turner's accusations about their constant lies, but the majority overruled them.

Before Cochran closed his computer and locked his office, he noticed he received an email with an alarming subject title.

STOP ALL YOUR PLANS OR SUFFER THE CONSEQUENCES

He read the brief message in the email.

We know what you're planning, and it needs to stop.
There will be no more warnings.
The Architect's Army

He shuffled upstairs to the residential quarters and made his way into the living room, using his cane for balance. His body could not stop trembling from the threatening message. He did not know who these people were, but just reading the name: *The Architect* brought a cold sweat over his entire body.

As he entered the living room, he saw his wife Estelle playing with their two grandchildren. He forced himself to put a big smile on his face.

"Estelle, I'm ready for dinner." Immediately, his two grandchildren, hearing their grandfather's voice, ran over to him, hugging his legs and almost knocking him over. They knew that it was time to read a story before their bedtime. As he lifted both children, his mind switched to his current problems, which he tried to keep out of his home life, but he found it difficult this evening.

Professor Cochran did not find it difficult to switch his personalities when home with his family, but at this moment, it was very difficult. He was a loving husband, father, and grandfather, never showing his brutal side to this family. However, what he had planned for the country he loved stressed him out. Yet, to the hundreds of thousands of his DRM followers, he was someone to fear.

Like it was yesterday, Cochran flashed back to before he fell in love with his wife. He was back when his path collided with Eric Kessler, a Nazi ex-patriot, and his brother Klaus when those men first took exile in the United States. They first met at one of his university lectures. They liked what they had heard about his dreams for the southern states and the classes he taught that every White man needed to feel proud of their heritage.

They became instant friends. While the Kesslers settled in Alabama during the early years, the brothers changed their surname to Stone and upgraded a plantation called Haven House to become the future White House of the South. The Professor realized these brothers could be just the catalyst he needed to help him grow his Domestic Revolutionary Movement. During those early years, Eric Kessler asked The Professor to mentor his son Charles and teach him the ways of the Nazis.

It was at that time that The Professor was introduced to the bastard grandson of Adolf Hitler. He learned that the Führer did not die in his bunker. It was his double that was the face of the Nazi movement. After the war, Hitler exiled to Argentina and created the Brown Shirt movement for his grandson. Wilhelm Hitler was just a boy at the time, but the Kesslers would be responsible for his grooming to be the new Führer to end democracy forever in the United States.

At first, the DRM movement needed Charles Stone to establish a mainstream White Supremacy movement. He did not quickly adapt to the ideology of the new Nazi Party forming in the United States.

Charles realized how wealthy he could become and had a different vision for the Domestic Revolutionary Movement.

In those early years, Cochran got hired by a Southern university that supported his racist beliefs. Moreover, the university's Chancellor tolerated how The Professor taught his young students the value of a needed race war, guiding them to be the new generation of White Supremacists.

Cochran snapped back to the present when he felt a tug on his shirtsleeve. "Grandpa, what about our story?" his young grandson pleaded.

He slid a wicker chair between their twin beds and opened their favorite story, *Little Black Sambo*. Cochran liked this story because Helen Bannerman was considered back then to be a racist beyond repair when she wrote the children's story in 1899.

It did not take long for both of his grandchildren to fall into a deep sleep. He dimmed their lights and shuffled out to the kitchen and gave his wife a warm kiss on her cheek.

"Sweetheart," Estelle said. "Tell me about your day?"

The Professor smiled and sat down at the kitchen table, thinking about what made-up story he could fabricate today.

8

Cochran was back at Blacks Landing Plantation, ready to monitor the planned attacks by his paramilitary militia. It had been two days since Paige Turner exposed the DRM's plans, setting off ripples within his organization. He had assembled his commanders so he could be assured their plans were still on schedule. It was strategic that these attacks went off without any disruption in twenty-seven states in the north.

"I think this will be a better way to start our race war and revolution," Cochran said. "These twenty-seven random shootings should be swift and brutal. Then, our followers in each state after the mass shootings will tell the authorities that they witnessed minority gangs leaving each scene. Then, panic will spread, and the police will begin to bust the heads of every Black man and Hispanic man they see on the streets. Once that begins, so will the riots and looting. Then, our supporters in Congress will open hearings and blame all the undocumented immigrants and the Black Lives Matter protesters, forcing all the local authorities to put in place curfews in areas where minorities live."

Godfrey Allen, the leader of the American Nazi Party, began clapping when Cochran finished talking. "When were you going to tell us about the warning you received from this so-called *Architect's Army* group you acquired yesterday," he said.

Cochran was stunned that Godfrey knew about the message. "I did get a threatening warning. How did you know?" he asked, puzzled.

"That's not important. I have my own connections within our movement," Godfrey replied.

The Professor gave Godfrey a strange look. "I believe whoever wrote this warning is a copycat group trying to move into the dead Architect's business space. What can a group of businessmen in suits do to our seasoned army of patriots?" Cochran said, a nervous edge to his voice.

Godfrey shook his head, appearing unsatisfied with Cochran's answer. He decided to change the subject. "Your new plan seems good on paper, but are you figuring out what the FBI might do once these small attacks happen? We don't have the firepower to go against the Bureau, as well as ATF and Homeland Security. What if President Thompson gets the National Guard involved?"

Cochran smiled at the question. "I'm hoping what we are doing will have them chasing their tails, plus we have the National Guard in the southern states that support our movement, on our side."

Godfrey Allen lashed back at The Professor. "We have another problem. President Thompson has asked Commander McAllister and his team to meet with him at Camp David. Charles Stone and the White Angels did not have a chance against the Commander and his Special Forces team. The Commander has the ear of a lot of influential Washington players who want to see our movement destroyed."

Professor Cochran was getting annoyed by Allen's remarks. "Don't you worry about my people or McAllister and his goons. Just you worry about getting your job done. I don't want to see you skipping out like you did when Charles Stone and Wiley Jordan needed you."

Johnny Ellis jumped into the conversation. "Professor, don't you worry about us. Me and my men have everything under control for tomorrow at the United Nations. You do what you need to do, and we'll do what we must do," Ellis said.

Godfrey Allen interrupted both men. "My Los Angeles group is ready to slaughter the commuters on the rush hour freeways in downtown Los Angeles. It should start another LA riot once the LAPD hears it was the niggers who slaughtered the commuters."

Cochran looked over at Billy Bob Crenshaw, the leader of their DC movement. "Do you have anything to add to all of this?"

Billy Bob shook his head. "Nothing, sir. My men are ready to go surprise the Capitol Police once again and deal with anything this Architect's Army group throws at us."

Cochran stood and walked toward the back door. He looked back at his team and shouted, "Let's kick some fucking ass and meet up back here in three days."

9

Three days after her podcast, Paige Turner and her Chief of Staff Rebecca Burns sat outside on Sam and Tiffany's deck at their Del Mar beach home. It was eight in the morning, midfifties, and the marine layer had not yet blown away. Paige found it uncomfortable introducing herself to two people she regarded as national heroes. As a junior investigative reporter and just a year out of Stanford, she had followed their remarkable careers. It was how they stopped Charles Stone and the White Angels, with the help from Commander McAllister, that became the motivating force that pushed her to stop Albert Dunham and his quest to become the next Emperor of the United States.

Tiffany noticed Turner's nervousness and opened the conversation. "Miss Turner, what brings you out to Del Mar? I watched your podcast the other day, and you must have rattled a few feathers in the Beltway?"

"Yes. All the way up to the President," she said, rolling her eyes. "I have a file I was given by an unknown source and wanted to get your opinion as to what to do with it."

Sam leaned forward, picked up the three-inch-thick folder, and started thumbing through the documents. "So, you haven't verified any of this but felt comfortable putting it out on the airways?" Sam said, his tone a little too aggressive even for him.

"That's correct," she replied. "I had waited too long to expose *The Architect*, and it almost destroyed our democracy. I wasn't going to do that again. What was inside the file scared me. I felt it important to alert the public first. Better safe than sorry, I always say." She shrugged her shoulders and grinned. "I wanted to talk with you and Tiffany first and get your take on all of this. I'm unsure what direction I need to go, as it seems these attacks are scheduled to happen any day now."

"Have you been to the FBI?" Tiffany asked.

"I tried after my podcast, but the FBI Director declined to see me. Something to do with him not being allowed to investigate unsubstantiated material. He can react after something happens, he said. Something about the new Freedom to Privacy Act legislation President Thompson signed into law a few months ago."

Tiffany and Sam seemed shocked at what she had just said. "Has the President forgotten that the FBI stands for the Federal Bureau of Investigation, not the Bureau of wait and see what happens?" Tiffany blurted out.

"Commander John McAllister will be joining us with his team. If anyone would know what to do, he's the man," Sam said.

Tiffany finished perusing the file. "When I was with the FBI, something like this we'd take very seriously. Are you sure you don't know who sent this to you?"

Paige slumped her shoulders, shaking her head, and tossed Tiffany the note she received inside the package. "I wish I did."

Before Turner could finish speaking, Commander McAllister and Bubba Jackson barged onto the deck. With no warm greetings, he ordered Sam to turn on his television. "We're too late," the Commander said.

On a seventy-five-inch screen in the Collins' living room, everyone sat silent as they watched and listened to the special news alert.

10

Professor Cochran and his DRM Generals were in their command center at Blacks Landing, staring at three large monitors. The random attacks would be watched simultaneously in Manhattan, Los Angeles, and Washington, DC. Today would be the first of many mass casualty shootings the Domestic Revolutionary Movement had planned over the next few days. Every attack was scheduled to happen precisely at 11:35 AM EST.

Professor Cochran, after careful planning, had put in place the best soldiers he had recruited to help him start his race war, as well as the civil war he so wanted. The digital clock above the three monitors was ticking down. In ten minutes, hundreds, maybe thousands, of Americans would be lying dead in the streets.

Cochran raised his hand, signaling his Generals to become silent. On monitor number one, The Professor watched commuters, schoolchildren, and tourists that were packed into Grand Central Station, the main hub for the Long Island Railroad and the New York subway system, walking briskly to exit the beautifully adorned terminal to get to their desired locations.

Today was extremely hectic as the UN delegates opened their session on the rising hate and terrorism worldwide. Security was on high alert. NYPD SWAT patrolled Grand Central Station and the perimeter around the United Nations building. Long lines of visitors stretched outside the UN headquarters. It was a beautiful day in Manhattan. The skies were a deep blue, and the East River was calm except for the five Coast Guard gunboats that patrolled the waterway. Paige Turner's podcast put every law enforcement agency on high alert.

The Professor knew that two hundred yards south on 42nd Street, just West of First Avenue, sat four of his men in a city utility van, monitoring a digital clock mounted on the dashboard. Their countdown matching to the command center's clock.

He watched Johnny Ellis, who had body armor under his uniform, speak in a low, calm voice to his men. "In ten minutes, our war starts," said the young, tattooed man. "Our brothers in two other strategic locations will concurrently begin their attacks. Today marks the day we finally take back what is rightfully ours. We have the honor bestowed on us by Professor Cochran to be one of three teams today that will set our race war in motion. Let's make our brothers proud."

Cochran noticed the other three young men, dressed in New York City utility uniforms, who had their body armor under their clothing. He noticed that they were sitting nervously, keeping silent as Johnny Ellis reminded them of what they had to do.

Ellis continued with his orders. "When the first explosion happens, each of you needs to go to your stations and start firing your weapons as the crowds run from the UN Building. Defend yourself from the police if you must, but don't back down. Now, go and wait for the signal."

Cochran watched his team, wearing their NYC Con Edison uniforms, take their positions. He noticed two men dressed in black approaching Ellis's vehicle. Their weapons at their sides. One of the hooded men tapped at the driver's side window with the barrel of his gun. The Professor tried to dial Ellis, but it was too late.

He watched Ellis, his eyes wide with fear, knowing he was about to die, press down on the detonator he held in his right hand a second before a bullet exploded through the center of his forehead.

The two men dressed in black turned their bodies toward the explosions ringing out inside the United Nations building and at the west end of 42nd Street, somewhere close to Grand Central Station. They watched in horror as three men dressed in Con Edison uniforms opened fire on the fleeing men, women, and children running from the buildings. Then, behind them, down near Grand Central Station, they heard more gunfire.

"Shit," one of the men in black cursed. "We need to help."

The other man said, "No. Finish your job. Then we need to report back to our team."

Cochran viewed in horror as one of the men opened the front passenger door and pinned a note to Ellis's chest. The camera in the vehicle facing his dead soldier made it easy for The Professor to read the bloody note:

An eye for an eye.
We are coming for all of you.
You need to stop killing our customers.
We know who you are.
The Architect's Army!

* * * * *

The two vigilantes walked calmly back to their unmarked black van and immediately called their leader. "We didn't stop the attack. Hundreds of innocent people, including children, are dead."

The leader of The Architect's Army continued to stare at his monitor. He couldn't believe what he was witnessing. Then, the hysterical reporter switched to her affiliate station in Los Angeles.

"Get back to our meeting place and wait for more orders," the man's voice said.

* * * * *

The Professor gazed at the inside of Grand Central Station, as more gunfire erupted. Ellis's team, unaware their leader was dead, opened fire, mowing down hundreds of commuters running to get outside.

When three SWAT officers opened fire on the men in Con Ed uniforms, their bullets had no effect. Ellis's men returned fire, killing one SWAT officer and wounding another. The third officer, realizing what was happening, decided that a kill shot to the head was the correct action and downed one of the shooters.

"Headshots work," he radioed to his team. "Shooters have full-body armor."

The attacks were over in less than ten minutes, and all the shooters inside Grand Central Station and outside the United Nations were dead. The carnage was hard to look at. Men, women, and young children lay twisted in pools of blood.

The commander of SWAT received word that more attacks had happened across the United States.

* * * * *

Cochran tried to remain calm, as he rewound the video on monitor two. He watched his Los Angeles group at 8:35 Pacific Coast Time initiate their attack on three of Los Angeles's most traveled freeways that merged in downtown Los Angeles. The freeways were close to maximum capacity as commuters inched their way to their office buildings. Overpasses were at a standstill, as gridlock was blocking every intersection. Car horns were blasting, igniting more frustration from angry drivers.

Cochran knew that his team of four men dressed in LAPD SWAT gear was waiting at a heliport about a mile from where the first attack would take place. He heard his team leader, Max Simon, speaking to his team.

"We have sixty seconds before the explosions are triggered," Max said. *"Liftoff will be when we hear the first explosion. That will be our signal to spray our weapons over all the cars and people running for their lives on the Santa Monica Freeway. After that, we will hit the Harbor Freeway, Hollywood Freeway, then the 60 Freeway, and reevaluate and survey our damage,"* the Leader of the White Lives Matter group said.

Cochran switched back to his men that were sitting in a black Ford pickup truck near the Los Angeles interchange. The men were from the Los Angeles White Lives Matter group. He listened as his team leader spoke to his men.

"We need to get into our positions, and when you hear the bombs go off, that will be your signal to start killing anyone you see, with emphasis on all Black men and women."

"Sir," a young boy, no older than seventeen, with alabaster skin and tattoos covering his neck and arms, interrupted. "What do we do if the police start shooting at us?"

Godfrey looked irritated. He didn't like being interrupted. *"Shit, Leroy, you're in full-body armor and we'll be so fast and efficient that the police won't be able to drive through all of the bullet-riddled cars stopped on the freeways. All of the bodies lying on the freeways will have them throwing up their lunch,"* he said, waving his phone above his head. *"We've got contingencies. If the police even come close, there are more overpasses we can blow up."* The team leader opened his hand, his fingers spread wide, and yelled, "Boom." He showed his phone's screen to the boy. *"It's time. Let's get the fuck back to the job at hand."*

Once again, Cochran sat horrified, seeing two men dressed in black walking toward his team. Before Leroy could open his door, the passenger door window exploded from a high-powered gun that shattered half of his skull. Godfrey tried to react, but another bullet entered his left temple from the second shooter.

The two men looked around to be sure they were not spotted. One of the men leaned in and pinned a note to Godfrey's and Leroy's chests. Again, the camera inside the car allowed The Professor to read it.

An eye for an eye.
We are coming for all of you.
You need to stop killing our customers.
We know who you are.

The Architect's Army!

While the two men walked casually back to their car, Cochran heard four explosions go off on the three overpasses at the merging freeways. Motorists were screaming and running for their lives. He noticed the two vigilantes looking up and pointing at two unmarked helicopters hovering over the panicked people. Within seconds, bullets began spraying from the helicopters, killing the terrified motorists trying to run for safety.

Fifteen minutes had passed since the Manhattan attack and Cochran was afraid of what he might see at the Washington, DC, attack as he rewound that video on monitor three.

The Professor could see Arlo Bennett, one of a dozen Captains inside the American Nazi Party, panning the Capitol Mall. Cochran was pleased to see hundreds of tourists taking photos and walking at a leisurely pace. He prayed this attack would turn out better for his team.

Cochran watched Bennett turn his body on the park bench to face Stanley Kipfer, his top lieutenant in his group. Cochran could hear his man speaking.

"Is everyone in place?" Arlo asked.

"Sir, I have fifty of our best men ready to initiate our attack. Some are strolling among the tourists. Each of our high-value targets has our men strategically positioned," Kipfer said, his voice calm and even.

Arlo squeezed Stan's shoulder, nodding, and showing his approval. "Very good. Today, what we are doing here, in Manhattan and in Los Angeles will go down in American history as the day the second revolutionary war started. In two days, we will hit Chicago and Dallas. The FBI and every police department will be scurrying around, trying to figure out what's going on. Then we will set off bombs at ten synagogues, five Black churches, and fifteen mosques around the country," Arlo said, anxiously standing up, feeling paranoid. He pulled out his cell phone and dialed his team leader Billy Bob Crenshaw.

Arlo sensed he was being watched. Something was making the hair on his neck stand at attention. He called his team leader. "Billy, something doesn't seem right here. I have a bad feeling we're being watched."

"Relax. All our men are in place—nothing to worry about. You and Stanley enjoy the sunshine. Everyone's in place and ready to go once you detonate the bombs," Crenshaw said, abruptly ending the call.

Stanley immediately noticed the concern on Arlo's face, too. "Something's bothering you," he said. "I can tell. Spit it out."

Bennett glanced at this watch and noticed there were two minutes left as his timer ticked down. "I'm sure it's nothing, just my nerves acting up."

Before Stan could reply, two men dressed in black approached the bench, their guns at their sides. One of the men pushed Arlo back, forcing him to sit. Then, without any warning, Kipfer felt the muzzle of a gun pressing on the center of his chest. Before he could react, the bullet exploded inside his heart. The other man, within seconds, did the same thing to Arlo. The detonator dropped on the grass.

Cochran watched in horror as the two men leaned both bodies together and pinned two notes to Arlo's and Stan's chests. The Professor could not read what the assassins pinned on the two dead bodies, but he had a good idea.

An eye for an eye.
We are coming for all of you.
You need to stop killing our customers.
We know who you are.

The Architect's Army!
Cochran noticed the assailants looking around, pleased that the tourists walking by did not notice the two dead men. They started to walk back toward the Washington Monument when three loud explosions shook the ground, causing

them to lose their balance. Off in the distance, they heard gunfire and people screaming.

The Professor leaned back in his high-back chair, sucking in deep breaths. "Gentlemen, while we made a statement today, we have lost too many patriots who will be sorely missed."

11

Fifteen minutes had gone by, and every major news station was covering the unthinkable attacks on American soil. Cochran threw his glass of whiskey across his office, glass crystals shattering everywhere. What he heard on the evening news did not please him. Losing fifteen of his most seasoned patriots was unacceptable. "How could anyone know where we were planning our attacks?" he muttered. Then, tapping his cane on his tiled floor, he thought about other possibilities. "I have a fucking traitor in my group."

He leaned back in his desk chair, listening intently to the news on three of the major news networks.

ABC's reporter on the scene at the United Nations found it hard to control her tears. *"Panic and confusion are everywhere in Manhattan and around our nation today,"* the reporter said, fighting back her tears. *"Not since 9/11 have New Yorkers felt so powerless. The same for the Americans in our nation's capital and Los Angeles. Over fifteen hundred Americans died today from one of the worst gun violence attacks in our country's history. Yet, the NYPD will not comment on who the perpetrators were or if they believe this was a foreign terrorist attack or one of the many domestic terrorist attacks our country has been hit with over the last few years."*

The reporter pointed her cameraman toward a car the police were investigating. *"It appears that two men, believed to be the leaders of this terrorist cell, appear to have been assassinated by a vigilante who left a note pinned to the chest of one of the terrorists:*

47

An eye for an eye.
We are coming for all of you.
You need to stop killing our customers.
We know who you are.

The Architect's Army!"

The reporter cupped her hand over her ear, the microphone shaking in her head. *"More on the shooting in Washington, DC, and Los Angeles. It seems that the same vigilante group assassinated more terrorists and left similar notes pinned to their clothing. Until we have more information from the authorities, we can only speculate on what's going on. This is Susan Williams, ABC news."*

After listening to every news channel, Professor Cochran called Wesley Jones, founder of a White Supremacist Church in Kentucky.

"Wesley, we have a big problem. We have a traitor in our group. We need to find this person immediately and deal with him!" Cochran shouted.

"Albert, calm down. What we accomplished today is precisely what we set out to do. Unfortunately, we lost some of our men, but they knew there would be risks. Look on the bright side; over fifteen hundred Americans died, creating panic and finger-pointing. Our surrogates are already telling the authorities that they saw people of color committing these heinous acts. It's what we wanted," Jones said.

"Let's wait and see what happens after the attacks tomorrow and Friday," Cochran said, abruptly hanging up, cutting off Jones before he could get in the last word.

The Professor stopped himself from turning off his monitor when a Breaking News Alert flashed on his screen.

The President of the United States, his eyes focused on the floor, walked over to his podium in the White House Briefing Room. When he raised his head, the cameras caught an exhausted and pale-looking leader of the free world. He adjusted his microphone, his hands trembling as he began addressing the nation.

"Today marks a sad day for our country. Vigilantes murdered patriotic citizens of our country in Washington, DC, Los Angeles, and Manhattan, New York."
Reporters sat there, shocked that the President was honoring the terrorists who

had just slaughtered innocent men, women, and children. Thompson just sucked in a deep breath and continued talking, his face ashen.

"Witnesses have come forward and provided the FBI descriptions of the domestic terrorists, and they were not White Supremacists that the media has reported. What we currently know is that different groups, gangs to be exact, were responsible for the heinous slaughter of innocent Americans."

President Thaddeus Thompson took a sip from his glass of water and leaned into the microphone. With a threatening tone, he said: *"The killers responsible for today's attack are on my radar, and we are coming for you."* After sipping again from his glass of water, he turned to his right and began walking off from the podium, refusing to take any questions. Then, to everyone's surprise, without warning, he collapsed, falling like a limp rag doll, his head bouncing off the carpet.

His Secret Service detail was immediately at his side, attending to him. One agent felt for a pulse, shaking his head. Another Secret Service agent screamed to cut the cameras and ordered everyone out of the briefing room.

* * * * *

Professor Cochran sat behind his desk in shock, his hands cupping his head. "What else could go wrong today? He was our biggest supporter."

With his composure coming back, Cochran called Wiley Jordan. "How fast can you rally your men to initiate Operation Self-Defense? I'm not so sure what we did today will ignite the race war we need. I'm confident that Operation Self-Defense will do the job."

Wiley didn't respond immediately, deep in thought.

"Are you there?" The Professor shouted.

"Yes. Give me a moment. I'm thinking."

"What's there to think about?"

"I want to be clear on what you're asking," Wiley shot back. "You want my men to patrol neighborhoods wearing our White Angels jackets in densely populated Black areas and, when confronted with one or a mob of Blacks, shoot first and claim self-defense?"

"Correct," Cochran said. "I'll have our attorneys ready to defend your men. What you will create are numerous distracting protests while we continue with our other attacks."

"I hope you're fucking right," Wiley barked. "I'm not ready to lose more men like I did when Charles Stone was alive and running the DRM. Why not let my men start fires as we did for Charles Stone? It's easier and safer for them."

"No more fires at this time. Operation Self-Defense strategy has worked before. And will continue to work if your men remain consistent with their responses."

12

Sam stood up, and the color drained from his face. He offered his guests something to drink. "Who needs a whiskey?" he asked, trying to conceal his shaking hands in his pants pocket. Everyone nodded. "How many fingers?" he asked as he walked toward the wet bar adjacent to the dining room. Everyone responded, indicating they all wanted five fingers of whiskey.

Carrying an oak tray with six glass tumblers, he gently lowered the drinks onto the coffee table. He exhaled a stressful breath. "How could this slaughter happen? And what just happened with President Thompson? Do you think he died of natural causes or something suspicious?"

Commander McAllister responded. "I had a man inside the DRM during their recent convention where their leader addressed his audience and talked about the unprovoked murder of innocent minorities. Nothing was said about an assassination attempt. All I know is that these attacks were coming, when or where was a mystery," he said sadly.

Tiffany squinted, with a confused look on her face. She addressed Paige Turner with her question. "Did you tell anyone at Homeland or the FBI?"

"I did. They said they couldn't do anything about it unless they had concrete evidence that was not from a spy inside the DRM. I'm not sure if they are hiding behind the new legislation President Thompson signed into law or if they are supporters of the White Supremacy movement in our country." Paige said, her tone a little testy.

"I got into a shouting match with the President over this same subject," McAllister said heatedly. "I feel terrible that my last words with the President were not very pleasant."

Paige was listening to everyone talk, trying to remain quiet, but finally had to add more in. "There are rumors inside the West Wing and the Hall of Congress that White Supremacists are in powerful positions that allow them to make decisions that will harm our democracy. It was believed that President Thompson was a White Supremacist sympathizer. That's probably why his last words did not condone these bastards," she said. "I'm trying my best to expose them, but fighting a losing battle on my own. I sometimes feel like Don Quixote swatting at windmills."

Sam bit his lower lip, drawing blood. "I need to call up some favors I had in the DOJ and see what I can turn up," he said. "Tiffany, maybe you can call some of your old friends at the FBI and see how morale is there now that Thompson is dead. You might be able to get a clue as to what is going on?"

Sam and Tiffany did not want to talk too much around Paige Turner. What they knew of her was that she would expose a good story if she had one, and they were not ready to trust her.

Finally, Turner could sense she was an outsider and excused herself.

McAllister and Bubba Jackson stayed behind and brought Sam and Tiffany up to date on what they had from their spy at the DRM.

13

The United States was on full terrorist alert after the tragic events from the East Coast to the West Coast. The intelligence community was asleep at the wheel, even though they had a warning from Paige Turner.

The sudden death of President Thaddeus Thompson rocked the free world and tanked the stock market. His comments about these attacks coming from gangs of color and not White Supremacists would sadly go answered in the halls of Congress.

There were protests in the streets calling for the DOJ, FBI, and Homeland Security to be able to act against all White Supremacist militia groups and gangs of color. The protesters carried signs demanding that President Thompson's Freedom to Privacy legislation be abolished.

By seven in the evening Eastern Time, eight hours after the attacks happened, Vice President Shannon Graham was sworn in as the forty-seventh President by Chief Justice Margaret Little. The Speaker of the House, Bradley White, was made the acting Vice President until President Graham could appoint her replacement.

President Graham immediately called the Joint Chiefs, her entire Cabinet, including the FBI Director, CIA Director, Homeland Security Director, and Secretary of Defense, to the Situation Room. Sitting in the back of the room were Godfrey Evans, the President's Press Secretary, and Graham's Chief of Staff, Martha Radcliff.

She wanted to be brought up to speed on the recent attacks and who these domestic terrorists actually were. She did not believe President Thompson was telling the truth before he died and needed to see who she could begin trusting in her new administration.

The meeting took over five hours, and President Graham was not pleased with her existing Cabinet Secretaries. By 7:00 AM the next day, the new President started asking for resignations. The first one she asked for was from the FBI Director. Then the Attorney General and finally President Thaddeus Thompson's Chief of Staff. As Vice President, she had too many policy issues with these men and wanted people who would have her back when needed.

After her Press Secretary announced these changes, the halls inside the West Wing looked like a ghost town. The once-animated offices were now silent, waiting for the next shoe to drop on their careers.

Later that day, President Graham was on the phone with Sam Collins and Tiffany Glass. She told them she needed their help and if they would consider working at the pleasure of their new President. While Sam and Tiffany did not agree at first, they said they would come to Washington to talk some more about what the new President wanted from them.

Later that day, Press Secretary Godfrey Evans leaked to the press that Sam Collins would be asked to come out of retirement and be President Graham's new Attorney General. In addition, Tiffany Glass would be asked to be the next FBI Director, and Martha Sweeden would be the new Chief of Staff for President Shannon Graham.

As expected, all the conservative cable news stations were calling for President Graham to be impeached for the rash emotional decisions she had made so quickly after taking office. A handful of House Representatives, all Republicans, tried to bring up an impeachment vote, which never saw the light of day.

After President Graham's first two days as President, the entire country and the world held their breath, waiting for more resignations as she addressed the nation on her third day in office.

14

Two days after meeting with Paige Turner, the Commander, and Bubba. Tiffany, and Sam were sitting on their beach house's large wooden deck that overlooked the pounding surf. They were contemplating what President Graham and the country were asking of them. It had been over ten years and three administrations since they retired from public life after they stopped Charles Stone's civil war. They promised each other that they would never put their family in harm's way again.

During that time, they had two children and built a consumer advocacy agency. Tiffany looked at Sam with a puzzled expression.

"Are we making too quick of a decision to get back into the political world we both despise?" she asked, while sipping her warm cup of coffee.

"I'm wondering that too. Over the last ten years, we've witnessed increases in hate crimes. We've watched how our political system has been turned upside down, and the country we love give illegal militias some legitimacy, especially the large number of White Supremacist groups like the White Angels." Sam appeared to be having a PTSD moment mentioning their name. "Shit, after Stone died, I thought we had eliminated them. What I can't fathom is that our current leaders, as well as a majority of White Americans, see White Supremacists as patriotic citizens," Sam said, unable to catch his breath.

"After Charles Stone was brutally murdered by the people who once called him leader, I too never believed the White Angel types who backed him would ever crawl out from the holes they scurried into," Tiffany said, tensing her jaw.

"While hate has been escalating, so has corporate corruption. Maybe if we are front and center in our new positions, we might be able to curtail, or maybe put our democracy back on the correct path," Sam said, breathing heavily. Anytime he mentioned Charles Stone, his blood pressure rose.

Tiffany noticed the tension on her husband's face. "We've talked about this subject many times. I agree with you, but until now, there was nothing we could do. We tried to help President Wilson during his last term in office, and it did not work. Will helping our first female President finally close the door on all the White Supremacists that want to destroy our democracy and rebuild their crazy Confederacy? Will she take the drastic steps to once and for all eliminate hate in America? That is one of the questions I need to get answers to so I can make a sound decision to be the next FBI Director."

Sam put his coffee cup down on the deck and took Tiffany's hand. "What about Irene and Michael? You just had our second child. Can you physically handle the long hours and travel expected as FBI Director?"

Tiffany smiled. "That's why I have you, Mister Dad. You're great with Irene and Michael, and during the day, we will take their nanny back to DC for them. She loves them and they love her too. Remember, Irene's in school, and Michael is getting easier as each day goes by."

Sam let loose a loud belly laugh. "Are you talking about our little Micky, the monster who's been terrorizing us all day long?" The moment his words flowed out of his mouth, adorable little Michael started screaming.

Irene, who was now ten years and acting like a teenager, came running to the deck. "Can you shut Michael up? I'm on a Zoom call with my friends," she barked and stormed back to her upstairs bedroom. She craned her neck and yelled back at her father, "Do something now, please."

Sam rolled his eyes at Tiffany. "Boy, she's so much like you."

"Go get your son, and I'll deal with Irene," Tiffany giggled.

15

Sam was feeding Michael on the back deck when Tiffany joined them. "See, he's a perfect little angel," Sam teased. "See, this is how you create the perfect child," he boasted, just as Michael flung his bowl of oatmeal. While Sam wiped the sticky cereal off his face and shorts, Tiffany tried to high-five her son, only irritating her husband more.

Just as Tiffany was pouring herself a second cup of coffee, a sandstorm overtook the three of them. The baby started screaming from the sand pelting his eyes. Sam covered him up in a beach towel, carrying him into the house.

Sam was puzzled that the swirling sand started dying down and was only happening by their beach house.

He and Tiffany heard the propellers get louder as a helicopter with the Presidential Seal came into view. It took only a few seconds for Commander John McAllister to jump out, holding his SEAL baseball cap, bending low as he jogged toward the two surprised parents.

Sam grabbed McAllister's arm and pulled him inside, away from the propeller noise. "What are you doing here?"

McAllister had a puzzled expression. "Haven't you heard the latest news?"

Sam looked at Tiffany. They both shook their heads. "What news?"

"There were ten bombings today around the country at churches, mosques, and synagogues. All when services were happening, I don't have a count of the dead, but it's in the high hundreds."

Sam sat down, his face flushed. "Do we know who did this? Or why?"

"No. President Graham wanted you at the White House yesterday. Pack up what you'll need. Air Force One is ready to take off at Miramar. We leave in one hour."

Fifteen minutes later, Sam had Michael facing forward in his snuggly that was attached to his chest. Tiffany had Irene by her hand. "John, can you help our nanny and grab Michael's bags and load them?"

McAllister looked at all the bags for Michael and groaned. "I took less on my survival missions. You're already too soft with your kid, Collins. Let me have a few weeks with him. I'll have him whipped into SEAL shape."

"He's not even a year yet. Just wait till he's awake. He'll have you giving him twenty before you get off Air Force One, you crusty old fart."

16

President Graham was uneasy sitting behind her new desk in the Oval Office. She appeared overwhelmed in the historic room as she squirmed in her chair. She forced a smile as Sam and Tiffany sat down in front of her desk. Commander McAllister remained standing behind his two friends, his hands locked behind his back.

"Sam and Tiffany, thank you for coming to Washington on such short notice. I followed your careers when I was a junior House Representative and have admired the work the two of you have done for our country. What you accomplished over ten years ago was a miracle," she said, noticing Commander McAllister point his index finger toward his chest. "Yes, yes, I know, Commander, what you and your team did to end Charles Stone's civil war as well as defusing the White Angels back a few decades."

Commander McAllister blushed, feeling embarrassed that he forced the President to praise him. Never in his military life did he need or ask for praise and felt bad acting the way he did. "Madame President, I was just joking and don't want you to think I need to be complimented for doing my job. I love our country and would die to defend it and protect our democracy and constitution."

"John, I know that, and I too was just joking," she said, holding back her smile. "Let me talk about why I called all of you here today. Our country is at the weakest point in our fragile history. Our grand experiment with democracy is being threatened by a large part of our population, as well as a political party that only wants to have autocratic authority over every citizen," Graham said, swiping a tear off her cheek.

She was known all her political career to be an honest politician who did not talk out of both sides of her mouth, a rarity in the halls of the Capital. She was known for working on both sides of the aisle. Every Representative and Senator knew she would listen to their side of an issue and then argue her point without burning any bridges.

"I was not ready to become President, but now that I am the first female Commander-in-Chief, I want to try to unite our country so we can save our democracy from these domestic terrorists before it's too late."

Tiffany instantly liked her and interrupted her pep talk. "President Graham, I have a general idea of what you want from me, but I need some clarification after witnessing these heinous attacks."

Before the President could respond, Sam jumped into the conversation. "I second that. What will you expect from me as your Attorney General?"

President Graham stood and started pacing around the room. "I'm glad both of you asked those questions. I'm sorry to say, I don't know what I need. I am hoping the two of you, with your experience with the last attempt of a civil war, can guide me and tell me how you can help me and our country."

For the next two hours, the most powerful woman in the world and three of the most popular heroes in the country laid out a plan to end the violence and bring the country back to a middle ground that every American would support.

* * * * *

As Commander McAllister headed out of the Oval Office, his cell phone pinged. It was from his spy inside the DRM, Jack Petry. "Jack, what up?"

"My wife and son were supposed to be at the synagogue that was bombed," he cried. "I've been calling Lea's cell and my son Seth's cell too and they are not answering or going to voicemail. I'm scared that they were inside when the bombs went off."

"Glad you called me. I'll check it out and get back to you," McAllister said. "Don't go there. You'll blow your cover." The Commander abruptly ended the call.

17

A Breaking News Break Alert using the Emergency Broadcasting System took over every television and radio station. President Shannon Graham was standing behind a podium in the briefing room, with Tiffany Glass on her right and Sam Collins on her left. All the White House Press Corps were speculating on what these two were going to do for President Graham in their respective positions. The room quieted down when the President started speaking.

"My fellow Americans, it is a sad time in our country when White Supremacists… homegrown domestic terrorists, murder innocent citizens because of the color of their skin. I'm appalled at how gun violence is at an all-time high and our Senate and House of Representatives are not sending me gun control legislation to sign. Average citizens, non-military citizens should not be able to buy military weapons to use on innocent Americans." President Graham sucked in a deep breath before continuing. Her emotions were showing as tears cascaded down her cheeks.

"From this day forward, these domestic terrorists will not go unpunished. I'll be issuing new Executive Orders to curb the sale of military-type guns, body armor, and other weapons that are for military use only. In addition, I am going to disband all militia groups that are not part of our National Guard. I am authorizing the DOJ and FBI to formulate a plan to neutralize these groups." President Graham paused and took a sip of water.

"Since both houses of Congress refuse to create legislation to prevent automatic weapons from being sold, then I have no choice but to sign an executive order placing on all automatic military weapons an excise tax of $10,000 per gun to help slow down or stop the sale of these weapons to average citizens," President Graham said, blotting her the tears.

"I have asked two of our country's most loved Americans, Tiffany Glass-Collins and Sam Collins, to help me arrest and remove these evil human beings from society." President Graham combed her fingers through her long red hair as she looked at the camera. "I'm appalled and frustrated with some of our Senators and House Members who feel these scum are patriots only exercising their First Amendment right to free speech. Let me be clear, any American citizen who randomly murders people of color, will be tried for murder with special circumstances of a hate crime, which under Federal law carries the death penalty." She tried to catch her breath as her heart kept racing.

"I am giving FBI Director Glass full authority to do whatever it takes to hunt down these animals and put an end to their reign of terror against our citizens. In addition to these Executive Orders, I've signed another executive order declaring war on domestic terrorists. If needed, I will institute martial law if these attacks continue," she said.

President Graham's hands continued to shake and she went on with, "In addition, I will have my new Attorney General, Sam Collins, issue as many subpoenas and no-knock search warrants to help the FBI do its job. I've temporarily suspended the Freedom to Privacy Act so our law enforcement agencies can do their job and protect all citizens." President Graham leaned forward toward the cameras. "White Supremacists and supporters of these groups, read my lips. Your time terrorizing our country is over. If you want to go to war with us, then be prepared to go against the full might of the United States military. You're not patriots, but traitors who will be treated as such. I'm coming for all of you. My warning extends to *The Architect's Army*. You are vigilantes and need to stop doing what you've been doing, or you'll be hunted down and locked up, too. I won't tolerate citizens taking the law into their own hands."

The President turned and walked off with her new FBI Director and Attorney General without answering any White House Press Corps questions. The three of them headed for the Oval Office.

* * * * *

Inside the Oval Office were the Joint Chiefs, the Secretary of State, the Secretary of Defense, the Homeland Security Secretary, the CIA Director, the President's Chief of Staff and Press Secretary, as well as Deputy Assistant Attorney General Mathew Heffron. President Graham sat behind her desk, shuffling a stack of papers.

"Everyone, please sit. We have a lot to go over and not much time," the President said, her face stone-cold serious.

Martha Sweeden, President Graham's Chief of Staff, handed everyone a file folder marked Top Secret. "After this meeting adjourns, these materials need to be left by your seats. Nothing inside your folders or what is said here today will leave this room," she ordered. "I also expect all cellphones to be turned off. I need to see your acknowledgment."

Everyone in the room nodded their heads.

President Graham started to speak. "We are at a crisis point in our country's history. Domestic terrorists have been percolating since the end of the Civil War. Their beliefs and actions against non-Whites have broader support today among other White Americans, especially within the halls of Congress and the judicial system. Their message of hate has become normalized to the point that the news media and certain Congressmen and Senators are labeling them as patriots. Even after all the attacks, we still have House Members and Senators pushing the notion that these animals were only expressing their First Amendment rights to free speech and normal political discourse." Graham took a quick breath and continued. "What galls me the most is that these domestic terrorists say they love our country, except for all the people of color that interact with them " The President paused and sipped from her glass of water.

"President Thompson accepted donations from at least a dozen of the most dominant hate groups and looked the other way after they committed crimes against humanity. I want to let every American know that we are at war with American citizens who are part of these illegal militias that preach hate and commit crimes against our country. No more will we look the other way. No more will we make excuses for these animals," Graham said as she blotted the perspiration from her forehead. "I am putting our new Attorney General Sam Collins in charge of ending this war legally, if possible."

The President looked directly at Sam Collins, pointing her index finger at him. "I expect you and your department to figure out how to redefine the term *domestic terrorist* and tie it into the wording of the constitution so these terrorists can be punished for treason, nothing less."

Collins noticed no one was saying anything, but he had a question for President Graham. "How do you classify those vigilantes, The Architect's Army, who appear to be doing what I sense is what you'd like to do to these White Supremacists?"

"Sam, that's a good question. While I don't condone any citizen taking justice into their own hands, I am conflicted about what to do about them. They are considered heroes by a majority of Americans. My problem is that they are calling themselves *The Architect's Army*. I need to know more about this new group and if they are affiliated with *The Architect's Manifesto*. If they are, then we have another problem that will need to be dealt with."

Sam shrugged his shoulders. "So, as your Attorney General, I can hunt them down too and arrest them?"

Director Glass wanted to make a comment. "Madame President, dealing with these White Supremacists won't be easy. What I know about them is that they are well organized and get financial support from inside Europe from our enemies. You need to make sure our Department of Defense and Homeland Security are monitoring all social media and emails and texts coming from Europe. Right now, we are vulnerable. Our enemies are waiting to find our Achilles Heel to attack us. I'll need to create a handful of specialized units to monitor and track the numerous hate groups hidden inside our country. Some of what I want to do will go outside the parameters of the law. With that said, I want to deputize Commander John McAllister. He'll be able to bend the rules, which will be a big help," Tiffany said.

President Graham was nodding her head. "Sam, you and FBI Director Glass will stay back with me after this meeting concludes. We have a lot to discuss regarding this *Architect's Army* group and our domestic terrorist problem."

After another two hours, President Graham ended her meeting.

18

Commander McAllister lost all control of his emotions as he bent under the crime scene tape at the bombed synagogue. The structure was still smoldering from the massive fire that had engulfed the congregation. He marched over to the paramedics carrying out the bodies from the burnt structure. The scene reminded him of bombed villages in Afghanistan.

The charred remains made it impossible to identify any of the victims. Then, the paramedic pointed him toward the large white tent a hundred yards away from the smoldering building.

"Additional bodies we've taken out are all over there," the paramedic said.

The Commander's pace slowed as he entered the tent and saw five rows of black body bags, ten deep, neatly lined up. The smell of burnt flesh made him gag. It had been ten hours since the massive bombings had taken place. The Commander's guilt blanketed his body, angry that his man hidden deep inside the DRM had sacrificed his family.

McAllister recognized the medical examiner and walked over to him. The medical examiner raised his head. "John, what are you doing here? You're looking for someone, right?"

"My friend's wife and son. They were supposed to be here when the bomb went off. He hasn't heard from them in almost ten hours, and he's terrified."

Woodman put his hand on McAllister's shoulder and gave it a gentle squeeze. "So far, we haven't found any survivors. Most of the bodies are burnt beyond recognition."

The Commander sucked in a deep breath. "I need some answers for him."

"It will be days before we can try to identify each body. However, we have a list of names that were inside and will do our best to identify each victim for their next of kin," the medical examiner said.

"Can I see the list of congregation members who were inside?"

McAllister took the list outside and scanned all the names. His friend's wife and son were not listed. He went back inside to find out if this was a complete list.

"Joseph, is this everyone who was inside?"

The medical examiner shrugged his shoulders. "That's the list I was given. Is there a problem?"

McAllister did not respond. He stormed off and jumped into his car. He needed to talk with Bubba Jackson. He wanted to know if they found out who did these bombings.

19

Tiffany and Sam were on their way to the Mayflower Hotel to see their children. As the new FBI Director, she needed to digest everything the President was asking of her. Before they could close the door to their four-bedroom suite, Irene jumped into her father's arms, complaining that her brother had been a real butt to everyone. Bubba Jackson looked worn out.

Tiffany looked at Bubba with a silly grin. "Did my little soldier wear you down?" she asked, unable to contain her laughter. "We told you Michael was a handful," she said, bending over to pick up her son.

Bubba Jackson tried to keep his mouth shut but could not. "Your son needs a few weeks on Coronado at the SEAL training station, like the Commander suggested," he barked, waving his finger at little Michael, who was sticking his tiny tongue out at his godfather.

Sam put Irene down and walked over to the living room couch. "Bubba, let's stop screwing around. We have a lot to talk about. Where's John?"

"He went over to the synagogue that was bombed. A close friend of his cannot locate his family who was supposed to be there at the time of the bombings."

There was a knock at the door. It was the nanny for the kids and Commander McAllister. The young woman immediately lifted Michael, cradled him on her hip, took Irene's hand, and led them to the small kitchen. "Does Michael want his bottle? How about Irene? Milk and chocolate chip cookies?" she asked sweetly. Both children instantly settled down.

Bubba looked pissed. "Is that a joke? Those rug rats don't deserve a reward," he growled.

Sam shook his head. McAllister too was shaking his head, his face showing his disapproval. "If you two are going to be their uncles, you better learn how to handle them with a gentle hand. Now let's get down to business."

Sam told Commander McAllister and Bubba Jackson that he'd was given free rein to fight the White Supremacists without any encumbrances.

Tiffany believed that as FBI Director, she'd be able to curtail the White militia groups by arresting all of them if Sam got them the warrants she would need.

Sam turned his attention to the Commander and Bubba. "I need your help again. Like we did when fighting the White Angels and Charles Stone. We need to do it again, this time focusing on the Domestic Revolutionary Movement." He was pleased that both men agreed to help.

Sam gave the Commander his first orders. "I need you and Bubba to find any possible connection that President Thompson's administration had with these White Supremacists as well as who inside the administration was connected to them. Also, we need to find out who's pulling their strings. They need money, lots of money to fund their operations. It's coming from someone."

Holding their beers, McAllister toasted the new FBI Director and Attorney General. "For the first time since learning about Haven House and Charles Stone, I feel safer now knowing you two are back protecting our democracy."

Sam nodded. "It seems like yesterday that we prevented a civil war that was being planned by Stone and a ghost going by the title The Professor. Unfortunately, a lot of bad things have happened since then. It continues to scare the hell out of me."

Tiffany jumped into the conversation. "I remember when Sam and I received Stone's severed hands and the reminder that even though we had won that day, the DRM would be back. We need to determine who their leaders are, especially this Professor, and do to them what we did to Charles Stone," she said.

"It's been just a few days since these attacks started, and we are no closer to figuring out what will be coming next. The key to stopping them, as I see it, is to figure out where they are hiding," said Sam.

Commander McAllister spoke up. "I'll talk with Raymond Stillwell. If anyone can build us a trail, he can."

Bubba Jackson stood and began pacing around the living room. "We need to stop talking and let me and my guys move on this quickly. We connected the dots on the White Angels, and there is no reason we can't figure out the organizational chart of the DRM. I think I need to go back to Haven House, where all of this started—" Before Jackson could finish, there was a loud pounding on the front door.

Bubba rushed over, his gun by his side, leaning forward to peep through the security hole in the door. When he saw who it was, a big smile cracked on his face. "I asked my men to meet us here today. I hope that was okay?"

Tiffany could not stop hugging all of them. They were the guys who saved her life and Sam's eleven years ago. "It's great to see all of you," she said, drawing all of them in for big hugs.

Sergeant Ron Arnold pushed away from Tiffany, uncomfortable with being hugged, and walked over to Bubba. "Sir, Wiley Jordan has been spotted in the backwoods of Georgia at the Blacks Landing Plantation."

Sam looked at Tiffany, his face ashen. "Shit. He's back?"

Sergeant Arnold handed the Commander his cell phone. "I have a video at the New York synagogue before the bombing. A mother and young boy were thrown into a van by men wearing hoods and black jackets with White Angel patches on their sleeves. My intel is confirming that the White Angels are active again."

"I'll bet the kidnapped mother and son are my friend's family," McAllister said. "If true, then he's been compromised and in danger. Check things out at the plantation and report back to me if they are holding a mother and son there."

"Copy that, sir."

20

Every news channel for the last forty-eight hours covered the recent mass casualty events and bombings across the nation. It appeared Paige Turner's warning four days ago was correct. The United States was again in the horrible grasp of domestic terrorists. What had started during President Woody Wilson's eight years in the White House while fighting Charles Stone and the White Angels had split the country into two fighting factions hell-bent on creating radical political divisions and using the disharmonies to raise money.

While fighting between both political parties was nothing new, *Dog Whistle* phrases were becoming a popular way of communicating to their loyal tribes. Words like *Cancel Culture*, *Karen,* and *Brandon* had specific meanings to certain classes of voters. The words or phrases signaled them to take action. Most of the time, violent action. The words *Fascist, Communist, and Socialist* had taken on different meanings when trying to describe a politician.

Paige Turner's *Corrupted Intelligence* theory had become another *Dog Whistle* phrase that helped the average American see the lies their leaders were saying.

Now with President Thaddeus Thompson's unexpected death and the appointment of the first female President, the media was skeptical that the first female President would not be able to unite a polarized electorate. A Camelot moment for President Graham had evaporated once the attacks escalated.

Dead bodies lying in the streets, places of worship on fire, and a vigilante group doing law enforcement's job were what the investigative reporters put front and center on the network news stations. There was no mention of the mass shooting and bombings by domestic terrorists. The country was at war and had no time to mourn for Thompson or call out the real perpetrators of these heinous acts.

The liberal cable news networks blamed the White Supremacists. The far-right cable networks, with the radical ultra-right officials in Congress, blamed gangs of color. The sad commentary was that many frightened White Americans believed what they were hearing allowed them to identify with the message of the White Supremacist groups carrying their automatic weapons and roaming openly throughout the country.

President Shannon Graham's appointment of Tiffany Glass to FBI Director and Sam Collins as Attorney General did not receive a warm reception from the Republican majority in the Senate and House. They had not forgotten what Glass and Collins had done to the White Angels, Charles Stone, and the Haven House Plantation.

Protests started popping up in all the states that experienced the recent attacks. Sadly, peaceful protests from the progressive left were met with fierce resistance from many White Supremacist groups carrying American and Confederate Flags, all dressed in military uniforms with patches on their sleeves and chest reading *Domestic Revolutionary Movement*. More mass shootings by lone gunmen and the killing of innocent protesters were becoming an everyday event. Law enforcement and the DOJ did not have the personnel or the budget to be able to handle the high volume of shootings.

21

Professor Cochran sipped his glass of Scotch, a joyful smile on his face. Everything over the last four days worked perfectly for the first two phases of his plan. However, losing key players within his organization group brought back memories of Albert Dunham, *The Architect*. He was sure the madman was dead and remembered *The Architect* had selected men in waiting that were loyal to his manifesto. The first person that came to mind was his number two, Frederick Ellison.

Before he could move forward with his next phase, he had to find out who these vigilantes were and dispose of them quickly.

Billy Bob Crenshaw was oblivious to what The Professor was going through and started clapping when he heard the positive comments from their supporters on cable news networks. "Professor, this is great news," he said. "I never thought so many Americans would support our movement."

"Billy, while some of this is good news for us, we have a bigger problem. With FBI Director Glass in a position of power and Sam Collins as Attorney General, as well as *The Architect's Army* movement picking up steam, we need to be cautious with the next part of our war against the minorities who are trying to replace us."

"Give me the orders, and I'll take care of Glass and Collins so that we can focus on *this fucking Architect's Army* group."

"I like your enthusiasm, but talk to Wiley Jordan first and let him tell you how hard it is to kill those two, especially with Commander McAllister and his team watching their backs."

"I'm sure he'll have some ideas on taking them out," said Billy Bob.

"Keep me in the loop," The Professor ordered.

After Crenshaw left, Cochran started to dial Freddie Blanton, who was running their Los Angeles Patriots. He knew if anyone could solve his problems, this man with his group could do it. Before Blanton could answer, another call was coming in. It was Wiley.

"I have the traitor's Jew bitch and his son. What do you want me to do with them?" Wiley asked.

Professor Cochran leaned back in his high-back chair and smiled. "Nothing at this time. You did well, Wiley. Now, we wait and watch to see how Commander McAllister reacts, believing his friend's family was blown up during religious ceremonies."

Wiley seemed puzzled. "Who is this Jacob Stein to McAllister?"

"He's a close childhood friend. He's our FBI spy going by the name Jack Petry."

"Then, I'll kill Stein's family and send him their Jew heads," Wiley cursed.

"In due time, Wiley, in due time," Professor Cochran said. "Let McAllister track you down first and then you can set a trap for them and revenge the killing of your men."

Cochran thought of calling Blanton, but decided to call Wilhelm Hitler, the leader of the Brown Shirts in Argentina. "Wilhelm, it's The Professor. We have a situation I might need your help with," Cochran said.

"I saw the news report on your recent attacks. You've done well. I am mobilizing my men and should be ready to invade after your next attack," he said.

"That's just it. I want you to hold off until I locate and destroy this Architect's Army."

"We can't wait much longer. The war needs to start as soon as possible," he said and hung up the phone.

22

Jacob Stein, a.k.a. Jack Petry, McAllister's CI, could not control his rage. "I can't believe my family is gone," he sobbed.

John McAllister sat down next to his friend, his arm around his shoulder. "Jacob, since their names were not on the list I got from the medical examiner, there is still hope they are alive. I might have a lead on their whereabouts. Let me find these bastards who took them. I need you to go somewhere safe as I believe your cover has been blown."

Stein lifted his head, his eyes red. "I know. If anyone can find them, you can. These sub-humans should not be permitted to roam the earth."

McAllister patted Jacob's shoulder. "I believe you've been compromised at the DRM. We are looking at them first for any leads."

"It's not going to be that easy from this day forward. They are looking for a mole inside their groups and if they did take Lea and Seth, then they are sure to be hunting for me," Jacob said, his voice cracking. "Too many agencies are hunting for the Domestic Revolutionary Movement maniacs that perpetrated these attacks. Their leader is shrewd and ruthless. He's hidden his identity from his groups because he doesn't trust anyone. He can walk without worry among us all, especially law enforcement. You've probably seen him within the halls of justice and even inside the chambers of Congress."

McAllister seemed puzzled. "How hard can it be to figure out who this guy is?"

Jacob smiled. "Very. He's a God to his followers and they would lay down their lives to protect him. Paige Turner, since releasing the information on their attacks, has their leaders scrambling. Now with a large swatch of Americans protesting and supporting the White Supremacy movement, exposing the DRM leader will be next to impossible."

"I will not sit back anymore and *shadowbox* with these traitors," the Commander said.

When McAllister's phone rang, his facial expression brought calm to the room. A silence came over the room. Everyone sat with their arms crossed.

"McAllister here. Are you sure?" he said. "Good job, Bubba."

The Commander smiled at Jacob. "My men know where your wife and son are being held. I'll update you later today after we assess the situation."

23

Keeping with their early morning ritual in Del Mar, Sam and Tiffany walked from the Mayflower Hotel to the Lincoln Memorial and strolled down the Mall toward the Capitol. Tiffany gave Irene a history lesson on the nation's capital while Sam, with Michael strapped to his chest, jogged ahead of them, triggering one of his son's incessant out-of-control laughing fits.

It was a cool May morning, and the Cherry Blossoms were in full bloom, with a clear ocean blue sky. A soft breeze was playing with the trees, causing pinkish flowers to gracefully float in the air, which excited Michael, who tried to catch a few petals.

While Sam and Tiffany knew that the Secret Service was protecting them while they walked, it was the Capitol Police in full-body armor carrying AK-47s that reminded them that the country was not safe.

Tiffany seemed disturbed as she walked back to where Sam and Michael were playing with the airborne Cherry Blossom leaves. "Sam, do you feel safe after what has been happening?"

Sam seemed puzzled by her question. "We've been involved with danger before while we tried to arrest Charles Stone. What's so different now?" he asked.

Tiffany bit her lower lip. "We didn't have children then. Being back in DC and leaving them at the Mayflower while we work is very scary," she said.

"Our nanny has been instructed on how to spot danger, and with Bubba's men and the Secret Service guarding them, they will be safe," Sam replied, his hand caressing Tiffany's cheek.

Tiffany inhaled a deep breath before speaking. "Today's our first day in our new jobs. I, for one, do not feel ready. I've been away from the FBI for almost eleven years. So much has changed that I'm not sure I can be very effective," she said.

"I'm feeling the same way," Sam said. "Once we give it a few days to acclimate ourselves, I'm confident we'll be up to full speed to get our democracy back on track."

"I hope you're right. I'm having my doubts about getting back to work so soon after having Michael. He's used to having both of us at home working," she said.

Sam had become skilled at reading Tiffany's moods after thirteen years of marriage. Their four-bedroom hotel suite at the Mayflower Hotel, with a full kitchen and three full bathrooms, as well as two thousand square feet of living space, would be more than adequate for them until they found the perfect second home in Maryland. They also had a full detail of Secret Service agents outside their door and throughout the hotel, as well as a handful of ex-SEALs who were working with Commander McAllister.

"Tiff, the kids are happy with their nanny. McAllister's men will be throughout the hotel looking for anyone who seems out of place and inside our suite."

"That's not what's bothering me. We've not worked outside the house since Irene was born. I'm not looking forward to her moods every time we leave to work."

Sam grinned. "Irene's a drama queen, and our little monster is happy anywhere he can intimidate anyone near him. The nanny is young enough to handle that little terrorist."

"Sam, you're a cold-hearted bastard, but you're probably right," she said.

Sam put his arm around his wife's shoulder as they went through the front door of their hotel.

Thirty minutes later, Tiffany was dropped off first at the Hoover Building and then Sam was off to meet with McAllister and his team before he introduced himself to his DOJ team. He wanted an update on where Wiley Jordan was hiding out with Jacob Stein's family.

This morning's meeting needed a solid plan to rescue the two hostages and, if possible, without jeopardizing the lives of Stein's family, kill all the White Angels, including Wiley Jordan.

Sam reviewed for the tenth time his list of items he wanted McAllister to set in motion. First, he wanted some of their plans to be leaked inside the halls of Congress to draw out all the traitors inside the executive branch.

When Sam arrived, McAllister spoke first. "Sir, Bubba Jackson is sure he's located Stein's family. We believe they are being kept in the woods near Haven House," McAllister said.

Sam nodded. "Are you sure Wiley Jordan has them near Haven House? It's a little ironic he'd go back to the place where they failed in their first civil war attempt."

"Nothing is logical with Wiley, sir. He's a very emotional man and doesn't see the irony in what he's doing."

"I assume you have a plan?"

"We do. After we complete this rescue, we have another problem that I don't have a handle on just yet. *The Architect's Army.*"

"What has you so concerned? Albert Dunham is dead. His movement died with him," Sam argued back. "These must be copycat militia trying to move into the DRM's territory."

The Commander frowned at Sam's indifferent mindset. "I read over the file the Justice Department created on *The Architect.* Something about his death puzzles me," McAllister said, biting his lower lip.

"Let me look at his file and see if I have your same concerns. Let's stay focused on our current task at hand and let me do my job," Sam said. "I'll call you later today for your update, and hopefully good news for Jacob Stein."

24

FBI Director Glass sat behind her desk, contemplating the enormity of being her country's first female FBI Director. On the floor behind her desk were ten banker boxes packed with all the evidence she had accumulated at the Haven House Plantation and from Silver Hawk insurance company. How her past investigation correlates with the Domestic Revolutionary Movement eleven years later puzzled her. In addition, she had twenty file boxes tagged, *The Architect's Manifesto*. She suspected that hidden inside these boxes was a connection between Dunham and Stone, as well as how The Professor had links to all the traitors inside the West Wing and Halls of Congress.

Tiffany hoped that the key to uncovering all of America's traitors was inside the Haven House logbook Charles's slave girl April had given her. Another conundrum she had was to uncover the traitors like her boss, Lawrence Colbert, who might still be working throughout the FBI. Where to begin was the million-dollar question, as well as who to trust.

She opened the Haven House logbook to the first page and began reading its appalling history again. After reviewing the first fifty pages, a person of interest, a man referenced only as *The Professor*, kept popping up. Handwritten by Charles's father and young Charles himself was a man they referenced as *The Professor*. Tiffany found it interesting that the logbook documented numerous dates that this professor visited Haven House.

Tiffany immediately searched the FBI logbook she created during her Haven House investigation and found where she, too, had referenced someone going by the title *The Professor*. *"Who is this person?"* she whispered. *"Is he the person behind the White Supremacy movement?"*

An idea exploded inside her head. She jotted down a reminder to find Charles's slave girl April and see if she might know who this Professor might be. Then, a loud knock on her office door startled her. "Enter," she shouted.

Rushing in was her Chief of Staff, Allison Monk. "Ms. Glass, there are mass casualty shootings happening right now in twenty states. Some have been lone gunmen, and some with multiple shooters." Allison was unable to control her emotions. "They are claiming they shot their weapons because they feared for their lives."

"Take a deep breath. How many deaths are we talking about?"

"First count shows approximately two hundred thirty-six dead. Little children are lying in the streets. At least eighty others are in critical condition. Why did they feel threatened by children," Allison said in disbelief.

Tiffany looked noticeably upset. "Get the President on the horn and get my team leaders in here ASAP," she ordered.

Director Glass was on the phone with the President thirty seconds later. "Copy that, Madame President. The Oval Office in one hour," Tiffany acknowledged.

Tiffany cupped her head with her hands, overwhelmed by all that has happened in under five days. Within a minute, her entire team marched into her office. She lifted her head, making eye contact with everyone. "Does anyone have any answers to what just happened?" A few of her people just shrugged their shoulders, and a few just sat there looking like they didn't give a shit. "I have to be at the Oval Office in thirty minutes and expect some answers from each of you, with solutions to combat this problem."

Director Glass dictated a list of items she wanted her team to have answers for when she returned from the White House. "I want the identities of all these shooters and if they were affiliated with any White Supremacy group. Second, I want to see all the case files police have on all the recent mass casualty events that started five days ago," she ordered. "We need to find any links to the DRM's leader."

After Tiffany left her office, Associate Deputy Director Walter Perle was reading notes the Director left exposed on her desk.

Her Chief of Staff, Allison Monk, shouted at Perle, "Walter, you need to remove yourself from the Director's office immediately." Allison texted her boss about the incident and that they must talk when she returns.

Tiffany immediately called Monk. "Call the US Marshal's office. Tell them to keep an eye on Perle. Let them know that I'll fill them in later."

25

It had been ten hours since Bubba and his team found Stein's family. Commander McAllister could not stop pacing as he surveyed Wiley Jordan's compound in the forest near the Haven House Plantation. Bubba and his team stayed focused, not saying a word. They'd seen him this way before when he was pissed and knew not to get in his crosshairs. They didn't know that he had just gotten terrible news about more mass shootings around the country.

McAllister barked out some orders. He briefed his team on the new attacks. He called Roger Stillwell and gave him orders. "Find out if The Architect's Army is responsible?"

Bubba walked over to McAllister and whispered in his ear. "As soon as I heard the news, I called Director Glass. No messages were left behind. She believes it's the DRM's signature. It fits what Paige Turner had uncovered, but they cannot confirm at this time. No one is claiming responsibility."

The Commander shook his head. "Are we ready to get Jacob's family back?"

"My guys are set and in position. Wiley's not in the camp. Just ten of his guards are patrolling the grounds. Only one guard is positioned by the entrance to the tent we believe has Stein's family," said Bubba.

The Commander spoke on his radio. "Team Alpha, you've got a green light. Team Bravo, neutralize all guards."

Within seconds, Bubba and McAllister could hear each pop from the suppressors on his team's rifles. He counted ten, and all went quiet. Then, over his radio, he heard, "All bogies down—no sign of Stein's family. Mother and son nowhere to be found, sir."

McAllister massaged his scalp, deep in thought. "Let's check out Haven House. It's possible that sick motherfucker Wiley would take them there to make a point." A cold sweat blanketed his body as he remembered all of the trophy skulls inside Charles's father's den.

Bubba released a small drone with a camera attached. It was a new advanced miniature model that looked like a dragonfly. It had a whisper mode that would allow it to go undetected. It took five minutes for it to travel the four miles to Haven House.

Jackson pointed the drone control monitor at the Commander. "Look. There are three Land Rovers and one black Ford van like the one that snatched Jacob's family. There are men inside by the big windows and three on the roof—all armed with military weapons."

"I thought President Wilson leveled that hellhole?" the Commander asked as they sped toward Stone's plantation.

"Our Southern Senators and Congressmen all protested. They said it was part of the history of the South. Some shit about their heritage. They wanted to make it into a museum for generations to learn about what went on there."

"It's been almost ten years, and it doesn't look like no fucking museum. I need a plan to recover mother and son safely," he said to Bubba.

Speeding up the dirt road that came out of the forest was a Chevy pickup truck. It came to a screeching halt, creating a dust cloud. The driver, dressed in military fatigues, jumped out of the truck and ran to the front porch. He shouted for Wiley.

Walking out from the front door was Wiley Jordan, holding young Seth Stein by the nape of his neck. The young boy looked frightened, but was not crying.

Wiley started howling after his man told him what had just happened inside their compound. He slapped Seth across his face, knocking him down. Lea Stein broke free from her guard and ran out to comfort her son.

Wiley was looking around and spotted the small drone hovering above the plantation. He scanned his surroundings and started yelling at the drone.

"You mother fuckers killed ten of my best men. You did this to rescue this Jew bitch and her bastard Jew son. You just made a big mistake." Wiley drew his gun from his shoulder holster and grabbed Seth from his mother's arms. "Watch how we handle Jews in my part of the world."

Bubba and McAllister watched in horror as Wiley lifted the young boy and pointed his gun at the boy's temple. "First the boy, then his mother," Jordan shouted.

They knew what that crazy man could do and needed to act fast. As Wiley's index finger started to press on the trigger on his pistol, an explosion erupted, shattering Jordan's hand. It was a direct hit from Sergeant Ron Arnold, the Commander's best sniper. As Wiley screamed, holding his bloodied hand, Lea rushed over and scooped her son up. Without thinking, she ran off the porch toward the woods like an Olympic sprinter holding her son's hand.

Two guards from inside Haven House rushed out, their weapons aimed at the backs of Lea and Seth, running toward the woods. Before they could get off a shot, their skulls exploded from two precise hits by Sergeant Arnold.

McAllister's team met Lea and Seth and surrounded them, rushing them into the forest for shelter where McAllister and Bubba were waiting. "Sir, should we go and capture that bastard Wiley and the rest of his men?" Sergeant Arnold asked.

"We'll save it for another day. We have what we set out to do. Let's reunite Jacob with his family."

McAllister called Sam Collins and briefed him on what had happened. "Yes, sir. Everyone is safe and unharmed. Just a bit shaken. Wiley Jordan is another story. We had to blow up his hand before he executed Seth Stein."

Sam seemed shocked. "He's not dead?"

"It was a rushed decision. Go for the headshot or Wiley's hand that held his weapon. I couldn't risk a reflex action that might have killed the young boy."

"Smart move. Let's get them back to the safety of their home," Sam said.

* * * * *

Wiley grabbed a towel and wrapped his bloody hand. He found three of his fingers and got one of his men to put them on ice. "Do we know who those men were?" he asked his man.

"You're not going to believe this, but it looked like Commander McAllister and Bubba Jackson."

Wiley kept chugging from his bottle of whiskey as he digested what he had just heard. "Get me out of here. I need to see The Professor immediately."

26

McAllister watched as Jacob started crying when he saw his wife and son. The joyful reunion released a waterfall of emotions.

Lea walked over to Commander McAllister and Bubba Jackson and gave both a big hug with a kiss on their lips. "I don't know how we can ever repay you for what you risked for us."

Young Seth walked over and gave both the Commander and Bubba a tight hug. "Thank you for saving us," he said, holding back his tears.

Jacob came over and shook McAllister's hand and then pulled him closer and hugged him tightly. He whispered, "Thank you. We need to talk later. I spoke with one of my contacts at the FBI who believes an FBI analyst gave my real name to the DRM."

"Do we know who that person might have been?"

"Not at this time," Jacob said.

"I'm going to put you and your family in my protective custody. The DRM will be looking for revenge, especially Wiley."

Jacob interrupted the Commander. "I can't let this go. It can't go unpunished."

McAllister put his arm around Jacob. "Trust me. It won't go unpunished. I've been fighting with these bastards for over twelve years. We made a few mistakes early on, letting our emotions guide us. Sadly, that didn't work, and their leaders disappeared. Now that they know you're the spy they've been looking for, you and your family are not safe."

"I must do something. I can't sit back and wait for them to find me," Jacob said.

"The previous administration did not want to lock up these animals, but our new President does. You need to trust me. There's a new plan in the works. We have Sam Collins, the new Attorney General working with us. I can't tell you more right now, but in a few days, I'm hoping to have more answers," the Commander said. "Here's an address for my safe house that should keep you and your family safe. Go there and try to relax."

Jacob shrugged his shoulders. "I'll try, but it won't be easy," he said.

McAllister whispered in Bubba's ear before they got into their vehicle. "These last few days don't make logical sense to me," the Commander said. "If the file Turner received is the DRM's plan for their civil war, why are they doing these attacks and not starting their stupid war? What are they waiting for?"

Bubba wrinkled his nose, deep in thought. "Maybe this was a test to see how the new President would react."

McAllister shook his head. "Something bigger is going to happen and I don't know what, and that pisses me off. Something about hearing *The Architect's* name after four years is raising some red flags and it won't be good for all of us."

They both got into their car and drove to talk with Sam.

27

In the heart of Budapest, it was day three of the *Wolf Pack's* secret meeting. They were discussing the uprising happening in the United States. Professor Cochran had gone outside their original plan that they had been financing for the last thirty years. Random killing, especially against people of color, was outdated and had no place inside their original manifesto.

The Matild Palace Hotel in the heart of the city had become their base of operations for their quarterly meetings. The group was worried that with all the instability in the United States, further infiltrating the economy and controlling the markets was becoming more difficult than they originally had planned. Over the last three decades, their group was able to manipulate most of the world's economy.

They trusted Albert Dunham, falling victim to his failed manifesto that set them back almost four years since his death. They were now having second thoughts about Professor Cochran's judgment and his obvious inability to get the job done after two drastic failures from Charles Stone and Dunham.

The Wolf Pack was formed before World War I. They believed economies grew from the top down. They influenced many leaders, especially the Republican Presidents since the early eighties. Money was power, and that was something they knew they needed at any cost. As a result, the legacy they created over a century ago for themselves and their families had become a perpetuating dynasty. Many American Presidents on the political right supported their philosophy, even though it wreaked havoc in the long run with America's budget deficit and national debt.

Currently, the *Wolf Pack*'s membership spanned from the United States and into Europe. However, their membership stayed in the shadows, never looking for the limelight and using elected officials to promote their dreams.

Each of their heirs was groomed to take over their family conglomerates and understood that their identities had to, at all costs, remain anonymous. As the upper 1 percent, they were able to mold governments to give their autocratic leaders the power they needed.

Albert Dunham had broken all the rules that bound their group. But, now that his brother Theodore was running the remaining Dunham enterprises, the *Wolf Pack* felt comfortable moving forward again. With Professor Cochran and his Domestic Revolutionary Movement, they were holding their breath, waiting for another failure to ruin their plans.

Their War Room, a small conference room at the Matild Palace, had an oval conference table with pop-up built-in computer screens so they could communicate with all their members worldwide. There were no security cameras or listening devices on the second floor of the hotel, giving them a fully secured meeting place. They were currently monitoring Professor Cochran's race war in the United States. They were not pleased with how it was going, especially with all the brutal slaughter of women and children of color.

Klaus Bergner, CEO of Apollo Pharmaceuticals, heard his phone beep with a new message. He turned bedsheet white reading the person's name who was about to enter their War Room. When he told the others who was going to crash their meeting, the other men in the room all began to squirm in their chairs, unable to say a word.

Elliott Martin, CEO of Swiss Financial, spoke first. "Is this a joke," he said. "He's supposed to be dead." Before he could finish speaking, the door to the War Room burst open.

At first, no one recognized the man in a blue pin-stripe suit and royal blue silk tie. Half his face looked deformed from severe burns. But, once everyone heard him speak, it was clear to everyone that Albert Dunham, *The Architect*, had returned from the grave.

"Gentlemen, it's so very nice to see you all working so hard. I've been monitoring your progress these last four years that I've been in hiding and I do not like who you are supporting. I am ready to restart my manifesto," Dunham said, with confidence, "and resume my position within the group. I've had enough time to reorganize and build a new and more powerful following with my new and improved army of loyalists."

He walked to the front of the room and laid his Berretta on the table in front of him. Three heavy-set men, dressed in black suits and dark sunglasses remained at the back of the conference room holding M16s and guarding the door.

Dunham was rubbing his hands together and an evil grin struggled to form on his scarred burnt face. "Let's get down to business. Unlike before, I'll expect full support from each of you, or you will regret it," he threatened. "You were disloyal to me before, and that will not be tolerated now."

Klaus Bergner tried to stand up to protest Dunham's arrogant attitude to the group. He was abruptly pushed back into his seat. He craned his neck, shouting profanities at the giant of a man. "Get your fucking hands off me…"

Dunham let loose a loud laugh. "Klaus, I don't think you'd want to get Bruno mad at you at this time. I meant everything I said a moment ago. Work with me, help me implement my new manifesto, or suffer the consequences as Professor Cochran has over this last week," Dunham said. "When you hear what I have planned and what I'll need from all of you, I think you'll see the light that my way is the best way to get even richer than you are now."

28

It had been two days since the recent bombings. The country was trying to heal from the loss of life that had been plastered on every media channel twenty-four-seven. Protests flooded the streets, along with looting from angry Blacks and Hispanics. Muslim and Asian people remained silent about the hatred given to them by all the White Supremacists.

It was Sam Collins' first official day at the Justice Department. His first order of business would be redefining sections of the constitution and how the Justice Department would prosecute the domestic terrorism that was tormenting the country and the courts. Clarify what the founding fathers meant when they wrote the Second Amendment, which he recognized would not be easy. While the Supreme Court had interpreted it many times, the final outcome always seemed to follow party lines and the pressure from the NRA.

Before he entered his office, his administrative assistant, Martha Wooden, texted him a message. "Sam, Paige Turner is waiting to see you with another gentleman, Dean Miller. She says it's urgent."

He texted her back. "Ask her if they can reschedule. I'm too busy to see them today," Sam wrote. He did not receive a response.

When Sam walked into his office, Martha was rolling her eyes at him, signaling that Paige Turner and Dean Miller were in his waiting room. He knew she was one of the most respected journalists. She had recently received a Pulitzer Prize for her journalistic piece on Albert Dunham and his quest to become the Emperor of the United States. Now he was learning that she was a brash investigator with no boundaries. *"So why was she here so soon after they first met a few days ago?"* he thought.

Sam walked right by her, saying good morning as he entered his private office. He buzzed for his secretary to get into his office.

"Martha, I thought I said no appointments today?"

Martha looked flustered. "I told her that, but she insisted. I couldn't say no. She's very pushy and has the ear of many Senators, Congressmen, and Presidents, both current and past."

"Okay. Wait five minutes and then send her in," Sam said.

Five minutes later, Martha buzzed Sam. "They are ready, Sam."

"Send them in."

Sam stood and walked to the door to greet the reporter and extend his hand to Dean Miller. "Mister Miller, your name is familiar. Where do I know you from?"

Miller forced a smile before responding. "I was a professor at Stanford teaching computer science back when you were there studying law," he said.

Sam nodded his head as his memory kicked in. "I remember now. You are the computer genius who created the software that Dunham stole and used against us," Collins said sarcastically.

"That's not what I want to be remembered for, but you're correct."

Paige could see that their meeting was getting off-track and interrupted the Attorney General. "Can we get back to why I am here?" she asked sternly.

Sam was taken aback by her forceful tone. Tiffany was the only woman he knew that could stop him in his tracks. When he first met Turner at his Del Mar beach home, she looked beautiful without any makeup, but today, she wore a floral sundress, her hair hanging down to her shoulders, and bright red lipstick with just the right amount of makeup to make her look stunning, even though she looked like she wanted to strangle him.

"Miss Turner, I thought we covered everything about your file you had gotten a few days ago?" he asked in a condescending tone. "My wife and I are still digesting everything you brought us. You know it's been a crazy couple of days." Sam was getting a little testy with the reporter.

Paige ignored Sam's rude tone. "We did, but something important came up and I felt you needed to see what Dean uncovered with his tagging software program," Turner said. "You and your wife inspired me to take a deep dive into the DRM and with Dean Miller's help, I've uncovered a bunch of links that connect to some very influential people."

Sam leaned forward, staring at Paige. "I'm listening," he said.

Paige crossed her legs, exposing her tanned thigh that distracted Sam. "I've been investigating political and corporate corruption in our country since stopping *The Architect*. I believe it is tied to what's been going on with our country's White Supremacist problem."

"You've got my attention," Sam said, leaning back in his chair and directing Turner to continue.

Paige opened a red manila file folder. "First, I don't believe Dunham is dead as first reported. I believe he's been building a new and loyal army of supporters these last four years. You've heard of QAnon?"

"Yes, I do. Justice is keeping an eye QAnon that is getting a strong foothold on social media."

"Everything about QAnon points to Dunham and his failed manifesto. I believe he's building an army of loyal followers that will do anything for their leader," she said.

Sam seemed puzzled. "If what you're saying is true, where is your proof he is alive and head of QAnon? Or is this some far-out conspiracy theory?"

Paige pulled out a typed piece of paper and started reading from it. "First, his remains were never found. There were no human remains or DNA, not even human ashes from when his home was incinerated."

"I know that, in fact, every American knows that. His ego was bigger than Charles Stone and I don't believe, if he did survive the bombing, he'd not surface and resume his quest to gain his power back," Sam said, his demeaning tone getting worse.

Paige rolled her eyes at him. Her blood pressure was rising as Collins talked. "His destroyed Maryland house had a bomb shelter and tunnel fifty feet under his property. Second, Dunham and his family were part of an international group of billionaires known as the *Wolf Pack*. It's a powerful group of CEOs and government officials spanning five European countries and our United States. Their regular meeting place is in Budapest at the Matild Palace. Third, the *Wolf Pack* that I was investigating back then went dormant after Dunham disappeared. Now this group is again active in Europe. I believe the *Wolf Pack* is supporting the White Supremacist movement here financially." Paige took an exhausted breath.

Turner piqued Sam's interest. "What would businessmen have to do with White Supremacists? It can't be good for business if they are exposed," the Attorney General asked.

Paige reached into her satchel and pulled out another manila file. "This is my *Corrupted Intelligence* file with proof that our most trusted leaders are leading our country down a terrible path that will destroy democracy as we know it."

Sam seemed puzzled. "Corrupted Intelligence? What's that?"

"It's the abuse of entrusted power," Paige said. "It's found in almost every aspect of life here in America and throughout the world. Even in every religion. It's a theory I have, and I believe it's the main reason we have so much division. We give powerful, wealthy people entrusted power and they abuse it for private gain, and we allow them to manipulate our lives and the environment by constantly believing their lies. Their followers hear these untruths for so long that it becomes truth to them, and they form a tribe that they cannot be swayed away from these powerful men and women," she said, emotionally.

"It's not illegal to abuse one's given power unless it breaks the law," Sam replied. "Do you have proof that these CEOs are doing something illegal?"

Dean Miller spoke up. "Mister Attorney General, while I created a dangerous weapon with my software, I've also created a state-of-the-art computer program that can track anyone around the world and who they are in contact with," he said. "Take a look at Paige's file and see what I uncovered."

Turner handed Sam her file. "I've made copies of my file and I'll leave it with you to read. After you've read it, we need to meet again. Something dangerous is brewing, and it's not just from the White Supremacists. Unfortunately, we don't have much time to stop it."

Sam lifted the thick, heavy file and put it in a basket on his desk. "Do you have a problem if I discuss this with FBI Director Glass?"

Tiffany sighed. "First read the file by yourself. If then you feel Director Glass needs to be involved, so be it. I know that within the halls of the Hoover Building and even your Justice Department, there are loyal supporters of the Domestic Revolutionary Movement and the *Wolf Pack*. So, I am skeptical that once the FBI gets a hold of my file, it will get buried under a backlog of other investigations that need to be completed. What needs to be done can't be accomplished through legal channels. I know what you're doing with Commander McAllister. Maybe run it by him first. Time is of the essence." With that, she was out the door.

Sam spent the next hour and a half reading over Turner's file. It read like a scary novel, except everything in it was true. He pressed his intercom button. "Martha, get Commander McAllister on the horn now."

29

Sam finished reading Turner's documents. He knew he would need to share them with Tiffany but not until he discussed them with McAllister first. He remembered what President Graham said after their meeting. The President needed plausible deniability and what he was holding fell under those instructions. His only problem is that he was the Attorney General and under a large magnifying glass. There was just so much he could do before he overstepped his authority.

Sam, when he got nervous, muttered to himself. *"There were too many items that appeared to have been gotten illegally. How Dean Miller connected these Senators, House Members, and CEOs to the DRM might have violated the new law on spying against Americans. In addition, Paige's report seemed unbelievable. The men on her list were well-respected Americans."*

He drew in a deep breath. He recalled how he felt when he was investigating Charles Stone, the White Angels, and the Domestic Revolutionary Movement over ten years ago and was alarmed that nothing had changed.

"Her Corrupted Intelligence definition fits Stone and Dunham exactly," Sam told himself.

Commander McAllister and Bubba Jackson were sitting inside Sam's office. Both men had just finished reading Turner's file, too.

"Well, what do you think?" Sam asked.

McAllister stood up and started pacing around the room, deep in thought. "There is a lot to digest here. I've never looked at our fight in this light. Our problem is bigger than I ever imagined. It's not just one Charles Stone or one Albert Dunham, but all their followers that have been easily manipulated to believe their lies," McAllister said, looking at Bubba. "Jackson, what's your take on all of this?"

Bubba sucked in a deep breath before responding. "As we did in Iraq and Afghanistan, we need to eliminate the abusers one by one. Arresting them will not solve anything. It would only make them martyrs and ignite their followers to start a war. Plus, I'll bet that soon we'll be seeing single-shooter incidents from ignorant followers of the DRM."

Sam's eyes grew wide with surprise at Jackson's remarks. "Are you saying that the approach of The Architect's Army group is our only solution?"

"What if Turner is correct and Dunham is not dead? He was very popular with tens of millions of Americans who accepted his lies after they received his money."

"I don't like what you're saying. I can't, as the Attorney General, condone killing the bad guys without first trying to bring them to justice," Sam said, unable to look at Bubba.

McAllister jumped into the conversation. "I understand how Bubba feels. During a war, it was killed or be killed. We are fighting a different kind of battle here. We are struggling to save our democracy, constitution, and way of life from the abusive behavior of our leaders, both political and corporate. Without remorse, they are untruthful, creating conspiracy theories to enrich their pockets. They are manipulating their followers to look the other way and only listen to their side of the argument, using weapons of mass destruction as the solution."

Sam cupped his hands over his ears. "I must digest all of this. I am shocked at what both of you are saying. I need to respect our judicial system. I took an oath a long time ago to defend our constitution and what you're thinking of doing is going against everything I believe in."

McAllister and Bubba dismissed themselves and told Sam they would have a blueprint on how they were going to fight their enemy. Before the Commander left, he turned toward Sam and spoke. "You didn't have a problem with how we all handled Charles Stone and the White Angels ten years ago, so why the moral high ground now, when thousands of Americans are lying dead in our streets?"

Sam just shrugged his shoulder, unable to produce an answer.

An hour later, Sam was sitting inside the FBI Director's office. He watched his wife reading all of Paige Turner's notes. Her facial expressions were void of emotion.

"I don't know what to make of what you brought me. I just finished reading the Haven House logbook. Paige Turner might be right about what she is saying. But, on the other hand, I am up to my eyeballs with all the brutal attacks by the White Supremacists. I don't have the human resources to spare to open another investigation into our elected officials, billionaires, let alone international ones," Tiffany said, dropping the large package on her desk.

Sam shook his head, showing his frustration, not with his wife, but that a variety of factors were slowly destroying the country he loved so much. "What about getting the FBI's National Security Department involved? It's within their purview internationally. Maybe they can investigate this *Wolf Pack* Turner mentions in her report?"

"That department is wrapped up with the attacks by all of our domestic terrorists. I'm not even sure the President will sign off on an international investigation and what that would entail. President Graham wants us to end domestic terrorism in our country first. That's her priority now," Tiffany said.

"Don't you think all of this is connected?"

"It might be, but if we start opening up investigations that reach into billionaires and some respected Senators and House Representatives, we'll look like we're a limp arm of our President." Tiffany shoved Turner's manila envelope back at her husband. "This is something you and McAllister can do. You can work with Paige Turner's theories and keep me posted."

"I'm not so sure you'd want me to condone what the Commander wants to do."

"What's that?" Tiffany asked.

"You don't want to know. Now, you do have an international division that could at least check out the *Wolf Pack* and then report back to you. At least then you'll be able to make a more informed decision as to what to do next," Sam said.

"Fine. I'll call the attaché in charge over there. Now, let me get back to my work. We can talk more at home tonight," she said, handing Sam the Haven House logbook. "Read this and see how it coincides with Turner's file," Tiffany said. "One other thing. Can you get McAllister's team to interview Stone's slave girl April? She might know who some of the players are inside the DRM. I really would like to know who this professor is."

Sam stood and leaned forward and kissed his wife goodbye. "See you tonight, sweetie. Take care of yourself."

30

Matild Palace, Budapest, Hungary,

It had been less than a week since Albert Dunham reared his head and three days since the attacks in the United States had started. He was very upset this morning with the news of what Paige Turner had been saying about him, Charles Stone, and all the allies he still had inside the federal government. *"That bitch needs her reputation shattered,"* he muttered before entering the conference room at the Matild Palace Hotel.

"I better see some loyalty from these bastards, or some heads are going to roll," he told his security detail, as he burst through the conference room door. Dunham marched toward the front of the room grim-faced. He panned the room and was pleased to see all the members of the *Wolf Pack* squirming in their seats.

"I rushed away the other day as I needed to attend to some important business. You all must be wondering why I would come out of hiding after what happened to me four years ago. All things happen for a reason. With everything happening in the United States, the country that I love, the implementation of my new manifesto will accomplish everything I tried to complete before," he said without taking a breath. "The current administration is swimming upstream trying to put out all the fires created by the DRM," Dunham said. Before he could continue, he was interrupted.

Klaus Bergner was the first to speak up. "Albert, your time has passed, especially since the world believes you died inside your home. No one missed you all these years, especially every member of the *Wolf Pack*. Our movement has moved on without you."

Albert pressed a few buttons on his phone. The door to the conference room opened, and five additional men holding Q Honey Badger pistols took strategic positions inside the room. Dunham began pacing, his hands locked behind his back while he walked behind each *Wolf Pack* council member.

"Gentlemen, if you think my time has passed and that I don't have anything to offer each of you… you are very mistaken. I've been watching and waiting while you set loose Professor Cochran's DRM. Supporting him was a mistake. Charles Stone proves my point. Our power comes from working with the adults in government, not the racist idiots who want to murder and create mayhem. Intimidating the masses is not a formula for success, especially for the uneducated citizens that have nothing to lose. I was once given the trust to lead, but other factors got in the way: Paige Turner to be exact. Once Turner's reputation is ruined, nothing she says will have any impact on our new manifesto. Then, and only then, will I be able to get back the trust I need to build our financial wealth."

Klaus, the color draining from his face as he spoke for the group, said, "Albert, what do you have in mind?"

Dunham squeezed Klaus's shoulder hard enough to make him cry out in pain. "Glad you asked," he said, patting Bergner's head. "First, I want to assume my rightful place on this board!"

Dunham looked at the other men. Their frightened expressions told him everything he needed to know.

"Good. Then, the first order of business is for Elliott Muller to give me access to my money at Swiss Financial. I believe my account has around five hundred billion gathering dust. Once I have my money, then I will tell you what I want each of you to do," Dunham said.

Muller raised his eyebrows with a look of confusion on his face. "Albert, I do not know of any money in your name at my bank."

Dunham started laughing. "My mistake. When the FBI was hunting me, I had my money deposited under an alias before my government tried to kill me. Here are the account number and the referenced name. I hope it won't be a problem?" His sarcastic tone caused Muller's hands to start shaking.

"This is highly irregular. My bank and our regulatory banking agency require identification to give you access. If you don't have it, then there is nothing I can do," Muller said, trying to project an air of confidence.

"I am sure you'd want to reconsider that. Look at my phone screen," Dunham said, sliding it in front of the banker. "That's your wife and pretty teenage daughter? Right?"

"What's this," Muller screamed. "Family is off-limits. That's our rule."

"Rules will be followed if you release what is owed to me within twenty-four hours," Dunham threatened. Then, without saying another word, he stormed out of the conference room, his armed security right behind him.

31

FBI Director Tiffany Glass was not totally on board with starting an international investigation into the *Wolf Pack*. She was in over her head with the attacks from White Supremacists and did not want to spread herself thin. Nevertheless, she trusted her husband's instincts and called her Special Agent in Charge in Budapest. "Agent Lassiter, this is FBI Director Glass. Do you have a moment to talk?"

"For you, Madame Director, yes, I do. Congratulations on your appointment. I was a new recruit when you were making a name for yourself. We studied you and your methods at the academy," Lassiter said. He heard the Director loudly clear her throat and realized he was talking too much. "Sorry for my rambling. What can I do for you today?"

"Have you heard of the *Wolf Pack*?"

"Why yes. My team is currently investigating the *Wolf Pack* with the help of Interpol. Why are you asking?"

"Are you telling me that an investigation has already started? When?" she asked.

"Yes. Interpol came to me after Dunham was killed and asked for our help with investigating the Wolf Pack," Agent Lassiter replied. "Why are you asking?"

"Have you heard of an American reporter Paige Turner?"

"Yes, we have, Director Glass. She was here in Budapest a few months ago trying to interview me for an article she was doing on her story: *Corrupted Intelligence*."

"Did she ask you about the *Wolf Pack*?"

"Why yes. How did you know?"

"Let me say she's a persistent reporter. Get me everything you have on the *Wolf Pack*, then I'll let you know what I will need from your team."

"Copy that," Agent Lassiter said just as the call ended.

* * * * *

Tiffany buzzed for her Chief of Staff to come into her office. Allison Heffron was a slender six-foot-tall career FBI Special Agent who was shot during the Charles Stone case. Instead of ending her career, Tiffany felt she could lend her expertise to the FBI Director.

"Allison, I want to run a few things by you."

"That's what I am here for, Director Glass."

"When we're alone, it's Tiffany. Okay?"

"Yes, Tiffany," she replied with a broad smile.

"My husband, Sam Collins, showed me a detailed investigation by reporter Paige Turner. She's working on something big for her *Corrupted Intelligence* theory and podcast. She recently released details of a pending attack by White Supremacists who are part of the Domestic Revolutionary Movement. Can you get me anything from our intelligence community before I meet with the reporter? I want to talk to her face-to-face again and compare what she has to what you can bring me. I need to determine if another attack is in the works."

"Tiffany," Allison said, leaning forward, her hand on her desk. "Paige Turner is the real deal. If she's working on something, you can be sure she's done her homework just like she did with *The Architect*. If she's concerned about something and thinks involving your husband is the right course, then we should all listen to her."

Tiffany combed her fingers through her long, wavy, jet-black hair. "See if you can get her here tomorrow. Have her bring everything she has on her *Corrupted Intelligence* theory."

32

In a booth at Martin's Tavern in Georgetown sat Paige Turner with her fiancée, retired US Marshall Scott Rogers. Sitting across from them was Dean Miller, the software genius who helped end *The Architect's* reign of terror with his advanced software tracking program. Every morning for the last ninety days, they had been meeting to discuss the political leaders who might fit into the Corrupted Intelligence theory.

Paige missed her California lifestyle, but her weekly podcast needed to air from the nation's capital. She wished she could slow down and have a normal life with Scott, but the world and all of its problems had taken priority.

Her adoptive parents had instilled in her high ethics and morals when pursuing the truth. Both her parents had died in a car accident when she was fifteen years old. It had taken her almost ten years to get over their death and marry the love of her life, Rick Turner. Her marriage ended when her husband, while he was reporting on the war in Afghanistan, was killed by a sniper's bullet.

After losing Rick, Paige decided she wanted to find her biological mother. She had lots of questions. She snapped back to the present when Scott tugged at her arm.

"Paige, come back to earth," Scott said.

She blinked her eyes and apologized to the two men. "I met with Sam Collins yesterday and handed him copies from my upcoming podcast," Paige said. "He was non-committal."

"Did he even react to your theory?" Scott asked.

"It was hard to read him. As the new Attorney General, he's attempting to arrest the White Supremacists responsible for the recent attacks by the Domestic

Revolutionary Movement. In addition, he's trying to identify their leader," Paige said.

"Did you show him my report and all the people connected to the DRM?" asked Miller. "He's an astute lawyer and will know what we've uncovered is crucial to his investigation."

Paige patted Miller's hands. "He recognizes that our country is screwed up. He said the FBI, before his wife Tiffany Glass became Director, was afraid of their own shadow and acted limp, trying to put all these bastards away," she said.

Scott Rogers seemed flustered with what Paige had been glossing over what Attorney General did not say. "Collins has a tough job. Being the number one policeman for our country, he has to navigate through the new anti-spying legislation President Thompson signed. His hands are tied if he wants to use Miller's data," said Rogers.

"He did say he wanted time to read over everything I gave him and will discuss it with Director Glass," Paige replied, letting out a stressed breath.

"Then, will you delay your podcast and wait to see if you have the support from the DOJ and FBI?" Scott asked.

Before Paige could answer, Professor Miller spoke up. "I've finished my trace on twelve of the top leaders within the radical militia groups you asked me to monitor. It isn't very comforting," Miller said, his frustration showing. He handed Paige and Scott a thick ream of paper that contained all his data.

Paige started thumbing through the first twenty pages and looked up at Dean. "Are you sure this is accurate?"

"The FBI has tapes that show White Supremacist members plotting more terrorist attacks," Miller said, sucking in a deep breath. "These domestic terrorists are planning to use a dozen upcoming pro-gun rights rallies to engage in mass murder and more bombings. Their goal is to start a racial civil war."

"Does the FBI have a plan?" Scott Rogers asked.

"They do now, since President Graham rescinded her predecessor's legislation barring the FBI from spying on these groups," Professor Miller replied. "Director Glass inherited a mess."

"What you're saying sounds promising, but your expression is telling me something is not right?" Paige said.

"It's not. I'm worried that if we expose all these White Supremacists, it won't shock anyone. There is a majority in the House and Senate that do not see these Americans as domestic terrorists, just patriots fighting for their freedom.

There are over a hundred million members supporting these militias, and a large segment of registered voters sending donations to these assholes. Our representatives won't go against the wishes of their financial supporters, which is leaving the DOJ and FBI with their hands tied," Miller said. "That's why my *We the People* movement' is getting some needed support from good people who want to redefine how our government and our democracy should be working. A third, very powerful political party is forming and should be ready to test the waters this next mid-term election," said Miller.

Paige started twirling her hair with her fingers, deep in thought. A nervous habit she had when a big story was about to break wide open. "After my upcoming podcast, will you come on my show and tell everyone about your new *We the People* movement? I think it will meld with my *Corrupted Intelligence* theory very well."

Dean smiled. "I'd love to. It would be a big help. I'm so fed up with both sides of the aisle. One party obstructs legislation that is good for their constituents and the other doesn't know how to message themselves to get things done. For almost a decade, much-needed legislation is not getting passed in both chambers," Miller said emotionally.

"Now, more than ever, my podcast has to air. I need to tell my listeners the truth about all of this."

Scott did not seem happy with Paige's plan. "If you think the threats on your life have been bad before all of this, just wait and see what they will sound like after you broadcast your story against these very powerful people."

Paige bit her lower lip before responding. "Scott, sweetie, I know how you worry about me, and I love you for that. What I am doing goes with the job. I won't walk away from this fight," she said, forcing a smile.

Scott's expression reflected his disapproval. He knew arguing with her would not work so he directed his concern to Miller. "Dean, if you thought your life was in danger when we exposed Dunham's manifesto, just wait, and see what might happen when you try to create a new political party to combat the White Supremacy movement and the DRM. Violence is the new normal with these radicals."

Professor Miller wanted to talk about the other important information he uncovered. "Scott, your concerns are well-founded, but there is more we need to understand," he said.

Paige glanced at her watch, tapping the face of it with her fingernail. "I've got a meeting in forty-five minutes across town with FBI Director Glass. Make what you have to say quick," she said.

"I'm not sure I can condense what I need to tell both of you. Here is the cliff notes version," Professor Miller said, mopping his brow with his napkin. "While doing my standard facial recognition search for a few of the known leaders in the White Supremacy movement, Professor Cochran popped up. He's a well-respected historian on the South and its failed Confederacy by General Robert E. Lee."

Scott interjected himself back into the conversation. "I know of this Professor Cochran. He's been very vocal on social media portraying these militia groups as American patriots, like the ones who fought the British during our Revolutionary War. His opinions are out there in looney land, but he has millions of followers who believe everything he says and will defend him both verbally and violently," Rogers said.

Paige stood. Before leaving, she gave Scott some orders. "Since you know about this Professor Cochran, see if you can get me a meeting with him."

Before Scott or The Professor could respond, Turner was walking out of the restaurant.

Scott looked at Miller. "I love that woman, but when she's on a story, she becomes overly focused and forgets about the people who love her."

Professor Miller chuckled. "Remember, that's what attracted you to her in the first place. I know she loves you, but she takes her work seriously and sometimes hurts the people close to her."

"I know all of that, but I can't forget that Albert Dunham almost killed her twice. Now, she is jumping right back into the shit that almost ended her life."

"Let's step up our security for her and our team. We can never be too safe," Miller said. "I'll have my tagging software monitor her phone and every security device she gets exposed to. I'll be able to see who is following her or tracking her movements."

33

Paige was escorted into the FBI Director's office. Sitting behind a big oak desk was Director Glass, reading Turner's file. Director Glass slowly raised her head and, without a word, pointed to a chair in front of her desk, motioning the reporter to take a seat.

Without any polite formalities, Director Glass started speaking. "Miss Turner, nice to see you again. Thank you for agreeing to meet with me today. I know you are busy with your investigations and podcasts. What you gave the Attorney General piques my interest," Director Glass said.

"It's my pleasure. I know how busy you must be with all the White Supremacy crap out there," Paige said. "Whatever I can do to help you and the Attorney General, I'm never too busy."

"You're well respected within the halls of justice and here at the FBI. What you've gathered within your *Corrupted Intelligence* theory, might be useful for my investigations. I just hope you are not going to broadcast any of what's inside this file on your podcast?" Tiffany asked. "What you have here is a National Security issue and President Graham would like you to stand down until we can get a better handle on what's brewing around the country. We don't want to panic the public after all they've been going through with the recent mass shootings and bombing." Tiffany noticed what she just said was not going over very well with the reporter.

Paige seemed puzzled. "I most certainly will use this," she said. "The public needs to know what's going on and whom they can trust. Too many important facts have been hidden from the American public that have cost hundreds of thousands of lives while Congress, the DOJ, and FBI debate what to do," Turner shot back.

"You can't use what's in this file at this time. My department needs time to investigate and if you expose this material, the leaders might go into hiding."

Turner abruptly stood up, both fists resting on the desk. "Director Glass, you don't know me very well. I will not bury a story for any government agency, especially the FBI, the DOJ, or the President. You're free to use what I've given you, but don't get in my way. The people inside this folder need to be named during my *Corrupted Intelligence* portion of my podcast," Paige said, turning and storming out the door before Tiffany could stop her.

* * * * *

After the reporter left her office, Tiffany called Sam. "I just met with Paige Turner again. She's a real pistol and ballbreaker. She basically told me to shove her file up my ass and not get in my way. Something about her seems familiar?"

Sam could not stop laughing. "What'd you do to piss her off? I thought you liked her after we first met her at our home?"

"Oh, I do like her. I just wanted to knock that chip off her shoulder and let her know who's in charge," Tiffany said.

"So how did that go?" Sam teased.

"Not well. I just told her to not release her story until I could verify and confirm her evidence."

"Don't you remember what she did to President Chesterfield and the FBI Director while she was investigating Dunham?" Sam asked.

"I sure do, but I wanted to see what she's made of. I like her and think she'll be able to help you and McAllister with your work," Tiffany said. "She's full of piss and vinegar and I like that."

"You need to curb your personality and not piss off people who want to help us and our country," he kidded. "See you tonight. Love you."

34

Six days after the first mass shooting event, Paige Turner's weekly podcast got preempted by a National Broadcasting Emergency Alert from the White House Briefing Room. The President's Press Secretary was recapping all that had transpired.

In twelve states, protesters for gun control became the target of White militia groups wearing military combat uniforms and carrying high-capacity military-grade weapons and Confederate Flags. It was unknown who instigated the fighting at each protest, but the militia groups, without warning, opened fire on the angry protesters, slaughtering hundreds of innocent men, women, and children.

Local SWAT was able to de-escalate the violence, but not before a handful of militia fighters were killed. The remaining shooters told the police that they felt threatened and were defending themselves when protesters started throwing bottles and rocks at them. However, before they could be booked and locked up, their lawyers posted bail for their clients at the local precincts, and they were set free with their weapons.

We have no comments from the House of Representatives and Senate members. They continue to dodge questions from reporters about gun control and the banning of military-type weapons. They were unwilling to answer questions that would condemn the violence. It appeared that they all were afraid to stir up more anger from the White Christian Americans who voted for them. Thousands of protesters were outside the local police stations chanting at the police to release the patriots they felt were protecting democracy and the constitution.

The Propagandists

President Graham, later today from the Oval Office, will be condemning the violence and vowing to get the FBI and the DOJ involved to determine the traitors who murdered innocent Americans.

Paige Turner sat behind her desk, a stunned look on her face. Then, trying to find the right words, she lifted her head and addressed her audience.

Sucking in a deep breath, she swiped a tear off her cheek.

"Everything we just witnessed… sadly was predictable. I've given the FBI and DOJ all the information I have on these groups, but like so many times before, they sat on their hands debating instead of acting, and innocent Americans paid the price. Today's events were the sum total of the last twelve years of how the White Supremacist movement has been infecting our country and striving for a civil war. We've all witnessed the first insurrection by Charles Stone and his White Angels over a decade ago. Then, we all witnessed how the billionaire, Albert Dunham, tried to become the next Emperor of the United States." Paige paused to sip from her glass of water. *"What our congressional representatives and other men in power are doing right now defines my Corrupted Intelligence theory to the 'T'. All of them are abusing the entrusted power we have given them. Instead of condemning this violence, they lie about these militia groups or just stay silent. It has to stop,"* Turner said, revealing an emotional side she had kept private from her followers.

"Dunham came close to accomplishing his goals and almost destroyed our Capitol. With his money and supporters hidden inside the halls of Congress, the West Wing, the DOJ, and the military, we were very close to losing our country to a madman. Today's events, and how they're being portrayed, are polarizing our country. How many of the men and women we trust continue to abuse their power over us? I'd like everyone listening to make an honest evaluation of the leaders you support and ask yourself, are they living up to what you elected them to do?" Turner challenged.

Before she could continue with her podcast, her monitors went black for ten seconds. Then, without warning, Albert Dunham's scarred face took control of Turner's monitor and every computer screen that was tuned into Paige's podcast.

* * * * *

Sam and Tiffany were at the Mayflower Hotel in the lounge watching the evening news and sipping Jameson's Whiskey when Albert Dunham's face appeared on the television screen in the bar.

"What just happened?" Tiffany asked.

Sam did not know what to say. All he knew was that Dunham's reappearing was not a good sign for the United States. "Let's listen to what this maniac has to say," he said, taking his wife's hand.

35

Albert Dunham, in front of a backdrop of the White House, stood in a secluded room broadcasting his worldwide message. Looking straight into the camera, he spoke.

"I am sure everyone watching this broadcast is shocked that I've been resurrected from my grave. To my loyal followers around the world and especially in the United States, the country I call home, everything you've read or heard about me was fabricated and manufactured by Paige Turner and supported by our government. She sold ex-President Chesterfield a bunch of lies and convinced him to put me on the FBI's most-wanted list. Whatever you believed about me was a lie. The President tried to execute me without a trial because of what I represented to their failed administration and what I was ready to expose. I narrowly escaped when President Chesterfield leveled my Bethesda Maryland home with a cruise missile," Dunham paused, blotting his eyes with a tissue.

He pointed to his facial scars. *"These are the scars I'll have to live with for the rest of my life. Ask yourself, did President Chesterfield, his FBI, or the DOJ offer any evidence for what I was accused of doing? Everything I tried to do back then was to make the United States a leader in the world and to share my wealth with the American people,"* Dunham said in a dramatic fashion pretending to wipe a tear off his cheek.

"America, your government, especially ex-President Chesterfield and investigative reporter Paige Turner, committed criminal acts against me and my family. Today, I am the only person who can stop all the attacks on our country. Your prior President, with his new legislation, the Freedom to

Privacy Act, has made America unsafe. I have the means and the army to end all of this right now. I will be in contact with President Graham in a few days to discuss the terms for my return to the United States, and hopefully, with a full pardon. To all my loyal followers, The Architect is coming home, and your way of life will soon be what I once promised you."

With that, all the television monitors went back to their normal programming.

Dunham turned to General Tucker Phillips. "Has my army fully infiltrated the DRM's paramilitary units?

"Sir, they are all in place and awaiting my orders. I can have them initiate your plan in each state," Phillips said. "Just give me the green light."

"I'm not ready just yet. I first need to have President Graham welcome me back, give me a pardon on all charges, and restore my reputation. Once that's accomplished, I'll then begin to use my army on those who were disloyal to me."

"What are we going to do about all the White Supremacist groups and Professor Cochran? They're in the way and should be taken out," General Phillips said.

Dunham rubbed his chin, deep in thought. "Maybe we show Cochran's militia they can't trust anyone inside their group," Dunham said, an evil grin on his face. "Knowing how politicians think, the new President just might take credit for stopping a White Supremacist group."

36

Sam was at the edge of his seat, biting his lower lip. "Could what he's saying be true? I always wondered how President Chesterfield got away with leveling Dunham's home with a ballistic missile."

"Dunham's story is more complicated than that. What I've read in his file paints a terrifying picture of one man's long-term ambition to overthrow our democracy and install himself as the emperor," Tiffany said. "With the DRM very active, and now with Dunham back in the picture, it just complicates matters for both of us."

"That's all well and good. But what I mean is, do we have factual evidence to back up these claims about Dunham's crimes?" Sam asked.

"Good question. I believe we do, but I have not reviewed the boxes of files we have on him since becoming Director. I've been a little busy," she said, shrugging her shoulders. "First, I'd like to speak with Paige Turner again and ex-President Chesterfield to hear their side of this story."

"You do that, and I'll get Stillwell to work his magic," Sam said. "If anyone can build a timeline of Dunham's actions, he's the one to do it."

"Maybe he can figure out where Dunham's been these last four years now that we have a current photo of him?" Tiffany asked.

Sam kissed his wife goodbye. He was off to see McAllister and Stillwell and get their take on what just happened.

An hour later, Director Glass got Paige Turner on the phone. "Miss Turner, Director Glass of the FBI again."

"I can only guess why you are calling?" Paige answered. "I am still in shock that Albert Dunham is still alive."

It was Sunday and Tiffany did not want to disrupt her time with her kids. "If you could, I'd like you to be at my office tomorrow first thing and bring all the files you have on Dunham," Tiffany asked politely. "I need your side and ex-President Chesterfield's side of *The Architect's* story. What Dunham is accusing you both of is very serious. If he can prove his allegations, or if the two of you can't, we will have a bigger problem on our hands."

"Madame Director, I can give you a detailed analysis of my investigation on Dunham, but getting all those records on such short notice will be next to impossible with my schedule," Turner replied.

"Need I say that this is a National Security emergency now? So please disrupt your busy schedule and please get me what I need," Director Glass said, her tone testy. "It's for your credibility and your reputation. If Dunham wins, no one will ever listen to you again."

Paige wanted to argue with the Director but decided to remain calm because she was right. "I don't know how we got off on the wrong foot, but can we start over? I agree that seeing Dunham is very upsetting. You know he tried to kill me more than once? So cut me some slack so we can work together on this problem," Turner said, her tone calm and collected.

Tiffany did her best to control her laughter to not appear rude to the reporter. "Miss Turner, we did not get off on the wrong foot the other day. When I am up to my waist in problems, I tend to come across as harsh. It's nothing personal. Maybe we need a girls' night out and get to know each other better?"

"Glad to hear that. I have the same problem. We are on the same team. I have a lot I can offer to help you and President Graham with Dunham and the White Supremacist movement in our country. So, will tomorrow around ten-thirty at your office work for you? And dinner one night would be perfect."

"That will be just fine."

Tiffany's stress levels kept rising as she contemplated her next steps. She walked over to a whiteboard in her office and started laying out everything that had transpired over the last seven days. Her gut was telling her that Dunham and Charles Stone had a connection to this Professor Cochran.

"Children are molded by their parents. Look to the fathers of these animals," Tiffany whispered to herself. She picked up her secured line and dialed a man she knew could help her.

"Raymond, Director Glass here. I need you to connect some dots for me," she said. "Sam and the Commander will be coming to you for another job, but what I need has to stay between the two of us for now," Tiffany said. "What I am asking you to do will be breaking the law."

"Director Glass, nice to hear from you. Congratulations on your appointment," Raymond Stillwell said. "What do you need me to do? I'm at your service. We did once before stretch the law a bit while we tried to take down Stone."

"I need you to investigate Charles Stone's and Albert Dunham's fathers. I believe there is a connection between them. I'm looking for a common link or person between these two parents. I believe the man known only as The Professor controls the DRM from behind the scenes, never showing his face. My gut is telling me he's the bridge between these two families. Right now, everything is pointing to Professor Cochran. Can you help?"

"I am not sure I have access to what I'd need. But I know of another geek genius who can help. Dean Miller is a friend and big supporter of Paige Turner," Stillwell said.

"I recently met him. Can he be trusted?"

"Professor Dean Miller. You might remember he created the software program for the satellite Dunham took control of," Stillwell said. "He also has a software program that he can use to build an organizational structure that will show everyone who is connected to these men. It's similar to how Ancestry dot com works, but without DNA and more accurate."

"Would Miller keep his findings 'for my eyes only'? I can't afford to have this leaked to the press before I have more facts," Tiffany said. "Can we all meet in a few days to discuss my idea?"

"I'll see what I can do. I make no promises. Miller is a family man who will not risk their lives again like he did when he helped Turner with the Dunham problem," Stillwell said. "He's also building a coalition for a third political party and very busy."

"Okay. Keep me posted."

37

Dunham had demanded another meeting with the *Wolf Pack* at the Matild Palace Hotel in Budapest. He had ordered Professor Cochran and his brother Theodore to attend. What he had to say to all of them could not be said in a Zoom call. He needed a secure environment.

Tucker Phillips had called his team, ordering them to travel to Budapest. He told them *The Architect's Manifesto* was back on track.

Minutes before Dunham arrived, the members of the *Wolf Pack*, plus Theodore Dunham, entered the same conference room they had occupied a week ago. The last person to enter the room was Professor Cochran. He did not appear happy being in Budapest, exposing himself to all the security cameras situated around the city. This was the first time he'd be in the same room with the entire *Wolf Pack* council.

After everyone took their seats, Dunham entered. He was followed by his security team. As he walked to the front of the room, he greeted everyone, letting his smile radiate over the group, especially at his brother, who he had not spoken to since his home was vaporized by President Chesterfield. Theodore Durham's smile evaporated when he saw his brother enter the conference room.

"Gentlemen. Thank you for attending on such short notice," Dunham said, panning the room to get a read on everyone's mood. He found none.

Dunham started to speak. "Our world needs a leader. A person who can unite Europe, Africa, and South and North America, as well as Russia, China, and North Korea," Dunham said unemotionally. "I will expect everyone here to show their loyalty to me and my new manifesto. I have a vision and it needs everyone's cooperation."

Professor Cochran spoke up, his tone exhibiting his anger. "Albert, your original plan to be the next Emperor of the United States failed badly for you and almost destroyed the DRM. What makes you think becoming the leader of the world can be accomplished now?"

Dunham stood and walked over to The Professor. "Professor Cochran, you're forgetting how close I came to accomplishing my original goal. It was you and your followers who turned your back on me and my plan. This time I will expect everyone's full cooperation and support or be labeled by me as a traitor."

"Brother, you are sounding crazy," Theodore Dunham said, slamming his palm on the conference table. "I can speak for the other members that we do not support anything you want to do. You will, this time, be on your own," he said.

Cochran, his face now beet red, stood and tried to leave the room. "Sit your ass down, Professor," Dunham said, pushing him harshly back down onto his chair. "As for you, my brother. You will do as I say or suffer the same fate as my departed wife," he threatened.

The Professor screamed, his face fire-red, "Get your fucking hands off me. I am the leader of the DRM with over five million followers and won't stand for your delusional behavior or demands. I worked with your father when you were a little boy, as well as Charles Stone's father. We built a worldwide organization that is almost ready to take back our pure White world."

"How well is your civil war going, Cochran? The way I see it, you're failing. I have over fifty million followers on QAnon and growing more with my new social media platform. Soon I will have many of your followers begging to join my army. If you want to see your plans mature into your goal of a new Confederate States of America, you will need me whether you like it or not," Dunham said angrily. "Without me as the leader, you will fail tragically."

Professor Cochran was at a loss for words. He had started tapping his cane on the tile floor.

It took Dunham a few hours to tell everyone his plans. The rest of the *Wolf Pack* looked surprised at what *The Architect* wanted to do. After three hours of listening to him map out his new manifesto, everyone in the room looked petrified.

After the meeting was over, every member of the *Wolf Pack* stayed behind. They tried to convince Professor Cochran to join them, but he refused. He wanted to get back to the United States and his DRM where he felt safer.

Klaus Bergner, CEO of Apollo Pharmaceuticals, was first to speak. "Dunham is crazier than he's ever been. There is no way we can support what he wants to do," Bergner said, out of breath. He took in some air and slowly expelled his breath through his caked lips, ready to continue. "We need to stick together. Maybe work with the FBI to stop this madman before he gets us all killed with his crazy delusions."

Elliott Muller, President of Swiss Financial, stood up and began pacing around the room. "Friends, it won't be that simple going against Dunham. He's threatened all of us, including our families. I'm scared."

Dunham's brother Theodore jumped into the conversation. "We all should fear Albert. He's a sociopath who will not hesitate to kill all of us. I think we should all go to our respective authorities and turn him in and tell them everything we know. If we ask for immunity, after this is over, we can go back to our respective lives and businesses. I will be increasing my security and I suggest each of you do the same," Teddy said.

After two hours of debating what they should do, they all agreed to wait and see what Albert Dunham was able to accomplish inside the United States first.

* * * * *

Inside a Mercedes Sprinter Van, General Tucker Phillips and Dunham were listening to the *Wolf Pack* plot their disloyal moves against him.

"We don't need these bastards," General Phillips said. "Just give me the word and they will not be in our way."

Dunham put his hand on the General's shoulder. "You're right, but now is not the right time. Once I get the first part of my plan moving forward, then they can all disappear, including my brother and his family."

"Copy that, sir," Phillips replied. "I'm still going to monitor all of them and make sure they are not moving against you too fast."

38

Sitting in their unmarked vehicle, three FBI agents who were part of the Bureau's international terrorist unit got clear photos of Dunham and General Phillips. Inside the Matild Palace Hotel, another agent captured photos of all the members of the *Wolf Pack*. One older gentleman, who was using a cane, was unknown to the agent. He had gotten multiple photos of this stranger's face.

Back at the Interpol headquarters where the FBI's International Terrorist team kept their offices, Special Agent in Charge Brian Lassiter looked over the photos his men had sent him. Seeing Albert Dunham parading around Budapest surprised him. The man was wanted by Interpol, as well as twenty other EU countries. Showing his face on worldwide media and acting like he was the victim of a conspiracy plot against him by the United States federal government was laughable.

Agent Lassiter dialed FBI Director Glass. "Director Glass, Agent Lassiter. I just sent the photos you requested. We can pick up Dunham anytime. Just give me the orders."

"Not just yet. I'm curious about what he has up his sleeve. I believe he's connected to the DRM and seeing him with the *Wolf Pack* worries me. Both groups so far have not shown any liking to *The Architect*," Tiffany said. "I'd like your team to monitor Dunham's movements, keeping yourself at a safe distance. I don't want him spooked and going dark before we figure out what his end game might be."

"Will do. Have you looked over the photo of the elderly man that was part of the recent meeting?" asked Lassiter.

Tiffany held up the photo. "He looks familiar. I'll run him through our facial recognition database and see if we can identify him. Is he still in Budapest?"

"One of my agents followed his car to the airport. He got on an American Airlines flight to JFK. If he had a connection, we could not determine by the manifest," Lassiter said.

"I'll alert my Manhattan office and get a team at the airport to monitor him when he lands," Director Glass said. Before she could end the call, Lassiter interrupted her.

"Director, I just got an alert that Dunham had a meeting with the head of Turkey's military and the head of Iran's Republican Guard. They looked very chummy."

There was a long silence from Director Glass. "Shit. What's that bastard up to? Keep me posted," she said, abruptly ending the call.

Tiffany immediately called a meeting with her team. Too many things needed to be juggled. With Dunham back in the public's eye, her brain was on overload. Her gut was telling her something big was about to happen, but what? This was the same feeling she had about Charles Stone that almost cost her and Sam their lives.

* * * * *

Thirty minutes later, inside a conference room at the Hoover Building, Tiffany's entire team was assembled. She was not familiar with most of them, but from what she read in their personnel files, they were all well-respected agents with clean records. In addition, Dean Miller did a massive analysis of their movements over the last ninety days, and they all appeared clean.

Director Glass sat at the head of the conference table and opened a thick folder. "Ladies and Gentlemen, I called you here today to figure out a plan to stop the domestic terrorist problem we have in our country. So much tragedy has befallen our country over the last seven days. Now, with Albert Dunham *The Architect* back from the grave, we have an added problem that has spread to Europe and beyond," she said. "I'm putting our entire agency on terrorist alert, both domestic and foreign."

FBI agent Rita Osborne, one of the agents on the FBI's domestic terrorist unit, raised her hand. "Director Glass, we all know we have a serious problem, but even with President Graham signing her executive order allowing us to investigate White Supremacists, the legislation the previous President signed into law continues to limit us," Agent Osborne said.

"I'm troubled by that too, but the DOJ has assured me that they will not be prosecuting any FBI agents for doing their job protecting our country and the constitution. Any other questions or concerns?" Tiffany asked the group.

FBI agent Adam Colton in the cybercrime unit jumped into the conversation. "Director Glass, my unit has been picking up a lot of chatter on social media from numerous White Supremacy factions. There's a new QAnon conspiracy gaining some steam. The militia groups are not very happy with Albert Dunham being back in the news. What we have are vague rumblings about what *The Architect* wants them to do to resurrect his failed manifesto," Colton said.

"Do we have any indication of what is being planned?"

Agent Colton shook his head. "Not at this time. If I didn't know better, whoever is leading the DRM has everyone tight-lipped."

Tiffany, for the next hour, threw out ideas to her team, trying to stimulate them to produce solutions to combating the White Supremacist movement and the paramilitary militia groups murdering innocent Americans.

"Let's all meet back here in three days. I'll expect no complaints but some solutions that we can act upon," Tiffany said, ending the meeting.

39

A few hours after the *Wolf Pack* meeting ended, Theodore Dunham strolled across the Chain Bridge, Budapest's oldest bridge connecting Buda and Pest over the Danube. It was a cool evening with a blue sky filled with stars. He needed to clear his head after seeing his brother alive and threatening everyone associated with the *Wolf Pack*. It brought back horrible memories of what an unspeakably nasty person he could be.

Teddy had a hunch that his brother did not die when his Bethesda Maryland home was leveled by the cruise missile. The way his wife Maggie died by hanging herself from the second-floor banister smelled like Albert's handiwork.

It was now after midnight and the bridge was empty of tourists. Teddy decided to go back to his hotel and get ready for his flight home in the afternoon. The streets were void of vehicle traffic.

Stepping off the curb, Theodore did not hear two men sneak up behind him and slip a black hood over his head. Both of his arms were yanked back. He felt a shooting pain radiate in both shoulders as his hands were zip-tied tightly. Before he could react, he heard a car screech to a stop. He was shoved into the back seat and the car sped away.

"What the fuck is going on? Don't you guys know who I am?" Teddy shouted.

"We sure do, Mister Dunham. Someone wants to speak to you before you fly home," the man said.

After what felt like an hour of driving in circles, he heard a squeaky metal garage door open. Teddy was pulled roughly from the car and guided up a short flight of metal stairs. He was forced down onto a wooden folding chair and ordered to keep quiet.

Five minutes later, he heard a door open, and a familiar voice ordered one of the guards to remove his hood.

Blinking rapidly, Teddy tried to clear his eyes from the bright light shining on his face. "Albert, what are you doing? Are you going to kill me like you did Maggie?" he shouted.

Albert started laughing. "If I wanted you dead, I would not have gone to this much trouble to bring you here to talk. I just want to get a loyalty commitment from you and your support for what I have planned."

Teddy was perplexed. "Talk? Support you? Why would I do that?"

Albert walked over to his brother and put his phone on his lap. "Look at the video and then tell me you won't cooperate with me."

Teddy's eyes grew wide with fear. "You're crazy. They are your family."

Albert patted the top of his brother's shoulder. He had an evil smile that brought chills to Teddy's body. "Hear me out first before you rule out aiding me."

"Not until I know my wife and children are safe," Teddy said.

Albert ignored his brother. "Within the next month, mass shootings and bombs exploding in some key European countries will make what Professor Cochran has done in America seem like child's play. On top of that, a new virus will spread throughout Europe, Asia, and Africa and I have the only vaccine that can curtail it. I need our pharmaceutical company to build a serum stockpile so we can get rich selling our vials to every country affected by this deadly virus that will be worse than any of the COVID strains," *The Architect* said.

Theodore was speechless. "You are one sick motherfucker, brother. I've always known since you were a young boy that you did not have a conscience, but something like this is the act of a lunatic," Teddy screamed at his brother.

"If you won't help me, then hundreds of millions of men, women, and children will die. Once the world sees what this virus can do and how fast it can spread, we'll make a ton of money holding the world hostage."

Teddy started shaking his thighs, jarring the phone to crash to the cement floor. He heard something crack and looked down to see that the screen of the cell phone had shattered. "You've gone mad. Don't you remember how devastating COVID-19 was on our country and the world? And you want to unleash another poison so you can make a ton of money?"

"I am not a heartless man. It's not that bad what I want to do," Albert answered. "Yes, I want to make billions of dollars. I'm only going to unleash the virus on my enemies. Those who are loyal to me will have the vaccine before any virus is released." He watched for his brother's reaction. "So, will you help me? Are you and your family going to be loyal to me?"

Teddy was deep in thought, trying to find the right words that would not ignite his brother's rage and harm his family. He knew what Albert was saying was mostly lies. He did not trust him. "I have no choice, do I?"

"Not really, if you ever want to see your wife and children again."

"I'll help you if you return my family to me."

"Not going to happen that way. You'll either help me or watch them die from the virus."

"Okay. Get me the formula so I can get started," Teddy said.

"That's not how it's going to work, either. I have a team of scientists who will be using your facilities. They are loyal to me. All you have to do is let them have full access to the manufacturing facility. No way will you get your hands on the vaccine recipe," Albert said. "When I feel confident that you're fully cooperating with me, then I will release your family."

Before Teddy could reply, the black hood was placed back over his head, and he was dragged out to the car and driven back to his hotel. He was handed an envelope with instructions on what to do next.

40

Paige Turner's weekly podcast had fifteen minutes until airtime. She was still shaken up after having her show preempted by Albert Dunham a week ago. Seeing his face and hearing his voice brought back a rush of bad memories. If there was any person who fit her *Corrupted Intelligence* theory, this man would be the poster child.

Dunham had a special hold on millions of people around the world who believe he was their savior with all the money he promised to give them. Turner knew better than most that *The Architect* was a charming individual who could lie without remorse.

Immediately after Dunham reared his ugly head a week ago, Paige was beckoned to the Oval Office. President Graham ordered her to pause her *Corrupted Intelligence* investigation. It conflicted with what the administration was doing to combat the attacks that kept escalating across the country.

Turner did not like orders, especially with an explosive story. "Madame President, I can't... I won't do that," she said in a calm voice.

The new President did not know Turner very well. If the President understood the mindset of the reporter, she never would have given her orders. "Are you saying that you won't cooperate with your President?"

"Madame President, before I say something I will regret, I'd like to table your request so I can think things through." Paige forced a smile before she continued. "Madame President, need I remind you that the press is not controlled by the executive branch," she said, her tone becoming confrontational. She took a deep breath to try to calm down. "I don't mean any disrespect, but once you get to know me, you'll find out I don't bury any story, especially one that has the lives of Americans at risk." She abruptly stood, said goodbye, and waited for the President to say something, which she didn't, and walked out of the Oval Office.

As she drove back to her office, she reviewed her actions and realized she overreacted. "I never should have been that rude to President Graham," she said to herself as she darted in and out of traffic.

Paige was not paying attention as she kept mumbling to herself. *"The public needs to know what's going on,"* she had told the President. *"I won't make the same mistakes I made when The Architect almost destroyed our country."* Hearing her words echo inside her head, she regretted letting her stubbornness overtake her emotions. Before she could react, a black Ford Suburban cut in front of her, fishtailing as it came to an abrupt halt. Two men wearing White Angel leather jackets jumped out of the truck, pointing automatic weapons at her. Off in the distance was Wiley Jordan, monitoring how his men were doing.

Seeing the two black unmarked vans cutting her off, set off alarm bells for Turner. Her heart started racing as she realized she was about to die. Scott Rogers's words echoed in her head. *"Don't do this story. Your life will be in danger."* Paige leaned forward and quickly popped open her glove compartment, pulling out the Berretta that Scott had given her. As she straightened up, explosions of gunfire surrounded her car, exploding her windshield, spraying her body with glass. It was over in a matter of seconds. Her heart would not stop racing as she saw the two men in White Angel leather jackets lying dead in front of her car. Four US Marshals ran over toward her and surrounded her car.

Her driver-side door opened, and Scott reached in and pulled her out, ushering his fiancée to his van. Once inside, he put his arms around her, squeezing her tight, whispering, *"I love you."*

Paige was in shock, unable to control her emotions. "How did you know where I was?" she asked.

"President Graham notified me, after you stormed out of her office, and ordered the US Marshals office to watch you. I'm glad she did," Rogers said, patting his glassy eyes. "Will you now back off on your *Corrupted Intelligence* theory like the President requested so you can be safe?"

Paige looked at Scott's tears cascading down her cheeks. "Never. Now more than ever, I need to take my *Corrupted Intelligence* theory to another level and let my podcast focus on the domestic terrorists plaguing her country. I don't care that the President and FBI Director will be pissed at me. I appreciate what the President did, but I am an investigative reporter first and foremost."

What she wanted to say on her podcast was forming inside her head. She imagined that it would bring Albert Dunham and the leader of the DRM out from the shadows so they could be arrested.

What she had in mind most definitely would upset President Graham. Her goal after her podcast was to have her followers talk about her *Corrupted Intelligence* theory, getting them to focus on Albert Dunham and the White Supremacy movement in America. She was confident *The Architect* would let his ego get the best of him, and make mistakes as he did before when his manifesto was leaked to the public and FBI.

Later that morning, sitting behind her desk, she watched her producer count down five, four, three, two, one, and point her finger, signaling that her podcast was live. Paige, with a casual smile, started speaking.

"Thanks to everyone around the world who chose to join me today to listen to what I have to say about my Corrupted Intelligence theory. Before I go on, I need to tell everyone that today after meeting with President Graham, two men associated with the White Angels White Supremacy group tried to kill me. They don't like what I've been saying about them and all the other illegal militia groups responsible for the slaughter of thousands of innocent Americans." Paige took a calming deep breath before continuing.

"For those of you who are first-time listeners, the abuse of entrusted power is the condensed definition of my theory. We all need to open our eyes and be critical of all the people we allow to have power over us. Our political leaders, media show hosts, and even the leaders you work for." Paige looked into the camera lens and gathered her thoughts. *"We need to have a skeptical ear when listening to every person who has power over us. We need to fact-check and fact-check some more before we accept what we've been told."*

Paige closed her eyes, catching her breath and looked up. *"Let's try to think about who we respect, who we turn over our power to so we can clearly see their Corrupted Intelligence that keeps us loyal to them. Let's think about a few past Presidents who might have abused their entrusted power we gave them. Let's look at President Nixon. He abused his power by breaking the law, lying to all of us to manipulate the outcome of his re-election bid. What about the political parties we support like sports teams? Don't they abuse the entrusted power we* give them? Studies have shown that societies with high IQs have less corruption. But I disagree."

Paige started combing her fingers through her long black hair, deep in thought. *"Our political parties overall are intelligent. Unfortunately, a high percentage of elected officials are corrupt and are good at drawing us into their special world of conspiracy theories and lies. These lies have created a loyal cult, a tribe of sorts, that believes everything they are told and will, like all manipulated groups, allow themselves to be called into violent action. These politicians have forgotten about the citizens who elected them, and only favor the large donors and lobbyists who keep them in office. While in office they are unable to support their voter's needs. Then, when they are up for re-election, the same cycle of lies and false promises and new conspiracy theories comes out of their mouths. And, when confronted with these transgressions, they blame the other party or their opponent and manipulate their followers to pick sides."*

For the next forty minutes, Paige laid out more examples of *Corrupted Intelligence* within the United States and around the world. Feeling confident she had built a solid case for her theory; she turned her direction toward the White Supremacists and Albert Dunham, *The Architect.*

"I want to sum up my podcast by focusing on Albert Dunham The Architect now that he's back from the dead. He's a perfect example of a person who abuses the trust he was given by his followers. He believes that repeating lies will become the truth to all the people loyal to him. Once he's confident he can do no wrong in the eyes of his faithful supporters, he begins to siphon off billions and billions of dollars from donations and government programs for his businesses." Paige flashed on her screen the URLs that point out the truth about Albert Dunham and reveal all his lies about being a victim.

Paige closed her file and looked straight into the camera. *"With Albert Dunham back in our lives, we all need to remember what he tried to do to our country four years ago. While he was not responsible for today's attempt on my life, he did try over four years ago to assassinate me twice.*

"Let's not forget what he's capable of doing to our democracy. He's a dictator and wants to shred our constitution and install himself as the first Emperor of the United States. That might seem laughable, but he came very close to achieving that goal four years ago. We need to scrutinize Dunham's words and clearly see all his lies. There is a frightening reason he's resurfaced,

and I promise you I will find out what it is," Paige said trying to take in a comforting breath.

"We need to remember the thousands of innocent Americans Dunham murdered while projecting himself as a philanthropist. It's important to understand that Dunham did not act alone. He had many elected officials helping him. The Architect, with his Corrupted Intelligence, has weaponized hate with his 'Dog Whistles', which will lead to more violence and death to innocent Americans. Albert Dunham is a criminal, a con man, and a traitor to our country. Whatever he has up his sleeves needs to be analyzed to make sure we don't give him, or the elected officials who support him, the power to abuse all of us again."

After sixty minutes, Paige ended her podcast. Her phone immediately started ringing. Her staff assistant rushed into her office.

"Paige, President Graham wants to talk with you, as well as FBI Director Glass. Both ladies sounded upset," said a nervous Rebecca Burns, ex-FBI analyst. "I told you to hold off doing this segment after you were almost killed. But no, you thought you knew what was best for your podcast."

"Relax. I know what I am doing. Do we have other angry messages?"

Burns dropped thirty messages she pulled off the answering machine. "By the looks of things, you have a lot of people very upset with what you said."

Paige picked up a few messages and smiled when she saw they were mostly from White Supremacists. One caught her eye. It was from Albert Dunham.

"Rebecca, I understand why you're upset with me, but trust me that I know what I am doing here," Paige said. She handed the Dunham message to her assistant. "Please get him on the phone. I really want to hear what he has to say."

41

President Graham was pacing around the Oval Office, looking like she wanted to punch someone. "Can I arrest Paige Turner for what she just did?"

Director Glass tried to answer. "Madame President, Turner is protected under the First Amendment. Plus, she didn't do anything wrong. The only thing she's guilty of is not obeying your orders or mine, which she had no obligation to do," Tiffany said.

"I thought saving her life today would have gotten her to show some gratitude."

"She doesn't think that way. She loves our country and is not frightened by threats and attempts on her life. Dunham tried a few times, and it didn't work for him. It only made her more determined to expose the truth," Director Glass said.

"Then how are we going to handle her?"

"We don't. Dean Miller intercepted a few of the angry messages Turner had received after her podcast. It seems that she's stirring up the cockroaches and bringing them out into the light. Even Dunham called her and requested a meeting. Let me and my team keep our surveillance on her and maybe we will cut a break," said Director Glass.

Before the President could dismiss the FBI Director, her Chief of Staff rushed in holding a piece of paper. "Madame President, Albert Dunham wants to talk with you. He says it's urgent. It's a National Security issue, Dunham said."

The President looked at her FBI Director. "Glass, what should I do with this Dunham guy?"

"Let me contact him on your behalf. If he's still in Budapest, I can have my team there arrest him, and then I can have a face-to-face with him."

As Director Glass left the Oval Office, her phone started beeping with a news alert. She stopped dead in her tracks, turning up the volume on her phone.

"Five hundred members of the American Nazi Party were found dead in the backwoods of Oregon. The cause of this mass casualty event is unknown at this time. A comment by the medical examiner was that it looked like a mass suicide. She wanted to first analyze the blood samples to have a clearer picture of what happened," the reporter said, noticeably shaken by what she had just witnessed.

Tiffany did an abrupt about-face and went back into the Oval Office. She could see the shocked expression on President Graham's face.

"Director Glass, I need your team up there to determine if this was a terrorist attack or maybe *The Architect's Army* striking again? Could this be what Dunham wants to talk about?"

"Will do. I really doubt *The Architect's Army* would do this. If it's mass poisoning against White Supremacists, we might be looking at the beginning of a race war for the recent houses of worship bombings," Director Glass said. "Give me a few days to get a handle on all of this."

When Tiffany got back to her office, she immediately called her husband. "Sam, it's me. Any thoughts on what just happened in Oregon?"

"Nothing at this time. I probably found out about the same time you did. I sent McAllister and his men to the crime scene. I also have Raymond Stillwell getting as much aerial surveillance to see who might have traveled to those Oregon woods. Someone must be cleaning house within the DRM. Do you think Paige Turner's publicity stunt shook up the leaders of the Domestic Revolutionary Movement?"

"The thought crossed my mind, but President Graham thinks it might have been *The Architect's Army* group or maybe Dunham specifically. Could we be looking at gangs taking matters into their own hands?"

"I don't have a clue. I wouldn't put it past Dunham's so-called army to murder these scumbags," said Sam.

"Sam, I need a favor. Can you talk with Paige Turner and find out what she might know about this attack? Dunham wants to speak with her. It's possible she might have some answers," Tiffany said. "I gotta go into a meeting. See you tonight."

42

In his office at his home, Professor Cochran sipped his Scotch on the rocks. Sitting on a large leather couch were Wesley Jones, Johnny Ellis, and Max Simon. They were planning their next move when they saw the special news alert. Wiley was pacing around the room, still smoldering about losing more of his men at the attack on Paige Turner.

"Cochran," Wiley shouted. "I'm sick and tired of losing my soldiers to your fucking vendetta against Turner," he cursed. "First it was Sam Collins and Tiffany Glass during your first uprising with Charles Stone. Now, this crazy insurrection has been doomed from the start. You don't know how to conduct a revolution. If you'd let me run the DRM, I guarantee you'd see better results."

Cochran's face was beet red listening to Wiley rant. "You're an idiot, Wiley. You can't even handle a simple kidnapping of Jacob Stein's family, or killing a runt of a female reporter. So don't mock what I've been doing for our people and our race."

Wiley's nostrils flared, looking like he wanted to strangle The Professor. "Then what the fuck just happened on your watch? Any idea who could have done this?" the White Angel's leader asked.

Cochran lashed back. "I bet it was Dunham and his fucking army. *The Architect* did threaten the entire *Wolf Pack* that this would happen if we were not loyal to him."

Johnny Ellis spoke up. "There has been a lot of chatter from the *Wolf Pack* ever since Dunham returned. I wouldn't put it past that asshole to do something like this."

Professor Cochran looked at each of his men, trying to find the right words to tell them about his meeting with Dunham in Budapest. "Gentlemen, I am sure this was the handy work of *The Architect*. After meeting with him in Budapest, he appeared ready to go on a killing spree that would get him back in the driver's seat with the current administration. He thought that Charles Stone was an idiot with mental issues and that he, *The Architect,* should have overseen the DRM, not Stone," Cochran said.

"If this mass murder of our patriots is *The Architect's* dirty work, then how can we stop him before he decides to kill all of us?" Wesley Jones asked. He was noticeably upset, which concerned The Professor.

"Let's assume this is the work of *The Architect*. I know how he thinks. We should be hearing from him very soon with his terms," Cochran said. "I wouldn't be surprised if President Graham will also hear from him with his demands for her. He always has an endgame."

Wiley stood up abruptly and started pacing around the room, noticeably upset with everything. He was holding his bandaged hand that had his three fingers reattached. "I can go to Budapest and kill that bastard. Then we can go back to planning our next moves."

Cochran shook his head at Wiley. "If you can't kill Paige Turner in the daylight, then what makes you think you can kill Dunham, who is surrounded by a well-armed security team?" The Professor said. "What we need to do is be calm, and not fly off the handle. That's what Dunham would like. We shouldn't give him the satisfaction."

"So, we just sit and wait until he begins targeting all of us?" Wiley said, slamming his good fist against the office door. "Do you think the *Wolf Pack* knew this attack was coming? I don't, and that's what scares me."

"The *Wolf Pack* is monitoring Dunham. They assured me they would let me know when *The Architect* leaves Budapest."

Wiley was not buying The Professor's casual attitude about Dunham. "If this was Dunham's doing, his reach extends across the Atlantic. I can't just wait for him to make a move. If I get the chance, Dunham is dust."

The other men all agreed with Wiley. They all wanted a pre-emptive strike before Dunham made another move.

Professor Cochran was not happy his wishes were not being respected. "Gentlemen, I understand your concerns. You need a well-thought-out plan, or you'll all be dead, and Dunham will win again. First, we need to understand how he infiltrated our heavily secured compound in Oregon. Let's meet back here in three days. Have a plan laid out for me to approve," said Cochran.

Once The Professor was alone, he called Theodore Dunham. "Teddy, Cochran here. I'm sure you've seen the news. Was this the work of your brother?"

Teddy answered nervously. "I can't talk right now. I have people here," he said, his voice cracking.

"Dunham there?"

"No."

"His men?"

"Yes."

"We need to meet, and discuss details, plans, share information."

"I'll call you in a few days," Teddy said, abruptly hanging up.

43

Tiffany was back at the Mayflower Hotel at six-thirty, just in time to eat with Sam and her children. She looked exhausted as she entered the suite. "I'm home," she called out.

"Back in the kid's bedroom," Sam yelled back at her.

Seeing Irene and Michael brought a big smile to her face. She was beginning to question her decision to be the FBI Director. She had known that the current division within the country was bad, but she did not anticipate it was so out of control.

Sam stood and gave her a big hug and kiss. He whispered in her ear, "I've got an update on the mass murder in Oregon."

Tiffany pushed herself away, biting her lower lip. "Let's talk about it after the kids are sound asleep. I need some mommy time with them right now."

An hour and a half after Tiffany had gotten home, they sat on their living room couch, sipping wine. Sam noticed how tired his wife looked.

"Honey, I've never seen you looking so stressed. What can I do to help you?" Sam asked.

"Give me a quick solution to stopping these domestic terrorists, Dunham, and finding the damn DRM leader," she said. "I am stressed, but nothing I can't handle. We have too many fires we're trying to put out before a new one pops up."

Sam put his finger to her lips to stop her from talking. "What I found out up in Oregon will not help you," Sam said, as he put his arm around his wife, giving her a loving hug. "The Oregon coroner ran blood samples and determined that what killed these men was a man-made genetic nerve gas that mutates so fast that within thirty minutes the body shuts down. He said he's never seen anything like this."

Tiffany did not want to tell Sam that Raymond Stillwell and Dean Miller were doing a facial recognition search so she could see who entered and left the camp before these men were murdered.

"Do the local authorities suspect anyone responsible for this mass murder?" asked Tiffany.

Sam shook his head. "Not currently. McAllister has Stillwell working on that problem and has been assured he will have something either later today or early tomorrow."

Tiffany frowned, wondering if Stillwell could still do what she wanted without alerting McAllister. "When you find out anything, I expect you to share it with my office," she said.

"I thought you and President Graham wanted plausible deniability about my investigations, especially the illegal spying?" Sam reminded her.

Tiffany took a slow sip from her wineglass, swirling the wine around in her mouth. "You're right. Just if you find out anything that might help my investigation, I think you need to share it with me anyway. I'll decide what I can use or not use."

Before Sam could respond, his cell phone rang. It was McAllister. "I've got to take this," he said and walked to the hallway. "Commander, what can I do for you at this hour?"

"Sam, I have some scary news about the nerve gas that killed that militia group," McAllister said unemotionally. "Bubba just got back from talking with Dunham's brother Theodore. He believes his brother killed those men. He said if his brother is true to form, he created this weapon as leverage for his overall objective: his revised manifesto."

"Does Bubba believe Theodore Dunham?"

"Yes, he said. Ex-General Tucker Phillips had traveled to Oregon during the timeline when these men died."

"Tucker Phillips? Why does his name sound familiar?" Sam asked.

"He's the traitor who tried to kill Paige Turner and murdered most of her staff," McAllister said.

"Why isn't he in prison?"

"He was, but escaped about a year ago with more of *The Architect's* henchmen, including his number two, Frederick Ellison. The FBI has not stopped looking for him."

"Are we testing the nerve gas? Any idea if there is an antidote?" Sam asked.

"Dunham's brother says there is one. Teddy says his brother wants to use their pharmaceutical lab to produce a large supply. If this is true, then *The Architect* is preparing for a major release of this weapon. He said that his brother has his own security team at the facility, as well as scientists from Russia and North Korea, to keep his secret secure."

"Is Theodore willing to cooperate with us?" Sam asked.

"As of this moment, yes. But his brother has threatened to kill his family, who he had kidnapped, and will kill them if he doesn't cooperate," McAllister replied. "Theodore remembers what his brother did to his wife who was disloyal to him. He's very scared."

"Can you and Stillwell figure out where Theodore's family is being kept?"

"We are currently looking for them," the Commander said.

"Keep me posted on your progress." Sam signed off with the Commander and walked back inside. "That was McAllister. Are you ready to hear what he's discovered?"

Tiffany gulped down her entire wineglass and leaned back on the couch after pouring herself another glass. "Fire away."

44

Professor Cochran's hands could not stop shaking as he looked at the photos of the dead bodies in the Oregon DRM compound. "I never imagined Dunham was this ruthless. These men were all patriots who would support *The Architect,*" he rambled to Wiley Jordan. "He needs to be stopped at all costs."

Wiley started shaking his head, disapproval written on his face. "I told you I should have gone to Budapest and blown his brains out. Now he's on the move and not leaving a trail to follow," an angry Jordan said.

"I'm sorry I didn't listen to you, my friend," The Professor said. "I'm in contact with the *Wolf Pack*. They are hoping to get a beeline on Dunham's whereabouts by tomorrow. Once we have it, I'll set you and your men loose on him and his team so we can get back to our insurgency plan and not have to look over our shoulders for *The Architect* and his army. When you find him, show him no mercy."

"What about Theodore Dunham? Should we interrogate him to find out what he might know?"

"That's a good idea. When I was in Budapest, I noticed he had a private meeting with his brother and might know what he's up to," Cochran said.

"He's still in Maryland, right?" Wiley asked.

"Yes. Here's his home address and the address of his pharmaceutical company." The Professor handed Jordan a piece of paper with the two addresses. "Be careful. I saw firsthand that Dunham has professional mercenaries who won't hesitate to use lethal force to protect *The Architect's* plan."

"Don't you worry about me and my men. We won't make the same mistake we did when we tried to kill Tiffany Glass and Sam Collins or Paige Turner. Once I terminate Dunham and his goons, the FBI Director and Attorney General, along with Paige Turner are next. Maybe Commander McAllister and his men, too. Don't try to stop me," Wiley boasted, his veins bulging on his face.

"I won't, but one thing at a time, Wiley. Our immediate problem is with Dunham and the bioweapon. Locate his brother and get answers."

Wiley looked frustrated with The Professor. "I want to get back to what we originally wanted for our movement. As Whites, we are the advanced race and are entitled to run the southern states and keep the niggers and others of color as second-class citizens. We need to keep it that way by any means possible," Jordan rambled with his hatred toward any person that's not a White Christian. He noticed The Professor was listening to every word he was saying.

Cochran wanted to speak, but Wiley put his hand up like a traffic cop, signaling him that he had more to say. "I don't like the billionaires of the world, like Dunham. They are trying to write us out of the picture. If they gain any more power and wealth, people like me and you, Professor, will become extinct. That's why *The Architect,* in my opinion, must be terminated before he takes control, like he tried to do four years ago."

The Professor started clapping. "Wiley, you surprise me with your intellect. I can't wait for you to tell me more about your life and background."

"Soon. One other thing. You need to start getting the southern Governors and their legislatures ready for their states to secede from the north," Wiley said and left The Professor sitting by himself.

Cochran immediately was on the phone calling Klaus Bergner, the head of the *Wolf Pack*. He needed to get them to work with him and the DRM to end Dunham for the last time.

45

Collins and McAllister sat at Martin's Tavern in Georgetown, going over everything that had happened over the last two weeks. They agreed that they did not have the manpower to deal with everything.

"Do you have any ideas on how we start to neutralize this White Supremacy movement and not break the law?" Sam asked.

"Our biggest problem is the billionaires. They have the money to promote their lies on social media and all the network news stations, keeping their followers loyal to them and their message of *We Won't Be Replaced*," McAllister said. "How I see it, we do not focus solely on Dunham or the Domestic Revolutionary Movement."

"I agree, but who do we target first?" Sam asked. "What do we do if the DRM or Dunham initiate another attack and stir up more racial violence around our country?"

McAllister put his arm around Sam's shoulder. "I'd like us to focus on the *Wolf Pack*, especially Theodore Dunham and his pharmaceutical company. I believe he is ground zero for *The Architect's* new manifesto. We need to let President Graham and FBI Director Glass deal with the militia groups and Dunham specifically. If we can destroy *The Architect's* plans with his new weapon, stopping the rest will be a lot easier," the Commander said.

"We don't really know for sure if this nerve gas came from Albert Dunham," Sam said.

"My sources, especially from Stillwell, point to *The Architect*. He's a sick motherfucker. This chemical has his signature all over it."

Sam once again opened Paige Turner's file she had given him. "After looking at what Turner gave us, she too believes that many men in power are favoring destroying our democracy and rewriting our constitution so they can accumulate massive profits. There are over a hundred Senators and House Representatives elected to office who have ties to White Supremacy groups. It doesn't stop there. This movement has infected our judicial system and over thirty State Legislatures. They have the support of the far-right cable news networks and their most popular commentators," Sam said, trying to catch his breath. "I'm planning to set up a domestic terrorist investigation team inside the DOJ and bringing enough of these traitors in front of a Grand Jury."

"Sam, relax, please. I know this is overwhelming, but we'll be able to curtail this movement once the additional men I've recruited get to Maryland. I've got over fifty patriots, ex-SEALs, and ex-Army rangers who will do whatever it takes to save our democracy and protect our constitution."

"This is the first I'm hearing about this," Sam said, surprised. "Are we going to fight fire with fire?"

"Something like that. When the time comes, you'll need to remain at the DOJ and begin arresting all the men we bring you or find some unmarked graves to bury them in. The men we are fighting are traitors and fit into Turner's *Corrupted Intelligence* theory. They are blatantly abusing their entrusted power and need to pay a price for it," McAllister said. "Boy, Turner has me repeating her message like it's mine. Sam, I've got a meeting with my team later today. Let's try to meet again tomorrow morning. What I have is a plan that will make you feel better."

"Tomorrow it is."

46

Dunham gave General Tucker Phillips a death stare. He was furious that he had unleashed the nerve gas without his permission. "What part of waiting did you not understand, Tucker? You've messed up my timing," he screamed.

The General just shrugged his shoulders. "I did what I thought was right. That militia group was Cochran's most dangerous group. They were getting ready to launch another mass shooting event at a county fair in Portland. You'll thank me for taking the initiative to convince that bitch President to grant you the pardon you so desperately want," said Phillips.

Dunham stood looking like he wanted to kill someone. "You work for me. You will never go against my orders, or you'll be dealt with severely," he said. He signaled for his security team to lift Tucker off his chair. Tucker tried to fight them off, but they quickly overpowered him. "Now, General, stay calm before one of my men accidentally hurts you. I have a new assignment for you and your team."

Phillips calmed down. "What do you want me to do?" he asked, pushing away from the men who were holding him.

"I want you to monitor Paige Turner and her fiancée, Scott Rogers. Cochran's crazy man, Wiley Jordan, tried to kill her and failed. I don't want her dead just yet. I need to destroy her reputation first," Dunham said. "Killing her is letting her off too easy."

"Just watch and do nothing?" the General asked.

"Yes. Send me daily reports on what they are doing and who they meet with as well as where they are at all times. Is that clear?" Dunham said. "Once I ruin her reputation, then I need to find the perfect place to release my weapon on her and her fiancée. I was thinking during one of her podcasts, but that might be impossible."

Tucker had a puzzled expression on his face. "Why is the timing so important?" the General said.

"It just is. I will never forgive her and Rogers for what they did to me. Then I will need the location of Professor Dean Miller and his family. I'll need his cooperation to recreate his satellite software. I never got to complete the best part of my manifesto."

"That's all you want from me and my men? If we notice they are planning to harm you, can I act and keep them out of your hair?" General Phillips asked.

"You will not do anything unless you have my okay. No gung-ho initiative."

Tucker did not appear happy, but nodded his agreement. "Copy that, sir."

After Phillips left, Dunham called one of his media supporters. "Albert Dunham here. Can we talk now?"

"I always have time for you. I was happy to see you broadcasting again," Randall Hunt said.

"I need you to tell your listeners how the past administration and Paige Turner lied about my actions. You know how to build a story with enough lies and conspiracies that will sound believable. In addition, I need you to paint a negative narrative on Turner and ex-President Chesterfield. I need this done quickly before I take a meeting with President Graham," Dunham said.

"It would be my pleasure. You're a true American hero who every citizen should respect and appreciate for everything you've done or plan to do for our country," Randall said.

Dunham spent the next forty-five minutes telling the American News Network talk show host everything he wanted to be broadcasted every day. He gave the media personality wild accusations about his enemies and all the people who wanted to harm him and his manifesto. Randall had the highest rating show on network media news. The commentator had over forty million listeners who only listened to the American Network News for their news.

Dunham's next phone call was to President Graham. He had heard from the FBI Director's office who was calling on her behalf, but he only wanted a face-to-face with the new President. He reviewed what he wanted to say and how he was going to threaten the most powerful person in the world.

47

President Graham had told her Chief of Staff that in no way would she have a face-to-face with Dunham unless he was ready to turn himself in to the FBI. Martha Sweeden relayed the President's message to *The Architect,* which was greeted with hysterical laughter.

"Madame President. Dunham basically told you to go fuck yourself. He said you'll want to talk to him and listen to what he has to say. He ended the call by reminding me about the four hundred-plus dead White Supremacists in the Oregon Forest. He wanted me to relay this message: *'More mass murders will happen every day if you don't agree to talk with me.'"*

President Graham's color drained from her face. "Was he admitting he killed those militiamen?"

"He didn't admit in those exact words, just implied he did," said Sweeden.

"I need my FBI Director Homeland Security Secretary and Attorney General here ASAP," President Graham shouted at her Chief of Staff.

* * * * *

Two hours later, Director Glass and Attorney General Collins were in the Oval Office, along with Homeland Security Secretary Kate Ambrose, waiting to meet the President.

"Did Sweeden clue you in on what she wanted to talk about?" asked Sam.

Tiffany just shook her head. "I can only guess it has something to with Albert Dunham and the militia lying dead in the Oregon backwoods. That's my best guess," she said.

Before Sam could ask another question, President Graham entered the room. "Thank you for getting here on such short notice. Our country is teetering on the edge of anarchy. We are surrounded by White Supremacists and an old nemesis, Albert Dunham, *The Architect*. Both entities are attacking us from all sides. In addition, I have a large group of West Wing traitors who are communicating with our enemies. We also have a group in Europe called the *Wolf Pack* who have become active," President Graham said, almost hyperventilating. Determined to get her point across, she kept talking. "My CIA Director briefed me and said that the *Wolf Pack* is sending financial support to the DRM and their new leader, this Professor character."

Tiffany spoke up first. "Madame President, my team laid out an organizational chart of everything that's been happening and determined that a major insurrection is about to happen. A civil war of sorts. *The Architect* is another story. While I don't have proof, I believe he's got a bioweapon that distributes a nerve gas, more severe than anything the Russians ever created," Director Glass said.

President Graham stood, her hands behind her back as she circled the room, deep in thought. "That's interesting. I just found out he's admitted to my Chief of Staff that he's responsible for the recent mass killing in Oregon. He also threatened to release his weapon every day on everyone who has been disloyal to him. He's holding me hostage if I don't meet with him."

Tiffany and Sam had shocked expressions on their faces. Tiffany spoke first.

"President Graham, I suggest you meet with him ASAP and find out what he wants from you?" Tiffany said. "This way we might understand his next move and his endgame."

Sam was shaking his head, showing his disapproval of his wife's plan. "Madame President, negotiating with this madman will not work. If he's anything like Charles Stone, he's got another goal that is not about killing but accumulating wealth. I've read the file Paige Turner compiled, and he is a very revengeful sociopath and will begin going after all the people he believes were disloyal to him or those who were successful in stopping him and his manifesto four years ago. However, that is not his endgame."

President Graham was nodding her head. "I don't disagree with what you are saying, Sam. I've read the file President Chesterfield left for President Thompson. It does confirm what you just said. It's a clear picture of a man hell-bent on doing anything to gain wealth and power."

"Madame President, my recommendation is to meet with him. What harm could it do?" Kate Ambrose commented. "Your first responsibility is to save lives."

Director Glass raised her hand. "Before you do anything, let me and my team figure out a way to capture him. Then you can talk to him while he's in custody," Glass said.

"You need to do that fast. The message he gave Sweeden worries me that he's ready to release his weapon again to make a point that he's in control. I'll give you two days, or I will meet with Dunham face-to-face," President Graham said.

48

Albert Dunham sat alone on a private jet, flying as far away from Budapest as he could. His security team had gotten an alert from one of the spies they had in the West Wing that the Bureau's international terrorist unit had orders to arrest him and bring him back to the United States.

Dunham knew that President Graham, as well as FBI Director Glass, were looking for him and tossing a large net over Europe and the United States. He was pissed that his recent demonstration did not motivate them to meet with him and was once again on the FBI's most-wanted list.

The Architect's destination after a few stops was the District of Columbia. The young pretty stewardess brought him his Irish Whiskey and a turkey sandwich on a brioche roll, with potato salad mixed with Dijon mustard.

"Thank you, sweetheart," Dunham said. As the strikingly beautiful flight attendant turned and walked back to the front of the plane, he couldn't stop staring at her short, tight skirt and her firm legs and rounded buttocks. It had been a long time since he had any intimate female contact. Maybe this one might give him some stress-release pleasure?

"Oh, to be young again," he said under his breath. He missed his wife and missed sleeping with her next to him. Even though she stabbed him in the back with her betrayal, he still loved her and all the wonderful memories they shared. When the flight attendant came to clear away the dirty dishes, Dunham slipped her a folded note with five one-hundred-dollar bills and watched her walk away.

From the galley, she turned and looked back at him and sent him a wink and a warm, friendly smile. She tapped her watch face, signaling him that she wanted to know what time he wanted to get together.

Dunham did not respond right away, feeling extremely nervous at the prospect of being with a beautiful young woman almost thirty years his junior. He had not gotten over having to murder his wife for her disloyalty. He still wished he'd had another choice. He blamed President Chesterfield and Paige Turner for making him do what he had to do. He knew President Chesterfield threatened his wife with prison if she did not help them destroy his manifesto and arrest him.

The Architect, for the last four years, had been plotting his revenge and comeback into public life. His first step would be to deal with all his enemies. Second, to get President Graham to give him a pardon for his alleged crimes, an important part of the equation. He had no second thoughts about using his bioweapon to show the President and FBI how effective and fast his nerve gas ate away at the body's internal organs. Third, after creating QAnon using one of his European surrogates, he now had a bigger and better social media outlet to spew his lies and build his loyal followers who were showing that they would believe any conspiracy he put out there. They just need the right Dog Whistle phrase, and they would defend him without regrets.

Dunham's thoughts kept slipping back to when his manifesto almost succeeded, if it were not for Paige Turner. Now, with her *Corrupted Intelligence* theory being accepted by her millions and millions of followers, *The Architect* knew he had to increase his own social communication with his loyal followers.

While Turner had her theory, so did Dunham. He always knew that politics was tribal and since creating his QAnon followers of uneducated, uninformed, and complacent Americans, it had become easy to manipulate them with lies and conspiracies. He knew those Americans needed a powerful leader to support their views.

The Architect kept mulling over the Paige Turner problem he had. Killing her or ruining her reputation, that was the sixty-four-thousand-dollar question.

Looking out the airplane's small window, Dunham thought about the next enemy that must go. He dialed General Tucker Phillips. He was pleased that the General answered on the first ring.

"Sir, I am so glad you called. Everything is in place for our next demonstration," the General said.

"Tucker, I'm glad you are ready to follow my orders. This demonstration needs to happen in three days. Not a moment sooner," Dunham reminded him. "Don't fuck this up."

There was a long pause at the other end of the phone line. "Copy that, sir. I still don't think my taking the initiative last week with the Oregon militia group was wrong. It's gotten the President and her FBI Director bitch scared as hell. Getting your pardon after this next mass killing should do the trick," Phillips said.

Dunham leaned back in his seat, a smile cracking on his face. For the first time in four years, he was able to see a light at the end of the tunnel for him to be able to walk freely and safe from arrest. *"Let's hope this next demonstration gets a rise out of President Graham."*

The Architect glanced at this watch. In fifteen minutes, a few of his enemies in Budapest would die a horribly painful death and his wealth would increase in the billions of dollars.

He leaned his head back and closed his eyes. He felt a cool hand slip inside his shirt and begin caressing his hairy chest. Before he knew it, the flight attendant had unzipped his pants and had her mouth around his enlarged penis. It took only a few minutes before he climaxed, and the young woman placed his trembling hand on her full and supple breast.

"Is that what you had in mind, Mister Dunham?" she asked.

With a trembling voice, he tried to answer. "Oh, that was more than I expected," he said, grabbing her other exposed breast with his free hand.

"I'm available anytime you need some stress release," she said, slipping a folded piece of paper into his pants pocket. "You have my phone number now, so call me, I'm always available for you. I'd like to feel your large cock inside me next time," she said.

* * * * *

Dunham sent a text to his best friend and the only man he could trust, Frederick Ellison.

"Will be landing in DC in an hour and a half. I have another demonstration for the President and her FBI Director. I need you to get me a meeting with Professor Cochran ASAP before he begins his civil war." AD

49

Sam and Tiffany were in the Edgar Bar and Kitchen at the Mayflower Hotel waiting for Commander McAllister, Bubba Jackson, Paige Turner, and Scott Rogers to arrive for their strategy session. They were able to grab a secluded booth near the back end of the bar.

Director Glass's objective for the meeting was to draw Dunham out in the open. After listening to Turner's recent podcast, she felt that working with the journalist and her *Corrupted Intelligence* theory was the smart approach. She was feeling an emotional connection to Turner that she could not explain. She made a mental note to discuss it with Sam.

Tiffany saw Turner enter the bar and waved at her. She was impressed that Paige wore a floral sleeveless sundress that fell just above her knees, exposing her slender legs to a strategy meeting, while she was wearing a dark three-piece suit. Walking by her side was Scott Rogers, ex-US Marshall. She leaned over and whispered in Sam's ear, "She's drop-dead beautiful with brains and with a handsome stud escorting her."

"But, not as beautiful as you, my lovely mother of my children," Sam responded. "I hope you are okay with her working with us. She's younger than us and could be our daughter if we would have started in our twenties," Sam teased.

Tiffany pinched Sam's inner thigh, making him wince. "That hurt," Sam yelped. "What did I say?"

"We would have had to have started when I was seventeen, you inconsiderate jerk. We'll deal with your stupid remarks in our room later," Tiffany said. What Sam had said triggered an unpleasant memory she had been hiding for over forty years. A chill blanked her body, remembering her sad past.

Sam noticed his wife was deep in thought. "You okay?"

Tiffany snapped alert and stood, extending her hand to Turner. "I'm fine. Thinking of a memory that continues to plague me," she said. "I'm happy you decided to join us. We need to figure out how we can all work together to stop Dunham as well as the DRM and this pending civil war."

"I'm flattered you even wanted to speak with me after I did not follow your orders," Paige said, shrugging her shoulders. She turned toward Scott and introduced him. "This is ex-US Marshall Scott Rogers. He was instrumental in fighting and stopping Dunham four years ago."

"Nice to meet both of you," Scott said to Sam and Tiffany. "At the US Marshall's office, we all studied how you ended Charles Stone's reign of terror."

Sam noticed that McAllister and Jackson had arrived and were listening to Tiffany and Paige trying to act polite. "Commander, so happy you and Bubba could join us," he said, trying to distract the two women.

McAllister didn't say a word. He turned and signaled the bartender to come by and get everyone's drink orders. The young barkeep rushed over ready to take their orders.

"I'll have four fingers of Jameson, and my friend," he pointed to Bubba, "will have any beer on tap," the Commander ordered.

The young man looked at the others. "What can I get the rest of you?" he said, taking out a small notebook. As he stretched his arm, a tattoo on his wrist was exposed. McAllister was first to notice it. It was the White Angels insignia.

Sam and Tiffany, oblivious to it, ordered two glasses of Pinot Noir. Paige and Scott ordered two glasses of champagne.

McAllister watched the direction the young man took and alerted two of his team to follow him and detain him without making a scene.

Collins was getting impatient and wanted their meeting to start. "Let's settle down now and get underway on why we are all here." Sam noticed he had everyone's attention. "Our country is on the brink of a civil war. We have millions of White Supremacist militia ready to attack and disrupt our fragile democracy. The NSA has been monitoring a lot of activity at our southern and northern borders. A handful of southern states are attempting to secede from the north. They have the support of over forty Senators and seventy-five House Representatives. We know that one man, going by the title *The Professor,* has been pushing for a civil war for over sixty years, but most recently during Charles Stone's leadership." Sam paused to catch his breath. "We believe he's active again and the leader of the Domestic Revolutionary Movement that's responsible for the recent attacks that have slaughtered over four thousand Americans. President Graham and the FBI Director are focusing their attention on finding this Professor and ending his White Supremacy movement."

Paige interrupted Sam. "I thought we were here to discuss Dunham and my *Corrupted Intelligence* theory?" she said.

Sam nodded and continued. "We are. I just need to address the DRM issue, as I believe they are somehow connected to Dunham."

Scott Rogers jumped into the conversation. "What I discovered about Albert Dunham when we were trying to destroy his manifesto, was that he could charm the pants off you while driving a knife into your gut. I've asked Dean Miller to work with Raymond Stillwell to find the person we all are addressing as The Professor," Rodgers said. "If Dunham has a bioweapon, I can see him eliminating his competition, that being the DRM, like he did in Oregon, so he can focus on his ultimate goal, being the richest and most powerful man in the world."

"I've scheduled a meeting with Charles Stone's mistress April," Sam said. "We have the Haven House logbook that has dates and times many powerful people were at the plantation. I'm hoping she can identify some of the players inside the DRM. I'll be seeing her in a couple of days."

Tiffany was getting anxious listening to everyone. "Let's get back on track and come up with a plan to bring Dunham out in the open and get our hands on his bioweapon and, hopefully, if he has any, his antidote."

McAllister jumped into the conversation, abruptly interrupting Sam and Tiffany. "I was able to pull some strings and bring in twelve ex-SEAL team members and a dozen more ex-Army Rangers. They are eager to get back into the action and help eliminate the DRM and Dunham." The Commander raised his finger, signaling everyone to be quiet. He pressed his ear mic, and a broad smile cracked on his face. "I have something to tell all of you. Our server will not be bringing us our drinks. Two of my men have him in custody. He's part of the White Angels," McAllister said.

"How did you know?" Sam's hands were shaking as he asked.

"When the young man extended his arm, his tattoo got exposed, revealing a White Angels insignia. I had two of my men monitoring the lobby and bar. With a little forceful persuasion, he confessed that Wiley Jordan had sent him to slip us something in our drinks," McAllister said. "I'm not very comfortable being this exposed. I suggest we go up to your suite and resume our meeting there."

Director Glass appeared shaken. "Let's move our butts. I need an organized plan ASAP that I can take back to the President. She's about to take a face-to-face with Dunham, which I disagree with, but unless I can show her a solid working strategy, she's going to listen to *The Architect's* demands," Tiffany said.

Paige looked confused. "What demands does Dunham have?"

"What we've heard is that Dunham wants a full pardon for all of his alleged crimes during the Chesterfield administration," Tiffany told her.

"That's a load of crap," Turner said, raising her voice. "I have enough evidence to back up everything he's guilty of. He's a ruthless murderer."

"We know that," Director Glass said. "Right now, he's holding all the cards with his bioweapon."

"Then why am I here? I am just an investigative journalist. What do you want me to do?" she asked.

"I need your entire Dunham file ASAP with every piece of evidence you have. You know him better than any of us. We need you to do what you do best; get under his skin during your podcasts," Tiffany said. "If you can focus on *The Architect* for the next few weeks, by getting your loyal followers and national news channels to start talking about *The Architect's Corrupted Intelligence* and how he abuses the power granted to him by his uneducated tribe, we believe he'll be pissed off and make mistakes."

Scott Rogers was becoming irritated at the FBI Director. "Does anyone here remember what Dunham did to Paige's coworkers? Or how many times he tried to murder her after she exposed his manifesto? He's got a bioweapon we don't know how to stop. I won't let Paige put herself in danger again "

"That's already happening. Our international unit in Budapest picked up conversations between Dunham and an unknown General situated in the States. I don't believe you can piss him off much more than he is already. I just feel getting under his skin a bit more will cause him to act irrationally," Tiffany said.

Paige, her face bedsheet white, slumped in her chair. "If it's the General, I think it is he's one crazy son of a bitch. He's a worse sociopath than Dunham or this Wiley Jordan," Turner said, squirming in her seat.

"I have an FBI detail monitoring your every move. If Dunham or this General try anything, we'll be there to stop them," Director Glass said.

McAllister stood and walked over to Paige, placing his hand on her shoulder. "We stopped the White Angel group today. I think my team can better protect Turner. We did a great job keeping you and Sam safe when Wiley Jordan and Charles Stone tried to kill you both on numerous occasions."

Before Turner could respond, a news alert flashed on four TV screens in the bar. Sam pounded his fist on the table, noticeably upset.

"The civil war has started. I'll bet this is the work of the DRM and Dunham."

"Riots are breaking out in fifteen states after local police were caught beating protesters at a Black Lives Matter rally and at a Hispanic parade." Then another news alert flashed out of Budapest. *"A mysterious substance has killed five very wealthy business leaders in Europe. This is Britany Fox reporting."*

Everyone was unable to speak about what they just heard.

* * * * *

A man wearing a janitor's uniform walked by the bar and smiled when he saw the news alert in Budapest, then pulled his baseball cap down to cover his facial scars. "That was so easy," the man said when he noticed the table with Paige Turner and Scott Rogers talking with Sam and Tiffany Collins. He did not recognize the other two men. Having all the people he had planned to kill in one place was a blessing, he thought.

"I wonder if they are talking about me?" *The Architect* mumbled to himself. He put his hand in his overall pocket and felt the vial he was intending to use at the hotel. Dunham slowly pushed his mop and bucket of soapy water toward a storage room. He needed a few minutes to think about how to modify his plan.

50

Dunham had slipped into the women's restroom mopping the tile floor when Paige Turner entered. "I need to use the restroom. Please leave and give me some privacy," she said politely as she headed for an empty stall.

Dunham's heart started racing when he realized the one person he hated the most in the world was no more than ten feet from him. He checked that he had brought his gun. *"This would be too easy,"* he mumbled. Before he could react, Tiffany Glass entered the restroom, calling out to Paige.

"Paige, finish your business. We've got to go," she shouted. She noticed the janitor acting nervously, holding his wet mop. "Sir, I need you to leave. You shouldn't be in here when it's occupied."

Dunham recognized Tiffany and thought about killing both women by emptying his gun into the FBI Director first and then Turner while she sat on the toilet. He thought better of it, spotting Glass's shoulder holster bulging under her suit jacket. "Yes, yes. So sorry," the janitor said in a raspy voice. He shuffled out, pushing his bucket and mop.

When Paige came out of the stall, she looked upset. "Can't a lady have some time for herself at this hotel?" she complained. "What's so important that you needed to rush me?"

"Dunham's been spotted at Reagan Airport a few hours ago. He's in DC now," Tiffany said. "He came in a private jet that left from Budapest. McAllister wants you upstairs in my suite ASAP. He needs to figure out how Dunham is moving around the Capitol."

Paige felt a cold shiver crawl up her spine hearing Dunham's name again. "That janitor made me feel uncomfortable. His voice sounded familiar," she said, a nervous edge to her voice. "Can you use your influence and get us to look at all the security cameras in the lobby and outside the ladies' restroom?"

Tiffany seemed confused. "What about the janitor bothers you? His face was partially scarred from burns."

"Something about him was familiar," Paige said.

* * * * *

Dunham noticed Director Glass and Sam Collins were talking to Turner, and everyone was acting alarmed. He took a closer look at the man he at first did not recognize and realized it was Commander McAllister giving his men orders. *"Could they know I am here?"*

Feeling the walls closing in, Dunham headed toward the service entrance. He needed to regroup. Before he opened the exit door, he spotted a hand sanitizer and emptied his vial, shaking it vigorously. "This is not what I wanted to do, but this will create a panic throughout Washington," he muttered. Outside in the alley, he jumped into a waiting car.

* * * * *

Paige and Tiffany were looking at a small security monitor, reviewing the last two hours of video in the hotel lobby and outside the men's and ladies' restrooms. "There," Turner said, pointing to the screen. "That's the janitor who was in the restroom when I was there. Can we get a clearer picture of his face?" she asked.

The security guard slowly reversed the video and finally found a better shot and zoomed in on the man's face. "That's the best I could do," the security guard said. "I don't recognize this man. He's not one of our janitors. I know every one of them."

Paige squinted and leaned in for a closer look. "That's some nasty burns on his face. He does look familiar to me," she said.

Tiffany asked the security guard to give her a backup of the tape. "I'll get our facial recognition software to run the man's face through CODUS. We should be able to get a match if he's in our system."

Outside the security office, screams were echoing throughout the hotel lobby. People were all running outside. Commander McAllister was shepherding guests to the closest exit, while his team rushed into the service corridor to see what had happened. Within thirty seconds, Bubba Jackson came out looking frightened.

"Call a hazmat unit. There are five hotel employees lying dead, blood oozing out of their mouths and nostrils. This looks like what happened in Oregon," Jackson said, his hands shaking.

Commander McAllister looked at his friend. "I've never seen you so shook up. You think this was Dunham's doing?"

"Once we get back the facial recognition on the janitor, I'll be able to confirm."

"Once the hazmat team gets here, please isolate yourself until you've been cleared," McAllister ordered.

Tiffany and Sam were speaking with the Commander when Turner and Rogers rushed over to them. "What's going on?" Paige asked after seeing the hazmat unit enter the hotel lobby.

"We're not sure. It looks like some type of nerve gas killed five hotel employees. Waiting on word from the hazmat guys," Commander McAllister said. "I've isolated Bubba until we know more."

"Do you think this is Dunham's handiwork?" asked Paige.

"I'd say yes, but until we identify the janitor, I won't say definitely," the Commander said.

"Do you think Dunham was here to kill me?" Paige said, her voice shaking from fear. "Could he be part of the White Angels?"

McAllister was shaking his head. "I doubt it. Nobody knew of our meeting today. It must be a coincidence."

"Then how do you explain all these frightening coincidences?"

"That's what my team is trying to figure out," McAllister said.

51

Professor Cochran had just finished a briefing from the five Captains who controlled his militia groups. Wiley Jordan remained silent, listening to everyone brag about what they had been doing.

Cochran had been told that the President, FBI Director, and Attorney General, as well as Commander McAllister, were looking for him and wanted to bring him in for questioning. He felt safe for the moment since they had not yet figured out he was the leader of the DRM. He was sitting with Wiley, trying to plan out their next move.

"We have something more serious than my identity being exposed. What Dunham did in Budapest scares me. This is his second attack using his bioweapon. It's obvious he's eliminating his competition," Cochran said, nervously clearing his throat. "I'm sure he's coming for all of us."

Wiley had a puzzled expression. "Do you know for sure that Dunham has this weapon?"

"Yes. I spoke to his brother Theodore, and he too is very scared. His facility has been secured by *The Architect's* security team, as well as the scientists who are working on a secret project," said Cochran.

"Did you ask his brother if he could help us get inside his pharmaceutical lab so we can destroy what they are doing or seize the weapon so we can use it?" Wiley asked. "I have enough men to overwhelm a small security team and a handful of scientists."

"Teddy said his brother has his wife and children hidden in a secure location. If anything happens to Dunham's men, his family will disappear permanently."

"Then we first need to find Teddy's family, and then kill *The Architect's* men," Wiley said.

"That all sounds good, but how will you locate them before Dunham tries to kill all of us?" Cochran asked.

"Not sure just yet. I need to think about it," Wiley said. "In the meantime, let's figure out how to keep your identity a secret so we can move forward immediately with our civil war."

"I'd like that," Cochran said.

Wiley started swaying while he paced around the room, a nervous habit he had when stressed. "Can you think of anyone who might know about your relationship with Haven House and Stone?" Wiley asked. "You spent a lot of time there when you were a young man."

Cochran thought a minute, then replied. He combed his fingers through his thick gray hair. "At this moment, I can't think of anyone. With the *Wolf Pack* members dead now, and losing our financing, I'm too stressed to think clearly," he said. "I think it's time to call Wilhelm, the leader of the Brown Shirts in Argentina and get them mobilized to invade."

Wiley wasn't buying Cochran's answer about Haven House or mobilizing the Brown Shirts. "Maybe this might jog your memory. What about April, Charles's nigger bitch?" he asked.

Hearing April's name turned Cochran's face bedsheet white. "I'd forgotten about her and her bastard boys. While I've never verified it, she might even be my daughter. Charles's father would have a young slave girl visit me when I stayed at Haven House. I know I fucked April's mother on more than one occasion. So, it's possible I am her father. Do we know where she is living?"

"Last time I checked, she was in Newport Beach living in a home Charles left for her with a healthy bank account of over five hundred million," said Wiley. "I've been monitoring them, along with Bubba Jackson who has been spending a lot of time with April and her boys."

"What's she doing every day?" Cochran asked.

"Not sure. Commander McAllister's second in charge, Bubba Jackson, has been with her a lot. After Charles's death, I've kept up with her from a safe distance. The FBI, at first, watched over her on Tiffany Glass's orders. All I know is that she's trying to make something of herself and is going to UC Irvine studying to be a lawyer. I didn't know that slave bitch had the brains to learn anything," Wiley said.

"She's a link to my past with Charles, and if she's shown a picture of me, she could identify me as The Professor everyone is looking for," Cochran said.

"Then April needs to die. You don't have a problem with me killing your daughter, do you?" Wiley asked snidely.

Cochran did not have an attachment to April. He'd never even spoken to her. "Kill her and her boys," he said without any emotion.

"Consider it done," Wiley said.

52

Bubba and his team drove up to April's house in Newport Beach. It was located on Balboa Island on South Bay Front between Ruby and Diamond. Jackson's men set up a security perimeter while he went to the front door. With his mallet-sized fist, he knocked three times. There was no answer.

After checking the backyard and looking in all the large picture windows, he determined that no one was home. The property butted up to the harbor with a small boat dock where a party boat had been moored. On numerous occasions, he and the boys would use it so he could spend the day with the boys playing games at the Balboa Fun Zone or walking the strand. With the boat being gone, he assumed that they were there.

Prior to Stone's death, he had only met her twice and became infatuated with her pretty face and intellect. He found it hard to believe a young woman who never experienced life away from Haven House could be so experienced with the outside world.

During those times Bubba spent with April and her boys, he had become emotionally close to them. When he'd leave them, an emptiness of not making time to fall in love and have a family consumed him. McAllister and his team had been his family for over two decades. He snapped himself back to the task at hand.

When he was back out front, he barked out orders to Sergeant Ron Arnold to have three of his men keep a watchful eye on the house and report back to him when April and her boys returned.

Bubba looked at his calendar on his cell phone and realized April was at UCI taking one of her law classes. "I've got to meet with Collins and McAllister in two hours, so you are in charge," he told Arnold. "Be alert. If we're looking for April, I must believe this Professor and Wiley Jordan are searching for her too," Bubba said. "Don't get distracted. Jordan's not a happy camper since you shattered his hand at Haven House. I'm going to stop by UCI and see if April is there."

"Copy that, Master Sergeant," Arnold said.

* * * * *

Wiley was driving on Marine Avenue thinking about how he would kill April and her two boys. He thought about having some fun with her, but he hated any woman with dark skin, especially a slave girl like her. As he made a right turn on South Bay Front, he stopped at Coral Avenue when he saw the big Black bastard who destroyed his hand. He noticed that Jackson's men were taking up positions around the house. He knew that this was not the time to try to kill Charles's bitch whore.

He looked at his notes and realized that April was at the University of California at Irvine, in a late afternoon class. He turned right on Sapphire Avenue and then another right on Park Avenue to Marine Avenue which got him to Pacific Coast Highway. He was twenty minutes away from the college.

Wiley called three of his men to meet him at the university. He told them this would be a catch-and-grab job. "I want the Black bitch alive so I can find out what she knows before we kill her."

53

Up in their hotel suite, FBI Director Glass was on a Zoom call with FBI Special Agent Lassiter in Budapest. "Agent Lassiter, has your medical examiner figured out what killed the *Wolf Pack* members?" Tiffany asked.

"We've run numerous blood labs. It's an unknown chemical. When it comes in contact with human cells, it begins to melt the internal organs within thirty minutes," Lassiter said. "We believe they were exposed to the bioweapon after using hand sanitizer in the restroom outside the conference room at the Matild Palace Hotel. It was a horrible crime scene. Our hazmat leader doesn't believe it's contagious. Once it's absorbed into the body, it stays there feeding on blood and tissue."

"That's the same conclusion our hazmat team came to at the Mayflower Hotel. We're analyzing the hand sanitizer from the hotel. I need you to overnight your samples to me. Our team is hoping to have some answers for us in a couple of days," Tiffany said. "Could this be something out of Russia?"

"I doubt it. We checked with our sources, and they say Russia is vehemently denying they had anything to do with this attack. They admit they created a nerve gas during the cold-war era, but their weapon only affected the nervous system, shutting down the body's vital organs. Nothing like what this chemical is doing. The Russians are worried they could be next. They know they turned their back on Dunham and refused to help him four years ago," Agent Lassiter said. "One other item. Klaus Bergner, the head of the *Wolf Pack,* is unaccounted for. He was not identified at the crime scene. We're searching for him. Right now, he is our primary suspect since he runs the largest pharmaceutical company in Europe and could be helping Dunham."

"I'm worried about this weapon. Dunham was seen talking with Turkey's and Iran's radical military Generals a few days ago. If they are working with him, then no country in NATO is safe," Director Glass said.

"I'll check with my friend at Interpol. She is well connected inside those two countries," Agent Lassiter said.

"In the meantime, send me everything you have from your crime scene. I particularly want to see the photos and compare yours to our victims."

"Director Glass, we are short-staffed over here. Investigations are going very slowly," Agent Lassiter said. "I need at least five additional agents who are trustworthy and have experience on the international front."

Tiffany paused, trying to think of a satisfactory answer. "I don't have the resources to be able to help. Our budget was cut under the last administration and the lack of funds is making it very hard on all of us to do our jobs," Glass said. "I have an idea that might help. I'll get back to you in a couple of days."

"Thank you. Anything will help," Lassiter said.

* * * * *

"I need your help. My Special Agent in Charge in Budapest needs help to investigate the recent murders of the *Wolf Pack* members. A fifth member is missing and currently in hiding."

Sam was scratching his head, deep in thought. "That's interesting. I thought the entire board was murdered?"

"Not Klaus Bergner," said Tiffany. "He's a person of interest as CEO of Apollo Pharmaceuticals. It's extremely possible that he's working with Dunham. He needs to be found and questioned."

"I'll call his company and see if they want to cooperate. Just a heads up. They don't trust our President or the DOJ, and that includes the FBI," Sam said.

"Why don't they trust us?" Tiffany said, sounding hurt.

"It's not you, per se. It stems from Presidents Thompson and Chesterfield. You should listen to their story," Sam said. "We might find out if Bergner is found."

"Sam, tell them that they can trust me. Remind them what we did with Charles Stone and the White Angels. Do what you can and let me know," Tiffany said.

Tiffany was interrupted when her daughter and son rushed into the living room inside their suite. "Mommy, Mommy, Michael is being a butt again," she whined.

166

Tiffany watched Michael jump into his father's arms, snuggling tightly in his father's embrace. Sam was doing his best not to laugh at Irene, but it was useless. "Irene, Michael is just eighteen months old, and you're his big sister. Have some patience with his little guy."

Irene was not having any of what her father was saying. "He's a little monster and a big pain in the butt brother," she said and stormed back toward her bedroom.

Sam tried to apologize to Paige and Scott, but Michael squirmed out of his father's embrace and jumped up onto Turner's lap, startling her.

With a special calmness, Paige began talking to Michael in a calm, soothing voice. "You must be Michael," she said. "I'm Paige. Nice to meet you." While she was talking to him, he started playing with her long silky black hair, while he calmly kissed her cheek.

Tiffany was shocked that Michael was so comfortable with the reporter. "He's never done that before," she said, waving the nanny over to take her son to the kitchen to give him something to eat.

After Michael was gone, she began apologizing to everyone. "So sorry for that interruption."

Paige, with a big smile on her face, replied, "That was a wonderful interruption. Both of your children are adorable. You and Sam seem to be great parents."

Before Tiffany could respond, she had gotten an urgent text from the White House. Sam had seemed to receive the same message. "It looks like we'll have to continue this meeting another time. President Graham needs us ASAP at the Oval Office."

54

President Graham's frustration with the progress her FBI Director was having trying to arrest the leader of the DRM had come to a boiling point. It had been seventeen days since the first attack and the only offensive against these White Supremacists had come from *The Architect's Army*.

"Martha, what's going on with FBI Director Glass? Does she have a problem being my Director?"

Chief of Staff Martha Sweeden was shaking her head at Graham's question. "She's working very hard at her new job. Director Glass is well qualified to be your Director, but with our intelligence agencies' inability to stay a step ahead of the active radical militia, and lack of funding, she is running in circles," the Chief of Staff said. "Now with Dunham's bioweapon, your FBI Director doesn't have the manpower or resources to handle this additional problem satisfactorily."

"Understaffed? How could that be?" President Graham asked, her frustration ready to explode.

"The past two administrations, with their Republican majority, drastically cut the DOJ's and FBI's budget," Sweeden said. "Furthermore, it is suspected that a majority of the radical right support what the DRM has been doing. If Dunham receives his pardon, I can imagine how the radical right will cheer his return."

"You do know that I was part of the last administration? It was a political decision by the House Speaker and Senate Majority Leader to defund the DOJ and FBI. I tried to advise President Thompson that taking away funding for those two agencies was a bad idea. Sadly, he wouldn't listen to me. He believed going against his party would hurt his upcoming re-election bid," President Graham said. "As for Dunham, I have no intention of granting him a pardon. I want him locked up in a Super Max prison for the rest of his life."

"Well, maybe you can right that wrong and show the American voters that you support law and order, and truly condone White Supremacy and everything the DRM and Dunham stand for by giving Director Glass enough money to bring in more agents," said Sweeden.

"I want my CDC Director here along with Director Glass and my Attorney General. I'm going to sign five Executive Orders and want them supporting my decision," President Graham said.

55

Dunham had snuck back to a small, secluded house he had purchased over thirty years ago outside of Bethesda, Maryland. After President Chesterfield leveled his mansion four years ago, he was able to hide in this safe house for the last four years. As he drove up his serpentine driveway and pulled into his three-car garage, he pounded his palms on the steering wheel. He was angry with himself that he missed an easy opportunity at the Mayflower Hotel to kill Paige Turner, the one person who got under his skin the most. "That bitch Tiffany Glass got in my way for the last time," he shouted.

Dunham's safe house had all the security safeguards anyone would need to stay under the radar of law enforcement, especially the FBI. Every window was fitted with bulletproof glass four inches thick. All entry and exit doors were armor-plated and had handprint sensors as well as iris readers that would only allow him to enter. The entire house was powered by a state-of-the-art solar system used by NASA.

Dunham's first order of business was to speak with Professor Cochran on a Zoom call and demand that he surrender his power and position with the DRM. If he objected, then more of his militia would die a painful death.

"Good afternoon, Cochran," Dunham said, greeting him with a friendly smile.

The Professor acted surprised that Dunham had taken over his laptop screen. "How the fuck did you hack into my computer?" Cochran said, his facial muscles showing his anger. "What do you want?"

Dunham smiled. "I'm glad you asked. But first I need to tell you a funny story that you'd appreciate. When I decided to return and claim my rightful place with the *Wolf Pack*, they basically laughed at me. I wondered why they would be so rude to me after all I had done for them over the last twenty years. I don't think I am a revengeful human being, but their insolence could not go unpunished," he said in a cool and calm voice.

The Professor seemed puzzled. "Are you admitting that you killed them the other day?"

"That's the funny part of the story. I had no choice if I was going to step back into power." Dunham laughed. "In war, there will be some collateral damage. That's why I am calling you today."

"If you think I will welcome you into the DRM with open arms, you're crazier than I imagined," Cochran said arrogantly.

"Now, now, Cochran old friend. You need me to help you achieve your goals with your civil war and reclaim the South once again."

Cochran burst out laughing, interrupting *The Architect*. "You'll never command the respect of my DRM members. You're a loose cannon who cannot be trusted. I suggest you step aside and go back to the hole you crawled out of and leave this war to me."

"Are you sure you want to do battle with me? The *Wolf Pack* board thought the same thing and look where it got them," Dunham said, his smile disappearing from his face. "Wasn't my demonstration in the backwoods of Oregon enough to convince you of my power?"

For the first time, Cochran was at a loss for words. "Are you going to kill all of us? If so, where will your army of patriots come from?"

Before Dunham answered the question, The Professor's computer screen had two small windows pop up. They showed two of his DRM militia teams. "Are you ready for a quick demonstration of my power?" he asked. "Or will you surrender your leadership role to me before I kill over fifty of your most seasoned fighters?"

Cochran was wiping the perspiration from his forehead. "You're crazy. You're sicker than Charles Stone."

"I'm sorry you feel that way," he said, sending off a text to General Phillips to release his weapon. "Watch and see my power you cannot defend against," Dunham said calmly.

"What am I waiting to see?" Cochran asked.

Dunham glanced at this watch. "Give it one more minute."

As the clock ticked down, The Professor watched in horror as his men started falling to the ground, screaming in pain as blood gushed out of their eyes, mouths, and nostrils while their internal organs melted away. He had never seen anything this gruesome in his life.

"You're one sick son of a bitch, Dunham," Cochran shouted at his computer screen.

"There is no reason for you to be rude and insulting to me. I just want what is rightfully mine. This demonstration is just the beginning of my quest to become the ultimate leader of the free world. There are different strengths to the weapons and I can use them to act as quickly or as slowly and painfully as I want," Dunham said. "I'll get back to you in a couple of days," he continued and abruptly ended the call.

The next two people he needed to speak with were General Tucker Phillips and Frederick Ellison. He wanted to make sure his next demonstration was in place and ready to happen on his orders. Realizing President Graham would not meet with him face-to-face, he booted up his computer, activating his hacking software so he could infiltrate the President's computer system inside the Oval Office. This would have to do as a face-to-face meeting.

56

Thirty minutes later, Dunham infiltrated the Oval Office computer system, demanding Martha Sweeden get President Graham so he could talk with her. A startled Chief of Staff tried to reason with the intruder, but to no avail.

"You can't hack into a White House computer. It's a violation of federal law," she said.

"Do you really think I'm frightened about violating federal law? I've already taken over your system and won't release it until you have the President speak with me. I think what I have to say, she'll want to hear," Dunham told her.

Martha left her computer and burst into the President's office. "Madame President, Dunham is calling again to speak with you from my computer."

President Graham looked puzzled. "Did you tell him I won't speak with him?"

"I did, but he won't take no for an answer. Dunham said he won't release the White House computer systems without talking to you first. He says you'll want to listen to what he has to say," Sweeden said.

President Graham looked at her FBI Director, Attorney General, and Commander McAllister, gesturing for some advice. "Do any of you have a recommendation?"

Also sitting inside the Oval Office were Rodger Stillwell and Dean Miller, both computer experts. They were there to help the President track down the leader of the DRM and to locate Albert Dunham.

"Madame President, if I may speak?" Roger Stillwell asked. "I think you should listen to what Dunham has to say. Right now, he's demonstrated he has the power to murder at will and take control of computer systems. If you keep

173

him on the call long enough, I might be able to locate where he is broadcasting from."

Dean Miller jumped into the conversation. "I have this thumb drive," he said waving it above his head, "that I can plug into Sweeden's computer, and it will sniff out and locate Dunham within sixty seconds. It's a new program I created to help businesses and government agencies from ransomware hackers."

"If you two are that confident, then let's hear what Dunham has to say," President Graham said.

Martha Sweeden returned with her laptop and placed it on the President's desk. Staring at President Graham with an evil grin on his distorted face was Albert Dunham.

Dunham's nostrils flared as he spoke. "Hello, Madame President. It is nice to finally meet you and have a chance to talk."

President Graham responded, "You did not leave me much of a choice. Now, what is so important that you had to force your way into the White House and threaten me?"

"Wow, settle down, Madame President. We're getting off on the wrong foot here. I wanted to speak with you and help you put an end to the White Supremacist problem you have, and the upcoming civil war The Professor is ready to start. If I could shut them down and stop their civil war, would you be grateful?"

"Mister Dunham, or should I call you Mister Architect?" Graham sarcastically asked.

"Albert would be less formal," he replied.

"If you could accomplish what you are saying, what would you want in return?"

"I like that you cut to the chase. First, let me give you a demonstration, then we can negotiate." Dunham pressed a button on his end of the computer and there was a split-screen showing what appeared to be a White Supremacist militia group in a Southern bar with Confederate Flags and Nazi flags hanging on the walls. "Madame President, please watch carefully. This is how *The Architect* deals with his disloyal enemies and the enemies of the United States."

Ten minutes later, everyone inside the bar started coughing and spitting up blood. After another five minutes, the entire tavern went silent, and all the patrons were lying on the floor in pools of blood.

President Graham and her Chief of Staff gasped. "You just murdered everyone without a second thought?" Martha Sweeden asked as tears rolled down her cheeks.

"Now, now. These men were the scum of the earth. They had no conscience when they set off bombs or sprayed their AK15s at innocent children. I just did what I know you would have done to them if you could," Dunham said, laughing.

"Every criminal deserves a trial before punishment can be rendered. You're a criminal, Mister Dunham, and I want you to turn yourself in to the FBI," President Graham said. She noticed that Dean Miller was giving her two thumbs up.

"That's never going to happen. I have the power now and you'll need to be nicer to me or become one of my enemies, like Paige Turner and your FBI Director. You've seen what I can do, so don't test me."

"I already know what you want, a pardon, right? Well, that is never going to happen as long as I am President," she shouted at her computer screen.

"Calm down, Madame President. I thought I was offering you a great solution to your current problems. Don't you want to save more innocent Americans?" Dunham yelled back at her. "Maybe another demonstration will convince you?"

Before President Graham could respond, her computer screen was showing a shopping mall in Bethesda, Maryland. A handful of mothers with their tiny children were coming out of a mall restroom. Within seconds, what happened in the southern bar minutes ago was happening to these innocent people.

"This is just a sample of what I can do if I don't get my pardon," Dunham shouted, and then the computer screen went black.

President Graham looked like she was about to pass out. Tears were cascading down her cheeks. She looked at her FBI Director, hoping she had some answers for her.

Tiffany was at a loss for words. Everyone in the entire office was speechless.

Dean Miller stood up and checked a few things on the President's computer. He clicked a few keys and said, "I should know where Dunham was broadcasting in about ten minutes. By the looks of it, he is somewhere in Bethesda. I'd suggest mobilizing a team. I should have the exact location very soon," Miller said.

57

Inside the Situation Room, Professor Dean Miller, with help from Roger Stillwell, set in motion Miller's tracking software. McAllister and Bubba Jackson were mobile, waiting for word on Dunham's location. Sam and Tiffany stayed back with the President and Martha Sweeden to discuss their next move against the DRM and *The Architect*.

Sam wanted to initiate a Grand Jury to investigate the workings of the DRM, as well as the crimes Dunham had committed. While he had the President's support, he was reminded that the two chambers of Congress were viciously divided and evenly split on what to do about the surging White Supremacy movement.

"President Graham, I do not believe we'll be able to legally stop the DRM and *The Architect*. They both have millions of followers, especially in Congress and in a majority of State Legislatures. Even our Supreme Court is soft on taking away their constitutional rights," Sam said.

President Graham appeared to have ignored what her Attorney General had just said, and instead opened a red file folder that was stamped Top Secret, Confidential.

"Tiffany, I'm concerned that you have not been able to stay a step ahead of the DRM or Dunham's bioweapon," the President said. She noticed that her FBI Director had gotten uncomfortable with her remarks. "Do you have anything to say?"

Director Glass looked at her husband, noticing he was about to talk back to the President about what he had just heard. She patted his hand, signaling him to back off. "Madame President, besides not having enough funding to manage a strategic fight against these domestic terrorists, I'm dealing with a few traitors inside the FBI who are giving the leader of the DRM a heads up on our plans," Glass said. "These traitors are staying one step ahead of me and my team."

President Graham did not seem interested in her Director's excuses. "I've known this for over two years when I was Vice President. President Thompson had been briefed on that problem but looked the other way so as not to upset his donors. That's why I asked for a whole slew of resignations after I was sworn in. I just thought you'd be different and begin arresting these White Supremacist bastards."

Tiffany pointed at the red folder. "Is there a list of traitors at the FBI inside that folder?" Glass asked.

President Graham nodded and pushed the folder toward her FBI Director. Tiffany immediately opened the folder and was shocked at all the names on the President's list. "Is this true? What you have here are over twenty-five seasoned Special FBI Agents." Tiffany sat there, stunned at the names on the list. "Why is this the first time I am seeing this?"

"That's why I asked both of you to stay back. I also have too many staff members here that I can't trust. So, I kept this file hidden until I could get a good handle on both of you to know if I made the right decision having you as part of my team."

"So, what have you concluded about me and Sam?" Tiffany asked.

"You two are the real deal and a big asset to me and our country."

Sam started squirming in his chair. "Madame President, you are looking at the most loyal Americans you'll ever have working for you…" Before he could continue, the President signaled him to stop speaking.

"Sam, I know you are one of the most patriotic Americans I know. What you did in California almost eleven years ago to stop Charles Stone and the White Angels was nothing short of remarkable. Your ability to get the California legislature to pass a bipartisan bill against the insurance industry was nothing short of amazing." President Graham stood and started pacing around the Oval Office. "Sam, I need… no, our country needs the Caped Crusader doing what you do best: threaten everyone on this list to either cooperate with me or be thrown in jail for treason. Inside this folder is the proof you'll need to get them to cooperate."

Sam blushed. "I'm honored that you believe in me. But understand that we first need to impanel a Grand Jury to indict them, then we can move forward with putting them away. However, our biggest hurdle will be to convince each of them to cooperate. They have many supporters within the halls of Congress that can help them delay the Grand Jury."

"Sam, the DOJ needs to have an advocate with no hidden agenda, pushing for legislation that would define domestic terrorism as traitors and write laws that deal with these terrorists. That's why I asked you to become my Attorney General. You'll have my complete support with whatever or however you want to accomplish this task."

Sam turned toward his wife. "Honey, you know this is right up your alley. You're a great litigator," Tiffany said, giving his hand a gentle squeeze.

"President Graham, I'll need to hire a few extra assistant Attorney Generals to help me with this problem, while I continue to try to stop Dunham and the DRM."

President Graham was nodding her head as she listened to Sam's demands. "How much funding will you need?"

Sam pulled out a piece of paper from his pocket. "I'm glad you asked. Five hundred million to start. I will share these funds with the FBI Director as she and her team are critical to our success."

A big sigh of relief came over the President. "If we all live through this, drinks are on me," President Graham said.

58

Maryland SWAT and the FBI were at Theodore Dunham's pharmaceutical facility serving a warrant. They had convinced a Maryland judge that they had probable cause that an illegal bioweapon was being manufactured at the facility.

Theodore Dunham accepted the warrant without protest. Twenty-five FBI agents, some in hazmat suits, spread out inside the facility looking for *The Architect's* bioweapon. After an hour of searching every corner of the building with drug-sniffing dogs, a frustrated FBI came up empty.

"That's right, Director Glass, no sign there ever was a bioweapon on the premises," the Special Agent said.

"Was Teddy Dunham there?" Director Glass asked.

"Yes. He was very cooperative. He's refused to be interviewed and asked for a lawyer," Agent Rita Osborne said. She was the FBI's terrorist expert, and her gut was telling her Albert Dunham's brother wanted to speak but was frightened. "Director Glass, I get this feeling Theodore wants to cooperate with us. Can I bring him in and interview him at a secure location?"

"Bring him to the Hoover Building so I can meet him," Tiffany ordered.

"I can't believe our intel was wrong. Dean Miller and Roger Stillwell don't make mistakes, especially with their software tracking program. I need you to gather up all the computers at the facility, including every employee, including Teddy's cell phone and electronic devices," she commanded.

"Madame Director, our warrant is specific. We are to look for only a bioweapon, not electronic devices," Agent Osborne said.

"Is it possible this bioweapon is on an electronic device?" Tiffany hinted.

"It's possible, but you are expanding the definition of this warrant."

179

"Let me worry about it. We have a National Security situation here and I won't take the chance of missing something. Who's going to complain, anyway? Not Albert Dunham. See you and your suspect back at the Hoover Building."

"Director Glass, don't you think it strange that they knew we were coming? Do we have a leak in our agency?"

Tiffany sucked in a deep breath. "I'll brief you when you return."

* * * * *

Simultaneously, in a remote residential area in Maryland, McAllister and his team were in a position to grab up Albert Dunham and bring him back to the Hoover Building. The Commander had positioned his men at each known exit point of the home.

Bubba Jackson was reviewing the infra-ray photo of the entire house. It confirmed that Dunham had not built any escape tunnels or safe rooms as he had done in his Bethesda, Maryland, estate. Jackson was concerned that the last infra-ray scan of the house showed no signs of life. It appeared Dunham was gone.

"John, I don't think Dunham's inside. How he got tipped off is puzzling. Only you and I knew of this operation until this morning. Either we have a leak inside our team, or we've been bugged," Jackson said.

"You're forgetting we discussed this raid with Sam and Tiffany inside the Attorney General's office. We know the leak is at the DOJ. This was a test so we can flush them out," McAllister said. "Let's go inside anyway and see if Dunham left some clues."

Dunham's home was around four thousand square feet and two stories. The entranceway butted up to the second-floor stairs, with a half-moon thin table at the base. On the table in bold black print was a note addressed to the Commander:

NICE TRY, BUT YOU SHOULD NOT UNDERESTIMATE WHAT I AM CAPABLE OF DOING. I AM NOT LIKE CHARLES STONE AND DO NOT MAKE MISTAKES.

YOU CAN SEARCH MY HOME, BUT TRUST ME YOU'LL NOT FIND ANYTHING THAT WILL HELP YOU FIND ME. FOR YOUR AGGRESSION, ANOTHER DEMONSTRATION WILL HAPPEN AT FOUR THIS AFTERNOON.

THE ARCHITECT

McAllister ordered his men back to their command base and told Bubba they were going back to the FBI Director's office. "Our traitor problem is worse than we imagined. Too many people inside the DOJ and FBI support Dunham and the DRM. We need to arrest these traitors before Dunham goes into hiding again."

Bubba Jackson nodded his head in agreement. "This problem has infected the West Wing and the Capitol too. This is bigger than anything Charles Stone tried to do," he said, looking like he wanted to kill someone. "How the hell are we going to stop these traitors?"

"If I didn't know better, I'd say our democracy and our way of life are collapsing," McAllister said.

* * * * *

Three national news stations were reporting the recent mass murders of DRM militia and innocent women and children in the Bethesda shopping mall. Each station had Congressmen and Senators from both parties being asked questions about the recent attacks and recently the use of some bioweapon on innocent Americans.

Senator Kenneth Jenkins was a longtime supporter and activist of the White Supremacy movement and advocate of the idea of a Southern Confederacy for a White Christian nation.

"Before more innocent patriots are slaughtered by our new President, a much-needed pro-Confederacy paramilitary force is needed to protect all Christian White Americans," Senator Jenkins said with a strong Texan drawl.

The commentator seemed shocked that a sitting Senator from Texas would be so bold. "Are you talking about a civil war? A new revolution?" she asked.

"These last few weeks are a good example that White Christian people are dissatisfied with how their country is going and treating them. I believe a reboot of our constitution and the destruction of our current society is necessary. First, President Graham has proven she is not up to protecting our liberties and must be removed from office." Jenkins looked into the camera and spoke directly to the President. "Madame President, make it easier on all of us and just resign before more bloodshed befalls our great country."

A shocked commentator, her hands shaking, asked a question. "Senator, are you threatening our President?

"No threats. Just a heads up as to what is coming if she doesn't resign," Senator Jenkins said abruptly ending the call.

Outside of the network's offices, Senator Jenkins allowed himself to be interviewed by two dozen reporters. "It is a sad day for our country when our first female President is unfit to lead our country. The Presidency is a man's job during a crisis like we have now. I call upon all loyal White Christian patriots to start deconstructing our current government, brick by brick, so a new Southern Confederacy can be our new nation. We have Professor Cochran, our new leader, who will stand with us. He's been silent for too many years and now is the time for him to unite all of us," the Senator shouted.

One reporter pushed his microphone toward Jenkins, almost touching his lips. "Sir, your words might be seen as treasonous. What do you have to say about that?"

"During the revolutionary war, everything said against the British Government and the King was treasonous, but if we are to have freedom from oppression, a revolution is the only solution. Understand that President Graham only became President due to the untimely death of President Thaddeus Thompson. She is not a friend of our pure White Christian brothers and sisters with her mixed blood. Change is coming," he shouted. "So everyone listening should choose your side." With that said, Senator Jenkins briskly walked to his waiting white Suburban and sped away.

59

General Tucker Phillips was listening to Senator Jenkins's speech and heard the Dog Whistle signals he needed. Now, his most seasoned mercenaries outside Paige Turner's studio had their orders to release the bioweapon at approximately four in the afternoon. All the General knew was that the timing had to be perfect for Dunham's next demonstration. He set the timer on his watch to start the countdown. Today, he did not want to piss off his boss.

Paige could not believe the brashness of Senator Jenkins. He was on her Corrupted Intelligence top ten list as the worst abuser of the public trust given to him.

She started making notes to analyze his speech on her show, adding him to the outline she had for her upcoming podcast. "Scott, I think this show will shake up Dunham and the DRM," she said. "I hope The Professor, after hearing Senator Jenkins, will finally rear his ugly head?"

Scott Rogers was totally against Paige doing any of this while Dunham was still out there. *The Architect* had come too close at the Mayflower Hotel for him to not be scared for both of them.

"Paige, I need you to stop being stubborn and take a rest from your podcast this week. Dunham keeps demonstrating his bioweapons power and I know he'll try to use it on us once again," Scott said.

"Scotty, you know me better than that. I don't run away from danger or hide like a little schoolgirl. My podcast will go on as scheduled at four this afternoon. My fans are expecting me to make sense of what's been going on. Just have your men watching over us," she said. "It's three fifty-five and I don't have time to argue with you," she said, pulling her long black hair back into a ponytail.

Scott marched out of the dressing room and radioed Paige's security detail who were monitoring the ground around the studio. "We are getting ready to start the podcast. Is it all clear?" he asked.

Walking through the studio door was FBI Director Glass. With her were four muscular agents keeping the Director inside their circle of testosterone.

Tiffany saw Scott and walked over to him. "Hi, Scott. I need to speak with Paige. It's urgent," she said. "Paige's life is in danger, and she needs to delay her podcast."

Scott was shaking his head. "I just had the same conversation with her not even five minutes ago. She's stubborn and won't run and hide when she has a job to do," he said, pursing his lips.

"Point me in the direction where she is and let me talk with her."

Blake Hunter, a Private Investigator and ex-Navy SEAL on Paige's security detail, had heard the alarm in the Director's voice. It only confirmed what he already knew.

"Ma'am, I need you and your men to follow me." He escorted Tiffany to Turner's dressing room, opened the door, and guided Director Glass inside. He stuck his head inside and shouted in a nervous tone. "Please stay inside the dressing room until I give the all clear. I just received a report that there are over fifteen men all dressed in military fatigues looking like they are about the storm the building. They are not friendlies," Hunter said. "Director, please get Paige somewhere safe and don't come out until you hear from me."

"Roger that. Do you have gas masks here just to be safe?" Tiffany asked.

Thirty seconds later, Tiffany was dragging a protesting woman into a storage room. "What are you doing?" she screamed. "I'm going to be late."

"Better late than dead," Director Glass shot back. "Now stop arguing and get your ass inside and lock the door. Don't open it up until you hear from me," Tiffany ordered. She drew her weapon and took a defensive position behind a desk in the dressing room. Her gun was pointing at the only door.

* * * * *

Blake Hunter noticed that General Tucker Phillips had ordered his men to breach Turner's studio. They were moving fast, their weapons at the ready. One man appeared to hold a metal case with a hazardous material label on the side.

Scott Rogers ran upstairs to the roof where three US Marshals had ten untested miniature drones fully armed and ready to repel a military assault. Commander McAllister had gotten the President's approval to use these deadly weapons for Paige's and Scott's protection. With the remote control in his left hand and one drone in his right hand, the miniature weapons were ready to go. Scott peeked over the edge of the roof that faced the west side of the property. The first one was released and began hunting for its target. Once the drone was airborne, his men released the other nine drones. On a small screen, Rogers could locate the enemy and steer the drone toward its target. Each drone had five hundred rounds of armor-piercing ammo.

Hunter's men were positioned perfectly to stop the assault from coming through the front lobby door. Each man wore a metal button that would let the drone know they were friendlies.

Blake signaled Aden Parker, a retired Secret Service agent for President Wilson, to neutralize the three men approaching the west side of Paige's studio. Then he called Rebecca Burns and her team to stop the five men running toward the south side of the building. They were outmanned but with the drones airborne, General Tucker Phillip's mercenaries had no chance of entering the studio.

* * * * *

The Architect hacked the President's computer once again while General Phillips's attack was underway and booted up his face that was smiling. "Ladies and Gentlemen, since you do not want to give me what I want, you'll have to witness another demonstration. One that will tear at your hearts," Dunham said, his voice projecting an air of confidence. "Your beloved Paige Turner and Scott Rogers have been pissing me off for some time and will now suffer the consequences of their actions."

Dunham held up a digital clock with the seconds ticking down to four p.m. "When this clock reaches four, my weapon will be released inside Turner's studio, and you'll be able to watch them die a most horrible death."

President Graham and Sam had not been briefed on what McAllister had set up with the drones and waited in horror. Each monitor got directed to Paige's studio both outside and inside. They could see fifteen men dressed in military fatigues running toward the studio.

While Dunham clapped like a schoolboy, laughing like a deranged mental patient, his men stormed the west side of the property. But they abruptly fell to the ground after bullets blew off the sides of their skulls. Then five more met the same fate.

Dunham had stopped clapping and his laughter turned to profanities. "You can't stop all of them," he screamed.

Then, from out of nowhere, the remaining seven men, including General Tucker Phillips, were torn apart by the ten drones that were flying like a swarm of angry wasps. As the last drone shredded the man carrying the case of hazardous material, he fell to the ground, causing the metal case to pop open. Five glass vials fell out, all shattering on the red brick walkway. A light vapor formed a small mushroom cloud and floated toward the front door.

Inside the room, huddled with Paige, the gunfire had stopped, and she assumed it was all clear. She grabbed Turner's hand and rushed to the front door to escape the building. The President and the Attorney General looked in horror at their monitors, shouting for the two of them to stay indoors.

Dunham's profanities changed to encouragement for the two women to open the front door and inhale his bioweapon. "Open the fucking door, bitches. Your time is up."

Rushing through the back door was Bubba Jackson, his large arms extended. He wrapped them around the surprised ladies and pulled them away from the front door. "That was close," Jackson said.

"Bubba, what are you doing?" both women yelled.

Relieved, he answered, "Just saving your lives. My hazmat team is outside gathering up the bioweapon and any residuals that might harm you guys."

Paige looked drained and exhausted. She looked at Tiffany, puzzled. "What just happened?"

Tiffany gave Bubba a big hug. "Thank you and the Commander again. I don't know how I can ever repay you for what you risked for us," Tiffany said.

"Just doing our job."

Paige, her hands shaking, tried to force a smile. With a nervous breath, she took Tiffany's hand. "How about you and me having that dinner you promised me, with some martinis?" she asked.

"I'd like that," Tiffany replied, stuffing her shaking hands in her pockets. "Let's do it at the Mayflower in our suite. I need to kiss my two kids," she said.

"I'd love that."

* * * * *

Dunham sat in a secluded warehouse in Maryland, his hands cupping his head. "How the fuck could they have known what I was going to do?" he shouted, his voice echoing off the metal walls. Then he remembered he had told his brother that Turner and Rogers were going to have the pleasure of testing his new weapon. "Teddy, you're a fucking traitor. Your family will suffer for your disloyalty," *The Architect* warned his brother.

Dunham was on the phone with Randall Hunt, commentator on the American News Network. "I need you to go ballistic with your smear campaign against Paige Turner. She needs to be destroyed. You have all the proof to make what you say believable. Keep her name on your station for the next two weeks," *The Architect* said.

60

Professor Cochran watched in horror the decisive actions President Graham had taken to protect Paige Turner and Scott Rogers. He was surprised she could be so assertive.

The President's actions shocked the press and every far-right cable media network. The slaughter of retired General Tucker Phillips and his American Mercenaries outraged half of Congress.

The General, even though he had been tried and convicted of treason during the time *The Architect* tried to become the Emperor of the United States, had hundreds of thousands of QAnon members who believed, as they did about Albert Dunham, that these men were the new Messiahs put on earth to save their world. They believed the bodies lying on Turner's property were staged and that General Tucker Phillips was alive and hidden in another secret location where all enemies of the United States were being held.

The coverage of what happened at Paige Turner's studio had been twisted and rewritten by the mysterious QAnon leader and half of Congress to be a false flag event by the FBI and Homeland Security. This only ignited an already polarized America.

On the American Network News, Randall Hunt was sprouting conspiracies about Paige Turner and how she had it in for him and, with the help from ex-US Marshal Scott Rogers, planted false information about Albert Dunham.

On three of the major national news stations, President Graham was being accused of slaughtering patriotic veterans. A majority in the House of Representatives tried to get a vote to open a hearing to impeach her. Chants to lock her up for what she did was gaining speed. More calls to divide the United

States and create the Confederate States of America were echoing in the halls of Congress.

Even Paige Turner was being accused of using the staged event to promote her *Corrupted Intelligence* theory. Calls to close her podcast had been put on the agenda of the Senate Judiciary Committee.

Protests had started to pop up around the country in every far-right state. Governors rushed to get on every media outlet that would hear their story. What seemed to scare everyone was that the President authorized retired Commander John McAllister to test out the military's new drone weapon without Congress's approval.

The attempted murder of Paige Turner, Scott Rogers, and FBI Director Glass, three of America's favorite heroes had been buried and not mentioned on any network news station. Nothing was said about how Albert Dunham attempted once again to use his bioweapon on American soil. The only item being aired was the murder of General Phillips and his patriotic mercenaries.

Professor Cochran could not believe the support his DRM was getting and how the calls for the South to become the Confederate States of America once again. What irritated him most was that his loyal followers were calling for Albert Dunham to be their next President.

Albert Dunham, immediately after the incident at Turner's studio, broadcasted his twisted message to his disciples around the world. He was once again acting like the victim and saying that President Graham, like President Chesterfield four years ago, felt threatened by his approval ratings and placed him and his men on a kill list. He told his supporters to not believe anything President Graham or FBI Director Tiffany Glass or Sam Collins said about him.

While he had disagreements with Turner and her *Corrupted Intelligence* theory, he respected her patriotism. He had sent General Tucker Phillips to her studio to protect her from the CIA who wanted to kill her and use her as a martyr against *The Architect* and all he wanted to do for the country he loved.

Cochran was tugging at his white hair, struggling with what Dunham was doing. "How the fuck could this be happening? Doesn't anyone see what a crazy sociopath he is and what he's promising are all lies?" Cochran said, pounding his desk.

The Professor did not see that he too had the same sociopathic tendencies as Dunham. He called Wiley Jordan. He needed an update on locating April and her two boys. The Professor knew he had to remain hidden for just a little while longer until his final phase for his race war was in full bloom so the civil war could start.

"Wiley, update me on finding April?" Cochran asked.

"When my men went to the University of California at Irvine to capture the bitch, she had already withdrawn from all her classes two days before. Nobody knows where she's hiding," Wiley said, expressing his frustration.

"We have to find her soon or our final phase can't happen. Do you think McAllister's team got to her first and put her in protective custody?" Cochran asked.

"I doubt it. The day I tried to get her, they too were at her house and university looking for her. She seems to know how to stay one step ahead of trouble. Something I am sure Charles taught her," said Wiley.

Contact all of our allies inside the West Wing, DOJ, and FBI. Maybe they know where she is?"

"Let's hope she is not being protected by the US Marshals office. Those bastards are the most loyal police force the United States employs. We do not have any men hidden in their ranks. If they have her, you're fucked, Professor," Wiley said.

"If that's the case, then screw April and Director Glass. We will move up our attacks and go nuclear with our civil war in a few days."

61

Sitting in the White House Situation Room were Turner and Rogers to brief the President on everything they knew about Albert Dunham's personality and the possibility of him using the nerve gas on millions of innocent Americans.

Lending support to the President were FBI Director Tiffany Glass and Attorney General Sam Collins. They had brought all the files they had on Charles Stone and the Domestic Revolutionary Movement. This planning session was to compare these two psychopaths. They also brought the Haven House logbook with notations going back to the Civil War.

Commander McAllister and Staff Sergeant Bubba Jackson were there with their team to fill in the gaps and help create a workable strategy to end the reign of terror on the United States by the DRM, Professor Cochran, as well as capture and arrest Albert Dunham.

On a large monitor were Dean Miller and Roger Stillwell, using their state-of-the-art software that was hunting for the DRM's professor and Neo-Nazi Wiley Jordan. Dunham had turned out to be another problem, as he had once again disappeared somewhere in Europe.

President Graham did not include any other Cabinet members, as she did not trust any of them at this time. Their punishment would come in short order.

A tired and exhausted President walked into the Situation Room with her Chief of Staff, whom she trusted with her life. "Are we ready to do battle with Dunham, The DRM, and half of Congress?" she asked, trying to force a grin.

Paige Turner was the first to speak. "I cannot express fully how I feel about all of you risking your lives to save ours. It was the most frightening day of my life," she said, unable to control her emotions. "Madame President, the courage you showed authorizing Commander McAllister to step in and arm my security team with the firepower to ward off an army of seasoned soldiers was amazing. I know you're getting a lot of heat from Congress, but once we explain why those steps were necessary, I'm sure the sane Americans who love our country will step up and support you once again."

"That's very nice, Miss Turner, but today we don't have time for hugs and kisses when our country and democracy are teetering on the brink," President Graham said unemotionally. "I needed all of you here today, including Miss Turner and Mr. Rogers." President Graham's last comment got everyone, including Scott, to burst out laughing.

"Ha, ha, ha, everyone," the President said. "We need to get focused right now and come up with a solid plan to save our constitution and country."

Commander McAllister jumped into the conversation. "Madame President. A few years ago, Master Sergeant Jackson and I created a veteran's group that has grown to over ten thousand retired soldiers from all four branches of the military. They continue to honor the oath they took to defend the United States from both foreign and domestic enemies as well as protect the constitution with their lives." The Commander noticed that the tension on Graham's face started to melt away. "What I'd like you to do today is sign an executive order reinstating these men and women with full pay and benefits and authorize me to lead them into battle to save our country."

"It sounds like you already have a plan?" President Graham said.

"Bubba and I do. It's better than you choosing to declare martial law, which could further divide an already polarized electorate. These patriotic veterans are the only people I can say I trust other than who is in this room today."

On the TV monitor, Dean Miller interrupted the Commander. "Hi, everyone," Miller said, waving his hand. "I know all of you have been chasing your tails, putting out fires everywhere over the last month. Stillwell and I have remained on task with our job of finding Charles Stone's mistress April. The good news is we have located her and her two boys. She is at an undisclosed safe house only Roger and I know exists. We showed her photos of men we believe frequented Haven House when she was enslaved there and you'll be shocked to find who we believe is the DRM leader," Miller said.

"Don't reveal this person until you are in the Oval Office later today," President Graham ordered.

"I'll send a few of my men to bring him and Stillwell here," Bubba Jackson told the President.

"Now, let's get back to the business at hand." The President looked at Sam Collins and gestured for him to make his presentation.

Sam passed around a workup of what he was proposing to redefine domestic terrorism. "I know my department is authorized to write legislation and send it off to Congress for their approval. Madame President, with a polarized House and Senate, it seems unlikely that whatever I write will get a majority vote," he said. "So, I believe our best shot at giving you the power you are looking for, and not violate the constitution, is to clearly define what a domestic terrorist is, so it conforms to what the founding fathers wrote in the constitution defining a traitor. Once I have your approval, my department will be able to prosecute these homegrown terrorists. We need to look at these traitors, these illegal militia groups, the same way we would look at any foreign invader."

President Graham looked uncomfortable with where Sam was going with all of this. "Mister Collins," she said seriously. "How can we justify arresting and incarcerating an American, or a group of Americans, who believe they are exercising their constitutional right to free assembly and free speech?"

Sam began nodding his head while he stared at the President. "Madame President, my clarification of domestic terrorism and illuminating what I believe is currently written in the constitution will not violate the rights of law-abiding citizens. We already have the Patriot Act and section 802 defines a domestic terrorist clearly. I am not proposing to eliminate this law, but to better describe who is a domestic terrorist and what constitutes an act of terrorism. Then I can fully prosecute these murderous pigs."

President Graham seemed confused. "If we have these laws on the books now, what's the problem?"

"Very good question. For the last three to four decades, our politicians and federal district attorneys have labeled these groups as militia, and not domestic terrorists, which they are. Our constitution has every politician, and military personnel swear an oath to the United States Constitution to defend our country from both foreign and domestic enemies. We have been afraid to call American citizens domestic enemies until now," Sam said, blotting the perspiration off his forehead with a napkin.

Director Glass jumped into the conversation. "Sam, you do know that a new definition will get tested in our court system. What you're proposing might not stand the test in the Supreme Court," she said, knowing what his answer would be.

"If each Justice said what was truthful at their confirmation hearing, then there should not be a problem. Sadly, from what I've witnessed over the last ten years, most of them have lied. So, yes, I believe what I am proposing will meet the challenges. Our judicial system being slow is my advantage, and who I arrest will be locked up until the courts decide their outcome."

"That seems too easy, Sam," President Graham said. "Why has this not been done before?"

"Our country has not been faced with the type of attacks we've experienced these last four weeks. We have never before had an American citizen release a bioweapon on innocent men, women, and children," Sam said.

Commander McAllister interrupted. "Sam, don't you remember how it was when Stone and his White Angels tried to kill you and Tiffany?" He noticed a puzzled look on Collins' face. "Nothing was done within the halls of Congress."

Sam blotted the perspiration off his forehead. "Yeah, I remember. During Charles Stone's insurrection attempt, the then Attorney General and President did not have any backbone to risk their popularity with a re-election pending," Sam responded. "By you signing an executive order to clarify the wording in the Patriot Act, will allow all of us to take the necessary action to stop the pending civil war. I'll be able to lock up all domestic terrorists. This includes Albert Dunham."

President Graham, for the first time, smiled and leaned back in her chair. "Sam, you've done a great job. Anything else you want to say?"

"Yes, Madame President. My office has also recommended a ban on all military-type weapons in the District of Columbia, except for federal law enforcement. This would include handguns—" Before Sam could continue, the door to the Situation Room opened.

Walking in were April and her two boys, escorted by Bubba Jackson, Dean Miller, and Roger Stillwell. Tiffany had not seen Charles's boys since that night on the Santa Monica pier ten years ago. When the older boy, who was sixteen now, saw Tiffany sitting with Sam, he strode over toward them and bent down, and gave the FBI Director a firm hug. He kissed her on the cheek. In a deep, low voice, he whispered in her ear. "I remember you saving our lives against mean Master Charles," he said and backed away, extending his hand and giving Sam a manly handshake. April tried to corral her son, but Tiffany waved her off and gave the handsome young man a kiss on his cheek.

62

When everyone settled down, Dean Miller and Roger Stillwell walked toward the President. She was handed a slip of paper with the mysterious Professor's name.

President Graham passed the note to Tiffany. "You've got to be kidding," the FBI Director said with a shocked look on her face. She passed it to Sam.

"He's a well-respected Southern leader. He's always holding speaking engagements, never exposing his radical side to the public," Sam said. "I never thought anything about it when he'd be in the same room with Charles Stone, but after reading the numerous entries referencing The Professor as Stone's mentor," he said out of breath, "it's all beginning to make sense."

"Can I see that piece of paper?" Turner asked, extending her hand, and like everyone, was surprised to see Professor Albert Cochran's name. Next to his name, it said he was April's biological father.

"I'm not sure I can arrest him for murder and treason," Sam said. "Do we have any concrete proof he's the person behind all of these attacks on American soil?"

Director Glass addressed President Graham. "If this is the man we've been looking for, it's going to be difficult getting anyone to come forward, or for that matter provide us evidence to lock him up."

"Let's first start arresting every member in these White Supremacist groups and see where it leads us," Sam said. "We already have hundreds of White Supremacist militia captured during their murderous rampage. I want their trials to begin immediately for treason."

"Albert Cochran has a lot of friends and supporters in the House and Senate, as well as on the Supreme Court," President Graham said. "If we thought we didn't have support now, wait until we arrest this sociopath."

Dean Miller raised his hand. "Madame President. When I first saw The Professor's name, I used my new software program and tagged some very influential people connected to Cochran. Even Dunham is connected to this man and the DRM," Miller said. "If I'm permitted to dig a little deeper, I might be able to give you the evidence you'll need to arrest him."

President Graham was rubbing her chin, deep in thought. "Is your program able to weed out the traitors working inside my West Wing, FBI, and DOJ?" she asked.

Miller was nodding his head. "I was able to do this for Paige to destroy *The Architect*, so I don't see why it can't be done now."

Sam was shaking his head. "Invading people's privacy is illegal under the constitution. I can't be part of that," he said.

"We can," McAllister said. "Give us the leads and then let us take it from there. Stillwell helped us with some government spying satellites to end Charles Stone's reign of terror. Now that I know who the leader of the DRM is, I'll bet he's the person who delivered Stone's severed hands to Sam and Tiffany. He did threaten that he'd be back. I'm confident my team will be able to put an end to all of this now that we know who the players are."

Dean Miller stood up and began pacing around the Situation Room. "Madame President, you have a bigger problem than the White Supremacists or Dunham. Almost 50 percent of good Americans do not trust the federal government. They watch all the fighting, name-calling, and false promises given by both sides of the aisle. They feel that they do not have any representatives who can give them what they need to survive."

"You're not telling me anything I don't already know," Graham said. "Is there a point to all of this?"

"Yes. I've been developing my software just for this moment. Five years ago, I formed a political action group that I named: *We the People*. As of yesterday, our membership has grown to over sixty-five million registered voters. I recently sent out a survey with a hundred questions. I was surprised by the response I got, especially with the answers," Miller said, holding up the results.

"Professor Miller, many Americans like yourself have tried to form an independent party and have fallen flat on their faces," President Graham said. "So can we get back to the problem at hand?"

"Give me one more minute, please." He didn't wait for an answer. "Those first attempts at a major third party did not have more than five hundred thousand registered voters. With my large paid membership and the positive acceptance I am getting, I believe that by the upcoming mid-terms and then the General election, the *We the People* party will have enough House and Senate Representatives to command the respect we'll need to make positive changes for every American citizen. In addition, our movement is seeing inroads into over seventeen State Legislatures. Change is coming and you need to get on board."

President Graham pursed her lips as she mulled over what Miller had said. "We need to talk after this meeting," she said.

"Can we meet in a week? I'd like to show you the platform we'll be offering to our membership."

"Fine," Graham said.

The meeting went on for another two hours. The President was very pleased with what everyone was going to do to end the reign of terror plaguing the country. April and her boys were put in protective custody until the DRM, especially Wiley Jordan, were eliminated. Joining them in protective custody was Theodore Dunham. He was the only one who could help create the antidote for the bioweapon. But first McAllister had to find the location Albert Dunham had his family before he'd help to create an antidote.

Sam went back to work on his drafts to define domestic terrorists and expand the language inside the Patriot Act that would coordinate with the US Constitution. He also had planned to talk in front of both chambers to harness their support for his redefined wording for a domestic terrorist.

FBI Director Glass had one assignment and one assignment only. Find Professor Cochran and put him in custody while Dean Miller and Roger Stillwell gathered the evidence the DOJ needed against both men.

After the meeting back in the Oval Office, President Graham sat with her Chief of Staff Martha Sweeden, sipping a brandy. "You were very quiet. Nothing to add to all of this?" President Graham asked.

"I had a lot to say, but thought I'd share it with you first."

"Feel free to speak right now."

"You have everyone doing some very positive things to help our country, but you failed to talk about what to do if the predicted civil war happens, which I'll bet will happen any day now," Sweeden said, gulping her brandy.

"We'll deal with that if and when it happens."

63

Professor Cochran was stunned that President Graham was able to find April and the boys before Wiley. "I have to believe my cover will be blown," he said to the White Angels leader. "If the President and Collins know I'm The Professor they are looking for, then I must strike a severe blow once and for all and get our civil war started."

"I think we should Eliminate Collins and Glass once and for all too. Then that bitch Paige Turner. Finally, I want to personally cut off the head of McAllister and feed it to his Black bastard friend Bubba Jackson. Then we'll have clear sailing toward our civil war," Wiley boasted.

"Let's take a breath right now. I remember what happened to you and your men the last time you and Charles tried to kill these cockroaches."

"No fucking breather. I've got my spies watching them and this time, it will be swift and brutal." Wiley stormed out, leaving for his command post in the backwoods near the Haven House Plantation to see his small army of patriots before he met up again with The Professor at Black Landing.

* * * * *

The following day, Professor Cochran gathered five of his Generals at Blacks Landing Plantation hidden in the woods in Southern Alabama for a three-day pre–civil war strategy session. In attendance were Wesley Jones, Leader of the White Supremacist Church, Godfrey Allen, Leader of the American Nazi Party, Freddie Blanton, leader of California's Aryan Alliance, Max Simon, leader of the National White Lives Matter group, and Wiley Jordan, leader of the White Angels. On a Zoom call was leader of the Brown Shirts in Argentina, Wilhelm

Hitler, bastard grandson of Adolf Hitler who was mobilizing his ten thousand mercenaries to invade the United States once the civil war started.

Professor Cochran was dressed in a black silk suit, with a black long-sleeved shirt and black silk tie. He wore his original Nazi cap he had gotten from his father when Charles Stone's father and uncle escaped Nazi Germany after the war ended.

"Gentlemen, patriots, today marks an important and critical time for our movement," Cochran said proudly. "The country we love, the country we want to raise our White children in, has been infected with inferior humans of color for too long. Before our President Thaddeus Thompson dropped dead on national TV, we were so close to having the support we needed to succeed with our dream of a White Aryan Nation." The Professor paused to sip from his glass of Scotch. He noticed Wiley squirming in his seat and pointed at him to speak. "Wiley, you want to say something?"

"I do, glorious leader," Wiley said sarcastically. "We are not ready to start our civil war at this time. Too much needs to be done, especially as I told you the other day, eliminating all the enemies who are currently trying to find us all. If we show our faces too soon, we'll lose," he said.

"That's why we must strike when we have the advantage of surprise. Once our attacks spread to every state, they will be on defense and putting out fires. Remember, we have allies in the CIA, Homeland Security, and FBI who will not try to stop us. They have been indoctrinated and believe that we're the true patriots who are trying to restore the United States to the greatest power it was before we had to live with all the inferiors."

"What about FBI Director Glass and Attorney General Sam Collins? We know they won't put their tails between their legs and run away, especially since they have Commander McAllister watching their backs," Wiley shot back. "As I told you, I want to attack these pigs first and then we can go after that bitch President Shannon Graham, who has some slant eyes in her blood."

* * * * *

Inside the White House, the alarm went off on Dean Miller's cell phone. "Wiley Jordan is in the backwoods of Alabama with four White Supremacist leaders." Miller's tagging software had a built-in program that continuously tracked the locations of specific targets.

Dean was immediately on the phone with McAllister. "My program has located Jordan and four other high-profile leaders of White Supremacist groups at Blacks Landing Plantation in Alabama. The coordinates are being sent as we speak. There is one unknown with them. I bet it's Professor Cochran."

"Good job, Miller. Let me take it from here," the Commander said.

64

McAllister and fifteen members of his team landed at Wetumpka City Airport in Elmore, Alabama. They were thirty-five miles away from their target. Waiting for them were five Humvees, fueled and loaded with enough weapons to stop a small army.

Also waiting at the airport hangar was CIA Director Porter Ramsey. "Commander McAllister, it's nice to see you again. What's it been, fifteen years since we worked together in Afghanistan?"

McAllister tried to control his surprise seeing this particular spook standing by one of the Humvees with a broad smile on his face. The Commander did remember working with him and all the innocent people, especially children he had gotten killed with his sloppy intelligence. "What are you doing here?" he asked, ready to lay him out on the tarmac.

"President Graham thought you'd need some assistance with your mission. I have some accurate intel that you will need before you breach this compound," Ramsey said.

"I remember the crap intel you gave my SEAL team in Afghanistan. It sacrificed innocents and almost killed me and my men." McAllister's loud voice had shaken Ramsey up.

"That was over twenty years ago. It was difficult getting accurate information back then. Now the CIA, under my watchful eye, has its act together," Porter lashed back.

Bubba, who remembered Porter, stepped in between the two men. "We have our own intel that we trust more than anything you could provide us. So, crawl back into the hole you came out of and leave us to do what President

Graham wants us to do." Jackson's tensed facial muscles had the CIA Director backing away, trying to hide his shaking hands.

"You two are making a mistake today. The President authorized my agency to run point on this mission since it falls under domestic terrorism," he said, his voice cracking.

McAllister, while Jackson had his six, called President Graham. "Yes Madame President, I understand. We'll be careful."

Inside the hangar, McAllister's team readied themselves for their mission, checking their equipment and putting on their body armor. The Commander saw Porter Ramsey walking over to his men. He waved him away with his automatic weapon.

Inside the command Humvee, McAllister gave instructions to his men. The caravan of five armor-plated vehicles sped away from the airport, kicking up a dust cloud, causing the CIA Director to cough.

* * * * *

"Wiley, I tried to reason with McAllister, but he hasn't forgotten when we worked together in Afghanistan. He does not suspect you were working for me back then. I forgave you for the mess you created. Now, is everything in place?" Ramsey asked.

"The landmines are set. They should impact them about a mile out from where we are," Wiley said. "I owe you big time for this. I hate McAllister and Bubba Jackson. Finally, I can have my revenge."

"Once it's all done, give me a status report."

* * * * *

Dean Miller's cell started buzzing. He stared at Tiffany and Sam. "Wiley Jordan is using his cell phone. Give me thirty seconds," he said, holding up his hand. "There. CIA Director Porter Ramsey just hung up talking to Wiley. I can't record their conversation, but I'll bet it's nothing good for the Commander and his team."

Sam immediately called McAllister. "John you're heading toward a trap," he said anxiously. "Wiley Jordan and the CIA Director just finished talking. We don't know what was said, but it can't be good."

"President Graham warned me about her CIA Director and with my history with him, I've already taken precautions," the Commander said.

"Please be careful. You're my kid's godfather," Sam shot back.

"Roger that, Sam. I still have a loyal friend at Pensacola Air Station. Commander Alan Baker, who tried to help me with my friend Rayford Miller, the guy you remember who escaped from the Haven House Plantation and exposed everything Charles Stone was doing. He has SEAL Team Four in place, led by one of our best SEAL Captains, and they have our backs. Gotta go. We're two miles out from our target."

65

Cochran had finished issuing his orders to his field commanders. The following day, all fifty states would be under siege by the newly formed ten-thousand-plus White Confederate Army. After successfully raiding ten armories at National Guard Military bases where he had supporters, The Professor felt his civil war was ready to happen. As a firewall, if things don't go according to plan, he had over ten thousand foreign mercenaries, The Brown Shirts from Argentina, waiting for their signal to cross the border and lend support to the Confederate Soldiers.

Wiley burst into the command center, out of breath. "McAllister and his men, fifteen of them are almost here," Jordan said, forcing a grin.

Cochran seemed confused. "Did I hear you right? An assault team is almost here?"

"I couldn't tell you or you wouldn't have come here. CIA Director Porter Ramsey, who I worked for in Afghanistan, owed me a big favor. He alerted me three days ago about McAllister and Bubba Jackson looking for you and me."

"This is bullshit, Wiley. You can't put our people in jeopardy like this. We don't have the manpower here to stave off an attack from a SEAL team commanded by McAllister."

"We are ready. I have forty of my men scattered in the woods forming a five-mile perimeter around you and your Generals. Everyone is safe. Trust me," Jordan said.

Before Cochran could respond, explosions could be heard inside the woods.

Wiley started clapping his hands, knowing what was happening. He wanted to go out and see McAllister's bloodied body and watch him beg for help.

"Sir, it's already started. It should be over in about fifteen minutes," Wiley said, with an air of confidence.

"Wiley, don't count your chickens before they're hatched," The Professor said. "I've heard your foolish bragging before."

Wiley did not say a word as he stormed out of the metal building. He was puzzled he did not see any of his men marching back carrying the severed heads of their enemy. He radioed his team leader.

"Status report," he shouted into his stat phone. He did it three more times. All he heard was a static buzzing. "Shit," Wiley screamed when he saw five Humvees about half a mile out speeding through the woods.

He rushed back inside to warn The Professor and his Generals, but they were nowhere to be found. He looked out the back door and noticed all the escape vehicles were gone. For the first time in his life, he realized death was knocking at his door. He picked up his assault rifle and ten clips. He had his Beretta fully loaded as he stepped outside to confront McAllister.

Inside the lead Humvee, the Commander noticed Wiley alone and fully armed. He looked at Bubba, shaking his head. "Is he crazy enough to take all of us on?"

"Crazy yes, but I'd bet he's going out as he lived. Let's give him what he wants if he won't surrender," Bubba replied.

McAllister had gotten off his stat phone with SEAL Team Four leader Captain Smith. "Roger that. No sign of Professor Cochran, just his four Generals. They attempted to resist arrest and fired their weapons at us. A very foolish choice on their part," Captain Smith said in a calm voice.

"Was lethal force necessary?" McAllister asked.

Captain Smith replied, "We had them cornered and demanded they surrender. It was a no-win scenario for them. They said no by getting out of their vehicles and firing their weapons at us. It was over in sixty seconds. All of them are dead sir. No sign of Professor Cochran."

"Captain Smith, thanks for your help. We owe you our lives," McAllister said. Before the Commander could put his phone down, Wiley started running toward the back of the building, looking back, and firing his automatic rifle. Bubba Jackson opened fire, hitting the back of his thigh. He saw Jordan fall down, screaming in pain.

"Go grab up that bastard and bring him back here," Jackson ordered his men.

Behind the building was a large pool of blood, but not Wiley Jordan. "Sir, the target is gone. There are motorcycle tracks leading into the woods."

McAllister was impressed with how Wiley always seemed to survive. He dialed President Graham to update her. "All four of Professor Cochran's Generals are dead, but Wiley Jordan was able to escape after being shot in the leg. He's going to need medical attention quickly or he'll bleed out. Professor Cochran is another story. He's nowhere to be found. Hopefully, Dean Miller can find him?"

"Great job, Commander. Please head back to the airport and deal with Porter Ramsey. I want him cuffed and brought back to me ASAP," Graham ordered. "I'll make an example of him and convict him of treason. I just got briefed by Sam Collins about Article III, Section 3 of our constitution. Since Professor Cochran has levied war on our country and aided the enemies of the United States, he's guilty of treason and punishable by death."

"He's probably handcuffed already. I alerted Director Glass, and she promised me that she'd have him restrained when I got back."

"I'm sure he won't cooperate, but see if you can get him to tell us who else is working for the DRM inside our government?" President Graham asked.

"He's already confessed to his crime. He wants to be held as a prisoner of war. He wouldn't shut up about his part in the new Confederate States of America."

"Excellent. He's made the charge of treason a slam dunk with his confession," Graham said.

66

Porter Ramsey, before talking with Wiley, had set up a foolproof escape route for Professor Cochran and his Generals. In the backwoods of Alabama's forest, General Robert E. Lee had the Confederate Soldiers build their own underground railroad, with tracks and a steam locomotive, pulling one small car that could hold twenty soldiers. It stretched almost fifty miles, sixty feet underground, crossing the border into Georgia.

The Professor tried calling Wiley, but it went to his voicemail. He then tried to speak with his Generals and got the same result. He had to assume all of them were dead. He dialed Godfrey Allen, leader of the American Nazi Movement's team leader Stanley Kipfer in Los Angeles.

"Stanley, have you heard from Godfrey?"

"Nothing yet, sir. What happened there?"

"Wiley's ego almost got me killed. I think he's either captured with the Generals or they are all dead," Cochran said, tapping his cane nervously.

"Does this mean our civil war is not going to start tomorrow?" Kipfer asked, sounding disappointed.

"Hell No. In fact, I think we should start today. Is our army ready and in position?" Cochran asked.

"We've been ready for almost two weeks now. Our men are getting anxious and needing to kill some non-Whites," Stanley said.

"Great. Let's catch everyone by surprise," Cochran shouted as his railroad car surfaced in a forest in Georgia. Waiting for The Professor were twenty combat veterans, along with five hundred domestic mercenaries, all fully armed and ready to transport their leader to their new compound.

Kipfer could hear Cochran barking out some orders as his train screeched to an abrupt halt. "Professor, send out your signal and we'll do the rest. Soon we'll have our country back," Stanley said.

"Give me five hours so I can hack into the National Emergency Broadcasting System and officially declare war on President Graham and her illegal government."

Professor Cochran, before he declared war, needed to alert a few loyal supporters inside the West Wing, FBI, Homeland Security, and the CIA. Their orders, once the attacks started around the country, were to arrest President Graham, FBI Director Glass, and Attorney General Collins.

Then Acting Vice President Bradley White, a lieutenant in the DRM would declare martial law and activate every National Guard unit in every state to support all the patriots fighting for the Confederate States of America. Once that was accomplished, they were to lower the American flags on the Capitol Dome and White House roof and replace them with Confederate Flags.

During these critical hours, Cochran would be airing his declaration of war to every American. His speech would ignite all the Domestic Revolutionary Movement supporters to take to the streets, shooting at all non-Whites so it would ignite rioting and looting by persons of color.

With the wheels set in motion for the civil war to begin, Professor Cochran successfully took over the Emergency Broadcasting System. The Professor sat in front of a bank of cameras behind a large oak desk, with a bust of General Robert E. Lee behind him and a Confederate Flag hanging on the wall directly above his head. On a tripod stand was a map of the new Confederate States of America with flags pinned to the exact place where the new Confederate White House and Capitol building were located in Richmond, Virginia. He held onto his new Declaration of Independence as he started to talk:

"My fellow Americans, let me introduce myself to all who do not know me. I am Professor Albert Cochran, the General of the new Confederate Army. We have come to a point in our nation's short history to right all the wrongs that you and your ancestors had to endure since our first Civil War. We are stronger and more organized now and today we will be victorious. Unlike what happened to our beloved General Robert E. Lee, I, as your new General, have been organizing and formulating our new democracy for over thirty years. Finally, we will have our own Confederacy in the States we lost to the Union Army.

"Four of our Generals have been slaughtered while trying to surrender to Commander John McAllister and his band of retired SEALs under the orders from our bitch President.

"President Graham will soon be arrested for treason, along with Attorney General Sam Collins and FBI Director Tiffany Glass. These two traitors brutally murdered Charles Stone, and it cannot go unpunished. Their children will be indoctrinated into our new way of life so they can help rebuild our country," Cochran paused, blotting his forehead with a cloth napkin.

"Before I end this broadcast, investigative reporter Paige Turner will be arrested for her part in the attempted murder of Albert Dunham, The Architect. It was her lies and planted evidence that convinced President Chesterfield to use a ballistic missile to level his beautiful home in Bethesda, Maryland. Dunham, like Charles Stone, is an American hero who I hope will come back to us and help form our new Confederate States of America." Cochran was looking straight into the camera. *"Mister Dunham, we have a place for you in the Domestic Revolutionary Movement."*

Before the broadcast ended, The Professor could be seen looking at his cellphone screen. Once Cochran was assured that all his soldiers were ready to begin the civil war, he sent out his signal for the battle to begin.

67

Dean Miller had been summoned to the White House. He had been asked to use his software to see where Cochran's civil war would be starting. With help from his son Allan and his wife Allison, the three of them had gathered enough information about what would be happening, primarily in all the southern states, at the Mexican border, and in Washington DC.

President Graham had been escorted into the White House bunker with her entire Secret Service security team that had been fully vetted by Commander McAllister. The Capitol Police were given orders to be alert and let the traitors make their moves before arresting them. The President wanted concrete evidence so she could try them for treason.

On the other hand, President Graham was distraught about what had been reported to her about ten thousand suspicious men, all in military fatigues and armed with assault rifles at the Mexican border. It was unconfirmed, but the NSA did not believe it was the Mexican army. Then who were these men and what were their intentions? She asked her Joint Chiefs, Secretary of Defense, and Homeland Security Secretary.

President Graham looked like she just got out of bed, waiting for some answers. "What, if any, are my options at our Southern border?"

"Madame President," Chairman of the Joint Chiefs, General Hawkins replied. "I've mobilized one of our Army battalions consisting of six companies with around one thousand soldiers. They are battle-ready to repel any attack that tries to invade our border," he said. "Once we know their intentions, then I can further access our next move."

"Very good, General Hawkins. I just hope we're not too late," President Graham said despondently.

"In addition, I've positioned two battalions that will form a tight net around the Capitol. We are ready for an assault by these domestic terrorists," the General said.

President Graham, for the first time since entering the Oval Office, felt relieved. She looked at Sam Collins and signaled him to brief her on what she had asked him to do.

Attorney General Collins seemed uncomfortable in his chair. He was fumbling with his notes. "Madame President, what you're doing with our military has never been done before. It's going to look like you've instituted martial law unilaterally."

"Sam, what would you have me do under these circumstances?" she asked.

"I'm not sure, but notifying Congress would have been my first step," he said.

"You're kidding, right? With the intel I've been given, a majority of Congress is in on this coup."

"I don't know what I was thinking. You're right, we are now in new territory here and our number one priority is to save our democracy," the Attorney General said. He looked again at his notes and began to brief the President. "I've issued enough warrants to serve on all your staff inside the West Wing and every Cabinet Secretary who we believe are part of today's insurrection," Sam said, his hands shaking. "Fifteen Senators and a hundred and sixty-five House Members as we speak are set to be arrested by our US Marshals immediately when these traitors make their seditious move to attack the Capitol and White House."

FBI Director Glass jumped into the conversation and assured the President that everything was in place around the border cities to stop the rebellion. Before Tiffany could continue, Professor Cochran had taken over their TV monitors.

After listening to Cochran's ranting, Sam, Tiffany, and Commander McAllister headed down to the Presidential bunker to analyze what the Domestic Revolutionary Movement's next steps would be.

"He's one arrogant son of a bitch," McAllister said. "Does he really think he has enough men to hold off the might of our military?"

"Whether he does or doesn't, it appears Cochran is going ahead with his plans," President Graham said. "Sam, do you have what I asked you for?"

"I do, Madame President," he said, handing her a confidential file that would allow her to authorize the use of the military against American citizens.

President Graham, at the one-month mark of her presidency, looked like she'd aged twenty years. She had not had one day to relax and enjoy her normal presidential duties. Her plans after she was sworn in, were to visit the states that needed economic help, talk to businesses about the investments she wanted to make to prop up the economy, or just have a relaxing weekend at Camp David. However, the non-stop attacks and slaughter of Americans forced her to abandon those plans.

Today, she was witnessing her beloved country falling into anarchy, with Americans willing to kill each other for a make-believe cause. She believed that Paige Turner's *Corrupted Intelligence* theory was the best explanation for the problems she was facing. She felt powerless against all of the lies and conspiracy theories being spewed by the radical right. She just didn't know how to message the point and change the minds and attitudes of the citizens who trusted the men and women leading them down a path to destroy democracy and shred the constitution she had sworn to protect and defend.

Her Attorney General had placed in front of her the papers she needed to sign to authorize the United States military to do battle with American citizens. President Graham tried to smile at the loyal Americans sitting in the Presidential bunker but couldn't. "Gentlemen and Ladies, today marks a very sad day in our history. Not since the Civil War, which was all about slavery, has our democracy faced such a tragic test to survive." The President signaled her Attorney General to address the group.

Sam opened his file folder containing the paperwork that would authorize the President to deploy the military. "I agree with President Graham. Today marks a day that none of us ever believed would happen in our country. The Insurrection Act of 1807 is a United States federal law that empowers the President of the United States to deploy the US military and federalized National Guard troops within the United States under particular circumstances, such as to suppress civil disorder, insurrection, or rebellion. Once the President signs these papers, the Joint Chiefs will mobilize enough troops to quell this insurrection as swiftly as possible. It's been over a hundred and fifty years since Americans died at the hands of our military. I can only hope we are successful and will not destroy our democracy," Sam said.

"Thank you, Sam," President Graham said. She turned toward her Joint Chiefs, looking to see if they had any comments they wanted to share. Before anyone could speak, Chief of Staff Martha Sweeden burst into the room.

"Madame President, turn on the monitor. Cochran's war has started," she said, blotting her soaked eyes. "It's horrible what these traitors are doing. They are slaughtering innocent men, women, and children of color. They have taken over thirteen Capitol buildings in the old Confederacy and have captured each of the Governors." She stopped talking once the insurrection came on the monitors.

"Martha, thank you. Leave us now," Graham said. Once her Chief of Staff was gone, the President pointed to General Ronald Hawkins, the Chairman of the Joint Chiefs. "Your assessment and action plan."

Thirty minutes later, President Graham addressed the nation from the Oval Office:

"My fellow Americans. Today marks a terrible day in our young experiment with democracy. An insurrection, by traitors who want to have the United States for White Christian men and women. Over a hundred fifty years ago, we fought with Americans who did not want to give up owning slaves, and as a young country then, won a most horrible battle.

"Today, we are fighting with the same ideology that wants to see our democracy destroyed and our constitution shredded and rewritten to only benefit those they believe are the chosen ones. As your President, I took an oath to defend and protect our country from both foreign and domestic terrorists, and effective today I am enacting the Insurrection Act of 1807 and authorizing our Joint Chiefs to take whatever action they deem necessary to end this civil war as quickly as possible. If it means killing Americans, then that is what they are authorized to do," President Graham said, and ended her address as abruptly as it started.

After she dismissed her Joint Chiefs, she asked her Attorney General and FBI Director to stay behind.

68

Professor Cochran's civil war had broken out in the south and a few northern states, while Albert Dunham watched on his cell phone as Cochran declared his war on the United States. What stunned him even more, was that he was asking him to join him and the DRM on National TV.

"The old man is crazy. Doesn't he know the train has passed him by again?" The Architect said under his breath.

Dunham started laughing loudly. He had always had a problem trusting people dating back to his early childhood and Professor Cochran, who turned his back on him when he tried to implement his manifesto, was the one person he needed to keep at arm's length. He knew that now was not a good time to show himself. He needed to become invisible until everything in the United States settled down.

* * * * *

The civil war had been going on for almost two hours. Every major news station had it covered. Some reporters were crying as they reported the slaughter that had happened, especially the brutal murder of one of their fellow reporters and crew by using their camera equipment to smash their skulls.

"I never thought I would live long enough to see something like this happen to the greatest world power, the greatest democracy on earth. But today the country I love is going down in flames," the female reporter from CNN said, her hand shaking as she tried to speak into her microphone.

Another male reporter from ABC expressed himself differently.

"What we are witnessing is not a civil war, not a new revolution, but an insurrection by uneducated angry White men who are racist and jealous of what everyone has, especially people of color. I hope our President and DOJ will arrest them and try them for treason or put them down like the rabid animals they are. Their leader, a once-respected professor Albert Cochran, should be executed by firing squad for his treasonous acts and willful murder of innocent men, women, and children," said the emotional reporter.

It was the same message from a dozen more news stations around the country. If the Domestic Revolutionary Movement thought they had the support to form a new Confederacy, today their dreams were evaporating.

Professor Cochran, from behind his desk at the original Confederate White House in Richmond, Virginia, felt revulsion at what his militia soldiers were doing to all people of color. They had become a wild group of murderers, not a liberating army like he planned. Even though he found what his army was doing disgusting, he was not motivated to try to stop them.

* * * * *

Marching up Pennsylvania Avenue were five hundred National Guard troops. Tourists were watching and taking photos, unaware of what was about to happen. A few of the young National Guard Soldiers pointed their automatic weapons at the civilians, targeting only the people of color. Shouts of anger toward the soldiers started to escalate and were then controlled by the Capitol Police, who thought the soldiers were there to help them.

Without warning, half of the soldiers broke off and took up positions around the Capitol, and the other half headed toward the White House.

General Stuart could be heard shouting out orders. "When you receive my signal, it will be time to storm the Capitol and White House. Stick to your assignments and initiate them with precision. If the Capitol Police resist, use lethal force. Once the Capitol is breached, I want the Speaker of the House and Senate Majority leader roughed up and in handcuffs."

General Stuart then led the remaining soldiers toward the White House. "I will take enough men into the White House and arrest President Graham and her Attorney General and FBI Director."

The General did not notice he was being filmed, and that his orders were captured on video. A camera crew from an earlier news segment saw what was happening and started to film the unusual event. When the reporter heard what the General had said, realized she was witnessing a coup. She started talking into her handheld microphone.

"This is Susan Miller from CNN reporting to you from the Capitol. Maryland National Guard Soldiers have entered the Capitol grounds with the intention of capturing the Speaker of the House and Senate Majority Leader," she said emotionally. *"They are planning to remove the American Flag and replace it with a Confederate Flag. What we are witnessing is another seditious act on our democracy."* Before she could continue, General Stuart pointed his gun at her head and signaled the camera crew to stop filming.

The General ordered the Black reporter to the ground, putting his boot firmly on her back with his pistol still pointing at her head. "You're here to witness true American patriots taking back our country." He started chanting, *We will not be replaced,* and then put a bullet in the back of the head of the young reporter. Then, without warning, the other two cameramen, one Black and the other Asian, were shot at point-blank range.

The General, showing no emotions, ordered his men to neutralize the two Capitol Police guards at the entrance to the White House. He then proceeded to march with his men toward the White House main entrance.

Waiting by the front door to the White House were six Senators and fifteen House Representatives, ready to assume their new roles in the new Confederacy.

"General Stuart, I'm glad to see you were able to rid our country of these fucking minorities," the House Minority leader said. "It's taken almost ten years, but the wait will be worth it," Congressman Parsons from Alabama said.

As the men discussed their strategy outside, inside the White House, Commander McAllister was receiving data from Dean Miller's son Allan.

McAllister, with assistance from retired US Marshal Scott Rogers, positioned his men at all entry points, with snipers on the White House roof. Young Allan Miller had been vital in his use of his father's software. He was able to pinpoint all the traitors with up-to-the-minute locations for each of them so the White House and Capitol wouldn't be taken by surprise.

Sadly, even with the coordination with the Joint Chiefs, McAllister and his men were initially too late to prevent the needless slaughter happening in Florida, Alabama, Virginia, Tennessee, Kentucky, Georgia, South Carolina, Arkansas, and Texas. Even though they were caught off-guard, McAllister had enough manpower to start pushing back against the insurrectionists and regain control of all the Capitol buildings. Loss of life stood at a little over four thousand, three thousand of the rebels and one thousand innocent Americans.

69

Sipping four fingers of whiskey, Professor Cochran watched how the attack on the Capitol and White House was going. He was able to watch what was happening, as numerous news outlets were there recording the bloodshed.

What confused him was that the Capitol Police were ready, with backup from the FBI and Maryland SWAT.

Cochran started tugging at his thin gray hair and, using his other hand, tapped his cane on the cold marble floor nervously. What he saw put a knot in his stomach. Six hundred National Guard Soldiers were on their stomachs, their arms zip-tied behind their backs. Ten Senators and twelve Congressmen were being secured in the rotunda handcuffed and forced to kneel. Their protests echoed inside the great dome as they were roughly pushed into a secure location by the Capitol Police.

What he saw back at the White House was another story. When General Arlo Stuart, who led the National Guard, burst through the White House front door carrying a Confederate Flag, he and his soldiers were met with a barrage of gunfire. It was over in a matter of seconds. The five Senators and fifteen House Representatives who were right behind him stopped dead in their tracks when they saw what happened to General Stuart. They panicked, and tried to escape outside, but were stopped at gunpoint by five US Marshals. Five Senators soiled themselves and two fainted. The House Representatives started cursing and protesting at Commander McAllister and Bubba Jackson.

"You can't do this to us. We're elected officials and can't be arrested."

Commander McAllister could not control the grin cracking on his face. "You stopped being Congressmen when you made the decision to overthrow the democracy and constitution you swore to defend," he said. "If you're lucky, your treasonous act might let you die by firing squad, not hanging."

Outside, the remaining National Guard Soldiers had laid down their weapons and kneeled, their hands locked over their heads.

* * * * *

President Graham had been escorted back to the Situation Room after her Secret Service detail got word the White House was secure. Sitting in the room were her Joint Chiefs, FBI Director, Attorney General, Secretary of Defense, and Homeland Security Director. Standing off to the side were Commander McAllister and Bubba Jackson. They were stone-cold serious. Everyone else looked tired and stressed.

When President Graham entered, she began clapping at all the heroes who saved her and the country. "Wow, it's been an utterly hellish few hours," she said. She looked at the Chairman of the Joint Chiefs, General Ronald Hawkins. "Please give us an update on what's happening in the southern states?"

General Hawkins cleared his throat. "Madame President, we have not been able to secure all the Capitol buildings these rebels have occupied and hoisted their Confederate Flags in. Four southern Governors, all Democrats, have been hung outside their respective offices. There is sporadic fighting that we're trying to curtail but are meeting with local resistance from supporters of Professor Cochran," he said.

"Are you talking about American citizens using lethal force against our military and elected officials?" President Graham shot back. "I'm ordering you to use whatever lethal force you need to stop this insurrection. Is that understood?"

General Hawkins, without any emotion, replied, "Yes, Madame President, I understand. One other item regarding the ten thousand foreign soldiers at our southern border. After checking with the Mexican Government, they denied these men are their military."

"Then who are they?" President Graham asked.

"Foreign mercenaries from Iran and Argentina. I deployed ten Apache helicopters to the border, and with a few warning shots that intentionally destroyed their military vehicles, ordered them to lay down their weapons and move away from our border."

President Graham looked confused. "You didn't attempt to capture them?" she asked. "What if they return?"

"The Mexican military has them in custody and will make them available for deportation to Guantanamo," General Hawkins said proudly. "The Mexican President will be calling you to discuss some immigration changes he'd like to see."

McAllister's cell buzzed. He looked at the screen. "President Graham, Dean Miller, and his family just arrived, as well as Paige Turner and Scott Rogers. Should I escort them in now?"

"That's perfect timing. I want to meet the young man who saved me and our country with his early warning and precise details of the attack on Washington," the President said.

70

Two days after Cochran's failed civil war, Albert Dunham was heading toward the Otay Mesa border crossing. A Mexican border patrol officer had been paid off to look the other way when *The Architect* arrived. Waiting at the Tijuana Airport in a remote hangar was a private jet fueled and ready to fly Dunham to Hungary. Waiting for him on the jet was his old team, who had been disbanded after his presumed death.

"Frederick, you've done well. With Cochran's big fuck up, and President Graham trying to put out all the fires from the insurrection, it is time for my new manifesto to be introduced," Dunham said. "As much as I don't want to help her, I want you and your men to distribute the nerve gas in every southern state Cochran is still calling his new Confederacy," Dunham ordered.

Frederick Ellison was the only person Dunham trusted, and said, "Albert, can I be candid with you?"

"Always, friend," Dunham said.

"After escaping prison, I found the original chip Gregory Wilbanks created for us that went into the weapons satellite. We tested it. It works perfectly with Miller's software. Even though we don't have the NASA computer to hook up the weapons satellite, I'm sure the software we were able to replicate and use with our chip will allow you to accomplish what you wanted to do on the international monetary highway."

A big smile exploded on Dunham's face. "Are you telling me I can get into the monetary reserves of any country and skim money out while it travels electronically from financial institution to financial institution?"

"Yes. It might take a little tweaking, but Edmund Bennet believes with a little more time, he can duplicate Dean Miller's program and get you the trillions of dollars you so want," Ellison said.

Dunham was rubbing his hands, deep in thought. "I think we should let President Graham have her day in the sun, healing her country. Then we'll return to relieve her of her duties."

The plane got clearance to leave and was heading down the runway on its way to a small private airstrip in Hungary.

"Frederick, I never thought that letting Cochran have his fantasy about a new Confederacy would turn out to be a benefit for us," Dunham said.

"It is amazing how things turn out. Four years ago, after you survived the missile attack, I told you to have patience and let things play themselves out," Ellison said, puffing on his cigar. "Lacing President Thompson's water was a genius move on your part, Albert," Ellison said. "It appears that the autopsy did not turn up anything in his blood. It just appeared he had a massive stroke."

Dunham leaned back in his chair, smiling. "Yeah, that was a brilliant move on my part. However, President Graham has surprised me with her TNS attitude. Soon she'll find out what I can do to her."

Dunham needed to make one call before resting for the long flight. "Are all the vials in place?" he asked his lead chemist in Budapest.

"Sir, every single one of them is in place at every Capitol building in the South, and every DRM militia battalion in the remaining fifty states. The timers are active and ready for you to activate them when you're ready," he confirmed.

"Very good. Now go to your designated safe house and wait for my orders."

Feeling confident the first stage of his comeback as *The Architect* would be happening once he destroyed Cochran and his Domestic Revolutionary Movement for good. Finally, seeing a light at the end of the tunnel, he was able to close his eyes for a much-needed rest.

Before he closed his eyes, to his surprise, Frederick had the lovely flight attendant come to him with a drink. "Mister Dunham, I'm very happy you asked for me. I look forward to helping you relax after we land," she said, allowing her slender hand with long nails to lightly caress his groin.

Dunham gulped down his Scotch and closed his eyes. For the first time in a long time, he felt at peace.

71

Dean Miller and his family walked into the Situation Room and were escorted to three chairs behind the President. Before they were seated, everyone stood and began clapping as father and son blushed at all the fanfare directed at them.

President Graham kept standing and extended her hand toward the young man. "What you did during this insurrection was remarkable. I wish I had more people in my administration with your cool and calm demeanor."

Allan blushed. He was normally shy around strangers, but being next to the President, in the Situation Room with everyone there, was too much for him to handle.

Dean Miller interrupted the President. "We are not out of the woods just yet. There are ten thousand foreign fighters from Argentina who are part of Hitler's old Brown Shirt Brigade being led by his grandson, Wilhelm. They have found shelter twenty miles inland with the largest drug cartel in Mexico. I believe an invasion is imminent."

The Chairman of the Joint Chiefs was getting impatient. "Madame President, can we stop worrying about a possible invasion and make a concrete plan to stop all the attacks that are still going on in our country?"

Admiral Roger Williams, Vice-Chairman of the Joint Chiefs, barged into the conversation. "President Graham. It's highly irregular to have civilians in the Situation Room, especially ones who have not gotten a security clearance," he said.

President Graham smirked at the two men. "We are not dealing with normal times right now. Almost half of the country wants to split us in half and create the Confederate States of America. We have too many foreign enemies that want to see our democracy destroyed and replaced with a new autocratic structure,"

225

she said. "I've spoken with Attorney General Sam Collins, and he agrees with me that Dean Miller and his family should head up my new Presidential Cyber Security detail. They will report directly to me and the FBI Director. Director Glass concurs with this decision too."

The President's announcement surprised Dean Miller, and especially his son Allan. "Madame President, I am honored you feel I can help you and our country, but I am not so sure I can work inside your West Wing," he said. "After what just happened, my full attention needs to be focused on the mid-terms and getting the *We the People* party in a position to make a difference for every citizen and our country. Our country is at a crossroads, and I feel I can be better served supporting the people of the United States of America."

"I know about your movement, and I support it one hundred percent. Our country is so divided by conspiracies and lies that the average voter does not know who to trust or who to believe. Your new position inside the West Wing will not interfere with what you want to do. In fact, it should help my administration accomplish what needs to be done to return our democracy back to the greatness it once was."

Dean did not look very confident with what the President was saying. "My movement will shake up the very foundation of our current two-party system. Do you really want to be associated with this?"

President Graham smiled. "Your honesty is exactly what I need inside my administration. You might not know this, but I am a Progressive Independent who has worked with both sides of the aisle for over twenty years. Your *We the People* movement is not too different from what I believe this country needs. So, take a day and think about my offer. Let me know tomorrow if you'll serve at the pleasure of your President?"

After the Millers left the Situation Room for their temporary quarters in the White House residence, the planning session got underway.

* * * * *

Paige Turner was waiting upstairs in the White House residence for the Millers. She already knew what the President asked of the Millers and her. She wanted to convince her friend that working inside the West Wing would be a great move to accomplish the next political party.

72

The Chairman of the Joint Chiefs and the Secretary of Defense were arguing about the method the military should use to stop and curb the rebel traitors who were murdering women and children of color and destroying property as they marched through the South. Both men saw things differently.

The crux of their argument focused on the National Guard in all the southern states who were supporting the Confederate Rebels and, in some cases, fighting alongside them. General Hawkins wanted to either arrest them and try them for treason, or go in with one swift move and kill all of them and save the country the heartache of a multi-year trial.

The Secretary of Defense saw the problem in a different light. "We can't arbitrarily murder American citizens, especially with our own military without a trial and letting justice do its job," Wallace Boyce, the Secretary of Defense, said.

General Hawkins bit his lower lip before replying. "Madame President. This is why having a civilian running our defense department is a piss poor idea. A military strategy needs to be implemented by career soldiers," he said. "Unless we act with lethal swiftness, thousands more Americans of color will be lying dead in our streets."

Sam Collins felt it was necessary to join in the argument. "There are always two sides to every argument. However, our circumstances have put all of us in a precarious position," he said. "My team has redefined what a domestic terrorist is and the punishment for being part of an insurrection—" before the Attorney General could continue, Secretary Boyce interrupted him.

"A large swath of our population believes these rebels are exercising their rights under the First Amendment and that like the founders who had their own insurrection against the British are nothing more than patriots trying to build a better America for their families," Boyce said.

Sam was getting livid at the comments by the Secretary of Defense after what he had witnessed by these traitors. "These animals can no longer call themselves patriots after they've murdered innocent men, women, and children. They are gangster terrorists and should be treated like them."

Secretary Boyce shook his head, unable to argue anymore, throwing his arms in the air. "I give up. Madame President, if you follow these men and go down this path, you are dooming our democracy forever."

FBI Director Glass jumped into the conversation. "As law enforcement, these rebels need to be dealt with speedily and harshly. They need to be made an example of so anyone or group thinking they should start a coup would think twice before trying to overthrow our democracy. Let them exercise their right to free speech and peaceful assembly and then use our court system to make the changes they want. Using hate and conspiracy theories to unite a vulnerable electorate will not be tolerated anymore," Tiffany said. "Voltaire said: *'Those who can make you believe absurdities can make you commit atrocities.'*"

The President's Chief of Staff for the first time spoke up. "Madame President, after we curtail this insurrection, we still have another more menacing problem: Albert Dunham, *The Architect*. He still has his bioweapon. If he's allowed to go into hiding, none of us are safe," she said.

The meeting went on for another three hours. The final solution for the insurrection was to end it like you'd stop an invasion by a foreign power.

* * * * *

SEAL Team 6 was outside the old Confederacy White House in Richmond, Virginia, getting ready to breach the building. Commander McAllister had been reactivated as well as his retired army of dedicated soldiers willing to do battle for their country one more time.

Commander McAllister signaled his team to hold back while he tried to communicate with Professor Cochran. He was unaware that The Professor was being interviewed by a popular right-wing media station with viewers of over a hundred million loyal listeners watching.

McAllister's cell buzzed. It was from Dean Miller. "John, call off your men. You'll have over a hundred million Americans watching live what you are about to do," Miller said.

"Shit," he said. He signaled his team leader to stand down. "Any idea when the interview will be over?"

"No clue," Miller said. "I think The Professor and the media network want to put you and President Graham front and center of murdering loyal patriotic Americans."

Commander McAllister and his SEAL team fell back to a neutral position until it was all clear to resume their attack.

73

Cochran had dressed for his interview wearing a replica of General Robert E. Lee's Confederate Uniform. He looked like he was fitted for the military uniform at a costume shop. It was so baggy it made him look like a clown. He had added the DRM insignia and a Nazi Flag patch to both his shoulders. He was not going to shun the racist beliefs that his soldiers supported.

The reporter started his questions by being very direct with the leader of the DRM. "General Cochran, that's what I should call you, right?"

Cochran nodded his approval. "Yes, General is perfectly correct. Hopefully soon to be the new President of the Confederate States of America."

"Aren't you getting ahead of yourself? It doesn't appear you're winning this civil war."

"We've already won," Cochran said. "We have over a hundred million Americans living in the South who support me and our movement. Remember that this country is trying to make Whites, like me, a minority, a second-class group that will be discriminated against so we can experience firsthand what people of color have been complaining about for hundreds of years." The Professor was breathing heavily unable to catch his breath. "We will not be replaced," he shouted into his microphone. He repeated it a dozen times. Each time, his voice got louder. "What I've accomplished is something General Lee could not have done—" the reporter cut him off.

"Wait one minute. You are still saying you won the war. The Confederate States of America has happened?" The reporter seemed surprised by Cochran's answer and arrogance.

Cochran was nodding. He glanced at his cell phone. His face turned bedsheet white. "I have to end this interview." He looked into the camera and in a raised voice said, "My loyal patriots, we have not lost. We have thousands of sleeper cells positioned around the country. I am ordering them to continue fighting while the Domestic Revolutionary Movement waits for reinforcements," and marched away from his desk. He craned his neck and started chanting: "We will not be replaced," holding his fist above his head.

The reporter, from a far-right network, looked into his camera, acting bewildered. "I am not sure what we just witnessed," he said. "While I was rooting for The Professor and the Domestic Revolutionary Movement to win this war, I am not so sure General Cochran is the right person for the job."

* * * * *

Professor Cochran was downstairs in the basement meeting with what was left of his Captains. "Is this true?" he asked.

"Sir, they were all stopped and arrested at the Capitol in DC, as well as the White House. General Arlo Stuart is dead. Killed as he tried to storm the White House. Our soldiers are surrendering and throwing down their weapons," he said. "Our congressional loyalists have been arrested for treason."

"I know about what happened at the White House. They can't arrest federal officials for treason. They were just performing their job duties to save our country," Cochran said.

The captain pursed his lips, afraid to contradict The Professor. "Sir, the Attorney General, Sam Collins, at the direction of the President has redefined what a domestic terrorist is and what acts constitute treasonous behavior. To make matters worse, all of your soldiers and loyal members of Congress are being transferred to Guantanamo for interrogation and then their trials."

Cochran lowered his head and threw his arms in the air, disgusted with how his revolution was working out. He walked off toward his residence upstairs to be with his wife. He did not want to be arrested and spend the rest of his life in prison. He had an escape plan; he just needed his wife Estelle to agree to come with him.

The Professor was in panic mode, sweating profusely in his Confederate Uniform. The last time he felt like this was when Charles Stone failed, and the FBI was closing in on him and the White Angels.

Sitting on a large, bright green and yellow floral couch was Estelle. She looked frightened. Looking at her husband, she knew after fifty-four years of marriage and supporting his racist views, there was pain etched on his face. "Albert, I've seen the news. You made a valiant effort, but your racial platform did not work again. The DRM failed ten years ago and then under *The Architect's* Manifesto failed again. You need to surrender and let your movement heal and regroup," she said.

"I'm not ready to concede. As a pure White man, I have rights and expect them to be honored by everyone in the United States," he ranted. "I need to escape and reorganize again as I did after the last two failures. It won't take much to convince our patriots in every state that our way of life is the only way for White men to raise their families," he said. "Now, pack a bag. We need to go now before Commander McAllister storms our residence."

Estelle was shaking her head at her husband. She was disappointed with him, and it showed on her face. "I guess you did see the announcement by President Graham. Commander McAllister was reinstated with full pay and rank. Albert, I'm not going anywhere with you. I haven't done anything wrong. I want the good life I still have, whether it's with you or not."

Cochran was squeezing the grip of his sword, his jaw clenching. He could not believe his wife was defying him. "You will either support me or die right here and now," he shouted.

Estelle had never seen her husband so enraged. "What are you going to do, kill me?" she yelled back at him. "Can't you see how crazy you sound?"

Cochran's voice was a low, menacing whisper. "Don't say that. You do know what I do to people who are not loyal to me?"

"Like you did to Charles Stone?" Estelle replied.

With the swiftness of a swordsman, Cochran pulled his blade out of his sheave and, with one quick sweep, decapitated his wife. The green/blue floral couch was splattered with blood from his wife's severed head. Estelle lay slumped over, motionless.

Cochran sucked in a nervous breath, said goodbye to his dead wife, and sprinted down the stairs toward another underground tunnel General Lee had built for his escape when the Civil War ended. As he jumped down the stairs two at a time, his mind swam back to when he murdered Charles Stone by decapitation. "Damn, it's getting easier," he muttered.

74

McAllister got the all clear and ordered his team to storm the building. With a perfectly timed breach, SEAL Team 6 and fifteen SWAT officers, with their weapons at the ready, entered from all access points of the old Confederate White House.

Before they could release their flashbangs, they were met with a barrage of fire from the few untrained Confederate Soldiers left inside the building by Professor Cochran. Undeterred, SEAL Team 6 and SWAT returned fire, and within seconds, the enemy lay dead inside.

Commander McAllister followed close behind his men and once he was sure the building was neutralized, he started his search for Professor Cochran. "Bubba, take your men and clear the basement," he ordered. "I'll check the residence upstairs."

Proceeding with caution, McAllister signaled his men to clear the approaching bedroom while he headed toward the living room. It was too quiet for his liking as he pointed his Berretta, ready for any resistance. When he made the left turn, what he saw caused him to gag.

Seeing the woman lying on the blood-soaked couch, her head resting next to the open wound that was once her neck, reminded him of the savageness that the Taliban left behind when they punished young girls and their mothers. "Bubba, get your butt up here now. Cochran killed his wife, the same way he did Charles Stone. These guys are animals," McAllister barked, his voice cracking.

He bounded upstairs and cleared the rest of the second floor. Cochran was nowhere to be found. He dialed Roger Stillwell. "Can you get our satellite positioned on this location and see who might have left the property? Use infrared. I believe The Professor had another escape tunnel. It's like Vietnam all over again."

Stillwell replied, "I anticipated your wishes, John. There's another large tunnel that stretches approximately two hundred miles south to North Carolina."

"Any movement in the tunnel about an hour earlier?"

"I should have my report in about ten minutes," Stillwell said. "What's it look like down there?"

"I'll tell you when I see you. It's disgusting what a human being will do to keep his power."

Bubba stood motionless over the body of Estelle Cochran. "How can anyone do this to someone who shared their life for over fifty years?" He caught himself before screaming.

Jackson met up with the Commander downstairs. "Stillwell says there is a tunnel under this house that stretches two hundred miles to North Carolina. I want you to take your team and one of our attack helicopters and find this bastard before he exits this tunnel," ordered McAllister.

The Commander was on his cell briefing the President and the FBI Director. "It was a slaughter down here. The men Cochran called soldiers were nothing more than uneducated White trash young boys with no combat experience. It's possible they had never fired an automatic rifle before."

Tiffany had a question. "John, how many prisoners do you have?"

"Approximately a hundred and fifty, and fifty soldiers who are in critical condition from either self-inflicted gunshot wounds or from combat."

"I'm sure you haven't listened to the news. Two radical news outlets are accusing President Graham of the genocide of Americans who were defending their right to protest and free speech," Director Glass said.

"That's a load of crap, Director. We tried to get them to surrender, but they refused and opened fire on us."

Sam spoke up. "Someone released a video of the slaughter that is not showing you and your men in a favorable light," the Attorney General said.

"Who was recording this?"

"It appears Cochran had security cameras positioned inside and around his White House. If what you say is correct and The Professor escaped, then I can venture a guess he released the video to stir up his loyal followers as he tries to regroup," Sam said.

"I'm sending you a video of what Cochran did to his wife. It's horrible. Maybe you should release it to see if it turns his ignorant followers against him," McAllister said angrily.

"We'll review the video and let you know. Don't get your hopes up. His followers believe The Professor is a God," Sam said. "Oh, a heads up. Paige Turner is on her way down to you to review the aftermath of the insurrection. Give her access to whatever she wants," Sam said.

McAllister blew out a loud breath. "I hope she doesn't get in my way. It's still a powder keg down here and she won't be safe. Turner is less popular than me currently."

75

Paige arrived forty-five minutes after McAllister finished briefing the President. She had brought her cameraman and administrative assistant. She wore blue jeans, an orange tank top, and a Los Angeles Rams baseball cap and was turning many heads with her hair pulled back into a ponytail and no makeup or lipstick.

McAllister knew how beautiful she was, but today in a war zone, she looked exceptionally radiant. "Paige, President Graham said to expect you and to give you free access to anything you might need."

Paige smiled and extended her hand. "Commander McAllister, thank you for your cooperation. I'm here to document what happened and give a truthful side to the insurrection."

The Commander became livid. "There is only one truth here." He pointed at the new Confederate White House. "This was the beginning of a civil war. There is nothing else to report."

Paige remained calm at the Commander's outburst, realizing he had just finished fighting for his life. "Sir, it's not even been a day and many Senators want a full investigation into what President Graham authorized against Americans," Turner said. "I am here to report the truth, nothing more. So let me do my job. I think you'll be happy with what I document."

McAllister looked like he wanted to shoot someone as his facial muscles tensed. "Are we going to have another rewriting of history with this insurrection?"

Paige shrugged her shoulders. "It appears these Senators and even House Representatives are the same ones who tried to paint the January 6, 2020 siege on the Capitol as just American patriots exercising their freedom to protest," she said. "There is talk of impeaching President Graham for authorizing the military to attack and murder American citizens."

"That's bullshit. There is enough proof that the Domestic Revolutionary Movement, led by Professor Cochran, has committed heinous acts by murdering thousands of innocent men, women, and children," McAllister said.

"That's why I am here. The actual facts need to be told," Paige said.

"Do you really believe that the truth will change the opinions of the DRM supporters?"

Paige shook her head. "That's a good question that I don't have an answer for," she said. "Let me get started with my investigation for President Graham, and then we can talk some more. Our country has been changing over the last twenty years, triggering voters to become desensitized to what each side is saying. I believe our country needs a reboot and our constitution needs to be updated so it deals with issues and rights that are relevant today," Paige said as she walked off toward a group of Confederate Soldiers cuffed and sitting under a tall oak tree.

Paige positioned herself and her cameraman with the sun behind them and sat down on a folding chair McAllister had set up for her. In a typical Turner expression, she smiled at all the soldiers.

"I'm reporter Paige Turner and I am here to get your side of this civil war you tried to accomplish. I'll be asking you," she pointed at all the soldiers, "what you were trying to achieve and where all of this hate for America came from."

Paige extended her microphone and asked a soldier who had bloodied bandages on his hands and head, "Tell me what the mission of the Domestic Revolutionary Movement is?"

Turner was surprised that each soldier seemed puzzled by her question. "You do know that you are part of the DRM, right?"

One soldier spoke up. "Miss, we joined because we needed the money to support our families. We were told that we are being *replaced,* and if we didn't try to stop the Jews from bringing into our country Blacks and Mexicans, we'd be working for Jews and niggers and cartel gangs." He crossed his arms in front of his chest and started chanting: "We will not be replaced; we will not be replaced."

Within minutes, the entire camp started mimicking the chant. After it quieted down, Paige tried to resume her interviewing with these men "Now that you have it out of your system, can you tell me where you get your news?"

Another soldier with three stripes on his sleeve spoke up. "We have been lied to by you people in the press for most of our lives. We now have our own honest news outlets on social media and network news stations that support our cause and speak the truth to us," he said.

Paige's eyes grew wide with disbelief as he spewed out his one-sided opinion. "Let me show you some photos of what your leaders have done to innocent Americans," she said as she passed around the pictures.

As the photos got passed around from soldier to soldier, what happened next shocked her.

"Little lady, these are fake, staged pictures. If they are true, then the Jews and Blacks did it to make us look bad," he said, tossing them back at Paige.

Commander McAllister had been watching Turner's interview and felt these prisoners were getting too wild even for her. He walked over and stepped in front of her, eclipsing the soldiers from her view. "Paige, it's time that these interviews ended. We need to move these men out and secure them in a federal Facility," he said.

Paige looked up at him, not objecting. "Yeah, I think I'm done here anyway. I've got more than I need to present to the President," she said.

* * * * *

Inside the command tent, Paige and McAllister sat with a warm cup of coffee. The Commander spoke first, breaking the ice. "How did your interview go?" he said, a smug look on his face.

Paige recognized his arrogant question and gave him a big, friendly smile. "Surprisingly well. I already knew the answers to my questions. I just needed these boys to say it aloud so I could video them."

"What will you do with these videos?"

"Show them to President Graham and then broadcast them on my next podcast. It's important that Americans see these animals for who they really are. They are not the victims they are making themselves out to be," Paige said.

"You really believe that the so-called rational Americans will do anything about any of this?" he asked.

"I sure hope so. If not, our country and democracy are forever doomed."

McAllister handed her a video camera and told her to watch as he pressed the play button. Paige looked at the Commander. "What am I watching?" she asked

238

"That's Cochran's wife Estelle. He decapitated her right before he escaped."

Paige looked like she would throw up. "Can I get a copy of this, please?"

"I already made one for you," McAllister said. "I hope you use it and get the far-right radicals to shut up about calling these murderers patriots."

76

It had been ten days since the resurrection started with over eight thousand Americans dead. Small pockets of single-shooter incidents kept popping up in every state. Other than that, the country was quiet, an eerie silence for the first time since President Graham took office.

The FBI and Interpol were actively hunting for Professor Cochran and Albert Dunham. It was as if they had vanished off the face of the earth.

It was a tragic time for the country. Six thousand domestic terrorists and two thousand innocent Americans were being buried. President Graham refused to label these traitors as Confederate Soldiers so as to not give them any legitimacy. She remained adamant that they were traitors and will be dealt with as such by her Attorney General.

Since President Graham had taken office, she had not been able to lay out her economic agenda nor have President Thompson lay in state. His cause of death could not be accurately determined, but the coroner wanted more time to run additional tests.

President Graham could not wait any longer and needed to get on with her agenda of how she would bring the country back together. She called a meeting with her entire Cabinet to review the fallout from the news outlets regarding the military action she took against American citizens. Calls for her impeachment were getting louder and picking up steam.

Every Secretary in her administration arrived at the Cabinet room early. Her Cabinet was filled with leftovers from President Thaddeus Thompson's short time in office.

President Graham came with the only people she currently trusted. Today, she knew she'd be making changes that would further rattle the halls of Congress.

In attendance with the President were her Chief of Staff, the Attorney General, and the FBI Director. Sitting next to her was her Press Secretary and her new cyber security chief, Dean Miller.

Commander McAllister and Bubba Jackson asked to be left in the field to hunt down the leads they had on Professor Cochran. Dean Miller and his son Allan discovered the glitch in their software and made the necessary corrections. They felt confident that The Professor would soon be found.

Cochran's last known location was a hidden room inside the tunnel under his Confederate White House in Richmond, Virginia. A forensic team from the FBI followed Commander McAllister down to Virginia to go over every inch of the Confederate White House, looking for clues that might indicate Cochran's next move.

Before her meeting, the President studied a file Miller had created for her that exposed the Cabinet Secretaries who supported the DRM and Professor Cochran. Heads were going to roll, and it wasn't going to be pretty.

The President looked up and smiled. "I'm happy to see all of you here today. With everything that's happened since President Thompson died, I haven't had a moment's rest to talk about my agenda and what I want my administration to accomplish in the next three years. It's very important I have people working in my administration who are loyal to me, and our constitution." Graham paused, hoping what she just said was sinking in.

She stood up and started pacing around the room, her hands locked behind her back. "I know there are some of you who support the Domestic Revolutionary Movement. Over the next few weeks, I will be weeding out all of our country's traitors," she said, stopping behind a few Cabinet Secretaries and pinching their shoulders. Then, she walked away and gave them a passing glance, and continued talking.

"Not since 1861, our first Civil War, have American citizens declared war on democracy and our constitution. For almost two decades, racist hate has been escalating to a point that it has now become mainstream with the far-right party. The Progressive Left Party verbalizes its complaints but doesn't do anything about the problems. Not addressing this problem makes all of us guilty. My top priority will be to call out all White Supremacists by name in the media and in the halls of Congress, so every American will be able to choose who they want to stand by. None of us can have it both ways. You're either a racist or you're not. There is no middle ground in my administration or in the country I was elected Vice President to protect and defend before I was thrown into the presidency after Thompson's death." President Graham was staring at the four Cabinet members who were acting uncomfortable.

"Over the next few weeks, I will be meeting with each of you individually and asking you to re-take your oath of office and to take a lie detector test to find out if you're a White Supremacist or not." President Graham noticed her Attorney General was ready to chime in.

Sam Collins knew ahead of time what the President was going to announce about a lie detector test. He had advised her that what she wanted to do was illegal, but she said it did not matter when it came to saving democracy.

The Attorney General knew the Secretaries on her list who were going to be called out and observed them fidgeting in their seats. He took a deep, cleansing breath before he started to speak.

"Gentlemen and Ladies, our country has gotten to a sad point with all the division and polarization that has been festering for the last ten years. Liars and spreaders of conspiracy theories in our government, on social media, and network media are out for power, money, and control. These leaders are abusing the entrusted power and are pushing their listeners to do the most unthinkable crimes. The most recent Cabinet member was our CIA Director, Porter Ramsey. He will be our first to be tried for treason and his seditious behavior.

"My office has focused our priorities on stopping any form of domestic terrorism and all illegal militia groups by redefining what a domestic terrorist is, and which militia groups will be classified as terrorists," the Attorney General said as many members started to squirm in their chairs. "When each of you comes in for your lie detector test, you will first be sworn in, and asked to tell the truth, the whole truth and nothing but the truth so help you, God—" Before Sam could continue, four Cabinet members stood and stormed out of the room, giving the President and Sam a single-finger salute.

President Graham was relieved that the four Cabinet members who were on Dean Miller's list revealed themselves on their own. She knew that her Secret Service detail would be detaining them as they left the room.

"Does anyone else want to object to what Attorney General Collins said?" President Graham asked.

The Secretary of Defense spoke. "Madame President, I applaud you. It's about time your office confronts White Supremacy. I hope you will put them in a coffin where they belong," Wallace Boyce said.

President Graham was pleased she was getting support from her remaining Cabinet Secretaries. "Sam, thank you for your commitment to rebuilding the DOJ to one of the most respected law enforcement agencies in the world. We all need to multi-task so our country can get back on track. Our war against White Supremacy is far from over, however; our economy needs to get back to how it was before the recent attack on America."

Sam raised his hand, wanting to speak. "Madame President, the DOJ has a clear definitive direction it will take to arrest and prosecute all White Supremacists and domestic terrorists. The Supreme Court can decide if what I will be doing is legal. It will be a good test of what our constitution meant when they gave all of us *Freedom of Speech and Freedom to peaceful protests*. I promise you I'll prosecute anyone who is a threat to our democracy, either through physical attacks or verbal attacks that incite people to commit crimes. That will include any media commentator or elected official who incites people to riot," the Attorney General said.

FBI Director Glass chimed in. "I'm thankful that the Attorney General and you, Madame President, have greenlit my department to take the battle to all illegal militia groups. I am sure I will be keeping the DOJ very busy." Tiffany said.

The rest of the meeting looked like a corporate board meeting, except that each Cabinet Secretary was given specific instructions on how to run their agency. The most stunning order was that it would be unlawful to be lobbied by any organization or corporation. No lunch or dinner meetings with Cabinet Secretaries. The bottom-line President Graham spelled out was that each department has a specific job to do, and she did not want any pressure from outside sources to influence how they performed their duties.

Before President Graham dismissed her Cabinet, she had one more thing to add to all these new guidelines. "Every ninety days, each agency will have an open hearing on C-SPAN so lobbyists can pitch what they need from all of you. Being open and attended by all lobbyists will allow the public to see how our government works for them," she said. "Now go back to your offices and get all of your staff on board with what I want. If you or your staff don't comply, then I will ask for your resignation or fire you."

Secretary of State Hanna Black made a comment about all the things the President wanted to do. "I've been working inside the halls of Congress, DOJ, and State Department for over thirty years, and what you are proposing will get you a ton of backlash from both sides of the aisle and every state Attorney General and maybe our foreign allies. You'll be buried knee-deep in lawsuits that will keep you from achieving your bold agenda," she said.

President Graham rubbed her chin, deep in thought. "I don't disagree with you. I'm ready for it. As a woman and ex-CEO of a large tech company, I know how to multi-task and get all that I want to be accomplished," she responded. "My objective is to reverse how our government is going and to have it finally work for the people who fund democracy with their tax dollars."

The Secretary of Commerce raised his hand. "Madame President. What you've proposed is all well and good, but businesses stationed here in America and around the world that do business here won't stand for paying more in taxes," said Daniel McGuire.

"Dan, I have a workable plan for all businesses doing business in our country," she said, opening a red folder. "First, let's be realistic about the corporations that are making billions of dollars and not paying any taxes to the country that is giving them a great opportunity to be successful," President Graham said.

Daniel interrupted her. "Ma'am, most businesses will disagree with you on that, too. They do pay taxes and they feel they are the ones creating their own success. They pay FICA on all their employees and tariffs on the goods they import."

Graham tried to contain her laughter. "That's hysterical. They've been using that argument for decades. I'm going to impose a minimum corporate tax that is higher than the one that's in effect today. It's a tax they can afford without having to raise prices or cut salaries. Like my predecessors before me, I feel they need to pay their fair share and contribute like all our citizens."

After the meeting ended, President Graham retired to the residence for a relaxing cocktail with her husband, Michael Graham, a corporate tax attorney.

77

Bubba Jackson was briefing McAllister that Professor Cochran had been spotted in North Carolina hiding out in an apartment building functioning as a women's shelter for abused women. Currently, young children and pregnant mothers occupied it. It was believed Cochran was hunkering down with twenty of his security team ready to use the women and children as human shields.

"Do we have any way of getting in and out without killing innocents?" McAllister asked.

"Sergeant Ron Arnold has three snipers on a roof across from the apartment building. The area where Cochran is holed up has all the windows boarded up. We have no visual," Jackson said. "Corporal Klein has ears inside and can hear everything Cochran is saying to his security team through their stat phones. If we breach the building, the security team has orders to murder as many Black women and children as possible."

"We dealt with this same thing in Afghanistan. You remember that we pumped in a gas that put everyone to sleep?" the Commander asked.

"Yes, but we still had some collateral damage when two pregnant mothers had an allergic reaction to the chemical. The higher-ups wanted to roast your ass for using that weapon," Bubba answered.

"Yeah, but nothing came of it since we freed all of the hostages. Can we get our hands on that incapacitating agent again?"

"I already have it. I anticipated you'd want to use it under these circumstances. It's a milder form of sleeping gas," Jackson said. "You going to brief the President? Sam or Tiffany?"

"President Graham gave me full autonomy while I am in the field. She wants results and I'm going to give them to her."

"What I secured for you is a chemical agent like the one used by Russia in 2002 when Chechen terrorists held over eight hundred hostages in a theater. This gas I secured is milder. It does not have fentanyl. Too many hostages died then. What I secured from my friend at the FDA is like what you'd get if you were having surgery."

"Tell Sergeant Arnold to have everything ready. Once we're there, I want a quick and swift breach with no collateral damage," McAllister said.

* * * * *

Cochran was once again on his favorite network media outlet, to the surprise of President Graham and Sam Collins. "Madame President, I'm not sure this far-right media station can be labeled as a domestic terrorist or aiding and abetting traitors," the Attorney General said.

"Then can we get them removed as a news outlet and barred from being on any national airway?" President Graham asked.

"I don't think so, plus the only Americans listening to these lies are their loyal followers, who would never change their minds no matter how many times we show them the truth," Sam responded. "Let's see what Cochran has to say."

"Friends of the DRM and loyal soldiers to our revolution, I am alive and well in North Carolina. I am being hunted by President Graham and her hired assassins, led by Commander John McAllister. They are trying to eliminate our people from the face of the earth and erase our wonderful heritage that helped form this great nation. I haven't had time to mourn my wife's gruesome murder by Commander McAllister and his mercenaries but will continue to fight on until we have our new Confederate States of America, which we can call our new home."

He pointed to a monitor that showed his wife and her decapitated head on their large floral couch. Cochran continued speaking.

"While I lost the love of my life for the last fifty-four years, patriots, don't hide, don't be scared. I'm not. We will prevail and have our own country very soon. Sleeper cells, you have your orders. It's time to strike another decisive blow to the heart of President Graham and her illegitimate government."

* * * * *

246

Ten minutes after Cochran ended his speech, Commander McAllister gave the order to release the sleeping gas. He watched on his monitor, waiting to see Cochran fall into a deep slumber.

"Good night, you butcher. When you wake up, you'll be in chains like the animal you are," the Commander said to the monitor.

It took only five minutes for the sleeping agent to work. McAllister's team, with an assist from the FBI, broke down the barricaded entry door and started zip-tying all the Confederate Soldiers. Bubba Jackson rushed up two flights of stairs to where it was believed The Professor was hiding.

Leaning into the apartment door with his muscular shoulder, Jackson stumbled in. Inside, four of Cochran's security team lay motionless. Bubba was surprised that Cochran was not in his apartment.

"Sir, Cochran is not on the second floor. I'll search every apartment, but I have a terrible feeling we've been fooled by that slippery old bastard."

After the entire building was searched, and the women and children were safe, Professor Cochran was nowhere to be found. Did Dean Miller's software have an error?

* * * * *

Cochran was never in North Carolina. He was hiding in a room in the tunnel at the Confederate White House. With his arms extended toward the blue sky, Cochran thanked God he had fooled McAllister again. He hugged his cyber expert. "I didn't believe you could do this, but you did," he said. "Can you continue to send false flags to Miller's software so we can continue our revolution?"

Lucas Jones was a soldier in the American Nazi Party and Silicon Valley cyber expert. He had worked for Dean Miller when he was a professor at Stanford. "For now, I'd say yes. If Miller or his son gets involved, though, there is no telling what they might throw at us."

78

Commander McAllister and Bubba Jackson, still reeling from another embarrassing attempt to capture Cochran, went back to the last sighting of The Professor.

On a hunch, they started ripping apart the living room where Estelle Cochran was murdered. They didn't know what they were looking for, but had a hunch The Professor's wife, a security nut, might have a few video devices hidden in the residence.

After the entire residence was searched, Bubba found a laptop inside a safe that was in Estelle's walk-in closet. She had it password protected. Commander McAllister asked Raymond Stillwell if he could unlock the computer.

"How long to unlock this laptop?" the Commander asked.

Raymond snapped out the hard drive and began copying the files onto a new hard drive. "This should take about thirty minutes. Then, if we are lucky, I will be able to read all the files Estelle had on her computer, providing her files are not encrypted," Stillwell said.

Raymond met McAllister downstairs and laid his laptop on the desk inside The Professor's office. "I guess Estelle didn't feel safe around her husband because she had a state-of-the-art security system installed throughout the entire house," he said with a big smile on his face.

McAllister knew Raymond very well and when he smiled, it meant he found something big. "Ray, in short, easy-to-understand sentences, what did you find?"

"A treasure chest of videos with sound," he said. He clicked on a file labeled security and let the McAllister watch what he had seen upstairs.

"Shit. We've got video of The Professor demanding his wife escape with him and when she refused, he swung his sword like a baseball player hitting a home run, connecting with his wife's neck." McAllister looked like he would throw up seeing her head fly in the air and land on the carpet by her feet.

"That's not all we have. We've got every phone conversation The Professor had with his Generals, supporters in Congress, and his militia in twenty-three states. If I didn't know better, we have the concrete proof Sam needs to lock up all these bastards," Stillwell said.

"I need to get this back to President Graham. She's not going to believe all the Senators and House Reps that communicated with The Professor about the planned coup and jockeying for a powerful position in the new Confederate States of America," the Commander said.

Stillwell was still smiling. "In this file, she recorded all the conversations her husband had with the West Wing staff under President Thompson and currently in Graham's White House. There are so many traitors in Washington that, when exposed, could tank the economy and open us up to attacks from our foreign enemies."

McAllister grabbed the hard drive from Stillwell and was out the front door. He jogged over to the attack helicopter and told Bubba they were going back to the White House.

79

In a secluded chalet deep in the mountains in Hungry, *The Architect* was having a meeting with his team. Fredrick Ellison, his best friend and right hand, was pressing keys on his laptop. He started humming. "Albert, with a little more tweaking, I think you'll have what you need to get everything back on track. You'll, I mean, we'll be rich beyond our imagination," Ellison said.

Dunham had gotten excited with the news. "You sure I'll be able to siphon money again into my accounts? What about controlling computer networks around the world?"

"Right now, this software can only infiltrate the internet highway where all money transactions flow. Our software can, how can I say it, re-direct small amounts of dollars as they move from one financial institution to another and from one country to another. To stay under the radar of any monitoring system, I will have to set it up where you'll steal approximately a hundred million dollars a day. That amount is under ten dollars per transaction, and it won't even get noticed until it's too late. Even then, they'll never figure out where their money has gone," Ellison said.

"That's billions of dollars each month," Dunham said. "You've done good, Frederick."

"Give me the word and I can get this started right now, while President Graham is hunting for Cochran and all of his conspirators."

"Do it. I need a timeline of when you'll get me control of the satellite again. It's crucial for my manifesto to work," Dunham said.

"Bennett is working on it as we speak. He needs more time. He discovered that ex-President Chesterfield wanted to destroy his weapon but found he couldn't. So, he had Miller put in a state-of-the-art firewall to keep any hackers out," Ellison said.

"Who can break into the firewall if not Bennett?" Dunham asked.

"Dean Miller."

"Okay. Send Julian Marshall and let him take the men he would need to kidnap Miller."

80

Sam and Tiffany were back at the Mayflower Hotel, cuddling on a large couch in their suite with their children. It had been too long since they had a moment to themselves and their children.

"Sam, I'll ask again. Are we doing the right thing?" Tiffany asked.

"Yes. Our country needs us more than ever," Sam said. "Who else will step up to do our jobs?"

"Do you feel safe with Professor Cochran on the run and Dunham somewhere in Europe?" she asked.

Irene had started to fidget listening to her parents talk shop. "Dad, what is Mom scared of?"

"Nothing, sweetheart. We're just talking about our new jobs. They are difficult, but we're able to handle it, sweetheart," Sam said, hugging her tight.

Little Michael started to stir from his nap. He opened his eyes and saw his sister staring at him with an angry face. He immediately closed his eyes and cuddled tightly on his mother's lap.

Just when Sam wanted to answer Tiffany's question, his cell phone buzzed, then his wife's phone buzzed, too.

"Yes, Madame President. We can both be there in thirty minutes," Sam said. "What's this about?" Sam could not believe what he was told.

"Tiff, I'll brief you on the way to the White House. And yes, now I am truly scared."

* * * * *

"Are you kidding?" Tiffany blurted out. "We have everything the DRM is planning on video and who in our government is supporting them. I know what

252

I want to do to all these traitors. I'll arrest them and you'll prosecute them, right?"

"I can. What's in our favor is that these elected officials have no protection from criminal prosecution for treason, felony, and breach of peace. I just need to be sure all of our ducks are lined up before we go to trial," Sam said.

"You have the tapes with their own voices incriminating themselves. What more do you need?"

"Not much more. I just need to dot the i's and cross the t's so the courts will rule in our favor. Remember, if we try these assholes for treason or sedition and win, the verdict will be appealed to the Supreme Court. With a conservative majority, I am not so sure we'll win based on their recent decisions that have favored the far-right."

Five minutes later, they were getting out of their vehicle at the front entrance to the White House, which still had crime scene tape where the front door was breached. They were escorted to the Oval Office, where President Graham, her Chief of Staff, the Joint Chiefs, and her Secretary of Defense sat waiting for them.

President Graham pointed to two folding chairs, motioning for her Attorney General and FBI Director to sit. "I'm sure all of you have reviewed the tapes Commander McAllister found at the so-called Richmond Confederate White House? What I need from all of you is your ideas on how I can arrest all these traitors without causing an economic meltdown."

Sam was the first to respond. "We have the videos and should release them to every news outlet that would want to air them. Hopefully, they will do their own investigation and move their supporters to distance themselves from the White Supremacy movement."

"I like that idea. I also want to release Professor Cochran's brutal murder of his wife. He's a perfect example of Paige Turner's *Corrupted Intelligence* theory," the President said. "He's a propagandist of the highest order."

FBI Director Glass asked a question. "President Graham. Are you now supporting Turner's theory?"

"She is the only person within the press to explain what's going on and why the uneducated would take up arms against their government."

The meeting lasted until late in the afternoon. The President felt confident she could begin the process of calling out all the traitors festering inside the halls of Congress and the West Wing. Getting to all the outlier militia would be another story. First, McAllister had to locate Cochran, and second, bring him in dead or alive.

President Graham did not inform her Attorney General or FBI Director about the message she had gotten from Albert Dunham.

President Graham, I hope you haven't forgotten about me? I know I haven't forgotten about you. Please get a handle on your insurrection and all the traitors inside your government or I will. You have two weeks to show me and the world that America is once again strong and prosperous... or I will deal with the traitors myself.
The Architect

Once her meeting was over, she and her Chief of Staff discussed the Dunham note. "Martha, any idea what Dunham meant by his threat?"

Martha Sweeden was biting her lower lip, a nervous habit she had when stressed. "Madame President, it could mean a whole lot of things. He still has his bioweapon and may be planning to use it if we can't get a handle on the DRM problem. I know we could use the help," she said.

"I'm not so sure it's that simple. I've read his old manifesto and believe he's trying to accumulate more wealth. It almost worked for him with President Chesterfield's communications satellite he got control of."

"He doesn't have it now, so how can he accumulate the wealth he wants?"

"Please get Dean Miller here ASAP. Maybe he might have some idea," President Graham said.

81

Paige Turner had finished reviewing the tapes of the interviews with the Confederate Prisoners she had done a few days ago in Richmond, Virginia, at the original Confederate White House. In addition, earlier today, she received a package from the White House. It was from the President with a personal note.

She was stumped that President Graham would give her such sensitive material, especially the video of Professor Cochran decapitating his wife. Turner was cautiously optimistic that the President was sincere to allow her to release all the videos to the media and to tell every investigative reporter to do what they do best, investigate.

Today her entire podcast would be directed at the insurrection that happened and how the leaders and supporters of the Domestic Revolutionary Movement use their fabricated lies with made-up conspiracy theories to control all their supporters. Paige was certain that Professor Cochran, his allies in Congress, and the radical right network media have become *Verbal Terrorists* that couldn't care less if their followers die for their selfish cause as long as they retain their power and wealth.

Paige was beginning to get worried that the world was tilting and everything that was once good was sliding off the edge.

Turner had one minute before her podcast aired. She noticed her fiancée Scott Rogers did not seem pleased with what she was about to do. He remembered all too well how she almost died at the hands of *The Architect*, now she was opening a new can of worms trying to expose the Domestic Revolutionary Movement, all their followers, and Professor Cochran, who appeared to be more ruthless than Albert Dunham.

Earlier that morning, Scott and Paige had gotten into a heated argument about the direction she was about to take. "Sweetheart, you can't do the President's job," Scott said. "Professor Cochran won't hesitate to gun you down in broad daylight because you looked cross-eyed at him. Shit, Paige, he decapitated his wife because she wouldn't escape with him; what do you think he'll do to you for exposing him for the lying bastard he is?"

She looked at Scott, unable to smile as she took his hand in hers. "You know I am committed to my *Corrupted Intelligence* theory. My followers are looking to me for some direction so they can make sense out of the twisted world they live in," she said. "I've always known my job is dangerous. I can't control the crazies out there. No matter what I say or do, they won't like me any more or less."

Scott lowered his head, unable to look at her. "I know you'll do what you have to do, but I don't like it," he said, kissing the back of her hand.

"I know how much you love me. I love you too. But I have a job to do and won't be deterred from doing it."

* * * * *

Paige's podcast had gone an hour and a half longer than usual. Before she ended her broadcast, she noticed FBI Director Tiffany Glass was sitting next to Scott. She noticed that Tiffany appeared overly serious.

Paige ended her podcast by introducing Dean Miller and his *We the People* movement. *"I want to end today's broadcast with something that is very dear to my heart. Our country, our democracy, has for too long been governed by two parties with agendas that don't help their constituents. We need a reboot and Dean Miller's We the People political party is what is required to right our ship. On my next podcast, I will have Mister Miller back on to lay out his party's platform and show everyone how he plans to work only for the people, not powerful lobbyists. For the first time, the average citizen will have a say in how they want their government to work for them,"* Paige said and ended her show.

Paige walked over to Scott and the FBI Director and extended her hand. "To what do I owe this honor, Madame Director?"

Tiffany extended her hand, forcing a smile. "We need to talk. Is there somewhere private we can go?"

"Yes. Follow me," Paige said. "Can Scott join us?"

"Absolutely."

Walking back to Turner's office, she could hear the phones at her studio ringing. Bradley Stevens, her friend and investigative reporter who lived through *The Architect* fiasco, rushed over to her, handing her a stack of messages. The messages were from over a hundred investigative reporters requesting copies of all the videos she had and any additional information to help with their investigations.

The phone calls were not limited to just reporters. Over fifty threats on her life were recorded and handed over to Director Glass. It was quite a nerve-wrenching morning.

Inside Turner's office, everyone took a seat, waiting for Director Glass to speak first. "What has you so serious that you needed to come to my studio unannounced?" asked Paige.

Tiffany waved the messages she had been handed. "These threats are why I am here. We have intel that Professor Cochran ordered Wiley Jordan to assassinate you and Scott. I have a protective detail with me to take you into protective custody."

Paige's color drained from her face and tried to respond, but instead, began rubbing with her fingers on a Saint Christopher medal she had worn around her neck since she was an infant. "I won't run away from a story, especially from these treasonous White Supremacists."

Paige noticed Scott looked worried and wanted to speak. "It seems your podcast triggered more attacks in Washington State, Oregon, and upstate New York. Pardon my French, but these animals were heard chanting *Fuck Corrupted Intelligence* as they unloaded their automatic weapons at shopping malls," Rogers said.

Paige shook her head, looking at Director Glass. "You really believe I caused this with my show? Don't you remember Cochran, before he escaped again, gave the orders to his sleeper cells to begin attacking non-believers," she shot back. "I will not stop fighting and we shouldn't either."

Before Director Glass could respond, gunfire erupted inside the studio. Tiffany drew her Glock 19M and Scott from his shoulder holster did the same.

Scott ordered Paige to get under her desk and stay there until he gave her the all clear. "Madame Director, please stay inside and protect the love of my life," Rogers ordered.

Tiffany immediately positioned herself behind the desk, her weapon aimed at the office door. With her free hand, she dialed 911 and demanded a SWAT unit to Paige's studio.

As Scott slipped out from the office, a barrage of bullets exploded through the door. Rogers was hit and went down hard. Tiffany heard her cell ping and read a text that McAllister and his team were in the building.

"Help has arrived," she told Paige, who was nervously massaging her Saint Christopher medal. "You were adopted?"

"Yes. My birth mother left this medal with me. I've always hoped by having this with me at all times my mother would see it and know I was her daughter. A silly dream, but one can only hope."

The color drained from Tiffany's face as she stared at the beautiful woman who might be the daughter she gave up at age sixteen. She wanted to hug Paige but needed to talk with Sam first.

The gunfire had increased in the studio, and then it was over. An eerie silence blanketed the studio, and then the office door burst open. Tiffany set her sights on a big bear of a man wearing a ski mask and army fatigues, his AR 15 fanning the office.

"Tiffany, it's Bubba," he called out, removing the ski mask.

Tiffany was relieved and happy to see a friendly face and one who had saved her life a few times before. "Bubba, I don't know how you do it, but thanks again for being in the right place at the right time."

Director Glass helped Paige to her feet. She immediately rushed out to find Scott. She stepped into a large pool of blood, not realizing it was Scott's. On a gurney, he was being attended to by a Navy doctor and corpsman. Chest compressions were being administered, and then he was shocked to restart his heart.

"Is he going to be alright?" she cried out.

The doctor looked up and shrugged his shoulders. "He's lost a lot of blood and I need to get his heart pumping so I can transport him to the hospital," the doctor said, with sadness on his face.

Paige stepped back, unable to control her tears. Tiffany came over and put her arms around her. "This doctor is the best trauma surgeon in the Navy. Scott has a good chance of recovery with his man," Tiffany said, using her motherly voice.

After two more shocks to Scott's heart, they got a heartbeat and rushed him to the ambulance. The doctor looked back and yelled, "You want to join us, Miss Turner?"

Paige ran over and took Scott's hand.

Tiffany walked over to Bubba. "Who did this?" she asked.

"By the patches on their sleeves and tattoos, the White Angels. It was Wiley's group." Bubba noticed that Tiffany was lost in thought.

"Did you tell Turner who you are?"

"What do you mean?"

"She's your daughter, right? You forgot you told me and the Commander all about your rape and giving up your daughter at sixteen."

"Yeah, but how can you be so sure Turner is my daughter?"

"It doesn't take a rocket scientist to see the resemblance and that you two have matching Saint Christopher medals. I loved the story you told about why you gave her one so one day if she still had it, you would be able to verify that she was your daughter."

"I need to discuss all of this with Sam," she said.

"I think he already figured it out."

* * * * *

Wiley got the report from one of his CIA contacts. "What do you mean all my men are dead? Your intel sucks," he screamed. "If I need a job done right, then I better do it myself," Wiley said, abruptly hanging up the phone.

He wanted to call Cochran, but thought better of it. Instead, he called his California team that helped him against Collins and Glass eleven years ago. This time, everything he wanted to do would be swift and painful.

82

An hour after Paige Turner's podcast hit the airways, every major news outlet frantically tried to piece together the facts of what really happened during the insurrection in Richmond, Virginia, and the District of Columbia. A small handful of reporters from the right were questioning if there was an actual attack or if President Graham overreacted by calling up the military.

Lawsuits escalated after the DOJ started to arrest all suspected domestic terrorists and supporters of the recent insurrection and slaughter of Americans who were heard on Professor Cochran's security tapes. The far-right, with support from the Supreme Court, was able to legally call themselves loyal patriots exercising their constitutional right to free assembly and the right to defend the whiteness they wanted to live under.

More calls for the President to resign or be impeached for murdering American patriots were spreading around the nation. From the other end of the spectrum, the left was calling for the FBI and Homeland Security to end the reign of terror by White Supremacists.

On a few progressive networks, Dean Miller was taking advantage of the turmoil to promote his new political party. Three of the major national news networks had begun talking positively about how the country might benefit from a third political party that would work for every American.

The RNC and DNC all protested the idea of a third party, stating that it would only make it harder to get things done. When Miller was asked to comment on those remarks, he responded in a calm and concise tone. "Right now, both parties are not getting anything done. Voting for legislation is done on a party-line basis, slowing every bill down or bringing it to a complete halt," he said. "Powerful lobbyists control the message, which doesn't help the average

American voter. The *We the People* party will get everything done because once we are formed and hold a majority in the House and Senate, we will finally have a political party that will work for the people."

83

Albert Dunham, during a meeting with his loyal security team, started laughing when he heard Dean Miller tout his new political party. "Ellison, is it too late to try again to kidnap Miller?" *The Architect* asked.

Ellison finished jotting down something on his notepad. "It's never too late, but why? We have the software and the chip you need to build your wealth. Isn't that your objective?"

"Not exactly," Dunham replied. "I still want to be the next Emperor of the US of A."

"Albert, are you crazy? That will never happen, especially if Collins and Glass have anything to say about it," Ellison said sarcastically.

Dunham gave his friend a nasty look. "Don't speak to me in that tone, Frederick. I know what's right and what can be done."

"Your crazy dream is what almost cost you your life. Let's first focus on the money part of the manifesto and then talk about this Emperor shit you want."

Dunham turned toward Edmund Bennett, who created the computer program he needed. "Bennett, is there a way to hack into Miller's software so we can use it?"

Bennett was shaking his head. "No. I would need him with us, and you'd have to get him to turn it over to us. He's under heavy security and living inside the White House."

"I'm not buying that. I want Miller and will not take no for an answer," Dunham screamed.

"Let's first see if my program will do what you want. If not, we'll try to get Miller to cooperate," Bennett said.

Two hours later, the first attempt to capture money had started. After twenty minutes, Dunham had dropped seventy-five million dollars into his offshore account. Bennett started clapping, and a big smile exploded on his face. He started to do some calculations and looked up at Dunham.

"Sir, at this pace, by the end of today you'll have upwards of five point four billion dollars in your account, and nobody would know it even happened."

Ellison looked at Dunham and patted him on the shoulder. "At this rate, you'll be the richest man in the world with so much power this Emperor dream shit will seem like child's play."

"You just don't get it. It's not only about the money. It's about revenge and payback on all the people who stopped me four years ago." Before he could finish, his cell pinged. It was Professor Cochran, calling from Blacks Landing Plantation.

"Cochran, what the fuck do you want?" Dunham cursed.

"We need to talk. Turner, Collins, and Glass are hunting for you and me and if they win, everything we've wanted to accomplish will evaporate and our legacy of a pure White Christian nation will be history," he said. "Collins has already arrested over seventy-five of our supporters inside the West Wing and Congress. At his rate, we'll be stranded with no allies to help us."

"Why should I help you after you turned your back on me before? I don't see things the way you and your DRM do. I never have and never will," Dunham said. "Now is not the right time for the mass murder of people of color."

"You and I have a bigger problem. If Dean Miller succeeds in creating his new third party, White Supremacy and the influence men like you can have in America will be over. We need to work together," The Professor begged.

"Maybe what you want has some merit. First, get all your soldiers back at their compounds within two weeks and have them ready to launch another mass casualty event," Dunham ordered. "We need to knock the President down a few notches and get her back to fighting and killing American patriots." Without saying goodbye, Dunham disconnected his call.

Ellison furrowed his brow. "Are you doing what I think you're doing?"

"Yup. I want to scare the shit out of President Graham," Dunham said.

84

President Graham's approval ratings had sunk to 25 percent. Voters were focusing on how she was illegally arresting all the elected officials named in The Professor's video. The President was convinced that every one of them either participated or provided the Domestic Revolutionary Movement support.

Her Cabinet Secretaries were another matter. At first, using a lie detector to weed out disloyal Cabinet Secretaries was being challenged in the Supreme Court. Using what she had from the videos showing all the people in her West Wing that were DRM members, and leaking it to the press, still did not help her ratings.

The only positive result of her drastic actions is that she was able to influence the replacement of the treasonous Senators and House Representatives with a majority of *We the People* candidates with help from Governors who supported Dean Miller's movement. The President had the truth on her side, but it did not matter as the lies and conspiracy theories from the right came across as more believable, igniting thousands of violent protests in every state, especially against the new third political party.

To make matters worse, the DOJ, led by Sam Collins, had arrested over twenty-five Senators and over eighty House Representatives for being part of the recent coup as well as for the murderous acts against innocent citizens. Their upcoming trials would be starting in sixty days. It couldn't come soon enough for the President and the Attorney General. The threats on their lives were unbearable.

The far-right tried to deflect from the heinous acts these elected individuals did by creating a new conspiracy theory that President Graham was lying so she could replace members in the House and Senate with officials that supported her policies.

FBI Director Tiffany Glass didn't have it any easier. She had her agents searching for Cochran somewhere in Alabama and Dunham in Europe. No matter how many leads she received, those two men were nowhere to be found. A handful of agents in some incidences were ambushed and assassinated. These heinous acts were planned and well thought out enough to release videos to the news media.

It remained frustrating for the President that a majority of Americans did not believe what the tapes revealed; even the graphic decapitation of Professor Cochran's wife did not sway them. The Professor was a God to his followers and could do no wrong.

"*What more does anyone need to do to change people's minds?*" President Graham emotionally said at a recent press briefing. That day she had looked straight into the camera and pleaded with every American. "*Does everyone listening really want a country that is run by racists, White Supremacists, and leaders that enjoy lying and creating conspiracy theories to stay in power? I still have faith in the American electorate and hope to see some positive signs that our democracy is still strong,*" she said, wiping a tear off her cheek.

Even though the tapes had been released exposing all the lies coming out of the DRM and Professor Cochran, the southern states still wanted to form their own country and government. There were protests in the streets from White Supremacist groups who did not wish to hide their racist beliefs anymore. Sadly, there were no counter-protests, except a silence from the progressive left that came across as excusing what was going on. The upcoming session in the House and Senate would be hearing the southern state's arguments to form their own Confederate States of America.

To make matters worse, QAnon was rearing its ugly head and filling the minds of the gullible that the federal government was not representing them and that they were going to be replaced unless they fought for their freedom. They were told that the only solution was to take up arms and form the new Confederate States of America.

After each series of lies was broadcast on national TV and social media, single-shooter incidents increased around the country. These individuals were not shy about expressing their bigoted beliefs and the reason for killing women and children of color.

With martial law being lifted, President Graham tried to address the sagging economy and the slumping stock market. She tried to inject federal funds into the States that helped her fight against the White Supremacists to give people some hope that the country could get back to normal.

The White Supremacist militia had become quiet, waiting for word from Professor Cochran to restart their civil war. They were all hunkering down in over twenty-five states conducting war games so as to be ready to attack on short notice. It didn't stop lone gunmen trying to make a name for themselves within the White Supremacist movement, with mass shooting events at schools, houses of worship, and shopping malls.

With calls to take away all assault weapons, especially from teenagers, the House of Representatives and the Senate remained silent as they'd done for over two decades. Their reasons remained the same, mirroring the gun lobby comments about the Second Amendment even though over 80 percent of voters on both sides demanded changes be made.

85

Albert Dunham had been following every news outlet, enjoying how screwed up his country had become. President Graham kept pushing her authority beyond the parameters of her sworn oath by arresting her political rivals for treason. *The Architect* hoped she would continue pushing the limits of her office, which would only make it easier for him to implement the next part of his new manifesto. While he waited for the right time to re-enter public life, he kept siphoning off billions of dollars daily.

Dunham was waiting for President Graham's upcoming news briefing on her progress in curtailing the active White Supremacist terrorists that continued to roam the streets with their assault weapons. Wherever protests by people of color were happening, these rogue domestic terrorists were there engaging them with their racist words and, in some instances, using their weapons in a murderous rampage. They told the media as they got arrested that they feared for their lives and had to defend themselves.

The Architect's plan needed to be timed perfectly, while the President and Attorney General spoke. For Dunham, it would be the most outrageous act he'd ever committed. Every detail he planned would be timed perfectly.

As President Graham stepped up to the podium in the White House Briefing Room, Dunham texted his men that were spread out in fifteen states that harbored Cochran's White Supremacist Militia. They all controlled their timers to go off two minutes after the press briefing started.

President Graham greeted the White House Press Corps and started talking:

"My fellow Americans, our once great nation is teetering on the brink of disaster. Our country has become polarized, pitting White Americans against Americans

267

of color. As I stop one White Supremacist militia group, three more pop up." President Graham blotted the perspiration on her forehead.

"I never thought I would see the day that almost half of our country supports all the murderous acts by our homegrown domestic terrorists. Our Attorney General has begun prosecuting these animals, but our judicial system works too slowly for my liking. Effective today, anyone harboring a known White Supremacist will be charged as an accessory to the crimes these animals have committed." Two minutes into her speech, President Graham leaned into the camera, ready to launch her threat. The TV monitors went black for ten seconds and Albert Dunham's scarred face came on the screen.

"Hello. For those who do not know me, I am Albert Dunham, better known as The Architect. I'm in exile in Europe hoping one day to return to the country I love. Your President refuses my help with your White Supremacist problem because I've asked for a full pardon for all the crimes I did not commit. I'm tired of watching so many innocent Americans die at the hands of these non-humans who enjoy murdering women and children of color. I am fed up with President Graham's inability to stop these animals." Dunham paused to take a sip from a champagne glass.

"Everyone is about to see how I will protect the United States from any threat from a foreign or domestic terrorist group. This will be hard to look at, but this is how these sub-humans need to be dealt with."

Every TV monitor across the United States and throughout Europe started airing thousands of White Supremacist militia collapsing and screaming in pain as their internal organs began melting inside their bodies. After twenty minutes, the monitors split into fifteen screens. Each one showed thousands of bodies lying in pools of blood. Then Albert Dunham came back on not showing any emotion for the acts he just committed.

"Our judicial system does not work when it comes to punishing men like these. Our Supreme Court Judges have never convicted an American for seditious behavior and crimes against humanity. I will once again ask President Graham for a full pardon so I can come back to my home and clear my name. To show that I am serious about helping our country get back to being the leading world economy, I am depositing fifty thousand dollars in every registered voter's bank

account who is earning less than a hundred thousand dollars a year. If President Graham gives me my pardon, then another fifty thousand dollars will be deposited every year for the next ten years."

The President and Attorney General briskly walked back to the Oval Office without answering any questions.

86

President Graham did not say a word after as she flopped down behind her desk, rocking nervously in her chair. She threw her arms in the air, as exasperation blanketed her body. "What the hell just happened? How can that sociopath do what he just did and seem happy about it?" she asked.

Sam responded. "We knew he was capable of using his bioweapon, but to wipe out most of the DRM militia groups makes no sense unless he's not supporting what Professor Cochran is planning," Sam said. "Are you planning to give him a pardon after what he just did?"

President Graham was deep in thought. "I'm not sure. He could give us more demonstrations of his power and maybe next time, it could be you or me. Right now, I might not have a choice," she said.

Tiffany stood and started walking around the room, her head tilted toward the carpet. "We can't give him a pardon. You can't negotiate with a terrorist and he's one of the most dangerous ones out there," the FBI Director said. "We've been working with his brother Theodore, and I believe we've created an antidote for his weapon. When testing it, the person is immune for approximately a week after receiving the injection. The only glitch is if you've not been inoculated, then we need to administer the antidote within fifteen minutes after being exposed. It's an impossible task. It's all that we have at this time," she said.

"What about making it an aerosol and distributing it using drones? If the bioweapon works from breathing in the particles, then we should be able to do the same with our antidote," Sam said. "Just a crazy suggestion from this frustrated Attorney General."

"That's not a bad idea. I'll run it by Teddy," Tiffany said.

"Are we any closer to finding his family?" President Graham asked.

Tiffany was nodding her head. "McAllister's team believes they have a location where they are being kept. Dean Miller's software, after some tweaking, was able to track them from the day they were abducted from their second home in Maryland. Dunham's paid assassin, Julian Marshall, has been working for *The Architect* for over ten years. We believe Theodore's family is in an underground bunker at Charles Stone's Haven House Plantation. There are over fifty heavily armed mercenaries ready to do battle with us," Tiffany said.

President Graham was tensing her jaw. "When are you going to attempt to rescue them?"

"Bubba Jackson and his team are on their way there to size up the situation and determine if it's possible to breach the bunker without jeopardizing their lives," Director Glass said.

"Do we know if Dunham has the place rigged with his weapon to go off if there are any intruders?" President Graham asked. "It could be a trap."

"Jackson's men will inoculate themselves when they get near Haven House. It will be our first test real test of the antidote," Tiffany said anxiously.

President Graham wanted to change the subject away from Dunham for a while. "Sam, how are we coming along with the clarification of the wording in the constitution? Are you sure we have the authority to do this?"

"What you have been doing, in my opinion, falls under the Emergency Powers Act. You can do this with an executive order and renew it every year. I believe the act of insurrection falls under the Emergency Powers Act since Congress is not willing to do anything under its authority. I say let's keep arresting these traitors and see where it takes us," Sam said. "I don't believe the remaining House or Senate members will object to you protecting our democracy from these animals, so they won't be seen as a branch of government condoning these horrible acts."

"I want you to speak with the American people and explain what we're doing and continue to call out all elected officials who are siding with the White Supremacists," President Graham ordered.

87

McAllister was monitoring his team as it approached Haven House from the forest that surrounded the plantation. They were in five Humvees. Two Apache attack helicopters were ready to land near the hidden retractable runway that Charles Stone had built.

"We're one minute out from breaching the bunker and neutralizing the mercenaries," Jackson said to the Commander.

"Are you all inoculated?"

"Roger that. We're good to go, sir. I have the extra antidotes for Theodore's family if needed," Jackson said.

McAllister had connected Tiffany to watch the extraction with him. "Director Glass, my fingers are crossed that our packages are safe and unharmed."

Tiffany's facial muscles tensed as Jackson and his men skidded to a halt outside the entrance to the hidden bunker. She glanced at Sam and then at the President. No one was talking as they nervously watched McAllister's men jump out in full-body armor with their assault rifles ready to do battle.

Before they could break open the metal doors to the bunker, they were met with gunfire from the roof of the plantation. Bubba was heard barking orders to the two helicopter pilots. "Snipers on the roof. Take them out."

The two pilots made a sharp banking turn and began spraying the entire roof, destroying whatever protection the snipers thought they had. "Sergeant, four snipers down and neutralized," the pilots confirmed.

Jackson then signaled his men to open the metal doors to the bunker. He was hoping to find one female and two teenage children safe. As the two metal doors slammed open, a loud explosion knocked two soldiers to the ground as a light vapor settled down on their bodies. The light mist floated back toward the rest of Bubba's men.

* * * * * *

Dunham watched his little trap work, and started cheering, proud he had such a powerful weapon at his disposal. He hoped that President Graham was watching these men die a slow and painful death. After five minutes, *The Architect* had a puzzled expression on his face. "Why aren't they dying?" he screamed. After another ten minutes, he realized that Teddy had created an antidote. "Fuck you, brother." At that precise moment, he pressed a key on his cell phone that triggered another loud explosion inside the locked bunker.

"This is what happens when you are disloyal to me, Theodore," Dunham screamed into his monitor.

* * * * *

Jackson heard the explosion and rushed down toward the room where Theodore's family was being held. It took him thirty seconds to breach the metal door. Inside, he found three scared people trying not to breathe in the vapor that engulfed the room.

Bubba and two of his men rushed over to Theodore's family and, without asking, jabbed three large needles into the carotid artery in their necks, pushing the antidote fluid into their bloodstream. Jackson watched, hoping he wasn't too late.

After five minutes, all three of them had no reaction. Then, after another five minutes, Bubba felt confident the antidote worked and escorted them up to the helicopters to reunite them with Theodore.

Tiffany, Sam, and President Graham started cheering and high-fiving each other. "Great job, Commander. Now, get your ass back here. We have more work to do," she said.

* * * * *

Dunham threw his champagne glass at Julian Marshall. "You couldn't get this simple job done for me?"

"You told me they didn't have an antidote. If I would have known that, I wouldn't have pulled my men. You were wrong about your brother," Julian said, his nostrils flaring.

"You'll have another try. This time I want Collins and Glass, along with their children, dead. Then, Paige Turner, McAllister, and that Black bastard Bubba Jackson," Dunham said in a rage.

88

Professor Cochran could not believe the number of his soldiers Dunham had murdered. He knew he had just one more opportunity left to win his civil war, but he would need a lot of cooperation from what was left of his congressional supporters, especially Senator Kenneth Jenkins. It was time for Congress to stand up and take a position to support the new White Supremacy movement and Senator Jenkins was the only elected official who could garner enough politicians to make it happen.

Cochran had helped get the Senator elected over forty years ago. He had become the first Neo-Nazi White Supremacist elected to the Senate. Jenkins had helped Charles Stone's father and uncle escape from Nazi Germany, allowing them to settle at the plantation Haven House and begin building the new American Nazi Movement.

Professor Cochran had a special relationship with the Senator. Their parents fled Germany running away from the war crimes they had participated in with Stone's father and uncle. Together, both men built a strong White Supremacy militia, using Charles Stone as the vehicle to legitimize their movement. They carried forward Hitler's methods of lies and conspiracy theories to convince White Christian Americans to commit atrocious crimes against men of color.

Cochran decided he needed to call Senator Jenkins and put the last phase of their movement into play before Dunham returned to the United States.

"Kenneth, Cochran here. We need to meet and discuss the next part of our plan," The Professor said. "We might have to mobilize our people in Argentina."

There was a long silence at the other end of the line. "Why are you calling me on an open line?" Jenkins asked. "Here is my new burner phone. Call me back in ten minutes."

In a silicon mask, Wiley Jordan listened as the Senator finished talking with Professor Cochran. "What did that old bastard want?" he asked.

Jenkins could not stop staring at the leader of the White Angels. "That's one interesting mask. Couldn't you make one that made you look better?" the Senator teased.

"Just trying to keep a low profile," Wiley responded, massaging his hand that had his fingers reattached. "Now answer my question. What did Cochran want?"

"I'm not sure. He still believes our movement can succeed. He wants to mobilize our Nazi ex-patriots in Argentina."

Wiley jumped up from his chair, walking over to the window in the Senator's office. "He's gone crazy like Stone and Dunham and needs to be stopped. Our dream of a new Confederate States of America is dead and can't be resurrected," Wiley said. "We need to rethink our strategy by taking over enough state capitols so we can import all of our White Christian supporters."

"Your idea has merit," Senator Jenkins said. "Cochran has become a liability. He's being hunted by every law enforcement agency and by Dunham. With President Graham arresting my friends in the Senate and House, it might not be that long before they come after me," the Senator said. "Only one person knows about all the times I was at Haven House meeting with Charles Stone."

"You talking about that nigger slave bitch April?" Wiley cursed.

"Yes. She could be a real problem for us," said the Senator.

"I know where she is hiding. I'll take care of her."

"April and Cochran are not our first priority. It's *The Architect* and his army. They are better trained than any group we have left and more disciplined," Senator Jenkins said.

"When you speak with The Professor again, set up a meeting and I will take care of that problem. Then, I will deal with Dunham on my own," Wiley said. "But first, I need to deal with Charles's slave bitch and her two boys. She knows who you are and if she hasn't already, can identify you."

After Wiley left Jenkins's office, Cochran called his burner phone. "Cochran, we shouldn't be speaking on any phones. Let's meet. Pick the place and I'll be there," the Senator said.

"I'll text you the location. Can you meet with me tomorrow?"

"Tomorrow will work for me," Senator Jenkins confirmed.

* * * * *

Dean Miller's computer screen flashed an alert. It was Professor Cochran talking with Senator Jenkins. He immediately called Sam Collins and Tiffany Glass. "Guys, Cochran has reared his ugly head. I don't know what it means, but he's talking with the Senate majority leader. The Professor is somewhere near The Blacks Landing Plantation. I'll tag his phone and the Senator's phone," Miller said.

"Can you give us the approximate location of Cochran so we can alert McAllister? He's in Alabama right now," Director Glass said.

"We have one other problem. Wiley Jordan knows where April and her boys are hiding. After tagging his phone, I believe he's heading there," Miller said, sounding alarmed.

89

John McAllister and Bubba Jackson waited for their team to report back from surveying the Blacks Landing Plantation for Cochran. They had been gone almost an hour and there was no word on their progress, which had both of them concerned.

"Should we head up there to make sure everything is all right?" Jackson asked.

Commander McAllister trusted his men and understood that an hour was not too long to assess the enemy's strengths and weaknesses before launching their attack. "Let's give them another thirty minutes," he replied. Before he could finish talking, he got a text from Director Glass.

Wiley Jordan knows where April and her boys are. He's heading there now. They need to be protected.

McAllister saw the worry on Jackson's face. "Take the helicopter and do what you need to do to protect April," he ordered.

* * * * *

Dunham's assassin, Julian Marshall, texted his boss about the situation at Blacks Landing. His message read:

Cochran's holed up at Blacks Landing in a secure bunker underneath the plantation. He has over fifty heavily armed men all wearing their Domestic Revolutionary Movement combat uniforms. My men will attempt to position the vials near the main house and release them before we breach the compound.

Dunham responded:

You need to get it done in thirty minutes. I'll be speaking to the American people and the President then. I want another impressive demonstration for the world to witness my power. After this, they better not doubt that I want a full pardon and nothing less.

Dunham signed off and walked over to his makeshift recording studio to get himself ready for another demonstration of his bioweapon's power.

* * * * *

Sergeant Ron Arnold had eyes on Julian Marshall and his twelve men camouflaged and equally positioned around the plantation. He noticed them positioning what appeared to be pipe bombs approximately ten yards from the main house.

"Sir, the situation here is very interesting. Dunham's head of security, Julian Marshall, has twelve men attempting to breach the compound," he reported.

McAllister did not reply immediately, deep in thought. "Are you in a position to neutralize them and not alert Cochran or his men?"

"It's risky. They are heavily armed and won't go down without a bloody fight," Arnold said. "I'm not sure we want to be exposed to Cochran's fifty men that are armed to the teeth. Let Julian Marshall do our dirty work. Maybe they might kill each other and save us the time and effort," Sergeant Arnold said.

"I agree. Hold your position. I'll call you back in five minutes," the Commander said. McAllister looked at Bubba Jackson, wanting his assessment of their situation. "Your thoughts before you go?"

Jackson started parading around inside their command tent. "You should run this by Director Glass and the President, but you don't have that much time. I'd opt to let Dunham's men battle Cochran's men and see who is left standing," Bubba said. "If these two factions want to kill each other, who are we to stop them?"

Before McAllister could call back Sergeant Arnold, he heard five loud explosions coming from the vicinity of Blacks Landing. Without any hesitation, he jumped into a Humvee and was speeding in the direction of the billowing smoke near the plantation. He looked back to see Jackson lift off to save April and her boys.

"Be careful, my friend," McAllister whispered.

* * * * *

Dunham had once again hacked into the National Emergency Broadcasting Network so every American, politician, and especially the President could witness his power once again. *"If this won't convince the world that I should be the first Emperor of the United States, then all that doubt me will be punished,"* he whispered.

Sam and Tiffany were back at the Mayflower, sitting on their living room couch with their two children watching the Disney movie *Frozen*. It was Irene's favorite. Halfway through the movie, a black screen popped up and then the face of Albert Dunham replaced what they were watching.

Tiffany immediately understood what was happening and ordered the nanny to take the children to their rooms and stay there until she gave her the all clear.

90

Dunham adjusted his bright blue silk tie and buttoned his navy blue pinned striped suit jacket as he stepped in front of his podium. He started cracking his knuckles, expressing a nervousness he had not shown before.

"President Graham and my fellow Americans. I am not comfortable having to demonstrate the effectiveness of my weapon once again, but your President has left me no choice." He walked back to the podium and found a large glass of water to sip.

"The United States is infested with vermin who are trying to divide and destroy our democracy and constitution. White Supremacy has no place in the United States or, for that matter, in the world. Hate does not improve anyone's life or put money in your pockets. If racists are not eliminated from the earth, our future will be in jeopardy. Professor Cochran is a murderous pig who wants to return to a time when every man, woman, and child of color had no rights.

"He's pledged to overturn our democracy and create an autocratic form of government. He's promised to create a new constitution, Bill of Rights, and new legislation naming all White Christian males and giving them authority over any person of color. All of this he'd sworn to do so he can rule his own southern group of states without certified elections.

"I am a privileged person who has never had to struggle. I've built my wealth from the dedicated hard work all of you listening here have done. I've never forgotten that, and that is why I want to reward each American with the $50,000 I promised you the other day. I want to share my wealth with the people who helped me become the billionaire I am today. By the end of today, each of you should have the money I promised you. With that said, I need to first rid our

country of the White Supremacist leader who has slaughtered almost twenty-five thousand innocent men, women, and children over the last two decades."

Without saying another word, Dunham switched the programming to Blacks Landing Plantation, where explosions had started to happen around the property.

Armed men, dressed in Confederate Uniforms rushed outside, their weapons at the ready, looking for someone to shoot.

Fifty men rushed around the perimeter of the plantation, taking up a position to defend Professor Cochran. Before these soldiers could settle in, a vapor cloud hovered over them and, in seconds, started raining down on them. One minute later, all fifty men were on the ground twisting in pain and screaming as blood oozed out from their nostrils, ears, and mouths. It was over in less than a minute. All of Cochran's men were dead, lying in a large pool of their own blood.

Dunham switched all the monitors back to his studio.

"I'm sorry I had to show you this, but this is how people who promote hate, especially White Supremacists need to be dealt with if we want to live in a society that is safe for our families, especially our children." Dunham looked directly into the camera, his eyes little slits of anger.

"President Graham, this is your last chance to honor my wishes, or I will start eliminating all the traitors inside your administration and within the halls of Congress. You have one week to let me know your decision."

With that last threat, all monitors returned to their original programming.

91

Bubba Jackson had texted April, warning her of Wiley's pending arrival. Over the last few weeks, they had become very close, building a love both of them had never experienced.

Bubba had given April lessons on how to use a firearm, as well as how to physically defend herself. While they had not taken their relationship to the intimate stage, it did not mean they both did not want it to go there.

The Apache helicopter landed in a small field a hundred yards from the safehouse. Bubba noticed three black Chevy Suburbans parked in front of the house.

Before the chopper landed and was still ten feet off the ground, Jackson jumped off and got into a waiting Humvee. His heart was racing, praying he was not too late to save April and her boys.

With his AR15 pointing at the front door, Bubba lowered his shoulder and burst through, doing a shoulder roll and coming to a squat position, panning the front room. Two bodies were lying face down, puddles of blood engulfing their heads. Bubba recognized both men. They were April's security detail.

Upstairs, he heard crying that sounded like the boys. Then he heard April's voice, screaming at Wiley to put her son down.

Bubba heard Wiley's loud, bellowing voice. "Hey, nigger bitch, I don't take orders from a slave girl, especially a whore like you," he shouted.

Rushing through the bedroom door, Bubba tackled Wiley, slamming him down the way a linebacker would sack a quarterback. The impact jarred his gun from his hand. With the agility of a gymnast, Jordan was able to free himself from the grasp Jackson had on him and came at him with a large hunting knife.

"I've been waiting a long time to skin your Black hide and bring your head back to Cochran as my trophy," Wiley said, with spittle at both corners of his mouth. The first swipe grazed Bubba's forearm, but the second one caught his left ribcage, puncturing his lung. Jackson fell back, hitting his head on a nightstand.

Once Wiley saw Bubba was out of commission, he picked up his pistol and pointed it at April and her boys who were cuddled in their mother's arms. "Nigger, you'll first watch your bastard boys die; then I'm going to have some fun with you and find out what Charles liked about fucking you so much."

Wiley had his back to Bubba and did not notice he was stirring awake. April was first to notice and began smiling. Her smile pissed Jordan off.

"What's so funny, bitch," he growled. Then he realized that she was looking at Bubba. He quickly turned around just when a bullet from Jackson's ankle holster gun landed dead center in Wiley's forehead.

Realizing Wiley was finally dead, Bubba fell back down and blacked out. April rushed over and felt for a pulse. It was faint but he had one. She immediately called 911.

In the back of the ambulance, April and her boys would not let Bubba out of their sight. She held his large hand tight, whispering in his ear that she loved him, and he better not leave her.

92

Commander McAllister got word that Bubba was in critical condition. All he was told was that he was fighting for his life and the surgery would take approximately four hours. He was happy he saved April and her boys, and that Wiley Jordan was finally in hell where he belonged.

The fighting at Blacks Landing Plantation had been going on for over an hour and Julian Marshall and his men were taking a lot of losses. While the bioweapon neutralized ten of Cochran's security detail, they were prepared with over a hundred soldiers with gas masks.

What surprised McAllister was that Dunham had underestimated Cochran and that his bioweapon could be less effective with protective gear. When Julian Marshall realized he was in a losing battle, he cut his losses and ran away with his tail between his legs.

Sergeant Arnold had taken a position with McAllister. "Are we going to capture Cochran?" he asked.

McAllister was deep in thought before he responded. "We don't have enough men right now. Let's regroup and figure out another way to get The Professor and stop his civil war."

* * * * *

Professor Cochran connected with the remaining member of the *Wolf Pack*. "Klaus, I was able to slow down Dunham and President Graham's efforts to eliminate me and the DRM," Cochran said. "While I have them on their heels, I think we should move with our final stage and mobilize our army and get them in position in all of our southern states."

Klaus Bergner replied in a slow methodical voice. "Professor, you'll need to convince me that we are done with *The Architect*. If he's still alive, we are all not safe," he said. "He's mobilizing his allies in Iran and Turkey, as well as a small rebel faction out of Russia."

Cochran was silent, thinking of a good answer for Klaus. "If you can locate him, then I can eliminate him once and for all."

"We know where he is, but he has over two hundred and fifty well-seasoned mercenaries protecting him. I am not ready to do battle inside Hungry. He's never without heavy security," Klaus said with a nervous edge to his voice.

"Get me his location and I'll handle the rest. I think President Graham might be willing to do our dirty work for us."

* * * * *

Cochran was on the phone with FBI Director Glass. "Madame Director, this is Professor Cochran. How are you today?" he asked sweetly.

"Are you ready to turn yourself in? If so, then my day is just peachy," Tiffany said sarcastically.

"Oh, that's very funny. I have a better offer for you than locking me up," he laughed. "If I can give you Dunham's location and a detailed layout of his compound in Hungry, could we have a truce on our fighting? I'm tired and need to regroup and figure out my next move," The Professor said.

"That's an interesting proposition," the Director said. "Let me discuss it with the President. Call me back at this number tomorrow around noon Eastern Time." She abruptly ended the call.

Tiffany looked at Sam and McAllister, biting her lower lip. "What do you think Cochran's endgame is? Should we negotiate to get Dunham?"

"After reading the Haven House logbook," Sam said. "He's the brains behind his White Supremacy militia. What was recorded about him and his father reflected he is a true Nazi down to his core. If I were to guess, his endgame is to split the United States in half and create an all-White Christian nation with a new constitution and governmental structure similar to what Hitler had envisioned for Germany," Sam said. "If he's smart, all he had to accomplish is having all the State Legislatures in each of his southern states filled with elected officials that support his movement."

"You might be on to something, Sam," McAllister said. "There's been a lot of activity within the Nazi Party in Argentina. I'm not sure you read this in the Haven House logbook, but Hitler, toward the end of the war, visited Charles's father at the plantation. The CIA believed Hitler did not commit suicide in his bunker and had his double sacrifice his life for the Furor and Motherland."

"You're scaring me," Sam said. "Didn't the CIA get permission to exhume his body and verify, using his teeth, that the body in his bunker was him?" Sam asked.

McAllister was grinning. "The teeth they verified were implants that could have been put into this body double. Hitler was paranoid and believed even if he lost the war, he'd be around to fight another day, which seems like he was able to do at Haven House."

"If what you're saying is true, then everything these last twenty years at Haven House makes perfect sense. Charles and Silver Hawk Insurance were attempting to divide our country with lies and conspiracy theories to polarize our politics to the point that our current democracy and constitution stopped working for the people."

"What about Dunham? Wasn't he part of Cochran's DRM?" Tiffany asked.

Sam answered. "Yes, he was at first, but his ego and quest for wealth did not match up with Cochran's and his Nazi plans."

"Everything happening inside *The Architect's* world and Cochran's are at opposite ends of the spectrum. Both men are still ruining our country and should be stopped at all costs so we can heal," McAllister said.

"I get the sense you're going to go rogue and handle this on your own," Sam said. "Don't you think President Graham needs to know what you are planning?"

"What I need to do can't be bogged down by committees. With Bubba fighting for his life, I need to do this to honor him and all he's done for our country," McAllister said. "Sam… Tiffany, please watch over him while I am gone," the Commander said as he rushed out of the FBI Director's office.

93

"Sammy, we need to talk about something not related to White Supremacy, Dunham, or Cochran," Tiffany said.

"I know you're not breaking up with me, so let's go have some lunch and you can talk to me all afternoon if you'd like," Sam said.

The Director's driver took them to Martin's Tavern in Georgetown, one of their favorite places since coming to Washington. Tiffany found a secluded booth in the back of the restaurant.

Tiffany was never one to hem and haw when she had something to say. "Sam, you remember I gave up my daughter at age sixteen and since having Irene and Michael, I've regretted not searching for her?"

"I do. I have a feeling you already found her," Sam said.

Tiffany's eyes had become glassy. "Yes."

A big smile cracked on Sam's face. "Let me guess. It's Paige Turner, right?"

Tiffany started crying. "How did you know?"

"Just looking at the two of you and how you both are with each other is a no-brainer," Sam said. "Have you told Paige yet?"

"There has been no appropriate time since Scott Rogers was shot. Will you be with me when I tell her?"

"I'd love to. Will she be my BSD?"

Tiffany wrinkled her nose at Sam's comment. "What's a BSD?"

Sam smiled. "Biological Stepdaughter."

"Very cute," Tiffany replied.

* * * * *

Sam got a text from April that Bubba was out of surgery and the prognosis looks good for a full recovery. "Tiff, we need to get over to Walter Reed and see Bubba. He's out of surgery."

94

Sam and Tiffany arrived at Walter Reed and proceeded to the ICU ward. Waiting for them were April and her two boys.

"Mister Jackson is doing remarkably well," April said, looking like she hadn't slept in a few days. "He was so brave, almost sacrificing his life for us," she sniffled as she put her arms around her boys.

"I know exactly how you feel," Tiffany said. "Bubba is a great human being." She was staring at April's eyes and watched her reaction when she mentioned his name. "It seems that you and Bubba have more than just a client/bodyguard relationship."

April moved closer to Tiffany and whispered in her ear. "I love him. No man has ever been so nice to me and my boys like he's been these past few weeks."

"He might look like a big bear, but he is a gentle giant with a selfless heart."

April had a worried expression. "Where will me and my boys go to be safe again? I'm afraid Professor Cochran will be very angry now that Wiley is dead," she said.

Sam chimed into their conversation. "I've gotten that all arranged. This time you'll have US Marshals protecting you and the boys," he said.

Walking off the elevator was Paige Turner, with Bradley Stevens, her closest friend and one of the best investigative reporters who helped end *The Architect's* Manifesto.

Tiffany immediately walked over to Paige, cutting her off from April. "What are you doing here? This floor is restricted."

"President Graham called and asked me to interview Bubba and April. Then you and Sam. She wants to take the fight to these White Supremacists in the media and airways. She felt it important that I interview all of you and tell each of your stories, from Charles Stone to Albert Dunham, to better explain what the DRM's long game is," Paige said.

Sam looked confused. "I thought that's what we've been doing," he said.

"Not exactly. Their decades-long plan to split the United States in half has never been told clearly or in easy-to-understand language. There is so much to talk about, especially what is inside the Haven House logbook and to tell April's story and the story of all the other slaves that were kept hidden at the plantation," Paige said, showing her emotional side.

Tiffany could not stop staring at her daughter and wondering when it would be a good time to tell her she was her mother. She leaned over toward Sam and spoke softly. "I need to tell Paige, but I don't know when the right time is," she said.

Sam kissed her on her cheek and whispered. "Now is as good as any time."

Tiffany noticed that Paige had started rubbing her Saint Christopher medal that was around her neck. In a reflex action, Tiffany started rubbing her Saint Christopher medal, and not taking her eyes off her daughter.

Paige noticed what Tiffany was doing and, without any warning, started crying. "Where did you get that medal?" she asked, her voice cracking.

Tiffany blotted away the tears cascading down her cheeks. "We need to talk somewhere private," she requested.

As the three of them walked toward a private waiting room, two male nurses passed them. The nurses were heading toward Bubba Jackson's room. One of the men reached behind his back and from his waistband, drew a gun and pointed it at April and her boys.

Sam and Paige were oblivious to what was happening, but not Tiffany. She drew her weapon from inside her purse and shouted, "FBI, don't force me to shoot."

The nurse with the gun turned, swinging his weapon and pointing it at Tiffany. Without another warning, the FBI Director, like she had been taught, placed a bullet in the center of her attacker's forehead. The second nurse started running toward the stairs, trying to escape.

Again, Tiffany shouted out orders to the other man. "FBI, stop running and get on your knees with your hands locked behind your head." The nurse did stop, but like his partner, turned and pointed his weapon, but this time it was at April and her boys.

Without any warning this time, Tiffany fired her weapon, aiming it at the center of the man's chest. He went down like a rag doll. Tiffany was immediately on her cell phone dialing 911. "This is FBI Director Glass at Walter Reed. Two active shooters in the ICU ward. Both are dead. Send the coroner and DC detectives to clean up the crime scene," she said in a calm and collected voice.

Sam and Paige rushed over to Tiffany. "Are you all right?" Sam asked as he took her into his arms. "I forgot how good you are in the line of fire, Annie Oakley," he joked, trying to slow down his heart.

Paige did not seem too rattled by what just happened. While Tiffany engaged the assassins, she had the presence of mind to video the attempted attack. "I got everything on video," she told the Director.

Bubba Jackson's female nurse briskly walked over to the Director. "Director Glass, are you okay? I'd like to make sure," she said as she forced her to sit down and started listening to her heart. She then slapped a blood pressure cuff on her left arm and took her blood pressure. "I'm impressed that your heart rate is sixty-five beats per minute and your blood pressure is one-ten over sixty-eight. What you did to save all our lives was remarkable."

Tiffany stood up. "It was nothing. I just did what I was trained to do when facing a difficult situation." She thanked the nurse and headed toward Bubba Jackson's room, where April and her boys were shielding the big man with oxygen attached to his nostrils and an IV dripping something she did not recognize.

Sam and Paige followed her into the room. Turner, once again, began videotaping the Director. She saw Tiffany look back at her and signaled her to stop using her cell phone.

Bubba's eyes were wide open and clear. He extended his large hand and touched Tiffany's forearm. "Are we even now, Madame Director?" Jackson said with a broad smile on his face.

Tiffany leaned forward and gave him a big kiss on his forehead. "We will never stop owing you for all you and Commander McAllister have done for us," she said. "We need to get you and April to a safe location until we figure out who is after the two of you."

"I can only guess it was the White Angels now that Wiley's dead."

Paige jumped into the conversation. "I checked their tattoos and they both had White Angel insignia inked on their arms and necks," she said, showing Bubba and Tiffany the video.

Sam interrupted the exchange. "I just got a text from President Graham's Chief of Staff. The President wants all of us at Camp David immediately. She is sending the Presidential helicopter to Walter Reed as we speak."

* * * * *

Two hours later, Bubba had gotten released from the hospital and was being taken out on a gurney by two Navy Doctors. With the type of wound he had, sitting was a struggle. They were escorted by five heavily armed Secret Service agents from the Presidential detail. They were airborne, heading to Camp David.

On the helicopter, Paige asked Sam if she could sit with her mother. She had so many questions. He just smiled and whispered. "Welcome to our family."

95

Outside of the main entrance to Walter Reed, crowds had formed. The hospital had been evacuated of all visitors. Rumors had begun to spread through the crowd. Most of the rumors were coming from far-right media news outlets. They had been shouting out conspiracy theories about what had happened in the ICU ward.

A far-right reporter, in a highly emotional state, was broadcasting unfounded rumors about what had happened. "Two male nurses were gunned down by FBI Director Glass," she said.

The conspiracy of lies escalated, getting the crowd inflamed. All the protesters heard was that American patriots were unarmed and trying to flee from two assassins that were sent by the CIA to finish off Bubba Jackson.

Another reporter yelled out to the crowd that Bubba Jackson had murdered Wiley Jordan, beloved leader of the patriotic White Angels. in cold blood.

Chants to lock up the FBI Director had spread through the crowd. The onlookers had now turned into a violent mob, throwing water bottles at the hospital security guards. Before they could storm the hospital, DC Police arrived and began cordoning off the area and ordering everyone to move back or get arrested.

Two pushy reporters who were the instigators of the lies, would not follow orders and were thrown to the ground roughly and handcuffed. They were put into separate police cars and taken to the local precinct while onlookers videoed the press being arrested.

On the National Evening news, the incident at Walter Reed took up most of the thirty-minute segment. On one of the network media news stations, all they could talk about is what Director Glass had done to two innocent nurses.

The White House Press Secretary spoke for fifteen minutes, focusing on the actions of the FBI Director. "What we know is that FBI Director Glass confronted two males impersonating nurses and stopped them from assassinating Bubba Jackson. I will not be taking any questions at this time since this is an active investigation that is still gathering evidence." The Press Secretary paused, taking in a nervous breath. "What we do know at this time is that the two men were members of the White Angels, and were most likely there to revenge the murder of their leader, Wiley Jordan." She thanked all the reporters for coming and she briskly walked away from the podium.

96

In a secluded villa in the hills of Mar Del Plata, Argentina, one hundred and fifty miles south of Buenos Aires, Professor Cochran had been summoned by the new leader of Hitler's old Sturmabteilung, The Brown Shirts, also known as the Storm Detachment. They have been around almost as long as the Nazi Party and were better known during Hitler's reign of terror on Europe as "Storm Troopers".

Cochran had never met face-to-face with any of these men, but knew of their history and influence throughout South and North America. These men were the children of Hitler's Gestapo, Storm Troopers, and Nazi Party leaders. Today they totaled close to two hundred and fifty thousand loyal patriots of the original Nazi movement.

The Professor could not control his nerves as he sat in a cold dark room, with walls of mahogany wooden panels. Red velvet curtains were drawn tight so as to not allow any sunlight into the room. The room was massive with its twenty-foot walls that had one large Nazi Flag and a large Domestic Revolutionary Movement Flag. Across the room from these two flags was a White Angels flag.

Seeing Wiley Jordan's flag surprised The Professor. However, it was now making perfect sense that these Brown Shirts with their long-range plan to divide and conquer the United States, created the White Angels for that purpose.

Cochran was piecing together the complicated puzzle that made up Wiley Jordan. He realized that Jordan's parents, like Charles Stone's parents, as well as his own father, were all Nazi Party members. It answered a lot of questions The Professor had about Wiley.

Cochran was startled when two very large wooden doors swung open and ten middle-aged men, all dressed in Brown Uniforms, marched into the room. They all took their seats behind a long white granite table, their expressions stone-cold serious.

"Professor Cochran, thank you for coming to meet with us. We have a lot to talk about, especially your progress, or lack thereof, of your civil war."

Cochran's hands started shaking while a nervous twitch under his left eye started to convulse. "I came down here with good intentions and want to know what you want from me and my DRM?" he said with a raspy voice.

"Professor. Let me clear up something first. The DRM is not YOUR organization, but OURS. You are its leader in the United States and nothing more than a figurehead. I recognize that it's been a long time since we spoke, or for that matter, met at Haven House twenty-five years ago. So, remember, WE control everything and will escalate OUR war on the United States with or without you. It all depends on what we hear from you today."

Cochran turned bedsheet white, realizing his life was in danger. "What do you want to hear from me that will convince you that I am a loyal soldier to your cause? I want the same things you want."

"Based on your results and your out-of-control behavior, we are doubting you have the same ideals as we do," said Wilhelm Hitler, great-grandson of Adolf Hitler.

"Then what can I do to convince you I am a loyal member of our new Nazi Party?" Cochran asked.

"I'm glad you asked, Professor. First, we need Albert Dunham, *The Architect* as he likes to refer to himself, eliminated, and his head sent to us. Second, we need inflation in the United States to soar and the economy to trend toward depression levels. Once this happens, then all that we've been working toward will happen and our new Nazi Party will be the largest political party in America."

Cochran was tapping his cane nervously. "First, killing Dunham will not be easy. He's becoming the richest man on the planet and with that, has an army of mercenaries protecting him as well as a new bioweapon he's used on fifteen hundred of my best militia. Second, there is a movement that is gaining followers. The *We the People* party, if allowed to go unchecked, will be the majority party in the United States," Cochran shot back at Wilhelm.

"Are you saying you can't get the job done?"

"I can, but you have another problem that will surely prevent you from even entering the United States—Commander McAllister, and his army of ex-military veterans. And don't forget about Sam Collins, Tiffany Glass, and Paige Turner. They are proving to be a firewall that is preventing my movement, I mean our movement, from succeeding," he said.

Wilhelm, whose face looked like it was on fire, stood up and marched over to where Cochran was sitting. "You keep telling me everything you can't do, so why do we need you anymore?" he said, pulling out his pistol from his waist holster.

"Before you summoned me here, I was about to meet with the Governors from our Confederate States to verify their progress about filing their papers for secession from the United States. While we know the federal government won't allow it, we are prepared to continue our civil war and open the doors for you and your Brown Shirts to invade and stand with us," The Professor said.

Wilhelm returned his gun to his holster and sat down next to Cochran on the couch. He put his arm around his shoulder and spoke in a calm voice. "I need this to happen in three weeks. I need it to coincide with what we are planning for Europe. Now go back home and make this happen or you won't get a second chance to live."

97

Sam, Tiffany, and Paige watched the news. They were all upset with the conspiracies and lies floating around. "I've got everything on video that will shut these fools up once and for all," Paige said.

Coming through the front door was Commander McAllister. "We've got a greater problem," he said.

Sam stood up and extended his hand. "Where have you been since Bubba was hospitalized?"

"Argentina. Hitler's original secret police settled there after the war ended and they have been the driving force behind the DRM and all that has been happening for the last thirty years," McAllister said.

"I don't get it. How are they involved with what's been going on?" Tiffany asked, puzzled.

"Hitler had a long-range plan to control all of Europe and then South and North America. The leaders of his Nazi Party had patience and kept spreading conspiracy theories. Now, after two decades, their lies have divided our democracy to the point that it is ripe for the taking," the Commander said. "Up until now we never realized how many state and federal elected officials are part of their DRM. We need a new strategy to defeat these animals."

Before McAllister could finish with his briefing, President Graham walked in, followed by six heavily armed Secret Service agents. She smiled and sat down behind her desk. "I am happy to see all of you in one piece. We have a lot to cover and not a lot of time before all hell breaks loose."

When Commander McAllister saw the President signal him to make his presentation, he first walked over to his close friend and brother, Bubba Jackson. He bent down and gave him a high-five.

Jackson was lying on his hospital bed, appearing alert. "Hey, John, this kissy, girlie stuff is embarrassing. Get a grip. I'm alive, well, and ready to join in the fight again," Bubba growled.

McAllister smiled at Jackson's words and started his briefing. "With help from Dean Miller and Roger Stillwell, I was able to track down the enemies, who want to see our country divided and ripe for the taking. It's happening in Argentina as we speak; a new Nazi movement from the grandchildren of Hitler's World War Two Nazi Party. My informant down there told me that all the attacks that have been happening these last few weeks have their origin in this group."

Sam was the first to ask a question. "Commander, do we know who these men are? Any names?"

McAllister was shaking his head. "Not at this time. They are very protective of their leaders as they are active politicians and philanthropists who are loved throughout Argentina," he said. "As I mentioned earlier, we have been barking up the wrong tree. When we stopped Stone, it turned out that he was just a small part of the overall plan these new Nazis have for the world. What's been happening in our country for the last two decades is not a Domestic Revolutionary Movement plan, but the long-range plan of these Neo-Nazis. All I know is that they are coming to America to install the new political Nazi Party as the majority party here. Also, they are coming for all of us, as we seem to be slowing their plans down," McAllister said.

President Graham cut off the Commander. "Back to why we are all here. As I keep my housecleaning inside the West Wing and the Halls of Congress, I need each of you to do specific things to right our ship," she said. "Everything I need can be done here at Camp David. It's the most secure place on earth."

The President spoke for almost three hours, covering everything from domestic terrorism to the economy and prosecuting all elected officials and militia members who were part of the recent insurrection. She gave Sam orders to begin speaking to the American public and selling the idea of saving the constitution and expose all the Senators and House Representatives who fall within the parameters of Paige Turner's Corrupted Intelligence theory.

"I trust most of our citizens have a moral conscience, but we need them to understand how their leaders they put their trust in are fooling them with conspiracies and lies." President Graham knew that the best spokesperson for that job was her Attorney General.

While Commander McAllister listened, his cellphone got beeped with a text message from his contact in Argentina. "The Brown Shirts are on the move and heading toward the Mexican border. Others are flying into Canada and plan on crossing at the Washington State and New York border crossings. They are coming with the firepower to start a small war.

"Madame President, it might be too late to do what you want to do at this time. The Brown Shirts are coming and should be at our borders in three days," the Commander said. "With your permission, I'd like to take my small army and confront them before they position themselves at our northern and southern borders."

President Graham looked angry. "I'll get the Joint Chiefs, Homeland Security, and our Secretary of Defense here tomorrow to figure out how we're going to take it to these terrorists and show them what happens to terrorists who try to enter our borders."

Tiffany was champing at the bit to say something. "How are we going to take it to these Brown Shirts in Mexico and Canada? I'm not too confident that the Mexican President will welcome our military crossing their border, especially with our strained relationship over immigration."

"Good point. I'll call him tomorrow and see if they will cooperate. These two countries have a vested interest to keep these White Supremacists animals out of their country too," President Graham answered.

98

Albert Dunham had fallen into one of his deep depressions. Frederick Ellison had witnessed these spells since they were both in Military High School. He was the only person close to his friend who could console him during these uncontrollable moods.

During these difficult times, Albert Dunham transformed himself into *The Architect,* becoming the sociopathic killer that made him happy. Today Ellison knew that allowing his friend to go on a killing rampage would mean the end of *The Architect*.

The siphoning of billions of dollars was going on without a hitch. No monetary agency had noticed the millions of transactions of loose dollars being redirected into Dunham's ten offshore accounts. After just three weeks, the computer software program had grown to over five hundred billion dollars.

Ellison remembered how his friend's behavior had gotten during his quest to be the next Emperor of the United States. If his friend stayed in *The Architect's* personality, the idea of a full pardon would evaporate. He knew he needed to act swiftly.

"Albert," Ellison called out in a calm voice. Shielding a syringe in his right hand that contained a sedative that would calm his friend down, he moved closer. Raising his arm, holding tight the syringe, and aiming it toward the side of his friend's neck. He'd done this before without any complications. For the first time, Dunham blocked his arm, twisting his hand and causing the needle to drop on the floor. Albert craned his neck, his eyes on fire with rage. He pushed his friend hard, causing him to fall backward, hitting his head on a coffee table. Frederick was out cold and breathing with shallow breaths.

The Architect picked up the syringe and expelled the fluid into Ellison's neck. "My friend, sleep well. I have a few things I need to attend to before *The Architect* is laid to rest forever."

Dunham went to his gun safe and extracted a Beretta with five clips, picked up his car keys to his Mercedes, and drove to a private airport where his Dassault Falcon 7X was fueled and ready to fly him to Washington DC. Waiting at the hanger were fifteen of his most seasoned mercenaries ready to do *The Architect's* bidding. The manifest had the name of another billionaire registered on the flight ensuring Dunham's identity was kept a secret.

The jet was airborne within fifteen minutes of Dunham's arrival. With everyone sitting in the main cabin, he opened up a file folder and jumped into what he wanted to say to his men.

"Our country is slowly crumbling, and President Graham, her FBI Director, and Attorney General are running around like chickens with their heads chopped off. While I do not want to help her, I must do something to right the sinking ship so we can come back to the United States free men," Dunham said. "Our biggest challenge will be Professor Cochran and all of his paramilitary units. They are now better organized." He paused to sip his whiskey.

"Cochran was smart recruiting a few retired Generals to help him build a disciplined military force. What we need to do is let Cochran start his revolution, so we can stop it and allow me to ride in on my white horse and become the new leader of the United States," Dunham said.

Dunham leaned his head back, closed his eyes tightly, and began dreaming about his longtime ambition to be the next Emperor of the United States. It made perfectly good sense to him that his country needed a re-draft of the outdated US Constitution. The experiment had tested many different roads to go down, but these last ten years had created a polarized country that was ready to explode into a horrible civil war that would leave America weak against an invasion from its enemies, both foreign and domestic.

99

Commander McAllister, with his team of fifty elite retired veterans, entered Mexico at the Tecate border crossing. They slipped across with twenty-five vehicles, two men in each car. Waiting for them was Felix Rodriguez General in the Mexican Special Forces.

General Rodriquez felt obligated to aid McAllister, who had helped get Charles Stone to leave his country eleven years ago.

At a secluded ranch approximately thirty klicks south of the border, they followed the General in a long caravan. The objective was to strategize how they would stop the Brown Shirts from crossing into the United States.

Mexico's President did not want any military action to take place inside their borders. The cartels were watching every move McAllister and General Rodriquez were making and threatened the President with swift retaliation if anyone brought harm to the Brown Shirts.

McAllister knew that the Mexican army was in bed with the cartels. He understood that if a battle broke out in Mexico, his fifty elite soldiers would not stand a chance. The Commander was on his tablet with the Secretary of Defense, Homeland Security, and the Joint Chiefs.

"Gentlemen, we have a serious problem down here. The current Mexican President has been looking the other way when it comes to the cartels moving drugs into the United States. I need a few drone flyovers to determine if I'm heading into a trap," McAllister said seriously.

General Ronald Hawkins was the first to respond. "I just released five of our drones to survey your surroundings. If you hear any explosions, then that will be your signal to high-tail it out of there and get across the border ASAP. That's an order."

"Copy that, sir."

General Rodriquez briskly walked toward McAllister. He did not appear happy. "John, I just received a disturbing text from my President's Chief of Staff. In addition to the Brown Shirts, five of the largest Mexican cartels are speeding toward our position. None of us are safe," the General said.

McAllister seemed too calm for the Mexican General's liking. When the Commander looked toward the northern sky, Rodriquez looked up too. "There, at two o'clock. I have five attack drones coming to back us up."

"You can't do that in Mexican airspace!" General Rodriquez said, alarm in his voice.

"I'd be surprised that you have an adequate warning system, especially with how you handle the cartels that cross daily into my country," McAllister said while putting his arm around his friend's shoulder. "Now watch and appreciate how my military protects its soldiers."

As the drones swooped past their position, they immediately broke their formation to begin hunting the enemy. Approximately five miles southeast, the horizon was lit up with explosions. Then, southwest, more missiles were released on the Brown Shirt encampment. After ten minutes of heavy shelling, it went silent, and the drones were seen heading back across the border as if they were never there.

McAllister's phone pinged. It was General Hawkins. "Commander, it's safe to cross the border and to the safety of America."

"Enemy count?"

"The five cartels with twenty-five men each, all heavily armed, were sitting ducks. They never saw us coming. No bodies standing. The Brown Shirts took heavy losses too and are heading back to Argentina. Once they cross into Guatemala, President Graham has given the orders to finish the job."

"Sir, thanks for having our backs. I think I need to bring General Rodriquez back with me. He's not safe here."

"Do what you think is right," the General responded.

100

Speeding back toward the Tecate border crossing was General Rodriquez and his small band of soldiers who were escorting Commander McAllister and his fifty elite soldiers. They were five klicks from the safety of America.

Off in the distance, heading toward their caravan, were twenty jeeps and dirt bikes with heavily armed men in ski masks. Sergeant Ron Arnold was the first to see them approaching from the east.

"Sir, we have company coming at our three o'clock and ten o'clock," he said, tapping McAllister's shoulder. "We won't be able to outrun them, and we should make our stand over there." He pointed toward a cluster of large boulders at the base of a grassy hill.

McAllister was communicating with General Rodriquez when a man from a speeding jeep launched his RPG at the first vehicle that contained General Rodriquez. It was a direct hit, and the explosion lifted the vehicle ten feet in the air and caused it to land on the highway in a large fireball.

Before McAllister could give his men orders, Sergeant Arnold jumped out of their moving car, did a shoulder roll, and got himself in a stance, ready to shoot. Without waiting for orders, he aimed his automatic weapon at the speeding jeep and blew the top part of the man's head off before he could release another grenade.

Commander McAllister ordered his team to take a strong defensive position and gave them a green light to neutralize their enemy. They were outnumbered, but that did not matter to these soldiers. They had the experience and the weapons to hold off a small army until reinforcements arrived.

"General Hawkins, we are trapped about four klicks from the border and taking heavy fire. Can you give me cover from our drones again and wipe these bastards from the face of the earth?"

"I was monitoring your progress back home and saw what was happening. Help should be with you in five minutes. Can you hold your position?" the General asked.

"No problem, sir. My guys need the practice," he joked.

Another RPG landed above their position, causing a small landslide of boulders to come crashing down on fifteen of his men. Sergeant Arnold found the soldier who was ready to launch another grenade at them. Like he did a moment earlier, he blew a baseball size hole in the man's forehead.

McAllister was relieved that the small landslide did not kill any of his men. Just some bruises. They signaled the Commander that they were okay to resume their fighting. Chance favors the prepared mind, and once again the Commander's battle decisions paid off. Picking the position to stand their ground was working out favorably. The morning sun had just crept over the hill and was directly in the faces of their enemy.

"Sergeant Arnold, take six of your men to the high ground. They won't be able to see you reposition yourself before it's too late," McAllister ordered. "Once you are in position, we'll stop firing, giving them a false sense we are out of ammunition."

"Copy that, sir. It will be over before the drones get here," Arnold said, his voice dripping with confidence.

As Commander McAllister said, these mercenaries started charging their position, running directly into the bright sunlight. Like shooting cans off fence posts, Arnold and his team had killed thirty of the charging men.

The leader of the cartel realized he was in a difficult situation and ordered the rest of his men to retreat and head back to their compound. That had proved to be a bad decision as the American drones swooped down and released a few hell-fire missiles, wiping out all of the speeding vehicles and the men inside them.

All fifty of McAllister's team were high-fiving and laughing at what they were still capable of doing. Commander McAllister did not like all the laughter but knew that today had been the first time they had been in battle since the Gulf War.

"I'm very proud of each and every one of you. You're all the bravest men I have ever commanded. Now, let's stop celebrating and get our butts back across the border. I need to brief the Joint Chief and the President. Our battle is not over yet," he said.

101

Commander McAllister and his team were back at Camp David the following day briefing President Graham on their mission in Mexico. Attending the meeting were the Joint Chiefs and Homeland Security Secretary. The Secretary of Defense was intentionally omitted from the meeting.

"Madame President, our country has a bigger problem than we ever imagined. Professor Cochran has a very large army of militia and foreign mercenaries. While we stopped them this time, I believe they are regrouping for a final and more devastating attack from the south and north," McAllister said.

General Hawkins jumped in. "What the Commander is saying is correct. NSA has been tracking excessive troop movements in Mexico and in Canada. With the White Supremacist paramilitary groups active, we might have a raging war ready to start in every state," the General said. "Like here, Canada and Mexico are having the same problems with White Supremacists."

President Graham, the color drained from her face, tried to control her shaking hands. "I'm not a military person. So, what are we supposed to do?"

Bursting into the meeting were Dean Miller and his son Allan. "Pardon my interruption. I've been monitoring all of the active remaining militia in fifteen states. Allan has been monitoring our borders and we've come up with a feasible solution that might nip this situation in the bud." Miller was speaking very fast. "Madame President, you need to reactivate the secret satellite President Chesterfield had me create. If I can get it functional again, we can use this to stop our enemies in their tracks. It was supposed to be a defensive weapon, but with a little tweaking, I can convert it to a functioning offensive weapon."

President Graham looked at her Joint Chiefs and Homeland Security Secretary. "Why don't I know about this weapon?" she asked.

General Hawkins responded, "We put it to the scrap yard out in space. It's a very dangerous system that Dunham had gotten control of and almost leveled the White House and the Capitol Building."

"I will need a complete analysis of this weapon and how we are to use it," commanded President Graham.

Surrounding the President were her Secret Service detail. Off in the back of the room, one of them was texting the Secretary of Defense. *"President Wilson's weapon is being activated. It has to be stopped."* As soon as his text was received, he deleted it.

Dean Miller's cell phone pinged. He read his screen, realizing someone in the Oval Office just texted the Secretary of Defense. He whispered to his son to run a trace so he could alert the FBI Director and the President.

102

Attorney General Sam Collins had convened a federal Grand Jury. Professor Cochran and Albert Dunham were still nowhere to be found. Nevertheless, he needed to bring these men to justice without delay.

Their popularity was growing by leaps and bounds. It did not matter to his followers how many American lives were lost by their actions. The belief that they were being replaced justified any collateral damage to people of color that Professor Cochran or *The Architect* felt necessary. Professor Cochran had become a God to his followers, a champion of sorts for White Supremacy.

Albert Dunham had become a beloved philanthropist, giving a majority of Americans fifty thousand dollars. It just had a catch to it. If he got his pardon and every American remain loyal to him, more money would come.

Before the Grand Jury proceedings, Sam was invited to speak to a joint session of Congress. They wanted him to address the DOJ's new wording and interpretation of a domestic terrorist.

Sam had left Camp David with an FBI and US Marshal escort. He did not trust the Secret Service, which had become too political for his liking. First, he needed to be dropped off at his office at the DOJ to pick up the file and speech he had prepared. He knew he'd be speaking to a large audience that would be filled with White Supremacist cohorts.

When Sam entered the large chamber, he was surprised to see every seat occupied by all the House Members and Senators. Behind him was the Speaker of the House and the Acting Vice President. His hand began trembling as he realized the enormity of what he was about to do. Like they do for the State of the Union address, Sam was announced as he walked toward the front of the room, taking his position where the President would stand.

Sam turned around and extended his sweaty hand to the Speaker and Vice President; he was embarrassed that he was showing them how nervous he was. He panned the large chamber and noticed that Tiffany had arrived with her FBI escort. She took her spot in the upstairs gallery.

Sam forced a smile and began talking. "Thank you for inviting me here to speak in this distinguished chamber. I recognized this is not customary for the Attorney General to address both chambers of Congress, but we are not in normal times. In less than two months since becoming our country's Attorney General, I have witnessed lawless Americans set off bombs, and engage in mass shooting events that have murdered over five thousand men, women, and children." Sam paused to blot his forehead with a handkerchief. "We are at war and sides have to be taken."

Sam sipped from his water bottle before continuing. "I am here to tell every one of you that this type of behavior will not be tolerated by the President or my office. Any person or group that plans and organizes the killing of people of color or, for that matter, any American citizen, will be considered domestic terrorists, and their behavior will be considered treasonous with the penalty of death as their punishment if found guilty."

Before Sam finished talking, five members stood up and stormed out. One of them craned his head and shouted, *"Sam Collins, you and your family are dead. We know you're a Jew and we will not be replaced."*

What had just happened did not surprise Sam. He was dumbfounded that these members would be so brazen about voicing their feelings when this proceeding was being televised nationally.

Without any hesitation, Sam continued his speech. "I'd like to remind all of you about our nation's motto: *E Pluribus Unum.* Out of many, one. Our country, when it was built, did not believe that all men were created equal. After hundreds of years of fighting for equality for women, people of color, and LGBTQ Americans, it appears we are going back to a dark and horrible period in our history. Our President and this Attorney General will not allow that to happen." Sam's voice had begun to get louder as he looked around the room, pointing at the House Representatives and Senators he knew were part of the DRM. He sucked in a deep breath and continued.

"Mutual acceptance of our constitutional principles and ideals, as well as the acceptance of all races, nationalities, ethnicities, and cultures, are the guiding principles of *Out of many, one.* The success of this experiment in a democracy lies with the responsibility of our leaders and teachers who are versed in our history and civics and the acceptance of our national motto. Sadly, what has been happening these last few decades and regrettably these last two months, is proving that our leaders and citizens have been infected with a form of Corrupted Intelligence. Too many of you sitting here today would be happier with an autocratic form of government because you are pandering to people's worst instincts."

Sam tried to continue. He was interrupted by the Speaker of the House, who called a thirty-minute recess. The Attorney General, while surprised that the Speaker needed a break, realized that he had shaken up the entire chamber with his words.

Outside in the hallway, Sam was escorted into a private office by his security team. He immediately called President Graham.

"Madame President, everything over here is going according to plan. I've made a big impression on a majority of the House Reps and a handful of Senators. Five members stormed out and one threatened me and my family," Sam said. "I hope Dean Miller was able to tag them and follow their actions after they left?"

"Miller and his son Allan immediately ran a trace on them and uncovered some very interesting people they called. When you get back to Camp David, we'll discuss," the President said. "Now go back in and close out my message to every member of Congress and every militia group in our country. Our war to preserve our democracy has begun."

* * * * *

Sam continued for another forty-five minutes, laying out the President's plan to rid the country of all White Supremacists and domestic terrorist militia groups. "President Graham is going to declare war on all domestic terrorist groups, the Domestic Revolutionary Movement, all illegal militia groups, and any American that is found to support these groups that promote violence against our citizens." Sam smiled at those Senators and House Representatives he knew supported the DRM and contained his laughter when he noticed them squirming in their seats. Sam intentionally paused and sipped from his glass of water for the dramatic effect his words were making.

"Thank you for allowing me to speak to all of you today. Our country is at a turning point in its history and a reboot needs to happen. Our two-party system is not working and needs to change. Our constitution is out of date and demands to be brought up to date, focusing on the needs of our citizens, not corporations. Over the next few months, I will be addressing these issues in more detail," Sam said, ending his talk and walking out of the chamber, passing a group of reporters who wanted to ask him questions.

"I will not be answering questions today, however, I will be holding a press conference tomorrow to announce all the Americans who will be questioned at our Grand Jury arraignment."

103

While Sam Collins spoke at the US Capitol, Paige Turner was getting ready for her weekly podcast. Today, she had planned to summarize the domestic terrorist paramilitary actions, the bloody attempt at a civil war, and the need for every American to stand up and be counted before the greatest country on earth was destroyed.

Scott Rogers, her fiancée, was finally out of the hospital after being shot during the assassination attempt by Tucker Phillips and Dunham's mercenaries at her studio. He was back, heading up her security detail. The threats on her life since then had escalated, but that was not deterring her from exposing all of the White Supremacists and their supporters who wanted to overthrow the government.

From the time she discovered Tiffany Glass was her biological mother, both of them had not had any time to sit down privately and learn about each other. For the first time in her life, she felt at peace that she had found the missing piece inside her heart. Having a family, and being a daughter and an aunt, delighted her.

She had one hour before her show would air and she took the time to review everything she had accumulated since receiving the anonymous package that spelled out the DRM's civil war. What she had garnered from reading the Haven House logbook was that Professor Cochran, since the early fifties, was laying out his plan for the new Confederate States of America. His lies and conspiracy theories were easy for his followers to hold onto, since these poor uneducated Southerners were indoctrinated at birth by racist parents, pastors, and teachers. After so many years of hearing the same lies over and over again, it became the truth that they lived by.

Paige read a report from her staff assistant updating her on the number of followers who watched her podcast. It had grown from fifty million to just under eighty million, and that was just in the United States. Throughout Europe, over a hundred million viewers listened to her podcast.

Inside the Haven House logbook were details of how the defeated Nazi Party, after the war, settled in Argentina, keeping their movement alive through Charles Stone's father and Professor Cochran. Paige was shocked at how Albert Dunham's father played a key role in promoting the Nazi Party and the White Supremacy movement.

It was unfathomable to Paige that these men were capable of creating a loyal tribe of soldiers who would commit heinous crimes because they were loyal to Professor Cochran and his Domestic Revolutionary Movement. The most frightening thing was that there were no Senators or House of Representatives willing to voice their outrage at all the racist killings that had been going on.

Paige remained lost in a deep trance, remembering everything that had happened since she received the package on the DRM's plan. She felt a profound sadness for the young Confederate soldier boys she had interviewed in Richmond, Virginia, after their failed coup attempt. They did not know why they hated people of color, it was that they believed they only belonged with The Professor and his warped dream of a White-only country. While she asked them questions, their lack of formal education stood out, making them easy prey for men like Cochran.

Bradley Stevens rushed over to Paige's desk, a look of dread on his face. "Boss, Albert Dunham is on the phone and demands to speak with you before your podcast airs."

Paige looked up with a blank stare. "Dunham? *The Architect* wants to speak with me?" she asked, puzzled. "Tell him I'll be with him shortly."

Watching Bradley run off, Paige looked at Scott, shrugging her shoulders. "What could he want?"

"The only way to find out is to hear him out. Give me a couple of minutes to alert Dean Miller so we can put a tag on his call," Scott said.

104

Paige could hear Dunham's agitated breaths that her keeping him on hold had created. "Mister Dunham, sorry to keep you waiting, but you took me by surprise with your phone call," she said, her voice overly perky, which only made him more agitated.

"Miss Turner, I know you don't think much of me or how I go about protecting our country—" he was interrupted by her loud laughing.

Paige was waiting for Scott's signal that Miller had connected with Dunham's call. When she saw his two thumbs up, she began talking. "You're damn straight I don't like all the killings you've done, or the assassination attempts on my life since your return from the grave. Can I convince you to go back there and die for real this time?"

Dunham let out an exasperated breath at her rude behavior. "I was hoping we could put down the hatchet and talk like adults. I have something very important to relay to you that will save America from a pending invasion from a foreign force that will test your military," he said.

Paige shrugged her shoulders at Scott. "I'm all ears."

"I will admit that I've had some spies inside your government helping me achieve my goals, but the Brown Shirts, Hitler's new army, has been infiltrating every department of the federal government. You can't imagine how many sleeper cells are waiting for their signal to open the gates of hell and bring the United States to its knees."

"Shouldn't you be speaking with President Graham about this?"

"I've been trying, but the bitch won't talk to me," Dunham cursed. "You're the only person in this fucked up country who can get hundreds of millions of

Americans to listen and prepare for the fight that is coming," he said. "I'm going to do my part with my bioweapon, but if I do, I need a favor from you."

"A favor? I knew there was a catch."

"I just need you to let every one of your listeners know what I was able to do to protect and save democracy. That's it," he said. "I've emailed you the specifics of what will be happening in two weeks." And with that, he disconnected the call.

Paige seemed devoid of emotion at what *The Architect* had told her. His pompous rant on the phone left her conflicted. "Do you think we can believe him?"

Scott was reading the email Dunham had sent. "If what he says in this email is true, then we need to alert the President, the Pentagon, and every law enforcement agency in every state."

Paige immediately dialed Dean Miller's cell. "Did you get your trace?"

"No. His signal was bouncing off multiple cell towers from here to China, Russia, Iran, and Israel. I'm not sure why he used Israel. Maybe as a joke?"

"Dean, thank you. I'm going to speak with the President about Dunham's call and warning."

* * * * *

Dunham took a hefty sip of whiskey after Turner's phone call. "Well, Frederick, do you think I'll get a rise out of Turner?"

"I'm sure she'll speak with President Graham. Once that's done, they will be distracted by the pending invasion and we'll be able to carry out your new manifesto," Ellison said. "Now, let's sit back and watch while I keep siphoning off the billions of dollars you'll need to become the next Emperor of the United States."

105

After speaking with President Graham, Paige set up a one-on-one meeting with Tiffany. The way the President ended their conversation left her with questions about how or if she would take any evasive action at our borders. Her neutral demeanor was opposite to what she had witnessed these last few weeks.

"If Dunham is telling the truth, something I am not sure he knows how to do, we don't want to be caught flatfooted if he's right," Turner said.

"I appreciate you telling me this. We know about the Brown Shirts and that they have become very active and mobile," Tiffany said, happy to see her daughter today. "I'll alert Homeland Security and the Secret Service. If something big is being planned, then these Brown Shirts will need a symbol to attack and the White House would be the perfect place," the FBI Director said. "Please keep a lid on this. We have too many compromised federal employees who we are still trying to weed out and arrest."

"Will do," Paige replied with a little giggle.

Tiffany had a puzzled look on her face. "Was it something I said?"

Paige shook her head. "I haven't adjusted to working with my biological mother. I have so much I want to ask you, but now is not the time."

"When everything settles down, I would like us to get to know each other better," Tiffany answered.

"I'd like that too," Paige replied and started twirling her index finger. "I need to change the subject. Have you ever had April look at photos of Senators and House Reps? Maybe she should look at other federal employees. She might be able to help us find the traitors under our noses a lot faster."

"We were getting ready to do that when Bubba got stabbed and April's safe house was compromised."

Paige headed back to her studio to prepare for her upcoming podcast, surrounded by her security detail run by Scott.

"I don't like you exposing yourself like this. Can't we set up your podcast at Camp David since President Graham authorized you to be there?"

"We could, but it would diminish what my podcast stands for," she said. "I have you protecting me. You're the only person I trust at this moment."

As their motorcades sped away from the Hoover Building, high on a rooftop were two snipers, their scopes zeroing in on Paige and Scott. "Sir, our targets are on the move. We have a clear shot. Affirm we can engage?" the sniper asked.

Professor Cochran paused before responding. "Hold off. I want to wait until my speech airs later today."

* * * * *

Tiffany was holding a meeting with her Deputy Director Mark Booth, her Chief of Staff Allison Monk, and Associate Deputy Director Walter Perle. She had asked Sam to attend.

"I need updates on our progress to arrest all militia groups that were part of the recent attack on our country," Director Glass demanded.

Sam spoke up first. "My department has issued all the warrants you requested."

Deputy Director Booth replied. "We have all the arrest warrants we need, but the resistance we're experiencing is putting our agents in harm's way. We don't have the manpower or weaponry to get the job done," he said.

Allison Monk passed a red file folder in front of Tiffany. "Here are some disturbing data on what we're dealing with," she said.

Tiffany opened the folder and started reading. "Are you kidding me? Arresting these criminals is making them martyrs and emboldening them to push their White Nationalism movement into other states."

Associate Deputy Director Perle jumped into the conversation. "My team is finding that these White Supremacists are riling up more followers on social media. We arrest fifteen and they gain fifty more. It's like trying to kill cockroaches. The more you stomp on them, only brings more out of the woodwork," he said.

"On top of everything else, conservative media companies are peddling misinformation and making the FBI look like a police state," Deputy Director Booth said.

Tiffany, her face drained of color, seemed at a loss for words. "Are we losing this battle?" she asked.

"We will if you stop being distracted by these sideshow antics of Professor Cochran and his DRM," Sam said. "We still need to arrest as many of these traitors, but not lose sight of the upcoming mid-terms. The DRM is becoming a strong political party, similar to what Hitler was able to do between 1930 and 1933. The German people were promised they would have a better economy, jobs, and regain their rightful position as a world power. To unite all Germans, Hitler directed the population's anger and hate against the Jews and other non-Whites. Inside the DRM are skillful propagandists promoting a series of lies over and over again until the untruths become normalized," Sam said.

Before Tiffany could respond, Sam's phone pinged with a special news alert. Professor Cochran was addressing the nation.

"Turn on the TV. Cochran is speaking again."

106

Professor Cochran sat behind a large oak desk, with a Confederate and Nazi flag on the wall behind him. He wore his Confederate General's uniform; the same one he wore when he declared his civil war.

"My fellow patriots and all White Christian militia groups. The country we love is being destroyed by progressives and non-Whites. Your jobs are being taken away by illegal Mexican immigrants, the Blacks, and the Jews who control all the money." Cochran took a sip of water before continuing.

"Today, President Graham and her police state are arresting all our patriots who oppose her way of thinking. With each arrest, our movement keeps growing. We have become a powerful political force. Change is coming at the mid-terms and by the general election, we will have our new White Supremacist President who believes in everything we stand for. We will not be replaced," Cochran said. "Jews and all inferiors, we are coming for you. The war has just begun. Our allies are coming to help us."

With The Professor's last remarks, the TV monitor went black.

Tiffany looked stunned, and Sam's face was beet red.

"What the fuck just happened? Did Cochran officially declare war on the United States again?" Sam cursed.

Tiffany was noticeably upset and attempted to act rationally. "We've been at war for the last ninety days and losing the battle in the press. Our message needs to be stronger as well as our actions against these traitors—" Before she could finish her statement, she got an urgent message from Paige to call her immediately.

Tiffany motioned for her staff to leave the room, except for Sam. In a whisper, she said, "Paige needs to speak with us. She says it's imperative we talk face-to-face."

* * * * *

Sam and Tiffany arrived at Paige's studio with their Secret Service detail and an FBI SWAT unit. Without any direction from the Director, the special unit secured the perimeter of the building and each of the floors in the three-story studio.

She noticed Paige's distressed body language. They briskly walked in and closed the door behind them.

"From the way you look, this must be very serious," Tiffany said.

"It is. Yesterday I spoke with Albert Dunham, and he informed me that a battalion of Brown Shirts, Hitler's secret police, are heading toward our southern and northern borders. Hitler's grandson, Wilhelm Hitler, is leading them. This relic of a radical hate group has been planning this invasion for over thirty years," Paige said, unable to catch her breath. "The scary part is that Wilhelm has been the shadow leader of all the White Supremacist groups in America and around the world."

"Do you believe Dunham?" Sam asked. "If he's anything like Charles Stone, lying is like breathing for him."

"I had my investigative team do some research, and everything Dunham has said has merit. Dean Miller got Stillwell to send me satellite photos of our southern and northern borders. After McAlister stopped the first invasion attempt and got chased out of Mexico, they regrouped with more men, especially from Iran and North Korea, with hardened mercenaries who want to see us destroyed."

Tiffany began combing her fingers through her long black hair, biting her lower lip as she gathered her thoughts. "I'm surprised the NSA or Pentagon is not aware of this pending invasion?"

"Stillwell found out that they are aware and are choosing not to do anything about it until they cross our borders. They are still receiving heat from the Mexican President for crossing into their airspace with our Apache helicopters and drones," Paige said.

"Does President Graham know about this?" Sam asked.

"I believe so. She, too, is being overly cautious to not start a conflict with Mexico."

"That's bullshit. We need to take the fight to these animals," Tiffany said.

"That might be hard as the DRM has mobilized their hundred thousand paramilitary militia at the border to lend these Brown Shirts some backup support," Paige said, her voice cracking. "I also discovered that Cochran's speech was filled with *Dog Whistles*. Those signals caused thousands of young men, wearing Brown Shirts and Khaki pants and carrying automatic weapons to flood their suburban neighborhoods."

Tiffany was at a loss for words. "I need to speak with the Commander and the Joint Chiefs."

"While I can only report the news as I see it and investigate pending problems, I am not equipped to figure out a solution for an invasion of this magnitude," Paige said.

"That's not your job. It's ours. Now, let's get back to Dunham and his reason for contacting you," Sam asked.

"He wants to help stop them and destroy the DRM once and for all. He just wants his pardon. If he is granted that within the next day or so, he'll set loose his paramilitary unit with his bioweapon and destroy the enemy at our doorstep. He needs at least twenty of our Kamikaze drones so he can weaponize them to distribute the nerve agent over a large area in Mexico and in Canada."

Tiffany stood up and began pacing around Paige's office. "We can't give Dunham those lethal drones," Tiffany said. "That's nuts."

"If we say no, then it's a deal breaker and Dunham will go back into hiding to wait for the dust to settle in the United States," Paige said.

Scott Rogers had been quiet while everyone struggled to find some answers. "Director Glass and Attorney General Collins, the way I see it is that we are on our own and need to take lethal action before we get caught with our pants down," he said. "I've spoken with Commander McAllister and the entire US Marshal's office. They are ready to fight and save our country."

Sam was shaking his head. "We do not have enough trained men to fight these highly trained and seasoned mercenaries."

"One more thing. Our Allies in NATO are willing to come to our aid. We just need to give them the green light," Scott said.

Tiffany stopped pacing and sat down. "Can we authorize this, or does it take President Graham's approval?"

"Our European Allies just need our okay and they will mobilize enough well-trained men in Mexico and Canada," Scott replied.

"This has never been done before," Sam said.

"We have never had a situation like this before, either. I would not be able to live with myself if I didn't do everything I could. General Hawkins, the Chairman of the Joint Chiefs is on board too and will, if needed, order the military to defend our borders."

107

On Capitol Hill, a committee had been established to investigate the criminal actions of President Graham, FBI Director Glass, and Attorney General Collins for their willful violation of the constitution. The charges ranged from authorizing the murder of patriotic Americans who had been exercising their right to free speech and assembly to making changes to the constitution without Congressional approval.

Subpoenas had been issued requiring all three to be available for depositions in one week. All the members on this committee, before sending out these requests, were on social media, cable news, and holding press conferences spouting untruths and conspiracy theories that during a trial could be easily refuted. But it did not matter to them. They needed to distract the President and her FBI Director and Attorney General so the invasion could go smoothly.

* * * * *

At Camp David, while still recuperating, Bubba Jackson and April had just gotten back from a long walk. Sitting down with a bottle of water, April and her boys started to watch their favorite TV show, Bel Air. It had been preempted by a major news alert.

The new bipartisan committee investigating the President, FBI Director, and Attorney General all stood behind a bank of microphones. April leaned forward, pushing her boys off to the side so she could focus on the faces of the twelve men looking into the camera. As they spoke, her hands started shaking.

"Bubba, come here quickly," she shouted. When Jackson sat down next to her, she began pointing her finger at the TV screen. "Those men, all of them, were at Haven House when I was there. They did horrible things to the women.

They went on many hunts, coming back laughing and high-fiving each other for killing a Black slave and chopping off the prey's head as a trophy," she said, unable to stop crying. "Each of them was at Haven House many times," she repeated.

Bubba looked at April and put his large arm around her. "Are you sure? These men have been in Congress for over three decades," he said.

"I am positive. Master Charles passed me around to some of them so he could get favors for his Silver Hawk insurance company."

That's all Bubba needed to hear. He was on the phone with Commander McAllister and briefed him on what April said. "I think we found a major link to the DRM. I'm ready to get back into the action," he said.

"Bubba, I've missed you, but I only want you back here if you're one hundred percent ready," the Commander said. "I'm going to brief the President on what you just told me."

108

President Graham was at a loss for words after listening to what Commander McAllister told her about the twelve men on the Judicial Committee. To top it off, she could not believe her NSA and Secretary of Defense during their last briefing did not mention the build-up of enemy troops at the northern and southern borders.

"Commander, what should I do about these two men who are supposed to be protecting our country?" President Graham looked like she was ready to shoot someone.

"Madame President, Dean Miller the other day, discovered that one of your Secret Service agents had been texting the Secretary of Defense about our meeting in the Situation Room," the Commander said. "This will not be an easy decision. If these two Cabinet members are working with or for the Brown Shirts, I think we should first monitor their actions over the next week," Commander McAllister said. "At this point in your administration, finding people you can trust is next to impossible."

"Advise me, please. I know of only a handful of people I can trust, and you are one of them."

"We'll closely monitor them, using Dean Miller's software and use Stillwell's connections to monitor our borders. One other thing, have you located the computer that controls ex-President Chesterfield's weapon's satellite? You'll need it to stop the invasion in its tracks."

"I have Dean Miller looking for it in the White House basement. It got mixed in with over a hundred old laptops from previous administrations. I'll need a quick lesson on what this satellite is capable of doing," she ordered.

"The '*cliff notes*' version I can give you now," the Commander offered.

"I'm all ears."

"Ex-President Chesterfield wanted to be able to neutralize any of our enemy's weapon systems, their internet, and stop all nuclear weapons from ever launching," the Commander said. "It can do a lot more, but those are the important benefits. One more thing. It has a powerful laser that functions as an effective weapon."

"I read in one of President Chesterfield's files on Dunham that *The Architect* got control of the satellite and almost leveled the Capital. That bastard also used the weapon to siphon off billions of dollars from Russia, China, and Turkey."

"That's true. However, after we thought we blew him up leveling his house, we were able to, with the help of Dean Miller, return most of the money he stole. That's why President Chesterfield wanted the software and laptop hidden deep inside the White House archives."

"With this civil war that's ready to start up again and the mercenaries at our borders, I need this weapon up and running without any delays," President Graham said. "Dean Miller should still be down in the basement. Meet up with him and get this weapon operative."

"Copy that."

109

At the Pentagon, Secretary of Defense Wallace Boyce and NSA Director Clayton Sawyer had just finished a secretive meeting that excluded the Homeland Security Secretary and Joint Chiefs. This was the last job they had to do for Professor Cochran. Just look the other way as the Brown Shirts inched closer to the borders.

Wallace looked exhausted and scared. "Clayton, are we doing the right thing here? We're leaving our country vulnerable to our enemies. I thought we were starting a revolution so our White race could regain its rightful place in the South."

Clayton patted Wallace's shoulder. "There, there, my little worrywart. Just like the French did during our first revolutionary war against the British, these Brown Shirts are here to help us by creating a firm hold in all of our Confederate States."

"I don't like it. What if these Brown Shirts turn out to be like the Nazis of World War II? I won't be able to live with myself if there will be concentration camps filled with people of color or any Americans our new government deems traitors," Wallace moaned.

"Our world as we now know it is changing. What is going to happen here in the states is happening throughout Europe and Africa. So, take a deep breath and smell the roses," Clayton said.

* * * * *

Roger Stillwell called Dean Miller. "I found the Secretary of Defense and the NSA Director. They had been in a soundproof room at the Pentagon. I need you to monitor their cellphones and put a trace on all of their activity for the next week."

"Is this coming from the President?" Miller asked.

"Affirmative. These two have been burying National Security threats. President Graham, before she arrests both of them, needs concrete proof of their treasonous behavior," Stillwell said.

"Will do. Good news. I located the satellite laptop that Dunham stole. I'm getting the software updated and should have the weapon active by tonight," Miller said. "Can we meet up in a few hours? I need to run something by you."

"I'll be at the White House briefing the President on the pending invasion. Let's meet in three hours."

* * * * *

Professor Cochran, using a burner phone, called Wilhelm Hitler. "Are you ready to invade in one week as we planned?" The Professor asked with a nervous edge in his voice.

"Cochran, we are ready right now, but will wait for you to get all of your troops in position. I don't want any fuck ups crossing the border," barked the leader of the Brown Shirts. "I have ten truck-mounted missile launchers, one hundred small weaponized drones, and ten thousand men ready to kill as many people of color as they can as they cross the border."

"I appreciate your help in our revolution and will reward you substantially before you return to Argentina," Cochran said.

Wilhelm did not respond immediately to what The Professor had just said. "Cochran, my old friend. What will happen in a week is the end result of everything I and my father helped you accomplish for the last thirty years. Once we have your Confederate States, I am not going anywhere. I will be marching toward Washington DC and then all the remaining states in the north."

"I don't remember that being our deal when we first met at Haven House in 2008," The Professor said, sounding annoyed.

"This was the agreement between my grandfather and father back in 1977 after I was born. So, unless you have a bad memory of what you agreed to back then, don't give me any shit. I am here to fulfill my grandfather's dream of a pure Aryan race in the United States without any inferiors getting in our way, including Jews." Wilhelm's voice had gotten agitated. "Don't ruin my plans or you'll be dealt with severely. Change is coming and your experiment with democracy is over." With that, the phone went dead.

The Professor stared at his cell phone, a blank expression on his face. "What the fuck have I started?" he asked himself.

110

President Graham had called an emergency meeting with her Secretary of Defense, NSA Director, CIA Director, and Homeland Security Secretary. Sitting with the President in the Situation Room were her Attorney General, FBI Director, and Secretary of State. She panned the room with a death stare.

"I'll get to the point of this National Security meeting." She started pointing at each of her Cabinet members. "Whose side are you on? There is only one right answer," she barked.

The Secretary of Defense and NSA Director started squirming in their seats. Sam noticed it first and whispered in Tiffany's ear. "I can't wait to see their expressions when the President has both of them in handcuffs, escorted out, and thrown in federal prison."

"Now, now, Sammy, let's give President Graham a little time to enjoy herself," Tiffany said.

"I will ask again and this time I want responses from all of you," she demanded as she pointed her index finger at each of them.

"Country first, Madame President," the CIA Director said loudly. "I love our country and will defend it with my life if necessary."

The Homeland Security Secretary said the same thing, but nothing from the Secretary of Defense or the NSA Director. President Graham opened a red folder that was marked *Confidential and Top Secret*. She tossed a handful of aerial photos at them without any explanation.

"I know the two of you saw these photos two weeks ago. Any reason during our many National Security briefings these last two weeks you failed to mention that over ten thousand mercenaries with military weapons were amassing on our southern border and five thousand more at the Canadian border?"

Clayton Sawyer replied first. "Madame President, you're not liked throughout the Beltway or by me. Our country needs a change so we can once again be respected around the world," he said.

President Graham looked at her NSA Director, her eyes like daggers. "Confession will save your soul, or so some would believe. I did not want this job and was put into it after President Thompson's death. I am not sure what you don't like about me or the job I've been doing unless you are pissed that your insurrection has been going nowhere."

Wallace Boyce decided to speak up. "It's too late for you to stop us. A new South is going to happen and all of you will be put in concentration camps while we decide what to do with you," he said with an air of confidence.

"Do you really think that our borders can be breached and your treasonous friends will succeed?" President Graham crowed.

"I think it's too late for you to stop our movement. It's been in the planning stages for decades," Clayton spewed out.

Sam Collins could not listen anymore to these racist bastards. "You tried with Charles Stone and then Albert Dunham. Just like how Hitler failed, so will this so-called civil war fail and all of you will be either dead or in a Federal Super Max locked away with no chance of ever seeing the light of day," Sam threatened. "We know what's happening at our borders and have already mobilized our military to stop the invasion before it even starts."

"We'll see how you stand up to Hitler's Brown Shirts that are coming to take all of you out," Clayton said.

President Graham was getting tired of these two traitors. She signaled her Secret Service detail to put them in shackles and hand them off to the US Marshals waiting outside the Situation Room.

"Get these bastards out of here. I don't want to see them again until their trial for treason," she ordered.

* * * * *

An hour later, President Graham sat in with her National Security team, which included Commander McAllister, Bubba Jackson, Dean Miller, Roger Stillwell, and the Secretary of State. Her CIA Director and Homeland Security Secretary had stayed with her from the earlier meeting. Everyone anxiously waited for Dean Miller to demonstrate how the weapons satellite could perform.

"What Miller will show us will not only astonish each of you, but will help us end this invasion by foreign mercenaries and end the insurrection by our homegrown domestic terrorists," President Graham said.

On the Situation Room's eight-five-inch screen, Miller had pulled up what appeared to be a small encampment south of the Tecate border crossing. What was visible were three missile launchers on the back of military-style trucks.

"Ladies and gentlemen, please watch closely." He began typing in some keystrokes on his laptop's keyboard and hit the enter key. Immediately, one of the missile launchers started swiveling on its base until it was aiming at the other two trucks. Miller once again started typing and hit the enter button. Two missiles shot off the back of the truck and blew up the vehicles it was aimed at. Then, with one swift stroke of the keyboard, the last truck self-destructed.

"This is just a small demonstration of this weapon's power and versatility," Miller said, letting a satisfying grin crack on his face.

President Graham started clapping, a big smile on her face. "If any of you had any doubts we will win this war on our democracy, I hope you feel confident we can soon get back to running our country and helping the average American achieve a good life."

The President dismissed her Cabinet and ordered them to be back in two hours.

111

In a meeting with the Mexican President, Wilhelm Hitler could not stop yelling at him. "You promised me that my men would be safe from President Graham and her military," he screamed.

The Mexican President had a puzzled expression. "How do you know this malfunction was President Graham's doing?" he asked.

Wilhelm was getting agitated. "Do you remember what Albert Dunham was capable of doing with the satellite weapon the United States created? He almost leveled the Capitol and White House before President Chesterfield regained control and turned one missile on Dunham," he screamed.

"If this is true, then what do you want me to do? Mexico doesn't have the weaponry or the military to go to war with the United States," he shouted back.

"You could get on the phone and rip that bitch President a new asshole for trying to start a war with your country. Show some backbone."

Alejandro Aguilar picked up the red phone on his desk and pressed the button that would directly take him to President Graham. Ten seconds later, a female voice answered. "President Aguilar, I assume you want to speak with President Graham?" Chief of Staff Martha Sweeden said. "I'll let the President know you're calling."

A minute later, President Graham greeted her counterpart in Mexico. "I think I know why you're calling," she said. "I was about to call you about the build-up at my border," she said in a raised voice.

President Aguilar was breathing loudly. "You sent missiles across into Mexico," he nervously said.

"I did nothing of the sort. The destruction of the Brown Shirts military trucks was done by their own weapons, not ours," she said. Before President

336

Aguilar could respond, President Graham shouted into her phone. "Is Wilhelm Hitler sitting there with you? If so, put the little shit on the phone," she demanded.

Wilhelm's face flushed with anger. He hated women in authority and especially hated this woman because of her bloodline. President Graham's mother was Chinese and as far as young Hitler felt, she was inferior to him and should not be in a position to fight with him. He yanked the phone from Alejandro's hand.

"Shannon, what you just did to my weapon will cost you dearly. I have enough weapons to level all the cities from Southern California to the Eastern tip of Texas. Once that's done, then I am coming to you at the White House and will drag you out of your Oval Office and hang you on the front lawn for all the world to see, you fucking bitch."

President started laughing. "Now, now, child. Temper tantrums are so like your grandfather and where is he today, you spoiled brat?"

"You can't talk to me that way. I'm the next leader of the new world order that's happening around the world as we speak. You soon will be on your knees begging for my mercy," Wilhelm shouted.

"I think you need another demonstration of our power. When you mess with the United States, we will bring the swift force of our military to wipe you out," President Graham responded in a low, calm voice. "Now watch your monitor in President Aguilar's office."

Dean Miller was streaming his next demonstration. Northwest of Laredo, Texas, in a small town called Piedras Negras, Mexico, Wilhelm had positioned his mercenaries from Iran and Turkey. Once again, Miller hit some keys on his laptop, positioning the satellite, so its lasers were focused on that small Mexican town.

Once Miller pressed enter, a wide red beam started sweeping the small town, incinerating each building it touched. Then the lasers found the military vehicles and caused them to explode. Once the dust had settled, over a thousand bodies, dressed in military fatigues, lay dead, smoldering from the laser.

"So, who's in charge now, my little friend?" President Graham said, her voice had turned icy cold. "Now, before I wipe all of your racist armies off the face of the earth, I want to see you immediately retreating back to the hole you crawled out of. If I don't see you leaving Mexico and heading back to Argentina within the next hour, I will unleash the full power of my weapon you've witnessed today," she threatened.

After the call, President Graham started asking her National Security team what needed to be done next to end this pending invasion quickly. "I don't believe Wilhelm Hitler will leave Mexico quietly. If he's truly been the shadow leader of the Domestic Revolutionary Movement, we haven't heard the last from him and his army," she said.

Sam Collins seemed confused about what the President was saying. "You really believe he's going to try to fight us?"

"Not in the traditional sense. He does have the support of over a hundred thousand Americans, citizens that don't trust our government. I'd like to have a plan that will neutralize the DRM and set them back to the Stone Age."

Before anyone could respond, Dean Miller was turning on the TV monitor. "We need to see this," he said.

A special news alert had preempted all normal daytime shows. Germany, France, and the UK were being besieged by White Supremacist groups carrying DRM and Nazi flags. Stores were being ransacked, and fires were being set around each city. These militias were heavily armed and were overwhelming the local police.

Then the news switched to Mexico City and the same riots were happening there. President Graham was shocked to see how easy it was for these terrorists to mobilize. "What can we do to help these countries?"

Tiffany suggested that the country needed to hear from their President and reassure everyone that everything is under control. "I suggest having your National Security team standing behind you might calm everyone down."

President Graham looked at her Chief of Staff. "Set it up now. I want to be on the air in fifteen minutes."

112

Wilhelm was unable to calm down from the humiliation he had experienced at the hands of President Graham, even though that woman was the most powerful person in the world. The degradation for him began when he was a young boy of eight years in Argentina, and his stepmother controlled him from the moment he woke up to the time he went to sleep. She'd shame him in front of his friends, relatives, and even his first girlfriend. At first, the verbal abuse he could take, but the beatings changed him forever.

His stepmother had been abused by his father after his mother had died from mysterious causes. Then one late night he was awakened by a loud gunshot and ran to his parent's bedroom where he saw his stepmother holding a pistol, smoke coming out of the barrel, and saw a large pool of blood on the pillow where his stepmother blew a hole in the side of his father's head.

Wilhelm was frozen at the doorway, unable to move or say a word. His first thoughts were not of his father's brutal murder, but the endless abuse he would be receiving from his only legal guardian.

When Wilhelm turned eighteen, his dislike for his stepmother had come to boiling point. The anger he felt inside his heart flowed through his veins to the point he felt he had to do something about it. On a cold wintery night in Argentina at his father's home, in a fit of rage, with a large butcher knife, he stabbed his tormentor over a hundred times while she was in the shower. It was his first kill but would not be his last as he assumed his rightful position as leader of the Brown Shirts.

Snapping back to his task at hand, he ordered his men to release a cruise missile at San Antonio with the coordinates to impact the famous River Walk shopping area. As he watched the missile head east, he smiled with delight.

He realized that if he got on the open road to return to Argentina, he'd be a target for President Graham's new weapon.

He dialed Professor Cochran to discuss their next move.

"Albert, after seeing President Graham's satellite weapon in action, I feel we need to move up our invasion. I don't trust that bitch to keep her word that we'd have safe passage home. I need to kill her in front of the entire world and let everyone know that we are the new Reich," he said.

"I'm not sure it's a good idea right now. My men are having doubts about letting you invade our country to create a new Nazi regime."

"I'm not in the mood for your whining, Professor. We've been planning this operation since Haven House had become our home base and you will not get in my way to fulfill my grandfather's and father's dream of a pure White nation," Wilhelm admonished. "I've already signaled our men on both borders to begin moving toward their targets. The war is starting, and if you want to be part of our new nation, you should mobilize your militia and begin the slaughter. Make sure you have all of the dump trucks and snowplows into position around Washington, DC, as well as the Pentagon."

113

The missile landed in the heart of the River Walk shopping district, leveling 80 percent of the retail shops and hotels. The tragic result was that over a thousand innocent shoppers, including two hundred small children in strollers, died from the massive explosion. President Graham was devastated that she had misjudged how her demonstration would impact Wilhelm Hitler.

Marching around the Situation Room, she went over to Dean Miller and rested her hands on his shoulders. "I need to stop this madman before he does anything else to our country," President Graham said, her frustration showing. "Can this weapon wipe every one of them off the face of the earth, even our own homegrown domestic terrorists?"

Miller was watching the news on his cellphone, unable to respond to her question. He handed it to her. "Madame President, we have a bigger problem than killing Wilhelm. The war and the invasion have already started in Washington State, Michigan, Texas, and California. The Brown Shirts have crossed our borders and have blended in with the DRM paramilitary militia groups."

The Joint Chiefs had all reacted to the news and began mobilizing all branches of the military. The Chairman of the Joint Chiefs General Hawkins, without getting authorization from the President, put all of the United States military bases on high alert and ordered all fighter jets airborne and sent fifty Apache helicopters to monitor the borders and if necessary, use lethal force to curtail the invasion. General Hawkins finished briefing the President on the actions he had taken.

President Graham thanked him. Without taking a breath, she began giving orders to her security team. "I want Commander McAllister to run point on this invasion with all of our Special Forces. I want FBI Director Glass to mobilize her SWAT agents and have them in Washington State, Michigan, San Diego, Texas, and Arizona. I'll put the National Guard on High Alert and declare martial law effective immediately," she said. "This is day one and by day five, I want this contained and all traitors and invaders either arrested or dead."

Attorney General Collins had been silent while the President gave her orders. "Madame President, you'll need to go before Congress and the American people and ask for their support with this counteroffensive you are planning," he said as any attorney would do for a client. "I'll call the Speaker of the House and Senate Majority Leader to have you before Congress in two hours."

President Graham gave Sam a harsh stare. "Do you really believe they will first, give me their support, and second, act in a timely manner?"

"It won't matter. This is just a courtesy visit. You took an oath to protect and defend the country and constitution from both foreign and domestic enemies. And this fits perfectly with your constitutional duties as President," Sam said. "I'd like to open the address to Congress first and remind everyone of the members of their oath of office and the DOJ's interpretation of domestic terrorism and the penalty for participating or even supporting terrorism in a form or manner," Sam said. He noticed the President agreed with what he requested as she left the Situation Room to prepare for her address to Congress.

President Graham turned around and shouted back at General Hawkins. "You have, on my authority, to take whatever actions you need to do to stop the invasion."

114

The Sergeant of Arms in the House Chamber announced the arrival of President Graham and Sam Collins. There was a hushed silence from every member.

The Attorney General and President walked side by side toward the podium, positioned in front of the House Majority leader and Vice President. The room was filled with every House Representative and Senator.

Sam stepped forward and opened his notes, ready to speak to everyone in attendance and every American who was watching this historic moment.

"My fellow Americans, distinguished members, and President Graham. Over the last ninety days, our country has been faced with mass shootings and targeted bomb attacks at places of worship in minority neighborhoods by White Supremacists. These groups have become the paramilitary arm of the DRM and Professor Cochran. During my short time as the Attorney General, I needed to redefine the term domestic terrorist to include all illegal militia groups, elected officials who support these groups, as well as any American who is found to harbor a White Supremacist." Sam paused to take a sip from his water glass.

"Some of you here today believe these White Supremacist militia groups are just voicing their First Amendment right to free speech. But what these animals are doing does not protect them under the constitution." Sam stopped and took another sip from his water glass. "Democracy needs dialog to air differences. When one party stops participating and using violence to get what they want, then autocracy threatens the freedom citizens believe they have."

Sam was interrupted by a group of House Representatives he spoke to when he was the Attorney General of California. He heard the shouts of *Liar, Traitor, Fascist, and Jew bastard. We will not be replaced.*

He turned his head toward the shouting and pointed his index finger at them. "So, the old dirty dozen from Charles Stone's era have reared their ugly heads," Sam shouted back, grinning. "If you think our country believes in your racist philosophy or that murdering women and children of color are patriotic acts for your revolution, then you are totally mistaken." His heart started racing to over a hundred and fifty beats per minute, per his Fitbit watch. "Right now, our four branches of the military are engaging with the enemies who have crossed our southern and northern borders, as well as the illegal militia groups who are aiding and abetting these foreign mercenaries. This little war will be over quicker than it started and most of you will be arrested for your support of these hate groups.

"If you believe that what you're doing is not a crime, first let me read to you the legal definition of aiding and abetting:
"The legal term aiding and abetting refers to a person's action to help, support, or approve of someone else's illegal act. 'Aiding and abetting' is a crime in itself, held against those who would somehow assist a criminal – short of physically contributing to the illegal act. In many jurisdictions, aiding and abetting is the same as an 'accessory' to the crime.

"My time is up for now, but be aware that the Justice Department is coming for anyone who is *aiding and abetting* White Supremacist militia groups or the foreign mercenaries who have invaded our country. One additional thing I need to mention. All of you here and you'll know who I am talking about, you need to stop inciting your followers to rise up and attack other innocent Americans. I have opened an investigation into your verbal actions and what violent results had come from your words." With that said, Sam turned the podium over to President Graham.

President Graham thanked her Attorney General and took the microphone. "I'll be brief as I have to get back to the Situation Room and monitor the uprising that is taking place in the north and south. I'm appalled that most of you here have remained silent about the attacks and killing of minorities that have taken place. I can't wait to see what your reactions will be about the civil war that has started and the foreign mercenaries that are helping our White Supremacist militia," she said, pacing nervously.

"I hope you've taken heed of what my Attorney General said here today. Trials will be starting for all the captured DRM militia during the first uprising weeks ago. If these traitors with their seditious actions are found guilty, our

344

nation will witness the first public executions in our country's history," President Graham said, her tone threatening.

She continued without taking a calming breath. "Aiding and abetting is not a subjective part of the law. It's a precise interpretation of your actions I am sure a lot of you know you are guilty of committing. A handful of you should be getting subpoenas after this session of Congress is over. The Grand Jury has been empaneled. You will pay for your crimes against our country and democracy." Without any closing remarks, President Graham walked off the stage and was escorted out of the chamber by her Secret Service detail.

115

Commander McAllister and General Hawkins were at the Pentagon's War Room coordinating the Special Force units engaging with the DRM's paramilitary militia, as well as Wilhelm Hitler's invading army.

McAllister did not look happy with the report Dean Miller handed him. "Are you sure this is accurate?"

Dean shrugged his shoulders, frustration etched on his face. "Four of our top National Guard Generals have been communicating with Professor Cochran and Wilhelm Hitler. Stillwell received aerial photos of the thirteen southern states Cochran wants for his new Confederacy and there are over a hundred and fifty thousand troops blending in with the Domestic Revolutionary Movement's paramilitary units," Miller said.

Commander McAllister started pacing around the War Room, growling under his breath. "Shit. We've known that there have been White Supremacists inside our military, but the numbers were small and insignificant. I can't believe that in the National Guard there are so many traitors," he griped.

General Hawkins was listening to the Commander's conversation and looking like he wanted to kill someone. "I thought we nipped this in the bud when the fucking Maryland National Guard tried to storm the Capital and White House. You'd think these fucking traitors would have learned their lesson," General Hawkins cursed.

Dean Miller handed the Commander another piece of paper that triggered McAllister to slam his fist on the metal table in front of him. He handed the piece of paper to General Hawkins. "I need to have my Special Force units hitting key locations in the north and south to slow down this advancement," McAllister said. "If we implement the same strategy with enough firepower as we did in

346

Iraq and Afghanistan, this could all be over in a few days. But I need to act now before The Brown Shirts and National Guard troops team up with more of DRM's paramilitary groups."

Roger Stillwell jumped into the conversation. "Satellite surveillance captured five cities that are engaged in heavy fighting with local SWAT units and local police. They are severely outmanned and outgunned. The Brown Shirts are very well armed with automatic rifles, RPGs, and ten truck-mounted SH-15 China-made Howitzer."

"Shit. This is worse than I thought. They seem to be well organized and have the support of civilians in each of these areas," McAllister said. "General, once I have my teams in place, Dean Miller will position our weapon satellite and disable their weapons. Then we can move in and neutralize the advancing armies."

General Hawkins surveyed the five large monitors, and when he saw the devastation the Brown Shirts were doing to highly populated cities, he gave the Commander the green light to move forward with his plan, but with one caveat. "Don't dismantle their weapons, wipe them out, including their armies," the General ordered.

* * * * *

Commander McAllister belted out orders to Bubba Jackson and his five SEAL units comprising fifty of the most seasoned and experienced soldiers with years of experience dealing with terrorists. This would be their first opportunity to stop an invading force that was crossing US borders.

"No arrests. Deadly force only. When you've stopped their movements, Dean Miller will position our satellite and destroy their mobile weapon vehicles," McAllister said.

"Sir, the Brown Shirts have grown with other foreign mercenaries and our own homegrown terrorists. Confirm if I have the green light to kill Americans as well as the Brown Shirts and the foreign mercenaries?" Bubba asked.

"Affirmative. Take no prisoners. These murderous bastards don't deserve room and board for life in our prisons."

"Copy that, sir." With that, the phone line went dead.

116

At all border crossings coming from Mexico, it was another tragic story. Wilhelm Hitler, with help from Professor Cochran's DRM paramilitary groups, Mexico's drug cartels, and mercenaries from Iran, Russia, Mexico, and Lebanon, had breached all of the immigration posts using snowplows and garbage trucks to break through, destroying all border checkpoints and leaving border patrol agents lying dead.

Three US military battalions with over three thousand men protecting the southern border had been surrounded by Wilhelm's approaching army approaching from the south and Professor Cochran's DRM militia groups from the north. The United States military was outmanned and outgunned by a well-organized assault.

General Tyler Fitzgerald, while not panicking, called General Hawkins. "Sir, we all miscalculated the size of the enemy advancing from Mexico, as well as the weapons they are using. I've lost over a hundred men so far, and it looks like that number will increase unless I can get some air support," General Fitzgerald said.

"I just saw from our aerial photos what is happening at the Mexican border. I've ordered twenty drones to your position, as well as ten Apache helicopters with orders to destroy the enemy," General Hawkins said. "At our northern border, we are experiencing the same situation. I don't like killing Americans, but these animals are traitors trying to overthrow our way of life. Hang in there, Fitz, help is on the way."

General Hawkins looked over at Commander McAllister, his face bedsheet white. "Commander, we have a war on our hands. It's not by untrained militia, but professional mercenaries that our enemies have sent to topple our government."

Before McAllister could respond, his cell started ringing. He glanced at the screen. It was President Graham. "Madame President."

"Commander, the Capitol and White House are under siege. The DRM is now occupying the Capitol building. The FBI and Secret Service don't know how long we have before they take over the White House," President Graham with a raspy voice said. "I am in my bunker and safe for now."

"I'll get Dean Miller to reposition our satellite and nip this in the bud," the Commander said.

"That won't work. Dean Miller and his family are missing. We suspect that his security team had some traitors and took him to an undisclosed location. If they get him to turn the satellite on us, our country could fall within a matter of hours," President Graham said.

"Miller was paranoid and had tracking devices inserted into his and his family's shoulders. Roger Stillwell will be able to find him, and I'll get him back to the White House," McAllister said. "Hang in there, Madame President."

"That's all I've been doing since becoming President. It's been a nightmare trying to save our democracy. I'm weakening and might give in to Dunham's demands and take him up on his offer to help," President Graham said.

"Madame President, that's a very bad idea. Once you open up that pandora's box, it will be next to impossible to turn back," McAllister said. "Give me a couple of hours before you make that decision."

"Two hours. Not a minute longer. I won't lose Washington on my watch to a bunch of invading mercenaries and our homegrown domestic terrorists."

117

Paige Turner was ready to air an emergency broadcast while the war was raging in the north and south. Her guest was going to be the leader of the Never Again coalition, a new group determined to end hate around the world and especially in the United States.

The Never Again leader had his face covered with a ski mask for safety reasons and had asked for this interview, citing that the war on hate must officially come to an end. He told Paige that his group was ready to take the battle to all White Supremacists, Nazis, and all supporters of domestic terrorists.

"Not sure what I should call you?" Turner asked.

The man at first didn't reply, then in a low voice said. "You can call me Major."

Paige smiled at his answer. "Major, it is a pleasure to have you on my show today. I agree with you on hate in America and around the world. You've got my attention."

"Miss Turner, thank you for having me on your show. While we've never met, I've watched you stand up for democracy when Albert Dunham tried to shatter the norms of the constitution. What you are trying to do by exposing the DRM for its terrorist activities is commendable. For many years I tried to stay in the background, hoping more people like you would step up and be counted to help with the struggles minorities have and the everyday hate they face from law enforcement, White Supremacists, and our own political leaders with their Dog Whistles labels. I've been fighting Anti-Semitism most of my life. With the rise of the White Supremacist movement in over twenty-seven states and throughout our government, I've brought together tens of thousands of Never Again ex-military men and women. They, like me, are sick and tired of all the hate growing in the country we love. While I am here talking to your audience, my paramilitary units are at the southern and northern borders lending support to our brave soldiers defending our country. We have men and women from every walk of life standing up and saying, '*we won't take it anymore*,'" The Major paused to catch his breath. "Here's a link I'd like you to broadcast to your followers that will show all the traitors and mercenaries that are killing innocent Americans as they use them as human shields."

Paige looked shocked when she saw the fighting that was going on at the southern and northern borders. What she didn't expect to see was civilians wearing body armor with painted letters on the back that read: Never Again Army. They appeared well-organized and professional as they took the battle to the DRM's paramilitary soldiers. Within thirty minutes, the White Supremacist militia ran to their vehicles, driving away from the fighting while still firing their weapons at innocent Americans.

The Never Again army had vanished into the surrounding hills to give the United States military the space to do their job.

As the DRM mercenaries drove off, seven American Apache helicopters that were positioned at the northern border started firing at the moving vehicles, turning the American traitor's trucks and cars into balls of flames. The military started capturing the remaining White Supremacists.

On another monitor, Paige witnessed the same scenario at the southern border. Once the Never Again army disappeared, eight Apache helicopters began firing at the Brown Shirt army. They were better organized than the northern DRM militia and return fire using RPGs, hitting two helicopters that had to make emergency landings. The other six helicopters retreated to a safe zone to await their orders.

The Brown Shirts, with their garbage trucks and snowplows, headed toward a small Texas town destroying cars in their wake. The local police were no match for the automatic weapons that ripped apart their bodies. Once inside the town, Wilhelm had his men collect all the hysterical women and children who had been playing in a grassy park.

Wilhelm looked to the sky and gave a single-finger salute to whoever was watching.

The Major looked at Paige, his eyes tearing up after realizing he underestimated Hitler's grandson. "Miss Turner, I have to go now and regroup.

I am not sure what our next move will be," he said, his voice cracking. "Thanks for having me on your show."

Scott Rogers came running into the studio as the Major rushed by him. "What just happened?" he asked. "Do we even know who this guy is?"

"Not a clue, but I hope my studio camera got a shot of his Jewish Star on his forearm. It was similar to what Mossad agents and Israel intelligence agents had tattooed on their arms."

* * * * *

Back inside the Pentagon War Room, Commander McAllister and General Hawkins were struggling with how the war was going.

"Who the fuck were those Never Again vigilantes?"

"I have no clue, but would like to get them to be part of our war movement," General Hawkins said.

McAllister was shaking his head. "I think they are already part of our war. I would like to be able to thank them for saving our men. Our immediate problem is the Capitol and the White House and getting our President to a safe location."

118

Professor Cochran had taken over all the networks and began speaking from the rotunda at the Capitol. Behind him were twenty-five Capitol Police officers, the Speaker of the House, and the Senate Majority leader. Several House Representatives, all non-Whites, were dragged in front of the podium; each had a gun pressed to the back of their head.

Cochran looked overly pleased with what he was about to say, tapping the microphone to be sure it was on.

"My fellow Americans, today a new America has emerged. Our country is back to its rightful place for all pure White Christian men and women. In front of me are the elite traitors who have been trying to replace all of you." The Professor lifted his bottle of water, taking a few relaxing gulps. "These eight elected officials are some of the most corrupt politicians making laws that protect the Blacks, Hispanics, and murderous A-rabs who are trying to replace us. Our new constitution clarifies what we do to traitors and people of color." With that said, he ordered his men to execute the seven House Members.

The explosion of bullets echoed loudly in the large domed hall as the seven crying men fell forward; the front of their skulls shattered as they lay in large pools of blood.

Professor Cochran, with a broad smile, started to speak again. "President Graham, the White House is next. I will offer you a pardon if you surrender and take your Attorney General and FBI Director and leave my country immediately, or suffer the same execution as these men," he threatened.

Walking up to the podium in full Nazi uniform was Wilhelm Hitler. He leaned toward the microphone with an evil stare at the camera. "We are methodically overpowering your military in the south and will soon have more soldiers crossing the border. More White Americans support our movement and welcome a revolution and a new beginning to your failed experiment," young Hitler bragged.

He grabbed the microphone and started marching around the large hall. "As America's new Chancellor, I will not be so gracious as Professor Cochran," Wilhelm said, holding back a laugh. "You have one hour to surrender, or I will level the White House and bury you inside your steel bunker. I will give you a quick demonstration of my power," he shouted.

Professor Cochran and his DRM soldiers rushed outside the Capitol, leaving the hostages inside. When Wilhelm was safely outside, he held up the device. With his thumb, he pressed a red button. Explosions could be heard coming from each corner of the building, then one large explosion blew the top off the dome. Like falling dominos, the symbol of American Democracy collapsed, creating a large plume of smoke and ash.

* * * * *

President Graham fell back in her chair, her head cupped in her hands. "How could this be happening?" she shouted.

Sam was the first to answer. "We underestimated how many traitors there were inside the halls of Congress," he said, looking over at Tiffany. "Are you thinking what I am thinking?"

Tiffany smiled, nodding her head. "McAllister and General Hawkins are up to their eyeballs with the battles raging in the north and south. With Miller and his family missing, getting the satellite up and running again will be next to impossible," she said. "We just need to position the weapon over Washington and destroy Wilhelm and The Professor before they can mobilize and breach the White House."

President Graham looked up, her eyes glassy. "I want to kill those fucking bastards and leave no one standing," she barked.

Tiffany texted Stillwell. "Find Miller ASAP."

119

Bobby Conrad, an NSA systems specialist, followed instructions from Dean Miller's son. He was able to reboot the computer and get the satellite up and running. With a few keystrokes, got the weapons satellite in position. He began streaming the satellite camera into the White House bunker. The front of the Capitol steps had Cochran and Wilhelm exposed. The monitor showed two crosshairs on the top of the two leaders' heads.

"Madame President, do I have a green light to engage the enemy?" Bobby Conrad asked.

President Graham, with a resounding voice, said yes. "Destroy these motherfuckers," she ordered.

Conrad quickly began typing and activated the laser weapon on the satellite. He had his index finger on the enter key when his cell phone rang.

"Yes, Madame President. Copy that," Conrad answered, confused.

President Graham did not seem pleased with Sam Collins at the moment. "This better be good," she said to him.

Sam sucked in a deep breath. "Madame President, killing them outright without a trial for the whole world to see, will anger their followers who consider them Gods and their savior," he said.

"Are you saying we should let them get away with murder?"

"No. Commander McAllister has a military unit five minutes away from the Capitol. We just need Bobby Conrad to take out Cochran and Wilhelm's men first. It will make it easy for the Commander to capture these two murderers," Sam said.

President Graham nodded. She was back on the phone with Conrad again. "New targets. Wipe out all DRM, Brown Shirt troops, and leave The Professor and Wilhelm to Commander McAllister's men, who are two minutes out. You have a green light, so get it done quickly," she commanded.

Typing in a few additional keystrokes and hitting enter positioned the satellite over the two hundred soldiers protecting their leaders.

President Graham, the Attorney General, and FBI Director all watched the laser from the weapons satellite do its job. A wide red beam blanketed the soldiers, causing them to vaporize. Within minutes, what was left of the soldiers were their bodies twisted in large pools of blood.

Standing in shock were Professor Cochran and Wilhelm Hitler, unable to move as the red laser beam formed a circle around them. Approaching from the street were twenty-five military SWAT officers, their weapons pointing at the two frightened men.

Camera crews from all the news organizations that cover Washington politics positioned themselves on Northwest and Southwest Drive and started to record what the weapons satellite had done. A few reporters were broadcasting the destruction and murder of over two hundred enemy soldiers, slanting their opinions, and naming the invading terrorists and domestic terrorist militias as freedom fighters.

120

Allan Miller leaned in toward his father and whispered. "I hope our tracking devices are working. I want to get out of here and away from this madman," he said.

"Depending on how busy President Graham is with her war, Stillwell should be locking into us very soon," Miller whispered.

Before Dean could console his wife and daughter, Albert Dunham was briskly walking toward them with a gun in his right hand. He was whistling an unfamiliar tune.

"Dean, I will only ask this once, or I will start shooting your family one by one," *The Architect* said.

Ellison was shocked that Dunham was not giving himself room to negotiate if Miller refused. "Albert, can we talk, now?" he asked.

The two men walked to the farthest side of the warehouse. "What is so important that you interrupted me?"

"You're not giving yourself any room to negotiate with Miller. Once you kill any of his family, he'll realize that everyone will die anyway. Then you will not get what you want," Ellison said. He immediately noticed a change come over his friend. "Is Albert back?"

Dunham took a deep, cleansing breath. "Yes, I am back," he said. "What do you want me to do?"

"Leave the Millers here with a small security team and use your bioweapon on the DRM and invading armies," Ellison said in a calm tone. "You don't need the satellite at this time, but with all the money you are siphoning off, as well as all the money that will be given to the loyal Americans who love you, you'll be closer to becoming the next Emperor of the United States. Then, as the Emperor,

357

you can get control of the satellite and protect your new dynasty from all your enemies."

"I like it," Dunham said. "Let's send out our signals to have the virus released."

Speeding out of Maryland, Ellison's cell phone pinged. A special news alert was flashing. He bit his lower lip and handed his phone to Dunham. "We were so lucky," said. "Watch this."

"In a warehouse in Maryland, Dean Miller and his family were rescued by The Never Again Group. It is believed that Albert Dunham, The Architect, was responsible for their kidnapping. Dunham seems to be desperate; if this is true, there is no telling what he'll do next," the reporter said.

121

Sam, Tiffany, and Paige were inside the Mayflower at the lobby bar. "It had been a harrowing day, but happy that the insurrection in DC was stopped and Professor Cochran and Wilhelm Hitler were captured," Tiffany said. "Sam, how soon until you bring these two murderous bastards to trial?"

"Bringing them to trial is the easy part. Getting them to Guantanamo Bay will be more difficult. While Wilhelm can be considered a foreign terrorist, incarcerating Cochran, an American domestic terrorist, will be another story," Sam said, sounding frustrated. "We have a current problem trying to curtail their supporters, who are already violently rioting in all the southern states," Sam said. "As well as the White Supremacist militia and Brown Shirts who are still fighting in the north and at the Mexican border, even though their leaders are gone."

"How come we aren't able to curtail these insurrectionists before they do more damage to our country?" Paige asked.

Tiffany seemed annoyed at how the conversation was going.

"Can we table this conversation for another day? I want to get to know more about my daughter and I am sure she wants to know more about me," Tiffany said.

Sam shrugged his shoulders. "Whatever you two ladies want is okay with me," he said.

Paige raised her hand. "It has my vote. I want to see my brother and sister," she said, squeezing Tiffany's hand and bringing it to her lips.

Sam had never seen his wife blush before, but it tickled his heart. Tiffany was at a loss for words.

"Before we go upstairs, let's stay here. I want to know everything about your life with your adoptive parents."

Sam excused himself and went upstairs to be with the kids. "I'll be upstairs getting the two monsters ready for dinner and then bed. Don't be too long," he said, throwing a kiss at Tiffany and then at Paige.

* * * * *

"Mister Dunham sir, the two ladies are remaining in the bar and Collins is heading upstairs to their suite," Julian Marshall said. "What would you like me to do?"

Dunham did not respond right away. "I'd like them all together in their suite so we can eliminate all of them, including their kids, with one swift blow," he said. "Alert me when they are all together. I want to be there when they die a slow, painful death by the hand of *The Architect*."

* * * * *

Scott Rogers had gotten to the suite earlier than planned and was there when Sam entered. With him were two US Marshals as well as the entire security team protecting Sam, Tiffany, and their children. After the Miller family was rescued, Allan wanted to help capture Dunham. He was sitting at the kitchen table in Sam and Tiffany's suite. He was working on this laptop, setting up a surveillance system that would monitor the entire Mayflower Hotel, including the lobby bar and every hallway on every floor.

Before Sam finished saying hello to Scott, they heard Allan, in a very loud voice, say, "I did it. The new surveillance is up and running."

Sam and Scott rushed into the kitchen to see what he was so excited about. "You seem very pleased with yourself, Allan?" Sam asked.

"Mister Collins, what you have now, what we have now, is a way to monitor every hallway, every corner of this hotel and simultaneously tag any suspicious activity and follow it in real time, with no delays," he said interlocking his hands behind his head with a broad smile on his face.

"Can we test it?" Scott asked. "Let's start with Tiffany and Paige in the lobby bar."

Allan, with a few rapid keystrokes, pulled up the lobby bar and hit a tab that had Tiffany Glass's name. Instantly, the screen was filled with the two ladies, laughing and being very animated. Before the young man could show them the screen, an alarm bell started ringing on his computer.

Allan immediately started hitting more keys on his keyboard. "Look here," he pointed. "That's Julian Marshall. Dunham's assassin. He's getting into the service elevator, and he's heading up to our floor."

Then another alarm went off, and this time it was in the hotel lobby bar. "Oh, shit, it's Albert Dunham sitting in the lobby on a beige couch." Then more alarms started going off.

Scott and Sam had become frantic. Sam was calling McAllister, and Scott called the head of his security detail.

"We need to get the ladies out of there and bring them back to the suite ASAP," Sam barked out orders.

Scott put his hand on Sam's shoulder. "My men are already on their way and will have the bar locked down," Scott said.

Sam asked Allan to show him where Dunham was sitting. The young boy pressed a tab labeled: *The Architect*, and instantly the screen had the entire lobby on the screen and a red circle around Dunham. "There that's *The Architect*," Allan said.

Sam and Scott could see that Dunham was talking on his phone and was very excited. "Who's he talking with?" Sam asked.

Again, Allan hit a few more keys and brought up an image of Frederick Ellison. He then pressed a few more keys, and Ellison's most recent calls popped up on the screen.

Sam leaned into the computer screen and was shocked to see all the Congressmen and Senators freely talking with Dunham's second in charge. "Why would Ellison be speaking to all these elected officials?"

"Maybe within *The Architect's* ranks there is a coup happening?" Scott said.

Allan interrupted the two men. "The hotel is being swarmed with *The Architect's* men. I guess this is his army."

122

President Graham had ordered the Secret Service to the Mayflower Hotel. Twenty-five agents took up a position at every exit point. The US Marshals with orders from Scott Rogers, started to evacuate everyone on the lobby level while the FBI SWAT team scooped up the FBI Director and Paige Turner.

Dunham had sensed that something was wrong and disappeared out the back service entrance before the Secret Service blocked his exit route. He was unable to alert Julian Marshall, who would be trapped somewhere in the hotel, and instead called Frederick Ellison again.

"Frederick, we've been screwed. Someone leaked to the FBI and Secret Service what we were going to do at the Mayflower," *The Architect* said, agitated.

Ellison drew in a deep breath before replying. "Albert, this is a sign that you should get back here and continue accumulating your money and not risk getting caught or being shot," he said, trying to act calmly.

"You know I can't do that. Glass and Collins have to die, as well as Paige Turner and Scott Rogers. Then I come home," *The Architect* said.

"How are you going to accomplish that tall order without getting captured or killed?" Ellison asked.

"Don't you worry about it," Dunham said in *The Architect's* voice.

* * * * *

Tiffany and Paige were reunited with everyone in the suite. Irene and Michael were preoccupied with Allan Miller and what he was doing at the computer. He was a patient boy, but they were getting to him, and needed to be rescued.

The young nanny saw what was happening and she rushed over and scooped up Michael and grab Irene's small hand, ready to take them back to their room. "I'm so sorry these two little rugrats drove you nuts," she said with a sweet smile.

Allan, a very shy boy, started to blush when the nanny spoke to him. "It was my pleasure to interact with these two guys," he said politely, patting both kids on the top of their heads.

Commander McAllister noticed that Allan was distracted by the cute nanny and came over to get him back on task. "Miller, I need an update on Dunham's whereabouts as well as Julian Marshall's. I need it ten minutes ago," he barked.

McAllister's strong voice startled the nanny, triggering her to rush away with the children. Allan scowled at the Commander but decided to go back to monitoring the hotel lobby and hallways with just a '*yes, sir*' retort.

Allan seemed upset at what he was watching. "Sir, Dunham is gone. I cannot find him with my tagging software," he said, trying to regain his composure. "I do have Julian Marshall on the second floor hiding in room 221. He is not alone."

McAllister started dishing out orders to the Secret Service and US Marshals. "Secure room 221 and either capture Marshall and his men or do whatever it takes to secure this hotel," the Commander said.

Bubba Jackson did not believe Dunham had left the hotel and asked Allan to let him see the video of when he was last seen. After watching for five minutes, Jackson called over McAllister.

"Sir, look at Dunham here. Now thirty seconds later, he's putting on a silicone mask, with a baseball cap, and walking out of the lobby. He's heading toward a utility door. That's where we lose him. Allan could not get the hotel to agree to put security cameras down there."

"Who at the hotel made that idiotic decision?" McAllister asked.

"Allan said it was the assistant manager. I have Allan running a background check on him to see if he's associated with Dunham in any way."

"Let's find him and we can do our own background check on him," the Commander ordered. "We need to get a hazmat crew inside the utility room to see if or what Dunham might have left behind for us."

McAllister was on his cell talking with President Graham. "Madame President, I need to evacuate everyone from the Mayflower and get the Collins family, Paige Turner, and my men helicoptered off the roof in fifteen minutes," he asked.

Bubba understood the Commander's concern and grabbed a canvas bag that contained the bioweapon antidote. Within ten minutes, everyone, including the children, were inoculated and shepherded up to the roof.

123

Inside the basement utility room, the hazmat team had begun their search for the bioweapon. The first area they wanted to search was the hotel's air conditioning system. It was a perfect distribution vehicle for the virus's vapor.

Dunham was across Connecticut Ave NW monitoring the utility room on his phone. He had left his own video device so he could time the explosion that would release the bioweapon throughout every floor and room at the hotel. When he saw the hotel being evacuated, he cursed under his breath and initiated the explosion earlier than he had planned.

Unbeknownst to *The Architect* was that his assassin Julian Marshall had not taken his antidote shot before he left for the Mayflower. All he knew was that his only mission was to kill everyone in the Collins' suite.

Just as the explosion happened, setting off alarms through the hotel, Julian had burst through the Collins' door, his AK 47 instantly spraying the living room. He was surprised that the suite was empty and rushed out toward the stairwell just as a light mist floated through the AC vents.

He heard people rushing to the roof and started taking two steps at a time, ready to complete his mission. When he burst through the metal door, he saw two Presidential helicopters loading his targets on board. He dropped down to one knee and took aim at Commander McAllister's back. Before he could get off a shot, a bullet shattered his left shoulder. Sniper Arnold had missed his headshot.

Julian fell backward, hitting his head hard on the metal door. He was a little dazed, but not enough to complete his assignment. With excruciating pain in his left shoulder, he switched the butt of his automatic weapon to his right and set his sights on the rotor blades of the first helicopter to lift off. His first shot missed, but with a slight adjustment, he landed a direct hit.

The helicopter started losing control and was spinning wildly above the roof. The pilot struggled to land while he spun out of control.

Julian watched as the helicopter missed the roof and headed down toward Connecticut Avenue. He waited to hear an explosion, but one never happened. He staggered toward the edge of the roof as the second helicopter got airborne and took off toward the Potomac River. Julian got off a few more shots, but was unsuccessful at hitting his target.

Leaning over the edge, he tried to empty his rifle into the fuel tank of the helicopter. He didn't notice that the second helicopter with Sam and his entire family circled back. The side door opened and Sergeant Arnold, with his sniper rifle, took aim at Julian Marshall. It took only one shot, and the assassin was laid out on the roof.

* * * * *

Dunham could not believe what had just happened to his plan. Seeing Julian shot dead turned his stomach. When he saw Turner and Rogers exit the downed helicopter, his rage got the best of him. He pulled his Glock from his holster and started shooting at everyone near Turner and Rogers.

Dunham did notice that four US Marshals were jumping out of the helicopter and rushing toward him, their guns drawn and firing at him. One bullet ricocheted off the cement sidewalk and entered his right thigh. Another bullet hit him directly in the middle of his chest, dropping him hard to the ground. Everything was spinning out of control. He kept telling himself to not black out and felt his chest for any blood. He was relieved that his Kevlar vest had worked.

Julian's security team, who was watching Dunham, returned fire and hit two US Marshals; the other two took a defensive position, taking fire. They watched two muscular men lift Dunham with blood flowing out of his leg. They placed him in a black van and sped off.

Scott walked back over to Paige and saw she was sitting on the curb, the color drained from her face. "Are you all right?" he asked, noticing a small pool of blood on the sidewalk.

Paige tried to answer before she blacked out and just fell to her side. Scott immediately bent down and started examining her shoulder and torso. His hand touched a wet bloody area just left of her heart. He yelled to his security team to call an ambulance as he tried to put pressure on the wound.

Paige had shallow breaths as the blood kept flowing out of her. He heard the sirens approaching and prayed the love of his life would survive.

Scott was lost in a trance when two paramedics pushed him aside and started helping Paige. "She needs to get to Walter Reed now. I can slow the blood loss down, but can't stop it," the young paramedic said.

Scott jumped into the ambulance, trying to hold back his tears as they had to shock Paige twice to get her heart back before they reached the hospital.

At the hospital ER, Paige was rushed to surgery, leaving Scott all by himself. He called Sam and told him what had happened. Then, he found a chapel and, for the first time in his life, he prayed.

124

President Graham ordered her Attorney General, FBI Director, and Homeland Security Secretary to the White House. She was not pleased that Sam and Tiffany had to see someone at Walter Reed.

"Get me Sam Collins. I want to talk with him," the President ordered, trying to contain her anger.

Martha Sweeden dialed Sam's cell and got him on the first ring. "Sam, Martha Sweeden. The President is pissed at you and Tiffany. She needs you here ASAP," the Chief of Staff said.

"We'll be there in the afternoon. My wife's daughter is fighting for her life, and we can't abandon Paige now," he said.

Martha was shocked at the news. "Paige is Tiffany's daughter?"

"We both found out recently. She got caught in the gunfire at the Mayflower." Sam's emotions were getting the best of him. "Tell President Graham I'll call her later this morning and bring her up to date."

"I'll say a prayer for Paige. However, I think you should call President Graham sooner than later. Something is happening in all of the southern states that she needs your counsel on," said Martha.

"So noted," Sam said, and ended the call.

As he was walking back to where Tiffany was sitting, she could not stop blotting her eyes with a tissue. Sam's heart sank, thinking the worst.

"Any updates?" he asked.

Tiffany slowly lifted her head, her eyes red from crying. "She's out of surgery, which was successful, but with the amount of blood she lost, they put her in an induced coma to let her body heal from the trauma."

Sam sat down and put his arm around his wife. "Sweetie, that's good news," he said kissing her on the cheek. "When did the doctor say they would be bringing her out of the coma?"

"Maybe late tonight or early tomorrow. They are monitoring her heart after being shocked three times, two in the ambulance and one during surgery," Tiffany said, unable to control her tears.

An exhausted Scott Rogers entered the waiting room and sat down across from Sam and Tiffany. Before he could say a word, Paige's surgeon came into the waiting room.

He removed his mask, exposing his sad face. Tiffany's hands started shaking as she scooted to the edge of her seat.

"Tell us some good news about my daughter, please?" asked Tiffany.

The doctor had no expression anyone could read. "Paige is doing better than I expected. Her vitals are improving and if she keeps improving, I should be able to take her out of her coma by this evening." He turned around before anyone could speak and headed for the door.

Tiffany yelled out, "When can we see her?"

The doctor stopped abruptly and turned around. "Sorry for my rudeness. I have another long surgery I have to go to. I'll have the nurse come get you so you can visit your daughter."

125

The insurrection in the north had over five thousand casualties. The DRM and Brown Shirts had sustained the most, which was estimated at roughly forty-five hundred. There were still some hot spots with single-shooter incidents, but the rebels were either captured or dead.

In the south, it was another story. Ten states from Texas to Florida, including South Carolina and Virginia, had been overrun by the Domestic Revolutionary Movement paramilitary militia and the Brown Shirts. The sad commentary was that a majority of Americans living in these states welcomed the liberating army that was going to give them the White Christian Nation they wanted.

President Graham was in a no-win scenario. She could accept the will of the people in the new Confederate States or turn the military loose on Americans who just want to live with people of their own kind. With the Supreme Court favoring states' rights, the White Supremacy movement might have found the perfect way to have its own Confederate States of America, but with all the support from the United States Treasury.

During a meeting with the far-right conservative branch of the Republican Party, led by Senator Kenneth Jenkins, President Graham was threatened with impeachment and possible war crime violations unless she stepped aside and allow what was happening in the South to move forward.

President Graham kept glancing at her watch, impatiently waiting for her Attorney General and FBI Director to get their butts to the Oval Office. She asked Martha to give Sam another call and told her to stress that the country was breaking apart and they were needed at the White House immediately.

* * * * *

Senator Jenkins, standing on the White House driveway, was talking to one of Wiley Jordan's men. The Senator was trying to keep the White Angels as a cohesive group like they were when Wiley was alive.

"Paige Turner will be making a full recovery at Walter Reed. I just found out that she's the biological daughter of Tiffany Glass. If you can get a few of your men into Walter Reed and pose as nurses, this could be the best opportunity for you to avenge Wiley's murder," Jenkins said.

Riley Baker, Wiley's second in charge, had assumed the role of the leader of the White Angels. "Sir, it can be done, but what's the point? We are getting the South as we wanted and maybe the fighting and killing should stop?"

Senator Jenkins did not like what Baker was saying. "Wiley would be turning over in his grave hearing how limp his White Angels have become," the Senator in a low voice said. "You need to remember that I am your superior in the DRM. Just do what I asked and then we can discuss making the White Angels a group of housewives of the Confederacy."

"I didn't say I wouldn't do it, I just thought that maybe it's time to build our new Confederacy," Baker said, his voice cracking.

126

Sam and Tiffany, along with Scott Rogers and Commander McAllister, finally got to the White House. President Graham looked tired. Her hair was uncombed and her clothing looked like it had not been changed for days. Bubba Jackson and a few of his men stayed at Walter Reed, securing the ICU ward.

President Graham, without a hello, started speaking. "Sam, we... I mean I have a big problem that I don't know how to resolve," she said.

"Madame President, I heard about the South and the threats you received from the Republican far-right. It's bullshit and I think I might have a solution you might like," Sam said.

President Graham noticed the sadness on her FBI Director's face. "Excuse my rudeness. How is Paige doing?"

Tiffany raised her head, forcing a smile. "First, she is still fighting for her life, but the doctor feels she has a good chance of a full recovery. We won't know until this evening," said Tiffany.

"Anything I can do to help?" the President asked.

"Not at this time. I really need to be with her."

"Why don't you go back to Walter Reed. I think we can deal with my problems without you for now," President Graham said. "Now go and be with your daughter."

Tiffany didn't argue. She bounced up, kissed Sam on the lips, and hugged McAllister. "Call me if you need me," she said as she rushed out of the Oval Office.

Once the FBI Director was gone, President Graham went right back to business. "Sam, I am all ears on how you think we can handle this southern states' problem."

Sam glanced at the notes he made on the way from the hospital. "These states have been planning something like this for the past decade. They've always known that a civil war would not really work for them or that seceding from the Union was even tougher. The recent attacks and bombings, as well as declaring war on the United States, were a distraction so they could unite their White Supremacy base in their Confederate dream of living among White Christian people," he said, pausing to catch his breath.

"Sam, are you saying I should let them have their Confederate States movement in those southern states?" the President asked.

"What I am trying to say is that we should call their bluff and let them be totally on their own without any federal government help. Can you imagine if they do not have any federal assistance for Medicare, Social Security, food program assistance for their poor, plus the hundreds of other federal programs that go to helping that region?"

"Can I do that?"

"I am not sure, but something like this has never happened in our short history as a democracy. In my opinion, they can't have it both ways. They are either part of the United States of America, or they are not. What do we have to lose?" Sam said.

"If we do this now, then maybe by the mid-terms and after about a year and a half of being on their own, their poor White Christian nations might want to come back?"

"I wouldn't hold my breath. I don't think the White Supremacy militia and the DRM will give up their power once they have it. I think when that happens, we'll need our military one more time to drive these bastards from our borders," Sam said.

"I want to hold a press conference for you and me to tell all Americans what is going on and what we're going to do at this time to stop all the needless killings."

127

The Architect was screaming in a lot of pain as the veterinarian pulled the first bullet from his thigh. Dunham had refused any pain medication or something that would put him in a twilight sleep. He didn't trust anyone and refused to be put under, especially in an animal hospital.

"Sew me up and get me ready to be out of here in thirty minutes. I have one last chore to finish up before I leave the country," he told the doctor.

Frederick Ellison was not pleased with Albert's attitude. "Al, you almost lost your life at the Mayflower and need to appreciate that you have another chance to achieve your manifesto goals."

"I can't stand knowing Paige Turner is clinging to life. I just want to hurry it along," he said without any motion.

"I've already sent two of Wiley's men there to take care of your business. I just need you to get on the plane with me so you can recuperate in Budapest," Ellison said.

"Just this one little job. I need to do it myself, after all that she's done to me these last four years," *The Architect* said. "Now get me out of here and take me to Walter Reed."

* * * * *

Bubba Jackson was sitting in Paige's room, guarding the door. Across his lap was his Beretta with five clips in his vest. She was still in her coma, but resting peacefully. Outside in the hallway were four US Marshals and in the main lobby were ten undercover FBI agents looking for any suspicious activity.

Dean Miller entered Paige's room with his son Allan. They dropped a three-page spreadsheet on Jackson's lap. "What's this?" he asked.

"We believe that someone is coming to the hospital to kill Paige. There has been a lot of chatter on White Supremacist social media that Wiley's White Angels want to avenge his death. You, Sam, Tiffany, and the Commander are also on the list," Dean Miller said. "We know that Dunham has been very active, and I wouldn't put it past him to try one more time to kill Paige."

Bubba was on his stat phone telling his team to be on the alert for White Angels and or Albert Dunham. He then called the Commander and brought him up to date.

"John, we might be the last hurrah for the White Angels and *The Architect*. Miller believes that an attack on the hospital is imminent."

"Initiate Plan B. Paige cannot be harmed at any cost," McAllister said. "I'm on my way over with Sam and Tiffany."

128

Four explosions at the Capitol Mall had the tourists running for safety while a dozen men, women, and children lay either dead or badly wounded. Within minutes, the mall was filled with SWAT units and Capitol Police. Sirens were echoing throughout the area. The President, Sam, and Tiffany were rushed to the bunker in the basement.

Tiffany was immediately on her cell, calling Bubba. "There's been a mass casualty event on the Mall. The injured are being diverted to Walter Reed. It's going to get crazy there, so be on extra alert," she told him.

Near the Lincoln Memorial Pond, a man was dropped there among the casualties. His leg was bleeding, as well as his scalp. Within minutes, two paramedics put him on a gurney and rushed him to an ambulance.

In a low, raspy voice, Dunham asked, "What hospital are we going to?"

The paramedic looked at his clipboard. "Walter Reed. Please lie back and let me put this IV into your arm."

* * * * *

Back at the White House, Commander McAllister wouldn't go into the Presidential bunker. With an AR-45 and a bulletproof vest, he jumped into his Humvee and headed toward Walter Reed.

"Bubba, these bombings are a distraction. I wouldn't put it past Dunham to kill more innocents so he can get his revenge. Have your men inside the ER looking for him. I'd bet my life on it that he's going to be there."

* * * * *

Six gurneys were rushed into the ER and directed to the appropriate room for their patients. One wounded man with a severe thigh injury and a gash on the top of his head was rushed past two FBI agents who were checking names on the charts. The man's face was partially covered with thick gauze that was soaked with blood.

Inside the exam room, Dunham checked his waistband for his gun. He laughed that no one checked him before bringing him to the hospital. *This is going to be so easy,"* he whispered. He texted Ellison to give him an update. *"I'm in the ER and should be on my way up to Paige's room within thirty minutes. Is the plane fueled and ready to take off when I get back?*

Ellison texted him right back as the plane sped down the runway. *Everything is set.* That's all he wanted to say as the plane lifted off the ground, heading toward Budapest.

Dunham looked at this watch and realized he had to leave the ER before he was recognized. He slipped off the gurney, removed the IV, and went into a closet marked for doctors only just outside his exam room. Inside, he found two white coats with ID badges. He took the one with the doctor's photo that looked more like him. He was now Doctor Brad Jarvis and headed toward the elevator. Trying not to limp, he shuffled in and pressed the fourth floor where Paige was in the ICU unit. He put on his M92 mask and advanced toward where Paige would be.

Down the corridor about fifty yards from the elevator, he saw Bubba Jackson leave a room. He assumed that was Paige's room. He briskly walked toward his target.

He checked the board outside the room to verify that Turner was in there, then slowly pushed the door open and observed all the machines working to save her life. He grabbed for his gun and fired five rounds into her bed. As the sheets filled with crimson red, he headed for the door.

Outside was Bubba Jackson, his gun drawn and pointing at Dunham's head. *The Architect* realized he was trapped, went back inside Turner's room, and locked the door. He had nowhere to run and decided he would make his final stand there, instead of being locked up in a Federal Super Max prison for the rest of his life.

He took a position on the window side of Turner's bed. He was ready for Bubba Jackson when he breached the door but wanted to see Paige's face with the bullets that riddled her body. He pulled back the sheet, ready to spit in her face, when he saw a plastic medical practice dummy staring back at him with the fake blood dripping on the mattress.

The door burst open as Bubba led the way, emptying his pistol at Dunham. *The Architect* was able to fire off two rounds that hit Jackson in his bulletproof vest. The impact caused him to fall back against the wall, but not before he was able to get off the kill shot that ended a long reign of terror.

129

The plane carrying Wilhelm Hitler and Professor Cochran landed on the tarmac at Guantanamo Bay. When both men walked to their waiting prison bus, two perfectly executed headshots blew a hole the size of a baseball in each of their heads. Sergeant Arnold, with orders from McAllister and President Graham, completed his mission with perfect precision.

"Sir, both men are terminated," Arnold told McAllister.

"Get your butt back here ASAP, we have another assignment for you and your men," the Commander ordered.

President Graham high-fived McAllister. "Good job, Commander. You've been the only person I trust to carry out what needs to be done," she said. "Are your men ready for the assignment?"

"Once Arnold returns, we will be sending our drones across the border to start wiping out the three biggest drug and human trafficking cartels in Mexico. General Hawkins has three Special Force units ready to help finish the job so we can all go back to getting our country run smoothly," McAllister said.

"I want to make a big statement to the enemies who want to attack Americans that they will be dealt with swiftly and without any mercy," President Graham said.

* * * * *

At Walter Reed, Sam and Tiffany were in Paige's new room. The doctor was bringing her out of her induced coma. "She's doing remarkably well for what she's gone through," the doctor said.

Sam, Tiffany, and Scott were all huddled at the foot of her hospital bed, anxiously watching. Bubba Jackson entered the room, looking exhausted.

379

Tiffany was the first to jump up and hug the big bear of a man. "Thank you again for saving our daughter," she said, as the tears cascaded down her cheeks.

"Just doing my job, ma'am," he said, forcing a smile. "Dunham's been taken to the morgue. Not sure who he should be handed off to?"

Before Sam could answer, Paige struggled to open her eyes. She focused on the three people at the foot of her bed. A smile formed on her face. "What'd I miss?"

130

Frederick Ellison's plane had landed in Budapest eight hours after Dunham, *The Architect*, was shot dead. President Graham promised him a safe passage reward for turning in his boss.

Waiting in a black Mercedes was Klaus Bergner the sole survivor of the *Wolf Pack*.

"We've done well today. Our group will take a sabbatical for a year to enjoy *The Architect's* newly accumulated fortune. Then, we'll get back to our original manifesto to control the world's economies."

Klaus had a curious expression. "Frederick, how are you doing after being instrumental in killing your longtime friend and boss?"

"I've tried to look the other way with his foolish quest to be the Emperor of the United States. His dual-personality would have destroyed our entire organization and I could not have that happen."

"I'm surprised you are not showing any, not even a slight sadness about what you just did," Klaus said.

Ellison took a deep, cleansing breath before replying. "In business, one that deals with trillions of dollars, emotions cannot get in the way. Dunham, as *The Architect*, was letting his need for revenge jeopardize everything we've built. I couldn't let that happen," he said.

"Where will you be staying for the next year?" Klaus asked.

"I'll tell you in a year," Ellison replied with a sinister grin.

* * * * *

Back at the White House, Dean Miller and his son Allan were showing the President a new and disturbing report their software created. "Madame

President, I can't tell you how Dunham was able to siphon trillions of dollars without the regulating agencies discovering it, but he did, and it is continuing as we speak," Dean Miller said.

"I thought the laptop and software he used before were in our possession?" President Graham asked.

"He must have created his own program with a little help from Edmund Bennett, one of my interns at Stanford."

"My first question is, can we stop it from ever happening again? And my second question, can we get all of this money back and return it to the countries it came from?" asked Sam.

Dean nodded his head. "Yes, to both of your questions. I just need permission from President Graham to tap into the monetary highway so I can first disable Dunham's software so it can't be used again. And, second, find the banks Dunham put these funds into and return the money to the countries *The Architect* stole from," Miller said.

"You have my permission. Keep me in the loop every day, but hold off on returning the money. I might need some leverage before our mid-terms."

131

Sam and Tiffany were walking back to the Mayflower Hotel from the White House, their security team keeping them inside their perimeter. They were both perplexed about what President Graham wanted to do with the trillions of dollars of stolen money.

"I'm not sure what her endgame is, but if she does what I think she wants to do, she's going to be breaking international law, as well as the trust our allies have with us," Sam said.

"I'm not so sure she's doing anything wrong waiting to see where all the money was stolen from," Tiffany said. "What would you do if you had billions of dollars from countries who helped the DRM and Brown Shirts with the invasion?" she asked.

"I wouldn't return it if that's what you're asking," Sam responded. "If your theory is correct that those countries Dunham stole from funded the insurrection, then our treasury should use these funds to help rebuild all the damage and life lost by the criminals who did this. Also, reparations to the families who lost loved ones during any of the recent attacks by Dunham or the DRM."

* * * * *

Later that afternoon, President Graham sat in the Situation Room with the CIA Director and her NSA Director watching the military action in three regions of Mexico. Each SEAL team, with perfect precision, was able to destroy ten drug labs and kill over a hundred cartel members. Three other SEAL Teams, with excellent intel from Allan Miller, were able to kill the three top leaders of the cartels.

President Graham started clapping when each Drug Czar was assassinated. "Are we finished wiping out these bastards?" she asked.

Her new CIA Director did not seem so happy. "Madame President, these cartels are like cockroaches. You kill a hundred and two hundred come out of the woodwork. Hopefully, we sent a strong message to stay out of our country."

* * * * *

The Senate Judicial Committee, as well as the House Judicial Committee, opened hearings on the lawlessness of President Graham. Witnesses had come forward, mostly from White Supremacy groups and DRM supporters. Every witness wanted the President's head on a stake, displayed on the White House front lawn.

Sam Collins called these hearings nothing more than a political stunt prior to the upcoming mid-terms in a year and a half. In a press briefing, the Attorney General did not hold anything back while defending President Graham.

"President Graham saved our country from foreign invaders from Iran, Turkey, and Argentina. Unlike past Presidents, our President had the courage to declare war on White Supremacy, domestic terrorists, as well as foreign mercenaries, never worrying about how her actions would harm her politically," Sam said. "I know how the House and Senate like to grandstand issues, but the DOJ will not. We have begun our trials and mark my words, any traitor found guilty will get the harshest penalty, including death." The Attorney General paused and scanned the room, looking for any sign that these reporters supported what he was saying about the President. Sadly, he saw none.

"With the DRM's leaders dead and the paramilitary wing of the group scurrying back to their caves, our country can now start healing and coming together to make sure this never happens again."

One reporter from CNN asked a question. "Attorney General Collins, what is President Graham going to do about the southern states who have passed legislation to become the new Confederate States of America?"

"That's a very good question and a difficult one to answer," Sam responded with a relaxed smile. "President Graham is grief stricken about having to turn our military on the insurrectionists. They were disillusioned Americans who were corrupted by verbal terrorism from propagandists. Every *Dog Whistle* spoken on social media, on the network news, and at political rallies was powerful and triggered our citizens to do horrible things to innocent Americans. What we've decided at this time, while our country heals, is to let these White

Supremacists have their own section of the country in the South, but without any financial support from the federal government. If they want states' rights, then they can use their own money from their poor citizens to fund their cause," Sam said. "Understand, these states will be welcomed back into the fold of our democracy once they denounce White Supremacy and everything it stands for." Without taking any more questions, he headed back to the Oval Office.

* * * * *

Inside the Oval Office, the President had brought in three TV screens. Sam was told that there was one more military action that had to be taken to move forward with rebuilding America.

President Graham signaled her Joint Chiefs and Dean Miller to get the satellite into position. Sam and Tiffany seemed bewildered by her orders. Then, when the monitor went live, they saw the caravan of military trucks and Humvees heading south toward Guatemala. A large laser beam, the width of the two-lane highway where the Brown Shirts were retreating, started moving with one swift brush stroke that painted the entire highway, causing every vehicle to burst into flames, incinerating Wilhelm Hitler's defeated army.

President Graham saluted General Hawkins and clicked off the televisions. "Sam and Tiffany, I know this looks bad, but the horrendous slaughter that these Brown Shirts did was too much for me to let slide. I made an executive decision that I don't regret, no matter the consequences," she said. "Now let's get started with our rebuilding and getting some positive work done for our country."

Epilogue

It was a year and a half since the civil war ended and America, except for the south, was prosperous and working for the majority of the country. The midterms were less than six months away, and Dean Miller's *We the People* political party was doing well in all the recent polls.

Tiffany decided to stay on as the FBI Director with the one stipulation that she could work out of the San Diego field office so she could be home most nights with her children. Sam resigned as the Attorney General and decided that his talents would be best served as the next California Senator.

Bubba Jackson married April and officially adopted her two boys. To everyone's surprise, April had gotten pregnant and was expecting a girl right before the mid-terms.

Commander McAllister was promoted to Admiral and was heading up the entire SEAL operation on Coronado Island. All the retired Special Force veterans who helped stop the civil war and the invasion were reinstated in the active reserves with full pay and benefits and assigned to work for the Admiral.

Paige Turner continued her weekly podcast but moved her studio back to Los Angeles. She was back living full time in her Malibu house. She and Tiffany grew very close, and she was enjoying being a big sister. After she got out of the hospital, Scott did not waste any time and asked her to marry him. To his delight, she said yes. They got married on the beach at Sam and Tiffany's Del Mar home. Irene was the flower girl, and little Michael was the ring bearer. Over a hundred and fifty people attended their beach wedding.

Paige's popularity soared through the roof when she announced on her podcast that Tiffany Glass was her biological mother. She now had over two hundred and fifty million worldwide followers, all calling out their political leaders for their Corrupted Intelligence and abuse of entrusted power.

Scott Rogers went to work with Admiral McAllister, heading up his new cyber security unit with Allan Miller. At first, he refused the offer, citing it was too far from Malibu. He wanted to be close to Paige, especially when he found out that they were going to have a child.

McAllister would not take no for an answer and sweetened the pot by providing a Navy helicopter as Scott's ride from Malibu each day.

While the country healed fast from the civil war, President Graham's political career appeared to be tanking as more and more reports surfaced about her ordering the killings of Americans. As it turned out, almost everything she did during the civil war needed Congressional approval. While a majority of Senators and House Members supported her actions, her approval ratings were in single digits.

The new Confederate States of America, after their first calendar year without any federal assistance, discovered that supporting their White Supremacist leaders had not improved their lives. No one wanted to work in the fields or pick up trash, which used to be what people of color did. The excuse of being replaced turned out, in reality, to be just another meaningless *Dog Whistle* that finally put all Southerners in the failing position they were currently in.

On the other hand, people of color in the north were prospering and not facing any racial discrimination at the workplace since a majority of the White Supremacist CEOs moved to the south. Over 75 percent of minorities had lifted themselves out of poverty, with enough disposable funds to send their children to good colleges, buy their first home, and finally realize the American dream.

New immigration laws were passed for the north that opened the border to day laborers and asylum seekers at the San Leandro border crossing. These people wanted to work and did not mind the type of jobs being offered.

President Graham was not seeing her popularity grow even after the recent low unemployment numbers, the record-breaking job numbers, and the fact that there had not been a mass shooting event in over a year or any hate crimes throughout the northern states.

In Budapest, Wolfgang Bergner and Frederick Ellison were meeting at the Matild Palace Hotel to review how much of Dunham's stolen money they were able to salvage. While President Graham was able to recover over seven trillion dollars that *The Architect* stole, Ellison, with some creative juggling, was able to hide over five hundred billion dollars. It was more than enough for them to begin rewriting the next manifesto.

Ellison put his arm around Bergner, giving him a gentle squeeze. "Wolfgang, we've been able to survive many times in the past, but nothing like this. After the United States mid-term elections are complete, I feel we need to put our money into the south and achieve Professor Cochran's dream. The United States is finally ripe for a new autocratic government.

"I agree totally with you. We're the only sane ones left from our *Wolf Pack*."

The two men shook hands and took the elevator to the lobby. Ellison had his security detail downstairs, waiting to escort them to their cars.

Sitting in the Matild Palace lobby was Theodore Dunham, his ball cap pulled down, shielding his face. He reached into his coat pocket and looked at the last vial he had of the bioweapon. He knew there would be collateral damage in the hotel lobby, but it did not matter. These two bastards had to die a horrible death.

Thank you for reading *The Propagandists*, book three in my Corrupted Intelligence Series. I would be very grateful if you could go to Amazon at:

The Propagandists

and give this book a review.